"We don't have to," he murmured.
"I told you I'd want to," she responded.

Lynne wasn't sure who initiated the move, but she found the strength and weight of his arms comforting. It had been two years since Alec had died, since she'd made love. She was filled with need, quaking with her inability to contain it. She knew she either had to break away . . . or remain and allow the next inevitable step to happen . . .

Berkley books by
Charlotte Vale Allen

DADDY'S GIRL
DESTINIES
INTIMATE FRIENDS
MEET ME IN TIME
PROMISES

Intimate Friends

Charlotte Vale Allen

BERKLEY BOOKS, NEW YORK

This Berkley book contains the complete
text of the original hardcover edition.
It has been completely reset in a typeface
designed for easy reading, and was printed
from new film.

INTIMATE FRIENDS

A Berkley Book / published by arrangement with
E. P. Dutton

PRINTING HISTORY
E. P. Dutton edition published 1983
Berkley edition / April 1984

ISBN: 0-425-06591-X

A BERKLEY BOOK ® TM 757,375
Berkley Books are published by The Berkley Publishing Group,
200 Madison Avenue, New York, New York 10016.
The name ''BERKLEY'' and the stylized ''B'' with design are
trademarks belonging to Berkley Publishing Corporation.
PRINTED IN THE UNITED STATES OF AMERICA

For Kate Conway-Marmo,
an extraordinary friend

PROLOGUE
December 12, 1963

❖❖❖❖❖❖❖

HE'D FALLEN ASLEEP again with the television set on. Lynne smiled as she walked down the hall to the bedroom, seeing the familiar blue-gray light flickering over the walls and floor as the images on the set changed. She was struck by the unearthly quality of the light and its strange shadows, accompanied by disembodied, unrelated voices and music, a small battle of light versus sound. After all her years working in television she still found it a little eerie to come upon a set, playing to itself, casting diffuse messages into a darkened room.

She paused on the threshold to look at the screen. A cowboy movie. Alec's fascination with them seemed limitless, almost as limitless as the supply the local stations seemed to have in their libraries. She glanced over at the bed to confirm that Alec was, indeed, asleep, and bent to turn off the set. The room was all at once too dark, too silent. She turned on the lamp on the dresser and put down her handbag and keys, looking for a moment at her reflection in the mirror. She looked every bit as tired as she felt. She and Dianna had spent the last nine hours reviewing the final editing, redoing segments of the sound track for their piece on the explosion during an ice show at the state fair grounds in Indiana on October 31. Lynne had edited miles of filmed interviews with the families of the sixty-eight people who'd died, and with a large number of the three hundred and forty who'd been injured. From the moment her unit had arrived in Indianapolis, she'd known it would

3

be a gruesome, emotional job. Once the filming got underway, she'd understood why a bigger budget than she'd expected had been allocated. It had taken two weeks longer than she'd estimated to complete the filmed interviews, now scheduled to air this Sunday.

She was looking forward to a month off before starting her next assignment for "Up to the Minute." Hoping Ned, the producer, would allow her to do a low-key piece on the Kennedy assassination, she was disappointed when he'd given the assignment to Greg Waldren and asked her to put together a piece on the closing of the *New York Mirror*, a lightweight story in her estimation. Ned had promised though to give her a more important piece if she'd cover the *Mirror* closing. She'd long-since learned to take the dogwork in her stride in order to land a plum piece every so often. As a point of principle, as a matter of integrity, she did her damnedest on whatever piece she did. Dianna balked, frequently and noisily, at some of the projects they had to do, but she too knew the futility of trying to fight not only Ned, as producer, but the entire male corporate structure of the network, from the executive producer right up to the network program director. She and Dianna simply weren't allowed the scope in their work that Greg and the half dozen other male associate producers had.

The fatiguing aspect of the job was that no matter how hard she tried nothing ever seemed to change. Dianna, with whom she did the majority of the segments, had been more bitchy and impatient today than usual, making the time drag. She didn't like arguing with Dianna; neither of them derived any particular satisfaction from infighting, especially when they had to continue to fight for every inch of progress they made on the show. Dianna was the only female regular among four male hosts, and Lynne was the only female associate producer, of the seven under contract. She and Dianna had, almost at the beginning, tacitly agreed to keep disagreements between the two of them to a minimum in order to concentrate on doing their jobs well.

Despite the fact that she was one of the very few women employed by the network in a producing and directing capacity, Lynne had no illusions about just how tenuous her position was. Frequently she and Dianna were called in to production meetings where their work underwent the kind of close, nit-picking scrutiny the men were rarely subjected to. With time, it had turned Dianna harder and tougher. It had made Lynne tired.

Alec, she noted, had gone to sleep fully dressed. There was an odd unpleasant smell in the room that made her wonder if there wasn't a dead mouse in one of the walls again. Once, about five years before, they'd had to suffer with the smell for weeks before it finally faded away. She debated waking him, wanting to tell him about wrapping the Indiana segment, and to discuss taking a couple of weeks to go away somewhere, perhaps to Arizona. She wasn't in the mood for crowds of tourists, and liked the idea of going somewhere warm and quiet. Six, almost seven weeks, four of them in Indiana, had drained her. Dozens of interviews, hours of film to be edited, a focal point to be strongly established, all had taken far too long and far too much physical and emotional energy.

She went across the room, noticing a brandy snifter on the bedside table. He'd probably been waiting up for her, she thought, touched. She sat on the side of the bed, reached for Alec's hand and at once dropped it. Leaping up, her heart slammed in violent response to the cold slackness of his hand. The smell was very strong here. It took her several seconds to connect the smell, and the chill weight of Alec's hand, the snifter, and the empty prescription vial sitting near the base of the lamp. Something in her brain short-circuited. Her thoughts had gone completely out of kilter; she felt as if all the parts of her were working against themselves.

Steadying herself, she switched on the lamp, took a deep breath and looked closely at Alec. There was a dark stain across his gray flannel trousers. He'd wet himself. That happened when someone died; the muscles relaxed. Covering her mouth with her hand she turned, looking for something; she wasn't sure what. She ran, still in her coat, to the living room, stopping first at the desk. Nothing. Then the bulletin board in the kitchen on the wall beside the telephone. Nothing. Just her shopping list, to which she added items daily until it was time to go to the supermarket. Then she would tear the list from the pad, stuff it into her bag or her pocket and, invariably, forget to refer to it once she got to the store.

Breathing hard, she raced back to the bedroom, and came to a halt in the doorway where she stood, holding on to the door frame for support, staring at Alec. Her body had entered into a palsied dance. There were things she was supposed to do. She'd have to call the police. The police. It seemed inconceivable that she should have to call the police about Alec. But who else would one call? No. Maybe she'd made a mistake. Maybe he was ill and she should call an ambulance, Alec's doctor. She couldn't be wrong. He was dead. She knew it. But where was the note? That was what she wanted, what was missing: the note. There had to be one. He couldn't possibly have done this without some sort of explanation, a letter, something. Again she went through the apartment, trying to take her time, methodically searching out every place where he might have left some words for her. She found nothing. The harder she looked, the more angry and frightened and confused she became. He *had* to have written something, even just a few words. How could he just turn on the television set, sit down on the bed with brandy and pills, and kill himself without offering any reasons?

She returned again to the bedroom, this time standing at the foot of the bed for several minutes before moving to the far side, studying Alec from every angle. Had he moved? No. When she'd thrust his hand away from her, his position had shifted slightly. That was all. He hadn't moved. She was breathing through her mouth, fast rasping breaths. Her lips felt parched. Her head ached. Her stomach was lurching up and down like an elevator out of control. Moving slowly, she inched her way around the bed to stand by Alec's side. He looked asleep. She touched her fingers to his throat. No pulse, only cool, yielding flesh. She looked around the room, trying to understand. It was no use. Perhaps she wasn't supposed to touch anything, disturb evidence. What had she touched? Nothing. She'd touched nothing, only Alec. Alec. He looked as if he'd just come in from the office. His tie was loosened but otherwise he was dressed as always for a business day.

She wanted to speak but was fearful of how her voice might sound, and perhaps if she didn't speak this couldn't be real, wouldn't be happening. Her eyes refused to leave Alec. Swallowing repeatedly, she remained positioned by the bedside, trying to think of what to do, of why he'd done this, of what he'd thought she'd do coming home to find him this way. No note, no words, no goodbye, just a dead Alec on the bed.

At last, she found the strength to turn and leave the room. She went to the telephone in the kitchen but couldn't remember the emergency number. She trembled, frustrated and more and more frightened, trying to remember, the receiver in her hand. Was it 999? Or 919? Had she waited too long before telephoning? Would they question her about the minutes she'd spent between the time she arrived home and the time she placed the call? She dialed the operator.

"I need the police," she said in a dry, shattered voice in no way recognizable to her as her own. The words seemed to echo off the walls, the high ceiling.

The operator put her through to emergency dispatch.

"My husband has . . . he's dead," she said, staring at the kitchen cabinets, old and yellowing, in need of a fresh coat of paint. She'd intended to spend a week repainting the kitchen but had never managed to find the time. She gave her name, her address, her telephone number. The voice on the other end said, "We'll send someone right away. Stay put."

Stay put. That was an odd thing to say to her. She replaced the receiver and went to stand in the hall near the front door, her eyes on the bedroom doorway. She felt like a small child, helpless and alone. She needed people to come and explain this to her, to release her from the noisy cage of her random thoughts and colliding desires. The voice on the phone had been quite right to tell her to stay put. Her instinct now was to run, to flee this apartment with its dead husband and his soiled deathbed. How could he do this in their bed? He hadn't thought about where she'd sleep, or even if she'd be able to sleep in the bed he'd died in, the bed he'd taken his life in. He'd killed himself.

It had to be a mistake. He couldn't be dead. Her coordination lost, she reeled drunkenly down the hall to the bedroom. Nothing had changed. He lay as before, his head propped against the pillows—all four of them, including her two—turned slightly to one side. He hadn't taken his shoes off. She stared at his feet, noticing a piece of blackened chewing gum on the sole of his right shoe. Always meticulous, Alec would be greatly irritated to know he'd died with a piece of chewing gum stuck to his shoe. The idea made her want to laugh, or cry. She didn't know what to do.

The buzzer sounded. She whirled around, her heartbeat gone crazy, to gaze down the length of the hallway. The police. She ran to lift the receiver on the intercom, wetting her lips before she said, "Yes?" She could still speak; it seemed astonishing.

"Police."

"Yes," she said, and applied her finger to the button that would release the lock on the lobby door.

She was still standing with the receiver in her hand and her finger on the buzzer when the knock came at the front door. She dropped the receiver and hurried to the door where two uniformed policemen stood waiting. Wordlessly she led them to the bedroom. The taller of the two lifted Alec's wrist, then pressed his fingers to Alec's throat, as Lynne had done. Expertly, Lynne thought, he rolled back Alec's eyelids to check the pupils. He nodded at the second man—a language comprised entirely of gestures—who asked, "Where's the phone?" Lynne pointed to the extension on the dresser. Perhaps only she and the first officer were symbol-speakers.

As she stood watching and listening, the second officer made a call. He turned his back to Lynne as he spoke in a low murmur. She felt unreasonably excluded, as if she and not Alec had done something criminal. She remembered reading once that it was against the law to kill oneself.

The call completed, the two officers directed her to the living room. While the second man sat near Lynne with a notebook propped on his knee and ballpoint pen in hand, the first man left the room.

"Where's he going?" she asked, alarmed, her mouth too dry, her body alternately hot and cold. Everything these two men said and did seemed highly significant. If she missed anything at all, she might lose some vital clue to what was happening here.

"He'll stay by the door. I know it's not a good time, but could you answer a few questions?"

She nodded. The questions and answers began: name, name of the deceased, time of discovery of the body, circumstances of discovery of the body, places of employment, both hers and the deceased's, on and on, questions she answered with mechanical detachment as if she were filling out a job or loan application. She had no idea how long it took—but before she'd finished responding the front door had opened and closed several times and men's voices moved along the corridor to the bedroom.

"What are they doing?" she asked, feeling now alarmingly excluded. This was her home, her husband, her private life they were entering so noisily.

"Coroner," the officer explained, "and a photographer. Standard procedure. They'll want to ask you more questions when they finish up. You okay?"

"I'm okay," she lied, grateful someone had thought to ask.

"You sit here and take it easy for a few minutes." He closed his notebook, returned it and his pen to an inside pocket, stood, and left the room. He had a gun in a holster slung around his hips, and a nightstick, also holstered. Alec had taken his life and now her home was overrun by taciturn officials and men with guns.

She had to see what was happening, and got up to go to the bedroom, but the corridor was blocked by the two patrolmen who'd arrived first. They glanced at her but said nothing. She felt like an intruder, an imposition upon the orderly routine of their militaristic days. She shrank against the wall, watching the new shadows shape and reshape themselves in the bedroom light. Photo flashes, movement. Then two men appeared in the doorway with a stretcher upon which lay Alec's tightly-wrapped body. The small procession approached the now-open front door. They were taking him away. It didn't seem right. She said, "Wait . . . !" and they came to a halt. Half a dozen faces turned inquisitively in her direction. She didn't know what she wanted them to say or do. She simply wanted Alec to end all this, to free himself of the enclosing—what was that? not a blanket, something more like canvas—wrap and announce that his joke had backfired, it was over now and they could all leave. Time hung in the air, filled with the slow, patient breathing of these strangers, suspended in their impersonal activity. They waited while her thoughts, like blind children in a schoolyard, ran explosively into one another. At last one of the men, a tired-looking, middle-aged man whose brown suit had a shiny, well-worn shapelessness, put his hand on her arm.

"Mrs. Craig?"

She looked into his face, discovering tired-looking brown eyes to match the suit.

"We'll just keep you a few more minutes. Why don't we step in here?"

She looked over at the package that had once been Alec and felt a cry rising through her body, gathering force. She closed her throat against it and allowed the detective to direct her back into the living room.

More questions, more answers. Then: "Is there someone who can corroborate . . . someone who can verify that you were where you say you were this evening?"

She stared at him, absorbing the implication. Could they possibly think she'd killed Alec? Did she look like someone capable of murder? It terrified her to think that the person she believed herself to be was not visible, could not be readily perceived by these men.

"Cigarette?" the detective offered casually, as if he hadn't just asked her that most offensive question.

She accepted the cigarette and drew on it, the first inhalations making her dizzy. She wanted and needed a drink, but thought it might be wrong, another semaphore to be misconstrued.

"I was with Dianna, Dianna Ferguson. I can give you her number. She'll tell you where I was." For a moment her mind was occupied by a bizarre scenario. The detective contacted Dianna, Dianna lied and said she hadn't seen Lynne in a week, Lynne was arrested, charged with Alec's murder. She was in a courtroom begging a tight-faced Dianna to tell the truth, but Dianna slowly turned her head away, refusing to hear, to admit that Lynne was innocent.

". . . there'll be an autopsy . . . as a matter of course. We'll let you know when the body's going to be released. You'll want to make arrangements. Is there anybody you'd like me to call, someone to come stay with you?"

She shook her head, puffing on the cigarette. The smoke was like sandpaper on her too-dry throat. She wanted to be left alone.

"We'll be in touch," he said, getting to his feet, his eyes all at once sympathetic. He seemed to be seeing her, now that he was preparing to leave. "Will you be all right?"

She nodded.

He left, closing the door quietly. She put the chain on the door, feeling hopelessly drawn back to the bedroom. Her head floating yards above her feet, she traveled the length of the hallway.

Alec's impression remained on the stained bedclothes, on the pillows. His keys and wallet sat on the dresser, near her handbag and keys. She hadn't noticed them before. On impulse, she lifted his wallet and opened it. Seventy-eight dollars in bills, half a dozen credit cards, no note.

Suddenly the smell and the heat and a ravaging grief overcame her. She had to get out of there. She cast a final accusing look at the guilty bed and tore down the hall to the front door, fumbled with the chain, got the door open, and slammed it shut behind her. In too much of a hurry to wait for the elevator, she ran down the nine flights of stairs to the lobby and pushed out into cold air that assaulted her like a physical blow.

She turned to look up the street, and then down, then back up. Third Avenue seemed a logical choice. But for what? She had no idea. She began to walk. At the corner was an all-night deli. She stood outside its steamy windows for several minutes. Behind the counter, a young bearded man sat on a high stool reading a paperback book. On the counter near the cash register was a styrofoam cup of coffee which he picked up from time to time, sipped at, then returned to the counter. Music was playing somewhere. Listening, she tried to decide where the music might be coming from. She managed to reposition her body in order to scan the street. Half a block away a woman stood waiting while her dog lifted his leg against a lamppost. The woman watched the dog intently, as if its activity was of paramount concern to her. Yet her physical attitude was one of utter boredom. Lynne, too, watched—both the dog and the woman—until at last they continued on down the street and out of sight.

Lynne returned her eyes to the deli window. For several moments she felt she was on the verge of losing control of her bladder. It seemed to swell, filling with her body's fluids. Then, the sensation was gone and she felt emptied, as if some invisible hand had scooped her organs from her body, leaving her hollow. She moved forward to the door and entered, causing a bell above the door to ring startlingly.

The counterman flicked his eyes at her before looking back at his book. She was interrupting his reading, and felt guilty. She'd buy something quickly and leave. She approached the counter and asked for a package of Marlboros—the first brand that came to mind—and watched the man set down his book, reach for the cigarettes, and slap them on the counter. She found money in her bag, paid, was about to leave when she remembered to ask for matches.

"Cost you a penny," the young man said.

She left a penny on the counter, and tucked the cigarettes and matches into her bag. That convict feeling was with her again, the feeling she'd had when she'd asked all those people to wait because there were things that had to be said, statements she'd wanted to make both to Alec and to the collection of strange men who couldn't possibly understand—not that she was sure she herself did—just what had taken place inside her home on this night.

Out on the street again, she got to the corner of Third Avenue and had to stop once more, directionless. A question had formed in her mind and was demanding her attention. *What am I supposed to do now*? She didn't know. She could hardly deal with obligations when she felt precisely as if she'd stepped off the table in the midst of a complicated and lengthy surgical procedure, neatly incised, the lips of the wound clipped tidily out of the way in order to facilitate access to the pulsing organs inside. Surely if she dared to unbutton her coat yards of intestine in slippery coils would come spilling out onto the sidewalk.

She wanted to weep. Her lungs heaved in anticipation of the relief of tears, but her eyes felt rusted into their sockets. She told herself Alec was dead and a part of her believed it absolutely, had seen the proof; another part of her longed to deny it, and protested actively her presence out here alone on these dangerous nighttime streets. She didn't care. Were someone to approach her now, intent on bodily harm or the theft of her possessions, she'd simply brush past and continue on her way. She turned the corner and walked into the wind, looking for the right place to go.

She sat in a booth in the 2 A.M. near-silence of a coffee shop on the corner of Seventy-seventh and Third Avenue. Three young men sat together at the counter and she could feel them turn every so often to look at her. Lynne studied the untouched cup of coffee on the table before her. Words in her brain ran in loops, circling endlessly. The whirring motion might be slowing, and she waited, knowing at the end would come a certain clarity. She'd be able to decide on an orderly way to proceed.

The sudden bass-pulsing blare of music from the jukebox shocked her and she looked up to see that one of the young men was standing by the machine, dropping more coins into the slot. The overloud music would play on for at least another half hour. She wouldn't be able to think here; she'd have to leave. She left a dollar on the table and slid out of the booth feeling giddy. Go slowly, she cautioned herself. No sudden, jarring moves. She felt as if she were moving through a haphazardly pasted paper construction that might disassemble were she to risk increased momentum.

She got to the door, opened it and stepped out into the street, buttoning her coat. The wind blew up her legs, her sleeves. She huddled inside the coat trying to remember where she'd left the car. Or had she brought it? She couldn't recall. She stared at the traffic on Third Avenue, amazed that there was always traffic on the streets of Manhattan, no matter what the hour. Where were people going at this time of the morning? To bars in the Village. That was possible. She'd once coerced Alec into taking her to a late-night rock show. It had cost them ten dollars to gain entrance but she'd found it worth every penny. For two hours she'd watched and listened, riveted, as a quartet of musicians, clad in the most outrageous outfits she'd ever seen, had gyrated and performed to their deafening music; the gaudy scene had been enhanced by the spectacular lighting effects and the rapt attention of the very young audience. She had been, for those two hours, encased perfectly in a capsule of under-standing, knowing in her late twenties what she hadn't been able to make sense of as a teenager: that she was merely a witness to most events and could, if she cared to make the effort, participate more fully than she'd realized. This dis-covery had seemed profoundly momentous to her, but when she'd attempted to convey it to Alec he'd merely smiled at her in avuncular fashion as if she were, in fact, a feckless teenager and not a grown woman trying to share something of importance.

The experience had eventually proved invaluable when, after working her way up from production assistant—hav-ing paid her dues first as a secretary, then as an assistant production assistant, while studying film technique at nights—to associate producer, she'd at last been allowed an opportunity to demonstrate what she'd learned. Despite the fact that her early assignments had all been dogwork, she'd applied her knowledge of editing, of lighting, of script blocking. Two years later, Ned had patted her on the shoulder, said, "Nice job," of a segment on which she'd labored extravagantly, and rewarded her with her first decent assignment. Believing she'd finally broken through to acceptance from her peers, she felt herself slam closed inside like a bank vault door when the assignment after that was another piece of dogwork. Nevertheless the rock show experience and her comprehension of her role as a witness paid off. She only wished she knew how to curb her eternal optimism, how to make herself accept that no matter how hard she tried or how good her work was she was never going to have the kind of freedom journalistically on "Up to the Minute" that she craved. There was something in her that insisted she could break through the imposed limitations with a carefully put-together filmed segment that would tear the tops off peoples' heads. She refused to be defeated by a power structure of men whose competency was inconsistent, whose vision was defined by the choices of other men, and who would never move over to make room for a woman in their ranks because that would be an admission, a recognition of her ability. At best her associates congratulated her from time to time on a job especially well done, but constantly distanced themselves from her, professionally, socially, and intellectually.

She'd forgotten Alec! Appalled, she looked about quickly, as if passersby might recognize how remiss she was. What was it she'd been trying to remember? The car. No, she hadn't brought it. She started toward the corner thinking she'd go home. It was all over now and safe to go home. Everyone was gone—the detectives, the coroner, the two patrolmen, the photographer, the ambulance attendants, and Alec. She couldn't go home. She crossed the Avenue and started walking down the east side of the street. At Seventy-second she spotted another open coffee shop and pushed inside. No music. Good. She slid into a booth and ordered coffee from the bored-looking, overweight waitress. Then she lit a cigarette. The trembling in her hands was worse.

There was so much to do, she thought exhaustedly, finally confronting the logistics. How could she possibly get it all done? She wouldn't have to worry about work. The next four weeks were free. Arizona. . . . The scream was threatening again to rise into her throat. She drew hard on the cigarette.

Alec's family, and her sister, their friends. . . . How would she explain this? How would they understand when she wasn't sure she ever would? Objectively she could put it together. If she suspended her emotional self for just a few moments, there was an alarming clarity to Alec's actions. All the reasons curved inward in her mind, folding protectively around a central core; reason upon reason layered thinly, one atop the other, forming patterns, curling, curving, crisping at the edges like yellowed newspapers. One atop another, reason after reason, the final, dried pages of someone's life.

She picked up the cup and took a swallow of the strong, bitter coffee. The bottom of the pot. Good coffee, her mother used to say, should never be allowed to stand for more than half an hour. How many pots of coffee had her mother poured down the sink in her lifetime of seventy-seven years? Lynne thought of the occasion when her old school friend Andrea had come to visit. Lynne had carried a half-pot of stale coffee to the sink and Andrea had let out a shriek of protest, exclaiming, "Don't throw it out! Reheat it! It's still good." Lynne had paused a moment, then smiled, saying, "I'll make fresh." Andrea, looking scandalized, had murmured, "It's such a waste."

Why think of that now? Because it was a waste. Angus Alexander Craig, known affectionately as Alec, took his life, ended it voluntarily, on this night of December twelfth, 1963. He took it quietly, she had to grant him that, in typical understated Alec fashion, choosing to sleep it away with a bottle of large red sleeping spansules obtained by legitimate prescription from his physician. The large red pills had been washed down with one or more snifters of VSOP brandy.

The detective who'd talked with her in the living room had observed that it was usually women who opted for sleeping pills. Men, he'd assured her, seemed to prefer louder or messier ways of ending their lives. But they hadn't known Alec. Given that there was choice involved, he'd have preferred the quieter, cleaner death. He'd have been incapable of placing a gun at his temple, or of leaping from the bedroom window. God! He'd thought of everything but her, of how she might react to coming upon his body, of how his electing their bed for the scene of his death had forced her out into the streets because just the sight of that bed might be sufficient to send her mad. She took another sip of the acrid coffee, then another puff of the cigarette. She hadn't smoked in two years. The smoke seemed to swell her head, to wizen her brain somehow so that, pea-like, it rattled ineffectually within the sere bone hollows.

How could she ever go home? Home no longer existed. Home had been a life she and Alec had structured attentively for seventeen years. They'd worked out their lifestyle over the years and made choices together, but he'd failed to include her in this decision. She brought her fist down hard on the tabletop, her eyes filling. The half dozen people in the place all looked over at her. She failed to notice.

There was so much to do, so many details to be attended to. Too clearly she could call to mind the countless things that had had to be done when her mother had died eighteen months earlier. The shock of that death was still with her; it didn't seem possible she now had yet another death to cope with. If she could just decide where to begin, perhaps it might all fall into some sort of pattern. There'd be an autopsy. After that, the body would be released to a funeral home of her designation. Should she call Dodie first? No. Alec's sister would find too much to relish in the drama; she'd beat her fleshy fists against her wealth of breast and create more drama. Tommy was in the West Indies, some island seething with political turmoil. Typical of Tommy; he liked to take advantage of situations. Political unrest, hints of murderous natives appealed to him. His motto, Alec had once said, could easily have been: Relax in a state of danger. "My brother Tom's never done anything ordinary in his entire life," Alec had often declared, not without a hint of pride. The amazing thing was that Tommy didn't look or act like someone who'd relish life's more unsavory aspects. From his appearance, and his old-maidish, rather finicky habits, he seemed like the archetypal English teacher, or accountant. In reality, he was president of a bank.

Having ruled out Alec's brother and sister, only his father, and her sister Amy were left. She glanced around the restaurant and spotted a telephone near the door. Leaving her cigarette burning in the ashtray, she picked up her bag, found some change and walked woodenly toward the telephone. In her mind, she could already hear the conversation, and anticipated the immediacy of Amy's warmth and concern. For a few seconds she saw herself and Amy, small girls in their nightgowns and robes, sitting on the window seat of the old house, watching the snow fall as they waited for their father to come.

The long distance operator told her to deposit her money. Lynne got the coins into the slots, and the ringing started at the other end. Lynne pictured the house in Greenwich, saw lights going on as, in alarm, Amy reached for the receiver. A call at this time of the morning—it was now two-thirty—could only signify bad news.

"It's me," Lynne said, almost before Amy finished saying hello in a sleep-encrusted voice. "I need to see you." Suddenly Lynne had the feeling again that her bladder might burst.

"What's wrong? What's happened?"

"I can't talk about it on the phone. I'm going back to the apartment to get the car. I'll be there in about an hour."

"*What's wrong?*" Amy nearly shouted. "Where's Alec?"

"Alec." She stopped to take a breath. Christ! she thought. How was she going to get through this? "Alec's dead. I'll be there in an hour." She replaced the receiver, her pulse racing. No one was looking at her; apparently no one had been listening. Why then did she feel so naked, so conspicuous, so guilty of some unspecified crime?

Thieflike, she stole back to the table to throw down a dollar before making her way quickly out of the restaurant. Her bones seemed to be getting smaller moment by moment; her skin was stretching so that the bones hung loosely inside her. Her coat felt several sizes too large, the empty spaces between the coat and her body puffed with pockets of cold air.

As she hurried along Seventy-fourth Street she fumbled in her bag, praying she had the spare set of car keys with her. She couldn't go back up to the apartment; she wouldn't. If she didn't have the keys, she'd stop a taxi and hire it to take her to Greenwich; anything not to have to go back to the apartment. She found the keys at the bottom of her bag and went past the doorman without bothering to acknowledge his greeting.

In the supposedly heated indoor garage she shivered as she tried to fit the key into the lock of the BMW. She felt now as if people were chasing her and it was vital not to be caught. She got the door open, threw herself into the driver's seat, fastened the safety belt, then started the car. She knew it was wrong, could hear Alec's admonitions against attempting to drive before the engine was properly warmed, but she simply could not attend now to things like properly warmed engines and observations of polite protocol, greetings to curious doormen. She had to see Amy.

The FDR Drive was clear, with very little traffic. She threw the shift into fourth and put her foot down on the accelerator, that feeling of being pursued even more pronounced. They might have called Dianna by now, and Dianna might, for reasons entirely her own, have lied about Lynne's being with her all day and evening. The police could easily be out looking for her. The sturdy little car jounced over potholes and took the badly-planned curves of the highway at a speed that would have frightened her had anyone else been driving. Once over the bridge and headed for the New England Thruway, she relaxed somewhat and again tried to consider all that would have to be done. She couldn't concentrate. Birdlike, her brain darted here and there, landing on random thoughts, memories.

The first time she'd seen Alec she'd loved him. Tall with sandy-red hair and a capacity for blushing that was one of the most endearing qualities she thought she'd ever discovered in a man; a quiet, even-tempered soul with a wry sense of humor and an inner core of finely-tempered steel pride. It was the pride, of course, that was to blame. If he hadn't been so rigidly determined to do it all on his own; if he'd allowed her to contribute financially, to contribute at all. But no. "I've never touched a penny of yours and I never will. I've never objected to your working and I'm not about to begin, but I won't take your money."

He'd refused to allow her to help and now he was dead. She was never again going to hear him speak or laugh. He would not be there in the morning when she awakened. There'd be no one to meet her on nights when she worked late at the station, no one to call her and ask how things were going in Indiana, or Florida, or Ohio, or any of the dozen other places she'd gone on assignment. He was dead.

She pulled over onto the shoulder and sat gripping the steering wheel, aware of the gentle hum of the car's engine, and the heat pushing out from the vents. She closed her eyes. She felt bewildered, devastated, dry; dry as if all the life-sustaining fluids in her body had evaporated in that moment when she'd mentally connected the empty brandy snifter and the topless vial with Alec's chilled rubbery hand. The lids of her eyes slid open and she stared at the highway ahead. It was so goddamned easy to die, she thought, sensing an anger she suspected would grow to enormous proportions in the days to come. It was such a cruel, thoughtless thing to do to the people you left behind. Unanticipated, the scream rushed into her throat and hurtled out of her mouth. She screamed until her temples throbbed and her throat gave out. Her fists pounded on the steering wheel until they, too, gave out. Then she lit a cigarette and sat, gutted by the loss of the scream, and smoked until the cigarette was done. After a few minutes she directed the car back onto the road.

INTERLUDE
December 16, 1963

❖❖❖❖❖❖❖

DODIE, ALEC'S SISTER, sat enclosed in grief and black broadtail, her substantial mound of breast heaving with the effort to repress audible sobs. Tommy, seated to Dodie's right, looked straight ahead as if speculating on the size of the minister's personal portfolio. In charcoal gray cashmere, with a pale gray shirt and black tie, Tommy was elegant and somehow obscenely alive. His eyes moved restlessly, guiltily meeting Lynne's for a moment before shifting away. He looked like a small boy prematurely aged, peculiarly comfortable in his expensive adult clothes, yet uncomfortable, overall, with having to play his adult role.

Dodie sobbed—an explosive, brief-lived gush of sound—at something the minister was saying, and Lynne returned her eyes to the front of the chapel, trying to find some meaning in the minister's roundly-spoken, mellow-toned and important-sounding words.

He was talking of the prime of someone's life, going on about that same someone's achievements. Lynne found herself more interested in Dodie's grief-stricken display. She looked again at her sister-in-law's profile, attempting, as she had countless times in the past, to locate some resemblance to Alec. It wasn't there. Nor was it there in Tommy. How had these two people come to be related to Alec? How had Dodie in her stoutness, and Tommy in his highly stylish elfin fashion, managed to be the products of the same parents as Alec? It didn't seem possible. There ought to have been something . . .

She turned her head—her neck felt solid, a little pillar upon which her skull had been set precariously—to look at Amy. At least, thank God, Amy looked not only familiar but recognizably related. She and Amy had the same coloring and height, similar profiles, big feet. She smiled inwardly, recollecting complaining discussions they'd had in high school about the ungracious dimensions of those pale, silly long things appended to the ends of their legs. She saw and heard herself and Amy rolling about on Amy's bedroom floor, laughing, as Amy shouted, "FOOTFOOTFOOT-FOOTFOOT!" over and over.

As if sensing her sister's thoughts, Amy reached over to take hold of Lynne's hand. The contact was upsetting and Lynne carefully freed herself, looking for a few seconds into Amy's eyes. Suddenly Amy looked no more familiar to her than the others. It frightened her. Perhaps it would be best if she gave up searching for recognizable qualities in the people around her. By the same token, she'd have to exercise caution, taking care not to allow anyone to see into her. If she kept her eyes averted maybe no one would question her failure to display appropriate grief.

It occurred to Lynne that a stranger attending these proceedings might readily assume that Dodie was the grieving wife, and not her. She could see—as if she were witnessing all this from a great height—that she was failing, in almost every way, to fulfill the expectations of those who'd elected to attend this service. Surprisingly, there were quite a number of people present: old school friends of Alec's, business friends, tennis friends from the days when Alec had belonged to the Racquet Club, clients, two former secretaries Lynne recognized. Once the minister came to the end of his recitation of what, to her mind, sounded like an often-repeated eulogy—only the name, age and circumstances of the deceased altered from one occasion to the next—those gathered here would attempt to speak to her, to express their sympathy. Realizing this, she suddenly filled with panic. She couldn't possibly cope with this. She had no idea of the names of most of these people, was unable to match faces to those names she did recall. She wasn't even certain that the people who belonged to the names she did remember were actually here.

She heard her name spoken and started guiltily, her eyes fixing on the tall, silver-haired minister. Mercifully, he wasn't looking at her, but at Dodie. Could he have mistaken Dodie for her? She glanced around to see if anyone was looking at her, and again encountered Tommy's pale blue eyes. He gave what she interpreted as an encouraging nod before turning away. She gazed, mystified, at his rather stubby profile, wondering if he were attempting, at this very late date when they were at least legally no longer related, to display some form of family unity. She could feel herself becoming angry at the hypocrisy of this possibility; she could also feel, like pinpoints of heat, someone's eyes, and she turned a bit more, scanning the assembly. There! Dianna was seated on the far side of the aisle, her eyes on Lynne. Shocked, Lynne shrank into herself and looked down at her gloved, tightly-clasped hands. Dianna. This was all wrong. It wasn't Dianna's style to do this, to be here. Her presence made Lynne feel bleached and fleshless, like one of Georgia O'Keeffe's New Mexico skull paintings. Lynne had asked, years back, to be allowed to film a segment on O'Keeffe, but Ned had said, "*Who?*" and that had been the end of it. However, Ned's ignorance had in no way reduced Lynne's fascination with the artist. It seemed almost appropriate at this moment to find in her mind an O'Keeffe image—an elongated steer skull adorned with exotic blossoms—to fit her present feelings, whatever they were. Her feelings were simply not to be trusted just now; they were too random, too arbitrary. But Dianna. She shouldn't, she told herself, have been as shaken as she was by Dianna's presence, and sat trying to understand what all this signified. It was serious, terribly serious. This was evidenced by the solemnity of everyone present, and especially Dianna. People died every day. But this time it was Alec.

Briefly, furiously, she thought about Alec. He'd removed himself, taken himself out of life. Yet he'd done nothing to cushion Lynne from the repeated shocks of his death. Nothing. How could he have done this? she wondered again. And why? Don't go into the whys! her inner voice warned. Don't go into all that again!

The words had come to an end, and there was the underwater motion all around her of people preparing to rise and leave the chapel. But first they'd approach her with their sober faces, their outstretched, sympathetic hands and consoling words. She wanted to scream, and reached instinctively for Amy's hand.

"I don't think I can do this," she whispered, her throat so narrow the words were barely able to travel its length.

Amy's hand squeezed her reassuringly, and Lynne hung on as she commanded her body to unfold itself from the pew.

"Half an hour at most," Amy said, "and it'll be over."

Amy had accepted Lynne's refusal to invite people back to the apartment after the service. "I've always thought it was a barbaric custom," Amy had said, three days earlier when they'd been planning Alec's funeral. "All those people coming by to stand around, drinking and eating and using all those 'sorry' expressions. We'll just go home and be done with it."

Why, Lynne demanded of herself, had she failed to anticipate the advancing crush of people, all intent upon making their particular statements? She felt as if she were standing, rooted, on a deserted beach in the direct path of a tidal wave. Her earlier panic rushed upward from her stomach and she looked longingly toward the door of the chapel, beyond which was freedom and through which, at that moment, Dianna was discreetly slipping away. Lynne was deeply grateful that at least one person had the wits not to hurry forward, overflowing with words.

Mechanically, she shook the hands that were thrust at her and nodded in response to the muted offerings of condolence. All the while, Amy was diligently propelling her up the aisle toward the widening aspects of escape. Behind them, Dodie and Tommy stood besieged by friends. Lynne could hear Dodie's tremulous, sodden soprano effusively thanking people for coming. Was her voice meant as a reproach to Lynne?

The hired limousine stood directly opposite the door, the uniformed driver waiting. Lynne could see him leaning against the right front fender of the immense, black Cadillac, her eyes scanning the crowd. She wondered if he had to memorize the faces of those he transported in order to pick them out, after the services, of the crowds of mourners. She wondered what sort of man could, for a living, provide a service directly related to death and dying. He looked like a pleasant, good-natured young man. Maybe he simply didn't think about it, or maybe each day brought a different assignment: a wedding on Monday, a Bar Mitzvah on Wednesday, a funeral on Friday.

As they arrived at the car—the chauffeur standing with the passenger door open—Lynne turned suddenly and gripped her sister's arm. "What the *hell* am I going to *do*?" she whispered urgently.

"Get in," Amy said softly. "We'll talk about all that."

"I feel so scared," Lynne said through clenched teeth. "I don't even know what I'm scared *of*."

"Get in, sweetheart," Amy repeated in the same soft tone.

For a long moment, Lynne continued to stand, her hand hard around Amy's arm, her eyes tracking the passage of the last of the crowd as it dispersed; the people slid into the stream of pedestrian traffic, blending, disappearing. She looked at the driver who stood with seemingly endless patience, waiting while Amy tried to get her to enter the back of the limousine. The pearl gray upholstery and dark-tinted windows distressed and frightened her. The interior of the car was altogether too coffinlike.

"We'll walk home," Lynne told the driver, then looked to Amy for approval. "Please?"

The young man also looked to Amy for approval.

Amy deftly repositioned Lynne's hand so that they were arm in arm, then told the driver, "We'll be walking."

As they moved along the sidewalk, Lynne said, "I kept looking at everyone the entire time, wondering what they were thinking. Did it make sense to you?" She glanced at Amy, and, without awaiting an answer, went on talking.

"Nothing makes sense to me. I mean, it does, off somewhere at the top of my head. But none of it makes sense."

"I felt that way when Mother died. Didn't you?" Amy said. "There's a part of us that knows nobody lives forever. But somehow that part's never connected to the part that's just not prepared for it actually happening."

"That's it!" Lynne said with more animation than she'd displayed in the past four days. "That's exactly it! I mean, when Alec and I were first married, if he was delayed, or forgot to be somewhere when he was supposed to be, I'd go through this little ritual in my head. I'd feel a terrible pain in my throat and an emptiness in my head: grief. That's not at all how I feel now. It's not the way it's supposed to feel; nothing is. God! I don't *know* what I'm supposed to feel!" She turned abruptly, coming to a halt, her hand again gripping her sister's arm. "I need you to help me. I've got to get his things out of the . . . I want to get rid of all of it. Every time I open a closet or a drawer, I can smell . . . I want to do it now, this afternoon."

"All right," Amy agreed.

"You think I'm losing my mind!" Lynne accused, sensing her reflection in Amy's eyes, feeling in all of Amy's reactions the strangeness of her own behavior.

"No, I don't," Amy disagreed calmly. "In a way, everything you've said makes perfect sense. Come on! Let's go home. We can stop by the supermarket, see if they've got any boxes."

Amy's agreeing to assist, her willingness, overcame Lynne as nothing to this moment had. Unable to help herself, she managed to reel several steps into a doorway where she sagged against the wall and surrendered to the hoarse, gasping noises that came involuntarily from her throat. No tears. Just this inhuman, wrenching noise that went on for several minutes while Amy hovered in protective closeness, appearing as helpless as she felt. Lynne wanted to speak, to indicate she understood how foolish Amy had to feel, but all of her being directed itself toward this painful and embarrassing wheezing.

At last, when she was able to breathe more or less regularly, Lynne managed to say, "I'm sorry. I didn't know that was going to happen."

"Why are you apologizing?" Amy asked, perplexed. "Don't do that! I'm not some stranger; I'm your *sister*."

"I'm sorry," Lynne said, apologizing now for apologizing in the first place. She wished she could explain the images of Alec that clicked on and off inside her head, and how those images drove her from love to anger to frustration back through love to an overwhelming sense of impotence, on and on. She was besieged by interior pictures and battling emotions. The effort to contain it all made her feel thin and weak.

"D'you really want to do that today? Will it make you feel any better?" Amy asked.

"Yes."

"Okay, then, we'll do it. They're bound to have some cartons at the supermarket."

At Lynne's request, Amy called the Salvation Army and explained the situation. It wasn't normal procedure, she was told, but under the circumstances, they'd arrange to have a truck make the collection within the hour. Amy hung up and returned to stand in the bedroom doorway watching Lynne tear Alec's clothes from the hangers and thrust them into the boxes on the floor. When the closet was empty, Lynne rushed to the dresser, threw open the drawers and dumped armloads of socks and underwear and shirts to the floor. Her movements were jerky and scarcely coordinated, like those of a frightened bird. The drawers empty, she took a step in one direction, then a step back, then darted from the room and ran the length of the apartment to the closet by the front door. She flung Alec's topcoats onto the floor. His old Dunlop tennis racket and a pair of ragged tennis shoes joined the pile, followed by some rubber overshoes, several wool scarves and a hat.

From her vantage point by the bedroom door, Amy stood watching as items flew past the open closet door, to accumulate in a heap. Watching all this, she felt as if her sister had moved into an area of reality that she herself had no concept of. Having a husband die was not at all the same as having a husband leave you for another woman. But perhaps, Amy reasoned, it wasn't all that different, either. Both ways it hurt and maddened. She thought, seeing Lynne reappear breathless and flushed from behind the closet door, that if she'd had the opportunity to savage her former husband's possessions as Lynne was now doing, she'd have done it.

Lynne kicked at the pile of coats, then whirled around and went through the living room directly to the bar. She poured half a glass of Scotch and drank it down, then poured some more into the glass, this time adding ice and water.

"I'll have the same," Amy said, upon returning from carrying the coats and shoes to the bedroom.

Automatically, Lynne fixed a duplicate drink for her sister, then left it on the bar as she wandered over to the window to look down at the street. Her body twitched with the need to do something more, to find every last thing that belonged to Alec and either destroy it or consign it to the items to be collected by the Salvation Army. "I'll feel better when it's all gone," she said. "I couldn't open the medicine cabinet because his things . . . I just got a garbage bag and threw everything out."

"Why don't you come back to Greenwich with me, stay for a few days?"

"I don't know."

"You don't want to stay here," Amy said reasonably.

"I've got to spend the rest of my goddamned life here! I might as well start getting used to it." A picture clicked into place: she and Alec at the closing, signing the documents, paying the money that purchased this apartment.

"Who said you've got to spend the rest of your life here?" Amy asked. "Did you sign some sort of lifetime covenant?" To her surprise, Lynne laughed. "Well?" Amy persisted. "Did you?"

"Of course I did," Lynne said bitterly. "It just happens that the lifetime was shorter than I thought it'd be."

"Come back to Greenwich with me," Amy repeated.

"I want them to take the bed, too. D'you think they'll take it?"

"I don't know. We'll ask."

"Don't let me forget! I want them to take it."

"We could drive back in your car. That way, you can come back whenever you're ready."

Amy's voice went on, making plans. Lynne found herself relying upon its insistent presence; it seemed to assist the surge of her thoughts in their hurried flow. If she could just maintain their momentum, something of importance might come clear to her, something that would get her past this moment. It was no good, nothing was clear.

"I've never lived alone," she said, still gazing out the window. "D'you know that? First we lived at home. Then I lived in the dorm. Then I shared that apartment on Seventy-first Street with Eileen. Then I married Alec. I don't know if I know how to live alone."

"It isn't difficult," Amy said from the sofa. "In fact, I know it's not the best time to say this, but it can actually be pretty damned good. I think we should leave as soon as they've made the pick up. We can eat when we get home."

"That's *your* home," Lynne corrected her, turning finally from the window to look at Amy. "*This* is supposed to be *my* home."

"It still is."

"I don't know. Why am I so *scared*? I'm not a kid. I'm almost forty years old."

"Thirty-eight," Amy amended. "Let's not rush it."

"But there's no reason for me to be so scared. I feel as if I'm never going to be able to . . . trust anyone. They'll say and do things I'm supposed to believe, but I know I won't believe anything I'm told because the minute I start believing, people will start doing things to . . . hurt me. . . . God! . . . the way this hurts . . ."

"You'll get over it."

"How do *you* know?" Lynne challenged.

"I just know. Why don't you come sit down?"

"I can't. I'm too . . . I don't want to sit down. I'll sit in the car."

Relieved to know that in Lynne's mind the question of her spending some time in Greenwich had been settled, Amy took a sip of her drink and relaxed somewhat.

"I wish," Lynne said slowly, "that I'd never laid eyes on him."

"You don't mean that."

"No." Lynne sighed and turned back toward the window. "I don't mean that. One minute I feel like I'm being pushed onto a roller coaster. The next minute I feel as though if Alec were alive I'd kill him for doing this! Did you see that Dianna was there?"

"I saw her."

Lynne shook her head. "That was real. Just that."

"There was a whole group of people from the network."

"Dianna was alone," Lynne said. "I know that." Once more she looked down at the street. "I know she was alone." The thought of Dianna, the memory of that moment when their eyes had connected, was oddly, unexpectedly comforting now.

The doorbell rang. Lynne jumped, causing the Scotch to splash over her hand.

"It's just the Salvation Army people," Amy said, rising from the sofa. "I'll look after it."

"Thank you," Lynne said, her mouth too dry, her heart beating too fast, too hard. A voice inside her head repeated Thankyouthankyouthankyou, while she wondered who she'd thought it might be at the door. Certainly not Alec, having forgotten his key. Definitely not Alec, returned early from a business trip. Never Alec, with a paper cone of flowers and that smile . . . the way he'd smiled. . . . Of course she'd expected it to be Alec.

FALL, 1965

❖❖❖❖❖❖❖❖

❖ *One* ❖

SHE STOOD NEAR the living room window watching the young man rake the last of the leaves onto a large canvas sheet he'd spread on the ground by the driveway. A dozen times he'd covered the sheet with a huge damp mound of leaves, then he'd folded the corners over diagonally, careful not to allow any of the leaves to escape. Finally, he'd grasped the four corners of the canvas and hefted the huge, rounded parcel off the ground and over to the pickup parked in the driveway behind her car. The truck, Lynne had noted, could hold four of these loads. After each fourth load, the young man wiped his hands down the sides of his well-worn denim overalls, climbed into the cab and drove off to the dump. This was his last load. The area now had the close-clipped, shorn look of a small boy who'd undergone his first haircut: a little embarrassed, but proudly trim.

She'd waited too long to have the leaves cleared. It had been a rainy autumn and the rain had turned the lower layer of first-fallen leaves to mulch. The young man had had to work hard and long—she glanced at her watch to see he'd spent almost eight hours clearing the property—to remove first the last-fallen, lighter layer, then the sodden, darker underlayer. Now he was finished. He'd take this last load to the dump and return to be paid.

The sky was already going dark. Daylight saving would end in another week and then night would settle in in late afternoon. For a few seconds she contemplated the warmth and glow of an imagined fire burning in the grate, the cozi-

35

ness of the cottage. It was a charming little place with unexpected nooks and a surprising feeling of spaciousness, considering its size. It had a fanciful nature, full of light, utterly unmenacing. She loved the squared-off living room with its fireplace opposite the front door, and the north-facing wall of windows. The real estate woman who'd shown it to her had explained that the paneled area near the small kitchen had once been a rear door. "You had to have a rear door two hundred years ago, because if someone died in the house, you couldn't take them out the front door. Of course the mud-room door doesn't count. That was added much later on."

Lynne had listened, fascinated, to the woman during her telling of this baroque bit of historical custom; she doubted its authenticity but was intrigued nevertheless by its possible truth. Death should never travel out by the same door through which it came in. Periodically Lynne would stop to stare at the area where the rear door had once been, trying to imagine small somber parties of people cautiously maneuvering their dead through that slim rectangle.

An area to the left of the front door had been made into a bedroom by the addition of a number of louvered folding doors. During the day the doors could be folded out from the walls to screen off the bed. At night, ritually, Lynne folded first one half of the doors and then the other back to reveal the bed, the night table, and the chest of drawers that constituted the furnishings of her bedroom.

The entire cottage was less than six hundred square feet, but had been cleverly renovated by the previous owner who had torn out the old kitchen and bathroom and installed plain white fittings and tiles in the bathroom, and all new white cabinets and appliances in the kitchen. In the small mud-room off the kitchen were the washer and dryer and an extra storage closet. Lynne had intentionally underfurnished the place to maintain the illusion of space created by the vaulted, beamed ceiling.

A deep porch ran across the front of the cottage and sometimes she sat out there and watched the occasional car travel past on its way to the old, elegant Victorian houses farther along Pear Tree Point. At high tide she could see the water moving on the far side of the road, on its way to fill Gorham Pond. She felt especially peaceful sitting out on the porch with a cigarette and a drink, observing the way the light fell on the water.

The young man slammed shut the rear panel of the pickup and prepared to climb into the cab. Lynne walked to the desk to one side of the window wall and sat down to write his check. He'd asked for thirty dollars for the job, but she was sure he hadn't imagined there'd be quite this amount of work involved. Thirty dollars simply wasn't enough. She was positive he'd put in twice as much effort as he'd thought he'd have to, so she made the check out for fifty and then went into the kitchen to put on a pot of coffee. He'd refused her offers of coffee that morning, a sandwich at midday, a beer in the afternoon. Perhaps he'd accept a cup of coffee now. He had to be hungry after all those hours outside in the damp, chilly air, brushing up against late-blooming bushes that had sent small cascades of water washing down his arms.

She'd give the young man coffee, and possibly a sandwich, then get back to work on the latest revisions of the rape script. Ned still hadn't given his okay for her to go ahead with the project, but she was determined that he would, and in the meantime she'd rework the script. Dianna was also eager to work on this segment, but so far Ned had blocked the proposal nine times. Lynne was convinced he'd never even passed her written proposal on to Keith, the executive producer, as he'd said he'd have to. "I can't approve this," he'd told her when Lynne had initially presented him with the idea. "Rape, for God's sake. Who the hell's going to want to watch a segment on that?"

More calmly than she'd felt, Lynne had replied, "Thirty or forty million women and girls, that's who."

"No go," he'd said flatly, and returned the proposal to her without even bothering to read it. "I want you to go up to Maine and do a piece on Margaret Chase Smith," he'd informed her. "It's already budgeted. Chuck'll be your unit manager. Get yourself a P.A., put the rest of the unit together and get up there as soon as you can. She's going after the Republican presidential nomination.'' He'd smirked, as if the idea of a woman running for president was laughable.

"I want to do the rape segment, Ned,'' she'd reiterated. "I'll leave the proposal with you.''

She'd left the pages on his desk and returned to her office to get started on the Margaret Chase Smith piece.

She'd presented the idea again five months later. This time he'd promised to think about the possibility, then put her to work on a retrospective, lightweight piece on Gracie Allen, who'd just died.

The Allen piece was nominated for an Emmy but didn't win. Lynne sat down to revamp her rape proposal and once more put it into Ned's hands. He'd assured her he'd discussed the possibility of the segment with the higher-ups and was still working on it. In the meantime, he was sending her with a unit to Selma to march with Dr. Martin Luther King and document reaction to this quiet demonstration for Negro civil rights. It was a good assignment. She put her unit together and they went off to Selma. It was one of the few occasions when she got to work with Harvey, the more popular, easier-going host of the show. He liked her script, added a few ideas, asked if he could be present when she ran the processed film through the Moviola prior to editing and, in the end, approved of and thanked her for her effort. The Selma segment marked her move slightly away from Dianna toward the inner circle of male associates. Dianna was no longer assigned to Lynne as a matter of course and on two occasions Lynne had specifically to request Dianna for segments she wanted to do.

Again she'd presented Ned with her rape prospectus. Again he'd told her he was working on it. Months passed, then more. As far as she was concerned, there was no such thing as an impasse. She'd do the segment if she had to stay with "Up to the Minute"—assuming it didn't one day get killed in a ratings race—until she was seventy years old. And Dianna would do the interviews. Lynne only hoped Dianna would be able to cope with it, when the time finally came. Dianna had, of late, taken to digging into their interview subjects, trying to ferret out their pretensions and expose them on camera. It was an inquisitorial style of journalistic reporting that the male hosts were engaging in more and more frequently—playing judge and jury for the benefit of the audience while maintaining bland, noncommittal facial expressions. It worked to a degree, but it was a style Lynne wasn't fond of and there were times when, watching the show from the control booth, witnessing Dianna's heavy-handed attempt to character assassinate an in-studio guest—she lacked the men's finesse and subtlety—she was tempted to lean over and whisper to Gus, the engineer, to throw the switch and go to dead air.

They got a lot of negative viewer mail, and it was becoming a regular weekly feature—one of Ned's clever ideas —to read letters from viewers at the end of each show, allowing the comments to speak for themselves. Often Dianna was lambasted for unnecessarily attacking someone, whether live or on film, and Harvey, who shared the on air reading of the letters with Mort Schneider, would smile as he read the condemnations. Surprisingly, the net result was to heighten Dianna's appeal. She generated more viewer mail than Harvey, Mort, Don, and Frank put together, and she was in no small way responsible for hiking the show's ratings.

The previous month had been the single most trying time for just about everyone involved in any way with television, due to the insane contest staged by the networks to air all the new shows as well as the returning programs in just seven days.

ABC had initiated the practice of a single week for the premieres of its new shows in the fall of '63. When they did it again in the fall of '64, the network went right to the top in the first ratings reports. The other networks weren't about to let it happen again, so everyone got into the act with premiere weeks. The result—certainly within Associated— was a state of panic unparalleled in anyone's experience. For weeks before, there were frenzied scheduling conferences, with shows being slotted, reslotted, re-reslotted in an effort to find the optimum placement. "Up to the Minute" went through two time-slot changes and was finally positioned in a very desirable early evening slot on Sundays, opposite "Lassie" and "My Favorite Martian" on CBS, "Voyage to the Bottom of the Sea" on ABC, and "The Bell Telephone Hour" on NBC. It was a carefully calculated risk that paid off. Associated's ratings climbed generally, and so did the show's. But everyone suffered from those weeks of crazed planning and scheduling. For seven nights, beginning on the twelfth of September, viewers had been faced with a staggering selection of thirty-five new programs and more than sixty returning shows. Once the week had ended and the first of the ratings had been released, it was generally accepted that this week of lunacy was destined to be repeated annually.

From Lynne's perspective, what had gone on within the network, as well as within the above- and below-the-line structure of "Up to the Minute"'s staff, seemed a sure indication that further radical changes were inevitable. This distressed her because she wasn't at all certain she wished to continue her involvement when it seemed television was bound to become as mediocre a medium as many of the products foisted on the public. If the season's new shows, like "Gilligan's Island," and "Gomer Pyle" were any indication of product quality, television could only go downhill. "My Mother the Car," "Please Don't Eat the Daisies," and "The Wackiest Ship in the Army" had to be shows that appealed to someone. But whom? The only show that had any appeal to Lynne herself was "Jeopardy," which, she thought with a smile, said a great deal about her personal taste. "Green Acres" and "O.K. Crackerby" and "Tammy" were all productions that set her teeth on edge. What had happened to good taste? Still, "Up to the Minute"'s ratings were holding, and for now, she'd continue to batter away at Ned.

A quiet tapping at the back door interrupted her thinking. She went through the mud-room to open the door, smiling at the young man.

"You've done quite a day's work. I've got your check ready. Come in for a moment."

The tall young man stepped into the mud-room and began energetically wiping his feet on the mat.

"I've just made fresh coffee," she told him from the doorway. "I insist you have a cup. And how about a sandwich? You can't work an entire day without eating or drinking something."

"I wouldn't mind coffee," he said, looking up at her through slightly lowered lashes so that, for a moment, he struck her as impossibly young. "Could I wash up somewhere?"

"The bathroom's just through there." She pointed and continued on her way to the desk.

He stood for a few seconds watching her walk away, experiencing an odd sense of expansion in his chest, a feeling like euphoria. He glanced at the bedroom, noting its contents, especially the double bed, and wondered if there was someone who came to sleep beside her in that bed with its pale blue sheets and soft-looking pillows. There was a photograph in an antique silver frame on the dresser, but he didn't feel he could risk taking the time to stop and look at it. He'd have liked to study everything very carefully, to examine those things with which she chose to surround herself.

He went to the bathroom sink, reached for the soap that sat in a small white enamel dish and began to wash his hands. He breathed deeply, relishing the mingled scents of fresh-brewed coffee, cut flowers, and her perfume which had a kind of a spicy edge to it that made his nostrils contract pleasurably.

The bathroom was spotless, and entirely white, even the towels and shower curtain. There was a clothes hamper beside the tub, and he was willing to guess it was empty. She didn't seem to him like someone who'd save up laundry—the way he did—until there was nothing clean left to use. Every two weeks he filled a couple of plastic garbage bags with dirty clothes and bed linens, drove over to the nearest coin-laundry and sat in one of the plastic chairs, reading, while he waited for his clothes to finish spinning through one cycle or another.

He dried his hands on one of the soft white towels and returned to the kitchen, liking the place. Everything was just right: the white-painted shutters on the kitchen window, the hanging plants above, the white-on-white linoleum, the ranks of white cabinets with porcelain knobs, the rack of copper pots by the stove. Everything was so clean. He had a sudden, irrational desire to step over to the cabinets and run his tongue lightly over the dazzlingly white surface. He shook his head, smiling to himself. Weird stuff, he thought, thrown by entertaining such a lunatic notion.

She tore the check from the book, thinking suddenly about Alec. He'd have objected to her paying this young man anything more than the agreed upon price, not out of any meanness of spirit but because when giving his estimate for the work the young man should have more closely investigated exactly what was involved in the job. But everyone made errors in judgment, she heard herself disagree. It wasn't fair to penalize someone for a temporary lapse in judgment. Certainly in her forty years little she'd witnessed and experienced had had much to do with fairness.

Her mother would have done what Lynne was doing: paid extra for a job well done. Her mother had had a strong sense of fair play and justice, but then her mother had been a woman who'd espoused causes. Not a dabbler at charity, nor someone given to token gestures, she'd picketed and marched and sat on cold pavements for the sake of peace. At the age of sixty-eight she'd placed her thin squarish bottom on the pavement outside the White House in peaceful protest against the treatment of southern Negroes. Her mother's courage and conviction had always been the ideal against which Lynne had evaluated her own actions.

John stood near the sink and watched her return from the living room. She was, he thought, an intriguing woman, lean and elegant and sad, with an aura of quiet strength. She looked, with her long blond hair and pale skin, her large blue eyes and strong, sharp nose, wide mouth, and firm jaw—definite, completely formed and finished. Not like the girls he sometimes dated who all looked half-done to him, as if they'd been taken out of the oven too soon. The edges of these young women seemed to him to be all runny, blurred like underdeveloped photographs. Lynne Craig looked completed, fully formed. He admired her tall angularity and wide shoulders, the suggestion of small breasts, long thighs.

"I made the check out to cash. I thought it would be easier for you." She handed him the folded paper.

"Thanks." He pushed it into his overalls pocket without looking at it. He felt he was staring and made a conscious effort to avert his eyes from her, taking in more details of the kitchen: an ashtray on the counter half-filled with cigarette stubs, a delicate streamer of dust up in the corner.

"Have some coffee," she invited.

"Well, okay. If you're sure."

"It's already made. How do you take it?"

"Cream and sugar, or milk. Whatever."

She smiled and again he felt that expanding sensation inside his chest. Her smile was very wide, almost girlish, yet it didn't reach her eyes. He wondered what had happened to put that mist of pain in her eyes. She did look strong. She was, he thought, the perfect end result of generations of intelligent breeding between physically excellent types: tall, clear-complected, decisive, generous, and obviously smart. The town was full of women like her. But most of them had blank eyes and tightly-closed pocketbooks. He'd met a lot of the women around town. He did their lawns in summer and their yardwork in the spring and fall. In the winter he plowed their driveways and came around with jumper cables to get their Benzes and Jaguars, their Alfa Romeos and Porsches started after the batteries had died down from sitting idle six or eight or twelve weeks while their owners wintered in Florida, or Jamaica, or the West Indies. Physically excellent types. It was something, he thought, that Snow would say. Snow had a passion for multisyllabic descriptive words; it was one of the interesting aspects of his character. Abie was forever teasing Snow for using three or four words where one might suffice.

They sat together at the table near the door to the kitchen. John wished he'd been able to change out of the overalls into something a little less damp and smelly; he felt uncomfortable, but after a few minutes he put it out of his mind. She was easy to be with. She didn't have any of that subsurface push most of the local women had; she didn't keep checking her watch, or recross her legs half a dozen times; her eyes didn't shift restlessly. She simply sat, both hands wrapped around her mug of coffee.

She stared at the young man, finding his face very beautiful. He had fine, almost delicate features that seemed very light in contrast to the rich, curling blackness of his hair, eyebrows, and lashes. His looks were so perfect that it was rewarding simply to be able to look at him. He couldn't have been more than twenty-two or -three, and had that enviable trimness and muscularity that only very young men seemed to possess. She found, gazing at him for a moment, that she couldn't conceive of ever again wanting to be so young.

"How about firewood?" he asked abruptly, looking so deeply into her eyes that she almost laughed aloud with delight. He was so very young; she'd forgotten until this moment the eager earnestness of young men. Alec had never had it; he'd always been the same—at forty-four he'd been precisely as he had at twenty-seven—without variation. But most of the Yale, Princeton, and Harvard men she'd known and dated during her early school years had displayed this same sort of near pathological sincerity. Or was she mistaken? Was she misreading his gestures and expressions? Since Alec's death she'd found herself more analytical of externals, of things and people who merely *seemed* to be a certain way while, in reality, it was she who'd applied her own appreciation and expectation to these things and people, tinting them with inappropriate tones. She was far more careful now than she had once been—about almost everything.

"I will be needing some," she said, looking past him as if at some critically diminished woodpile only she could see. "What do you charge?"

"I can get it for you at sixty a cord. It's good mixed woods for burning. I'll stack it for you, too, if you like."

"How much d'you think I'll need?" she asked, still contemplating that unseen woodpile so that he felt free to study the soft curve of her lips and the tautness of the skin over her cheekbones, the thrust of her chin.

"Think you'll be having a lot of fires?" he asked, his eyes measuring her breasts, then moving quickly to rest on her wide, long-fingered hands.

Her eyes returned to him. "Not a lot," she said consideringly. "I think a cord should be more than enough."

"I'll deliver it Saturday, if that's all right."

"That'll be fine. Are you sure you wouldn't like a sandwich, or some soup?"

"No, thanks. I've really got to be going." He didn't want to go. He'd have liked to stay for hours just looking at her, watching her, whispering his thoughts into the air between them and then examining her responses to the words he might say. He gulped down the last of his coffee and got up. "I'll be by on Saturday. Thanks an awful lot for the coffee."

She walked with him to the back door. As he was about to climb into the pickup, she called out, "What's your name again?"

"Grace. John Grace."

"John," she repeated, and watched him drive away. Grace. The name suited him. She closed the mud-room door and leaned against the washing machine, looking into the kitchen. In two hours Ross would arrive to pick her up. The thought of it set her on edge; she couldn't help feeling it had been a mistake to accept his invitation.

From the moment of their introduction a week earlier at a cocktail party her sister Amy had given for the members of her tennis club, Ross had displayed a keen interest in Lynne. Within half an hour of their meeting he'd asked her out to dinner. She wished now she'd refused. In the past two years she'd accepted quite a number of dates, at first with a kind of frantic zeal, as if she were being offered entrée back into her old life, or perhaps into some exotic new one. Nothing remotely like that happened. There were men who seemed content simply not to have to eat alone;

there were others who believed the answer to all a widow's problems lay in having her obviously repressed sexual appetite satisfied. These men attempted to lay claim to her body like quietly crazed prospectors discovering a mother lode. They reached for her breasts, sought out her mouth, stroked and caressed, and were all, ultimately, rejected. Since she had no desire for any man, she'd all but lost interest in dating. She was tired of saying no, of plucking hands from her body; tired of being made to feel guilty for wanting to say no.

She shivered, feeling a draft coming around the edges of the mud-room door. Rubbing her hands up and down her arms, she moved into the kitchen and picked up her notes from the counter. She'd get another hour's work done before she got ready for her evening out.

Waiting for the light to change on the Post Road, John reached into his pocket for the check. Fifty dollars. He looked at the endorsement for a long moment before carefully returning the check to his pocket. He heard the honking of horns and jerked his head up to see in the rearview mirror a row of cars behind him. He threw the shift into first and accelerated. He wondered what she'd do if he asked her out. Probably laugh in his face and tell him to get lost. No. She wasn't like that. She'd turn him down nicely, politely, regretfully. And that'd be the last odd job he got from her. He told himself to forget it. He'd call Lizzie and go out for hamburgers, some beers. What, he wondered, would Abie do? Or Snow? Snow would call her up on the phone, charm her with four- and five-syllable words. Abie would show up on her doorstep with an armload of flowers and an irresistible smile.

He didn't have the right words, or a smile women found tantalizing; he wished he did.

She settled in the rocker with a fresh cup of coffee, her notepad, a file of articles clipped from newspapers, medical journals, and women's magazines, and tried to concentrate. She read several of the articles then stopped, realizing she had no idea what she'd read. She went back and forced herself to pay attention. At six o'clock, she put her notes and the file aside and got up. She'd present the idea to Ned for the tenth time and for the tenth time he'd lie and tell her it was being considered upstairs, or spin her some story about trying to find a place to fit it into the schedule. She'd leave the proposal with him for another week or two, and then she would, as she'd been planning, make arrangements to do the segment independently. She'd put aside enough money to cover the cost of a bare-bones unit, and Dianna had agreed to moonlight. Someone, somewhere had to be willing to air an important piece that concerned all women.

It was time to get ready for her evening out with Ross. She yawned, wishing she were about to settle in for a quick dinner of scrambled eggs followed by an evening of reading or television. She would not think again about Ned today, would not think about her mounting frustration not only with him but with everyone connected with the program. It was legend that all directors—in her case, associate producer and director—waged ongoing war with all producers, doing battle on behalf of the crew, on behalf of the script, fighting for budget money, for time, for quality, for the right to artistic integrity in a business that understood only ratings, commercial sponsors, tepid topics guaranteed to offend no one, and sit-coms geared for ten-year-olds. She sighed and walked toward the bedroom.

❖ *Two* ❖

"WHY WON'T YOU give her the okay on the segment?" Dianna asked, leaning across Ned to retrieve her Scotch. "It wouldn't kill you. It'd probably make you into a hero."

"Why do I have the feeling I'm being engineered here?" he asked sharply, his attention momentarily diverted by the soft heavy sweep of her breast against his arm.

"Because you are," she said simply, gulping down the watery residue of her drink. "You owe it to her, to us. How the hell many times now has she given you scripts, proposals, outlines, and all the rest of it? Eight, nine times? Why're you stalling?"

"D'you honestly think just because you give great head I'm going to roll over and play good doggie?"

"Thank you." She smiled at him. "Yes, I do. If you won't do it for Lynne, do it for yourself. It's about time the show got a little bolder. Eventually, you know, people are bound to get fed up watching weekly political exposés and the latest medical scam. D'you have any idea what the rape statistics are? Have you ever even looked at Lynne's proposal? How would you feel if it happened to your wife or maybe one of your kids?"

"C'mon, Dianna. I'm not going to buy dramatics. Nobody wants the piece done. Nobody but you two pains in the ass. Can you see me going to Keith and asking for a budget for a *rape* segment? He'd laugh me right out of the goddamned office, right out of my goddamned *job*."

"Christ! It was bad enough when I thought maybe you were a fag, I never dreamed you were a coward too."

"Watch your mouth!" He grabbed hold of her wrist and held it hard. "I think maybe this would be a good time to call off this show," he said evenly, his hand closing tightly around her wrist. She made no effort to free herself but just stared at him. Her lack of reaction forced him to ease his grip somewhat, but not to release her.

"No more matinees?" she asked coolly.

"This is a fucking joke to you," he declared.

"It certainly isn't. I've never believed in mixing business with pleasure. This was your idea. I've always wanted to think I could get along without sex altogether. After you, maybe I will."

"Relax," he said, letting go of her, knowing it was the truth. He had been the one to pursue her. It had been a challenge to see if he could get her into bed. Instead, he'd wound up addicted to their "matinees" as she called them. "Your job isn't riding on this."

It sure as hell is, she thought.

"Maybe you'll tell me why you've suddenly decided to start championing Lynne's cause," he said, lighting a cigarette, taking a puff and then putting it out. He was trying to quit smoking.

"Because it's about time you stopped treating her like the house nigger and started giving her some decent assignments. She's better than most of the men and you damned well know it."

"I know it," he admitted surprisingly.

"You know it!" She stared at the complacent expression on his face and wondered why she'd ever allowed herself to become involved with him. Sure, part of it had been political in intent, and that was the dangerous part. Having an affair with the producer could blow up in her face, see her out on the street looking for a new job if he decided that was what he wanted. She wasn't a kid, certainly didn't have the face or body of one, so it never failed to surprise her that he continued to want to go to bed with her. As far as she could see, she'd trapped herself and could only go along with the situation until it ended one way or another. She should have turned him down that first time.

But she hadn't. She'd been flattered, and curious, and it had been months since anyone had wanted her. "If you know it," she said, "why don't you approve her proposal?"

He shrugged, and she wanted to wrap her hands around his throat and choke him. There he sat, in her bed, with his head resting comfortably on her pillows, idly scratching his thigh, dismissing Lynne as if she were a mosquito, dismissing her, Dianna, as if she were a slightly larger, more annoying mosquito. Who the hell are *you*? she thought, studying his faintly scarred cheeks, his too short nose and too small eyes, his short upper lip. A vain little man who'd already suffered—he'd talked long and loud about it— through two bouts of dermabrasion to rid himself of old acne scars; an arrogant little bastard who'd been a total loss as a unit manager, and then as an associate, so instead of firing him as they should have done they'd promoted him to producer, putting him in charge of the whole damned shooting match, thereby giving him the power he'd always craved. He appeared to believe it was he, and not the seven associates and four hosts, who did all the work, who spent twelve-hour days on location, and fifteen-hour days in the editing room. He took credit for anything and everything, except of course problems, mistakes of judgment, and less than perfect production. She continued to see him because she was more than a little frightened of him. He was capable of carrying his personal feelings over into the professional arena. She taunted him; they played a mutually satisfying game; but in reality he pulled all the strings and she knew it.

"The producer," she said slowly, then repeated it, stressing each of the syllables. "The pro-du-cer. You're amazing!"

He smiled, complimented.

"What would it take to get you to approve the segment?" she asked, placing her hand flat on his chest. He did have a good body, firm and smooth; he played tennis several times a week and worked out regularly. He was tireless, willing to go on and on making love until she had to ask him to stop. She wondered, not for the first time, what would happen if she failed, just once, to ask him to stop. Would he go on making love to her until one or the other of them died of it? She suspected he just might. There was a lot of pride tied up in his ardor. He liked to lean on his elbows above her and, smiling into her face, observe, "That's five times I've made you come." At first she'd found it novel that he could be so aware of her, but as the months passed and she became accustomed to him, she came to recognize that his supposed awareness was part of a pattern. She was positive he'd done all this, said all these same things to dozens of other women. He'd noted the number and quality of their orgasms and commented upon them; he'd dipped his fingers into them and then, with a dreamy expression, had popped his fingers into his mouth; he'd "gone around the world" on them the way he had on her, repeatedly, as he'd murmured compliments about the various parts of her flesh with which he was involved. He was a walking, breathing sex manual, complete with running commentary, hand, facial, and vocal gestures. He knew more about making love than he did about the women with whom he involved himself. She was beginning to loathe herself for continuing to see him. He made her feel like a performing seal, like a freak. He had an uncanny instinct for commenting on those aspects of her physical self she least liked—her superior height, the size of her breasts, the length of her neck, and the erotic qualities of her too-wide mouth. She wished he'd grow tired of her and put an end to the whole business.

"Let her do it, Ned," she said, stretching out on top of him.

"Why?" he asked, at once engaged with her body, his hands shaping her buttocks.

"Because *I* want to do the segment. I need to do a really serious piece. I need to establish some credibility. I'm getting a reputation as the show's heavy. This piece would be sympathetic. Do it as a favor to me."

"What's it worth to you?" he asked, grinning.

"What's it worth to *you*?" she countered, touching her tongue to his chin, the seal performing right on cue.

"A farewell present maybe," he said, his hands sliding up and down her waist.

"Farewell? From what?" For a second or two her spirits soared, thinking he might announce his intention to leave the show, that he'd landed something bigger and better and was moving on.

"Us," he said, grounding her spirits instantly. "This is getting tricky. Let's call it off with no hard feelings. You be a good girl and behave yourself and I'll send up the proposal for budgeting."

"It's a deal," she said, wondering if she could trust him, wondering too why she felt so angry at his calling off the affair when she'd been hoping he'd do so.

"You're a bitch," he whispered, urging her up on her knees. "You know that, don't you? You're one of the biggest bitches I've ever known, in every department. But you fuck like a bandit."

"So why call it off?" she asked, hating herself for giving in and asking.

"Not my idea," he said, playing with her breasts as if they were made of plasticene. "I was given a little talking-to by Keith. Apparently somebody saw us and made a point of mentioning it. I alibied, said we were working something up." He smiled, pleased with his little joke.

"And I'm a bitch?" she said, eyebrows lifted. "You're a fucking coward!"

"Absolutely true," he conceded. "But I can't afford to blow the job. I've got my eye on certain things."

"Jesus Christ!" she exclaimed. "So you're buying me off."

"Not altogether. We'll see."

"I should've asked for more."

"You bitch!" he laughed. "You were never asking for Lynne."

"You're not giving it to me for Lynne." He pressed his hands into her belly, maneuvering her to his satisfaction and she wanted to strike him, deal him a blow that would send him to the floor. She had to remain acquiescent, though, maintain the pretense that she derived pleasure from his measured thrusting. She wished she'd never raised the subject of Lynne's proposal, not because she didn't want to see

Lynne get the assignment but because she felt she had, in some indirect fashion, soiled Lynne by discussing her project while naked and in bed with this untrustworthy, treacherous little son of Sammy Glick.

After he'd gone—hurrying to catch the train from Penn Station to Great Neck—she ran a bath and sat in the tub with a glass of Scotch near at hand, considering what she might have gained from extracting his so-called promise. He wouldn't dare renege, she told herself, thinking about how neatly he'd dumped her. Well, she wasn't sorry. Three months with Ned and it felt as if she'd used up her lifetime's ration of lust. Ned liked to use people, and he'd used her. He wasn't going to get away clean. She'd make him deliver that segment if it was the last thing she ever did.

She remained soaking in the tub for over an hour. Then, a little high, she pulled on her robe and went into the bedroom to call Lynne.

"Ned's going to pass your proposal on to Keith for budgeting," she told Lynne.

"When did you hear that?" Lynne asked.

"This afternoon. He told me he was going to."

"I don't believe it. Why after all this time would he suddenly pass it on?"

"He *said* he'd do it." Lynne's skepticism was making Dianna angry. "What the hell d'you want, a signed affidavit?"

"From Ned, yes. What made him change his mind?"

"Maybe you just wore him down. Who knows? Anyway, he's agreed to let me do it with you. You'd better ask for Gloria from the pool right away. Once the budget comes down, we'll be able to put a unit together and get going."

"I'll get on it tomorrow. Dianna, are you sure?"

"All this doubtful female crap drives me crazy. Will you for chrissake stop it! He said he'd pass it through. What the hell else d'you want me to do?" I ate him like candy to get him to do it, she thought furiously, tempted to say this to Lynne. Like a goddamned ice cream cone.

"Why are you angry?" Lynne asked quietly. "You know Ned as well as I do. I'm surprised you're taking his word on this."

"Listen, you want something, go the hell after it! How d'you think assholes like Ned get ahead? You think they sit around worrying about why people do what they do? You wanted the piece, you've got it. Why the hell did I bother?"

"I take it I have you to thank for this, is that correct?" Lynne paused, then said, "I'm not going to ask you what you had to say or do."

"No, don't!" Dianna said crisply. "You wouldn't enjoy hearing about it."

"I wouldn't have let you . . ." Lynne began.

"You don't run my fucking life!" Dianna cried.

"Oh, God," Lynne sighed. "I hope he doesn't shaft us again."

"Over my dead body."

"I'm beginning to wonder if it's worth this much grief."

"Don't you go crapping out on me now!" Dianna warned. "Not after I finally managed to convince the son of a bitch to sent it up to Keith."

"I'm not crapping out. You know I've got my own money set aside."

"Yeah," Dianna said, calming down. "I know that. And you'd be an idiot to use your own money. Let *them* finance it! It's their goddamned show."

"I've got to go. I've got someone at the door."

"Go. We'll talk tomorrow." Dianna put down the receiver, picked up her glass, and went for a refill. Nothing was going the way she'd hoped it would. Lynne was supposed to be thrilled not doubtful. Ned wasn't supposed to dump her that way. She returned to the telephone to call Tricia. She wanted to talk to someone who'd be friendly, someone who belonged to her. She had to wait on the line while the girl who answered the phone at the dorm shouted for Tricia. Minutes went by and then Tricia came on.

"How's it going, baby?" Dianna asked.

"It's okay. You sound sloshed," Tricia accused.

"Maybe I am a little. Does it matter?"

"I wish you wouldn't call me when you get that way. It's so embarrassing."

"A couple of drinks and I'm an embarrassment? The kid that answered the phone can smell my breath?"

"Well, how are you?" Tricia asked patiently.

"I just wanted to call my daughter and find out how she is."

"She's fine. How are you?"

"Fine. D'you need anything, sweetheart?"

"You just sent me a check."

"I know that, but do you *need* anything?"

"No. Listen, I've got to go now. Okay? I'm studying. I've got a psych exam in the morning."

"Will you be coming home this weekend?"

"I can't. I've got an assignment that's got to be handed in on Monday. Trudy says she won't be coming either."

"When did you talk to Trudy?"

"The other night. I'll call you. Okay?"

"Okay." Dianna said flatly.

"Well, I'll talk to you later then. Okay?"

"Yup. Okay."

"Bye." Tricia hung up.

Dianna dropped the phone back into its cradle. She wouldn't bother to call Trudy now. Talking to the girls didn't help anything. She wondered why she always thought it would. They didn't want to hear from her, she was an *embarrassment*. Christ! she thought. If you knew the things I've done to keep you in those goddamned schools, to pay for your clothes, your braces, your mid-term trips to here, there, and everywhere but home.

She walked into the kitchen and turned on the light, opened the refrigerator door and peered inside. There was nothing she felt like eating. She shouldn't have called Tricia. Kids were so damned sensitive. She closed the refrigerator door and wandered into the living room where she slumped onto the sofa, cradling her drink in her hands, staring straight ahead. Not yet eight o'clock. The empty evening yawned in front of her. She looked down to see that her glass was empty, and she'd left the bottle in the bedroom. She debated going for it. Another drink and she'd be plastered. She was already dizzy from three drinks on an empty stomach, worn out and sore from two hours in bed with that insatiable prick Ned. She got up, set the glass carefully on the coffee table and went to the bathroom where she leaned in close to the mirror to inspect her face. Without makeup she looked totally washed out. There were patches of broken veins, one on the side of her nose, two on her cheek. Her eyes looked watery, and her roots needed a touch-up. She shrugged off her robe, and turned to confront her image in the full-length mirror on the back of the door.

Fuck like a bandit, she thought, studying her body. What you fail to understand, little Neddy, is that you've got to use what you have. The thing is, what I have is going fast. A couple of years and I'll be fifty. By then, I've got to have everything in place in my career because I won't be able to peddle the bandit anymore. Look at me! Big goddamned sagging tits with nipples turned brown from nursing two kids who grew up to find me embarrassing; stretch marks, and thighs turning flabby.

She bent unsteadily to pick up her robe, turning her back on the mirror. Belting the robe, she found the Scotch on the bedside table in the bedroom and carried it to the living room where she scooped up her glass from the coffee table, uncapped the bottle, and poured herself a hefty slug of amnesia. She laughed. She'd been calling booze amnesia for seven or eight years now. She was mighty damned careful with the stuff, but every so often, like now, a good dose of amnesia was just what the doctor ordered. She'd get quietly pied and then go to sleep, put everything out of her mind.

She awakened and looked at the clock. Just after one. She pushed the pillows up behind her head and reached for the telephone. It rang twice on the other end and then he answered. She located her glass and positioned it on her chest as she spoke, pausing every so often to take a sip. He listened for a time, then said, "Sleep it off, Dianna. Put the phone down now and sleep it off." Softly, almost noiselessly, he hung up. She wiped the tears off her nose and sat in the dark finishing her drink.

✤ Three ✤

Ross Fairstone sat abstractedly drumming his fingers on the all but empty file Brad had laid on his desk fifteen minutes earlier. He stared out the window not seeing the familiar view of Manhattan spread below. He was a little bothered by the lack of material in the file. His instinct insisted there should have been more. She had an excellent credit rating; she was a widow with a sister—Amy, whom he'd known through his late wife, Ella, for a number of years—in Greenwich; she was an associate producer on the television program "Up to the Minute," of which he was a fan; she had a Connecticut driver's license; the car, a late-model BMW, and the house in Darien were registered solely in her name. She'd paid just under twenty thousand cash for the cottage, she owned the BMW outright, and her salary was listed at twenty-one thousand a year.

The paucity of information disturbed him somewhat but not nearly as much as this routine of checking out every new person he met. Company policy had long since overrun his life, but he had no intention of calling off his date with Lynne. Despite the insistent feeling that the file was incomplete, he believed she'd told him the truth. Her husband had died close to two years earlier, and she'd moved from a co-op in Manhattan to the house near Pear Tree Point.

He swiveled around to press the intercom button. Brad responded at once.

"Send flowers, will you?"

"The usual?"

"Something different, I think."

"Yes, sir. Anything else?"

"I don't think so, Brad. Thanks."

Ross turned again to look out the window, this time noticing the flurries that had begun to fall. He watched the snow drift past the window, still feeling unsettled. There were times, like this one, when he heartily disliked the automatic cloak-and-dagger reactions he'd been obliged to adopt over the years. It struck him as ludicrous that his immediate instinct upon meeting someone, anyone, new should be to have that person thoroughly investigated. Yet that very instinct for precautions had saved the corporation untold sums of money and trouble; it had also spared him personally from several potentially embarrassing situations.

All in all, though, it was a pretty dismal way to live. If anyone had told him twenty-five or thirty years before that he'd live his life like some classic paranoid, suspicious of everyone from busboys to parking lot attendants, he'd have laughed at the sheer foolishness of it. At twenty-three he'd seen his entrance into the corporation as an exciting challenge, an opportunity to gain insights into a world that held a strong appeal for him. At fifty-five he viewed the corporation as a game gone out of hand, and his role in it was part of an existence to be survived until he could retire and leave behind the suspicions, the paranoia, the hypertension, the gladhanding, the artificial bonhomie. He felt tired, and often distraught; more and more frequently he couldn't seem to remember who he was, how he actually felt. Everything he saw, thought, did, and ate seemed to have been commanded of him via some interoffice memo or a friendly word of advice from some member of the board. The point was, of course, to protect the corporation, to ensure the continued growth of an organization that had at one time engaged in the very ordinary manufacture of tool and die parts. Today the tool and die plant no longer existed. The corporation, however, existed. It lived by taking over companies which were then either enlarged or improved, or were disbanded and dissolved. The corporation had evolved into a banking establishment, lending funds, carefully watching the prime rate, engaging in the purchase of certificates of deposit and, all the while, using its enormous wealth to its own convoluted purposes. Ross was thoroughly wearied of the game. Often now, he thought longingly of the old Long Island plant and trips out there to see how things were going, chats with the men, some of whom had been with the company forty and fifty years. They were all gone now, and the plant had been torn down in fifty-two to make way for a warehousing facility used exclusively by one of the corporation's subcompanies. Presently, there was heated discussion among board members as to the feasibility of razing the warehouse and erecting a more modern storage complex, possibly as part of an entire industrial park. Ross sighed and turned from the window. His hand still lay on Lynne Craig's file. He opened it and idly turned the half dozen pages inside.

He missed Ella, and the boys. The house sometimes daunted him with its silence, its everpresent dust that Mrs. Wain just seemed to skim over with her frivolous feather duster. She probably scattered more cigarette ash around the place than any ten heavy smokers could manage were they entrants in an ash-scattering contest. She was forever leaving half-empty coffee cups around the house, and Ross would come upon them—sometimes days later—to find whitish crusts growing across the stale remains of the coffee. She liked to sip at a tumbler full of Scotch while she prepared meals, and managed to get through a fifth of Red Label every four or five days. But her cooking was incomparable; she seemed to have limitless recipes stored in her memory. And she was always cheerful, even if she was somewhat haphazard in her housekeeping.

The boys were home less and less often these days. Ross Junior was talking about staying on in Boston after his senior year, and Bill was spending a post-graduate year at Cambridge, in England. That left Craig, and even Craig seemed to prefer spending his school breaks with friends, or skiing in Colorado. They'd all be coming home for Christmas, even Bill to whom Ross had sent a first-class ticket although Christmas was still a couple of months off.

After Ella's death, he'd found he had to set things up to look forward to. Christmas this year was one of those things. The year before it had been an outing over the Easter break to Palm Beach. He hoped Christmas wouldn't prove as disappointing as the Palm Beach trip when Craig backed out at the last minute to go to Vail, and Ross Junior had been sulky, brooding about something he'd refused to discuss. Ross knew he didn't have the right to pin his sights on the boys to the extent he did, yet without them, without that holiday or some outing to look forward to, he felt adrift.

He closed the Craig file and looked at the time. Three-forty. He was picking Lynne up at seven-thirty. They'd probably have a drink at her place and then go on to the club for dinner. He'd asked her out because she reminded him a bit of Ella, although Ella had been shorter, rounder, more given to laughter. Their coloring was similar, though, and he liked the husky tones of Lynne's voice. She was a physical type he didn't usually take much interest in. Yet despite her fashionably lanky appearance, he found her subtly sensual.

She felt odd, her insides unsettled, and tried to calm down, but she couldn't. She recalled her senior year at college, the production of *Romeo and Juliet*. She'd played the nurse. Waiting in the wings she'd been overcome by a combination of anticipation and dread, a feeling so strong it had turned her insides liquid, caused her hands to sweat and quiver, made her mouth and throat go dry, and she'd wished to God she'd never given in to the impulse to test her dramatic potential. She remembered none of the details of that performance beyond her interminable wait in the wings, listening so closely for her cue that she'd missed it altogether and only a shove from the stage manager had propelled her out onto the stage. That was all she remembered: someone else's strength providing the momentum to get her out there.

Arbitrarily she wished she were about to spend the evening with that beautiful young man. What was his name? John Grace. She'd have been content simply to sit studying his features, the contrast of his black hair to his creamy skin. There was something so wholesome and honest about him, something that spoke of little direct contact with the more sordid aspects of life; he seemed relatively untouched, untainted. His wholesomeness had the same effect upon her as the first snow of the season, or the sight of the first spring flowers: she wanted to freeze the moment, hold it captured forever so that she might endlessly restore her spirit with the sight of these things.

She threw open the closet doors and examined the clothes hanging inside. Where would Ross take her? Somewhere expensive, but quiet. Men like him were discreet about their evenings out; they didn't like too-public places. Ross's life, she thought with sudden insight, must be dreadfully routine: no spontaneous shifts in direction, no leeway for impulses; everything circumspectly correct. Could he possibly enjoy it?

She selected a pair of black wool slacks and a black silk shirt, laid them across the foot of the bed, then went into the bathroom to fill the tub. She paused on the way to raise the thermostat and heard the small surging noise as the furnace turned itself on. The days were already getting cold. One morning soon she'd step out to pick up the *Times* and see each blade of grass and all the shrubberies white with rime, surreal.

There were elements of her single life she found unexpectedly pleasurable: tending the small garden at the sunny side of the cottage, sitting on the front porch in the evening breathing in the salty air from the Sound, leaving Manhattan after work instead of traveling uptown to the apartment, the silence of mornings, many other things, and because they gave her pleasure she felt guilty. She was a widow. Her husband had ended his own life. She was still not entirely satisfied that she was blameless; she was still angry. Yet not only had she learned to function on her own, she actually enjoyed most of it. It seemed immoral that Alec's death should result, however indirectly, in her discovery of previously unsuspected resiliency, and of small personal pleasures. Therefore, she felt guilty.

Often she wanted to turn to include Alec in yet another discovery, but of course he wasn't there. Death was so damned bewildering. She would never acclimate herself to the stunning absence of her parents, of Alec, of the several school friends who'd died. She still remembered their telephone numbers, clothes they'd worn, things they'd said. How could they be dead when she knew so much about them?

The telephone rang and she went to answer, surprised to hear Dianna state, in her usual peremptory tone, that Ned was going to go ahead and present the rape proposal for budgeting. It struck Lynne as odd that it should be Dianna who'd break this news to her rather than Ned himself; it also struck her that Dianna had to have compromised herself in some fashion in order to get Ned to agree. She had so many conflicting reactions to this piece of news that she lied, saying someone was at the door, in order, first, not to get into an argument with Dianna, and secondly, to have some time to consider the numerous ways in which Ned might seek either to steal hers or Dianna's thunder, or to sabotage the segment altogether.

She climbed into the tub and looked down the length of her body, pallid and thin beneath the bathwater's oil-slick surface, and was repelled. Why did men claim to find women attractive? Only small children had perfect bodies; adults were assemblages of flaws and personal disappointments. The only woman she'd ever met who'd been completely content with her physical self had been the twenty-three-year-old *Playboy* Bunny who'd arrived at the high point of her life by being acclaimed Bunny of the Year, with the attendant seminude multipage spread in the magazine. She'd had the brain of an eight-year-old and the perfect, translucent prettiness of a still photograph. Dianna had asked how she felt about posing nude and the Bunny, in the trilling little voice of a toy made in California, had replied, "It's perfectly natural, isn't it? I mean, we're all the same, aren't we?"

Frank, the sound-man, had snorted, rolling his eyes. Lynne had laughed aloud, knowing they'd have to edit this bit out, and Gloria, who'd been assisting on this assignment had groaned, murmuring to Lynne, "Let me go over there and kill her. Please?" The camera still running, Dianna had, with typical panache, observed, "Some of us are more perfect than others," which had sent the entire unit into shrieks of laughter. The bewildered Bunny had looked over at Lynne to ask, "Is the camera still running?"

Ned had agreed to let her go ahead with the project. She wanted to believe it, but didn't dare. She wouldn't accept it as real until Ned himself told her it was okay, until the budget had actually been allocated. What, she wondered, had Dianna done? Lynne had suspected for several months that Dianna was having an affair with Ned. Dianna was subtle enough, and so was Ned, but there was a certain chemical reaction that occurred when the two of them were together at the office or in the studio. It was so damned dangerous! Dianna ought to know better. Lynne couldn't condemn her, though. It wasn't up to Lynne to make value judgments, especially where Dianna was concerned. But everyone said that the most important of Dianna's contracts had been signed and delivered in someone's bed. She seemed the least likely of women who'd seek to climb in this fashion, yet her exploits were common knowledge. Or was it, Lynne asked herself, just the typical gossip indulged in by everyone and anyone in the industry? The men were talked about too, in essentially derogatory tones. So-and-so was a queer; he'd been caught with some producer after hours in the editing room. So-and-so had just walked out on his wife and moved in with a twenty-year-old production assistant. So-and-so was angling for a contract with CBS and would be making the big announcement soon. There were new rumors every ten minutes, and a fair share of them were about Dianna. Perhaps she'd never done any of the dozens of things Lynne had heard her accused of. Lynne didn't want to believe that Dianna would stretch out naked for a hateful man like Ned in order to secure his promise that he'd pass on Lynne's proposal. She didn't want to be beholden to anyone for approval of the segment.

She climbed out of the tub and wrapped herself in a

towel, then stood watching the water swirl down the drain, momentarily hypnotized by the motion. The doorbell rang. Startled, she grabbed her robe and hurried to the door to accept a flower box from the delivery man who looked plainly annoyed at having been kept waiting. She carried the box to the kitchen where, feeling a queasiness, as if she were about to witness an autopsy, she prepared to open it.

John could hear the jukebox downstairs. Big business in pizza town, he thought, smiling. There was usually a rush between five and eight when the takeout business boomed and every table in the place was occupied by mothers with kids, the kids all bouncing around in their seats, demanding to know when they were going to eat. On weekends it was busy right from five until about midnight. Then it would slack off until closing at one on Fridays and two on Saturdays. Sunday the place was closed. It was the one day of the week when his apartment didn't reek of mozzarella cheese and tomato sauce and garlic; it was the one day when he could try to work in relative peace.

When he'd first moved in seven months earlier he'd been enamored of the idea of living over a pizza parlor. It had struck him as romantic in a totally twentieth-century fashion. The romance, however, died after the first weekend when the noise and the music and the smells had become overpowering and he'd sought refuge at the movies.

It wasn't a bad place, though. It was big: three large boxy rooms, a kitchen and a bathroom. The window frames had been painted so many times that there were only three windows in the entire place that would open. The wiring was pretty dicey, and there were legions of bugs—spiders, silverfish, cockroaches. Aside from the smell, what bothered him most was the potential for fire. With the wiring as screwed-up as it was, it seemed amazing that the restaurant hadn't yet gone up. He'd bought a small fire extinguisher and hung it in the kitchen on the wall near the stove. He hoped that if there was a fire he'd have a fighting chance of grabbing his typewriter and manuscript and getting the hell out before the place burned down.

He was about two-thirds of the way through his novel. He probably would have been finished by now but the noise from the jukebox distracted him to the extent that he was unable to work in the evenings until after eleven when the restaurant closed. Since he had to be up most mornings at six, he couldn't get a lot done, except on Sundays. So he was really only working on the novel one day a week. At this rate, Abie and Snow would be old, old men before he finished writing about them. And the thought of spending another year on the book robbed him of his interest. He wished the jukebox would break down, even if for only a few days. Then he'd be able to get a little bit ahead.

It would never happen, he told himself. Besides, when he went down for something to eat, he always jammed money into the damned thing himself. Without the music the place was so sad somehow he didn't like to eat there. Joe was a good guy, though, and Gina, his wife, had long-since stopped charging John for his meals. The two of them worked like crazy, what with putting pizzas together for takeout, and serving the dozen tables and booths. After school and on weekends their two kids would come in to help out and occasionally, when business was really good, John would go out on deliveries with the pickup. He'd make eight or ten dollars for a few hours' work and Joe would always throw into the bargain a pizza somebody had ordered but hadn't picked up. They were good people, honest, hard-working, and strict with the kids; always smiling and laughing, ready for a joke. On slow nights, Gina would come sit with him at the table while he ate. She'd smoke a cigarette and drink coffee and ask about his book. It wasn't a bad situation, all in all, if he could just put some more time in on Abie and Snow.

He remembered the check and pulled it out of his pocket. Lynne Craig. Obviously she'd realized he'd worked a lot longer than he'd thought he'd have to. Most of the people in town would've held him to the estimate, but she hadn't. He put the check on the corner of his work table and weighted it down with a ladybug rock he'd picked up last year at the Tokeneke school fair where he'd taken his nephew for the day as a favor to his sister, Cathy. The kid was wild, spoiled rotten. John had been glad when the time had come to take Luther—Luther, for God's sake!—home to Cathy, and had vowed he'd never babysit the kid again. Seven years old and Luther had already been held back for a second year in grade one because the school people had felt he wasn't ready for second grade. He was such a disruption that Cathy spent half her time at the school arguing with the teachers and principal on Luther's behalf. When, John wondered, was Cathy going to stop fighting and start accepting that maybe some of what people had to say about her kid was true?

He shook his head and sat down behind the desk looking first at the stack of completed manuscript pages and then at the check. Twenty dollars more than he'd asked for. Maybe he'd throw in some extra wood or something. He didn't feel right about the money, even though he'd worked for it. He didn't believe in taking what wasn't coming to him. He wanted to do something to show that he appreciated her gesture. But what?

Closing his eyes for a moment, he could summon her up. She stood in the kitchen smiling at him. He opened his eyes and looked around the room. He wanted to ask her out, to spend time with her; he wanted to touch her. Man! He shook his head again and pulled the manuscript toward him.

She had little lines around her eyes, very faint ones, and her skin looked soft, as if it had been well lived in. How old could she be? Thirty-four, thirty-five? She wasn't that much older. Maybe she wouldn't say no if he asked her out.

❖ *Four* ❖

Ross HAD SENT freesias. Red roses would have been more in keeping with her expectations of him. Freesias were a little mystifying. She felt both elated and confused. She wanted to believe the flowers were Ross's personal choice, that he hadn't had some corporate lackey call the florist. Were that the case, it signified more than professional, habitual good manners; it could mean that he was genuinely interested in her. But Ross struck her as the sort of man who'd have a cleverly skillful assistant, someone who'd instinctively sense what to send to whom. The card enclosed was simply one of Ross's business cards, which confirmed her suspicion that an assistant had done the ordering. She wondered, smiling, if the florist had files of business cards and simply attached an appropriate one to each order.

It was trivial, she told herself, of no importance. Yet it was important. Since their initial meeting the previous week she'd had the feeling that events were going to shift direction; she was standing on the brink of something. Again she felt guilty. Every time she went out on a date with a new man she felt disloyal, as if she were actively betraying Alec by accepting the attentions, no matter how slight, of other men. There were times when, angrily, she wished Alec would finally die for her so that she'd be free to live without guilt or anger. As it was, he was an unseen presence, sitting in judgment, commenting on the men she saw. Now Ross had entered her life, with his offering of freesias and his invitation to dinner, and she wanted to approach the situation with an open mind, but she couldn't stop processing Alec's thoughts and applying them to much of what happened in her life.

The truth was she'd found Ross attractive, appealing. More than that, she'd found him desirable. For the first time since Alec's death, she'd met a man who stimulated not only her brain but her nerve endings. It seemed dangerous, as if by admitting to more than a passing interest in a man other than Alec she was revealing a treacherous, trenchant vein of weakness in her nature.

Rather than continue to go through these enervating analyses of her actions, she frequently thought it would be far safer and less exhausting simply to stay at home alone. She felt furious with Alec for dying and leaving her alone to discover territories inside herself that might have been better left uncharted. She longed to be free, to be able to go out for an evening without the seemingly everpresent doubts that turned her every thought and action suspect. Ross had sent freesias and she wished she could just relax and enjoy the damned flowers.

Ross wondered why he had failed to remark upon her good looks. He found her exquisite. Perhaps it was the all black outfit that pointed up the silvery blondness of her hair, wisps of which escaped enticingly down the nape of her neck and in front of her ears. Her skin looked flawless, pale with a pearly sheen. When she walked across the room to pour him a drink he watched the way her body moved inside her clothes, the slight sway of her breasts, the side-to-side shift of her buttocks, and silently complimented her on her good taste, her natural attractiveness. He'd been trained to examine "product" and she was top quality. For the first time in a long while he found himself profoundly interested in a woman's potential. He sat comfortably on the sofa, taking his time to look around, perennially intrigued and charmed by the atmosphere of a woman's home. There were invariably subtle differences, a certain delicacy of scent and selection, between the homes of men who lived alone and those of women. His house, by contrast to

Lynne's, was lacking in texture. He'd concentrated so much on the look of things that he'd omitted considering how those things might feel. He'd been unaware of his error until this moment, and knew he'd go home this evening to touch the various fabrics in his house, and to study the color schemes.

"This is really charming," he complimented her, turning to study the smile she gave him before she said, "Cheers," and touched her glass to his.

"Thank you for the flowers. I like freesias."

"Well, good," he said, wishing he had, for once, taken the trouble to select the flowers himself. "Good. Tell me"—again he looked around—"we didn't have much of a chance to talk the other evening, and I'm curious. What do you do? Are you a career girl?" He thought he sounded like a pompous old fart, and despaired of having to carry out this charade of ignorance.

"When I was twenty-two," she said carefully, "I was a career girl. At forty, I like to think of myself as a woman with a career."

"Point taken." He smiled, glad of her confidence. "I stand corrected."

"Asking about my career. Is this where we display our credentials for one another?" she asked, bored at the prospect of another predictable evening.

"God, I hope not," he said, stretching his legs out in front of him. "I suppose most single people have to go through that. Personally, I don't have the energy anymore. After a while you even stop listening."

"That's true," she agreed, "you do."

"What was your career at twenty-two?"

"Credentials?" she asked, with a half smile.

"Interest, curiosity."

She sighed and looked over at the fireplace, took another sip of her drink, then returned her eyes to his. "I started with the network as a secretary. An opening came up in production. I applied for the job, as a glorified errand boy with a title, and got it. Once I got the job and had a chance to be involved in actual production, I became fascinated. I started night courses in film technique—editing, production, whatever was available—and began paying very close attention to what was being done, and how. I had visions of being one of the few dynamic woman producers.''

"And you succeeded."

"Only to a degree." She looked closely at his eyes. There was no hint of condescension in his expression. He wasn't a handsome man; his features were all mismatched, nose a shade too large, eyes dark and deeply set, mouth too—what? Mobile. He was attractive, though, and he did have good, broad shoulders. She could hear her mother telling her years before, ". . . watch out for narrow-shouldered men. You can't lean on them, can't rely on them to be there when you need them. I've always mistrusted men with narrow shoulders; it's like a visible character flaw." Alec had had broad shoulders, but he'd always been too thin, his chest slightly concave, giving him a tubercular look when he was younger. Ned Booker had narrow shoulders. Funny, she'd never thought about that before. "I'm the only woman," she explained. "They give me a lot of the less important work, the pieces they think have a 'woman's angle.' Alec was forever telling me I was beating a dead horse, that they'd never give me a chance to do anything more. I'm beginning to think he might have been right."

"How long were you married?" he asked.

"Seventeen years. I was twenty-one."

"And how long have you been a widow? D'you mind if I smoke?"

"Not if you offer me one. I don't feel like getting up to go for mine."

He lit two and handed her one.

"Two years," she answered, accepting the cigarette. "Thank you. And you?"

"Five."

"It ages people," she said philosophically. "I used to look young for my age, but in the past two years I've caught up with myself. It's probably that, and the strain of coping with everything alone, without anyone at home to explode at."

He chuckled. "I know what you mean. Although I'd like to argue about how old you look."

"And the awful part of it," she continued, electing to ignore the implied compliment, "is all the well-meaning friends who want to fix you up, who want to see you happily married again with someone new so they can stop thinking about you, stop feeling guilty, stop having to invite another odd person so the table will be balanced at dinner."

He nodded. "Nobody *talks* about it. Have you noticed that? People are so damned dishonest. They want you off their hands, off their consciences." He stared at her for a moment, liking her more and more, then smiled. "We're off to a pretty morbid start."

"We're off to a truthful one," she said. "It's a nice change. I've grown so used to people saying one thing but meaning something else that half the time I'm afraid to believe what I'm told. This is probably the most refreshing conversation I've had in the last two years."

"I'll drink to that." Again he touched his glass to hers, then reached for the ashtray and placed it on the sofa between them. "I feel very relaxed with you. I'm not sure what to think about that."

"Oh?"

"Corporate jitters," he explained. "Never trust appearances and most of all never trust your instinct to relax."

"Christ!" she exclaimed. "That's it exactly! I think you're the first man I've ever heard admit that. I think men would like women to believe that they don't feel that way, and that because we do—even if we don't broadcast it—we're inferior. Why do you keep on with it?" she asked.

"You start out as one thing and thirty-odd years later you've ended up as something else, but you've fallen into the habit. What's your work schedule like?"

"I've been off for the last few weeks. Between assignments," she explained. "Actually, I've been trying for close to two years to get the producer to let me do a segment on rape, and he's blocked me every time. Dianna . . . do you ever watch the show?"

" 'Up to the Minute'? I do, as a matter of fact."

"You already know about the show," she realized. "Did I tell you about that last week? But I must have. I'm sure I did. Why did you just ask me about my career?"

"I'm a little absentminded," he lied ineptly, promising himself he'd done the last rundown he was ever going to do on anyone. he loathed finding himself in a position where he had to lie with every other breath. "Anyway, you were about to say something about Dianna."

"Dianna phoned about an hour or so ago to say that Ned—he's the producer—is going to pass my proposal, finally. I'm afraid to believe it."

"Why?"

"Because he's an opportunist, and an operator. He'd say something like that just to get someone off his back."

"And you think Dianna was on his back?"

"Something like that," she said cautiously, fearful of being indiscreet.

He felt her pull back on the subject, and decided to shift the direction of the conversation to help her out. "What interests you?" he asked.

"This is starting to sound like an interview," she said warily.

"I'm sorry."

"Do you have children?" she asked, then laughed. "I suppose we've got to get all this out of the way."

"I don't mind," he said. "Three sons. You?"

"We decided not to have children."

"It takes a lot of guts to defy the conventions."

"No, it doesn't. I have an old college friend who never married. We were talking one afternoon and I said I thought it showed a lot of courage on her part, never marrying. She told me it didn't have anything to do with courage. It had to do with deciding what was best at the time. When I thought about it, I still had to say I thought it took courage. Then she laughed and looked a little deflated and admitted that no one who'd interested her had ever proposed. That made me mad, and I said so. It's awful to hide your disappointments under a noble light, allowing people to endow you with qualities like courage when the truth is we're none of us any different. We don't think noble or courageous things when we do what we have to do.''

"We're all cowards in one way or another," he said. "And we're all looking for someone, whether we admit it or not.''

"You're still looking?" she asked, disarmed by this admission. "Why?"

"Not actively," he qualified. "There's just an awareness that's always alert, always on the lookout for the possibility. Whether or not I'd ever do anything about it is a whole other ballgame.''

She felt a small stab of satisfaction. He'd just confessed to a vulnerability she hadn't thought he'd have. It made him seem more accessible, less of a cookie-cutter businessman.

"I'm hungry," she declared.

"I'll feed you." He downed the last of his drink, stubbed out his cigarette and moved to get up.

Watching him, she said in a low voice, "Don't look to me. I'm really *not* looking.''

He picked up her coat from the rocker and came toward her holding it out. "Liar," he said gently. "That's the first dishonest thing you've said.''

He wasn't, she was pleased to see, a heavy drinker. He had two glasses of wine with dinner and offered her a liqueur after but declined to have one himself. "A Scotch before dinner and a glass or two of wine and that's my limit.''

"Mine too," she said. She was discovering that he was anything but predictable.

"You're not typical," she said in the car as they headed back to her house.

"Neither are you.''

"No, I mean it.''

"So do I." He smiled over at her. "I thought you'd be one of those women on a perpetual diet. It did my heart good to watch you eat.''

She laughed. "I've always had the appetite of a trucker. My friends in college despised me. Half of them would gorge themselves on pizza and beer, then slip discreetly into the nearest john and throw up. I'd eat an entire pizza, drink three or four beers and an hour later want to go out for Chinese food. A manic metabolism," she explained.

"All I have to do is look at food and I start growing a paunch," he said. "I sometimes wish I had the courage not to look like a businessman, that it didn't matter to me."

He directed the car into her driveway and put the shift into neutral before turning to look at her. He hoped she'd invite him in for a nightcap or some coffee; he wanted to spend a little more time with her. When she didn't say anything, he said, "Will you invite me in?" He took hold of her hand, startled by its coldness.

"Not yet," she said, allowing him to chafe her hand. He was very gentle in his gestures. "The truth is I haven't made love to anyone since my husband died. If I invite you in, I'll want to. And I'm not ready."

Taken aback by her directness he couldn't say anything for a moment, so he continued warming her hand, trying to find the right words. "I was only," he said finally, "hoping for some coffee, a chance to talk with you a little longer."

"I know that," she said.

"You know that," he repeated, looking into her eyes. "You're quite a woman. Are you always so direct?"

"No," she answered truthfully.

"Well." He released her hand. "I'm going to have to go home and think about all this. I'll try to call you tomorrow."

"Good. I'd like that. Let me give you my card with the office number." She opened her bag, found a card and gave it to him. "It was a lovely dinner, and I enjoyed talking with you. Truthfully, more than I expected to. If you do find time to call tomorrow, I'll enjoy talking with you again."

"Saturday night," he said on impulse. "Will you come out?"

She paused, thinking. "Out where? I'll be honest again and tell you I've come to hate all the little local gatherings for cocktails, the paddle tennis club get-togethers. I only went last week for Amy's sake."

"I see. How does this sound? I have a housekeeper who

cooks like a dream. She can't clean to save her life but her dinners could inspire poetry.''

''It sounds wonderful.''

''Pick you up at seven?''

''Good.''

She stood in the driveway watching him reverse out into the road. She waved, then moved toward the door. Neither the man nor the evening had been what she'd expected. Mercifully, Alec had remained in the background. She let herself into the cottage considering some of what she'd said to Ross. She'd surprised herself, saying what she had about making love. Why on earth had she blurted that out? Because, she told herself, she really was fed up with all the nonsensical aspects of dating. She was tired of subtlety and innuendo, of the giving and receiving of credentials, of the feeling she usually had at the end of an evening with some man that nothing she'd said had really been heard, that she'd been indulged, patronized, in return for which she might gratefully offer her body. She didn't care if she never went out on another date as long as she lived. If Ross liked her, fine. If he didn't like her, fine. She liked him well enough to be truthful. It was up to him how he chose to proceed.

John sat on his bed and listened to the night sounds, cars passing less and less frequently on the road outside. The restaurant was closing. He heard Joe and Gina shut the front door; a moment later their car started up and they drove off. Silence. He looked over at the table, at the open Random House dictionary, at the stack of yellow manila copy paper, and the completed pages. He told himself he should walk across the room and get a few hours' work done. But he wasn't in the mood.

He folded his arms behind his head and thought about the cottage near Pear Tree Point. It was a great little place, exactly the kind he'd live in if he had the money. She'd done a nice job fixing it up, hadn't made it all cute and chintzy the way a lot of women would have.

She looked like someone with a career. She had the decisiveness, the attitude of someone used to being in control. The only discrepancy was her sad blue eyes.

He yawned and slid a bit further down on the bed. Gazing at the ceiling, he tried to imagine what it would be like to have his book accepted, to see it in print, bound between hard covers. Maybe it'd be a best-seller. "Hah!" He laughed aloud. Some joke. He'd be lucky if it even got a reading. No matter what happened, though, he wasn't going to quit. He wasn't going to spend the rest of his life odd-jobbing for the locals, jump-starting cars and delivering cord wood. If he bombed out with the book, he'd move into the city and start trying for editorial jobs. At least he'd make a halfway decent salary and be able to afford a better place to live.

He thought again of Lynne Craig and felt anew that expansion in his chest, an interior spasm of sorts. No one had ever had this kind of an effect on him. She was so vivid in his thoughts, so fully fleshed and intimately detailed he could almost touch her. He wished to God he had an irresistible smile, or a way with words.

❖ *Five* ❖

PEOPLE WERE HURRYING self-importantly between the production staff offices of "Up to the Minute." The momentum would have been impressive to someone unfamiliar with the inner workings of the show. To Lynne it was a sure sign that not very much was happening. The lulls, when they came infrequently, were filled with motion; people scurried from one office to another carrying canisters of film or stacks of files; heads bent together, deep in murmured conversation. In reality, when the place was nearly silent and not many people were in evidence, the greatest amount of work was being done.

Even the Teletype machines, hooked up to the wire services, worked only sporadically. A secretary walked past, paused to tear off an item, and continued on her way.

Lynne went along to her office, which was situated between Greg Waldren's and Tom Herbert's, and hung her coat on the back of the door before glancing through the stack of mail on her desk. An American Express bill, a Diner's Club bill, several magazines; nothing that couldn't wait, although the charge bills reminded her that she'd have to prepare her expense account. Each month it was something she intentionally forgot to do, an annoying few hours of paperwork, tallying up receipts and listing the names of people she'd taken for drinks, or meals, and for what project. She went out into the central area again—the production assistants' desks were out here—to get coffee from the machine against the far wall, near the Teletypes. Only Julie and Gloria were at their desks. Carrying her coffee, Lynne made her way through the jumble of desks toward Gloria who sensed her approach and looked up.

"Hi!" Gloria smiled. "D'you just get in?"

"Just now." Lynne pulled over a chair and sat down. "I got the word last night from Dianna that Ned's going to send my proposal up to Keith for approval."

"You're kidding!"

"According to Dianna."

Gloria groaned softly and looked at the papers covering her desk. "Boy, I sure wouldn't want to go out and buy stock on that tip."

Gloria's remark served to confirm Lynne's own sentiments. "Well, we'll know for sure soon enough. If we do get the go-ahead, I just wanted to let you know I'll get the paperwork in early so we can have you in the unit."

"I don't know," Gloria said. "Tom put in a request for me yesterday. They want me to work on the Sealab segment."

"When's it scheduled for?"

"Wait a sec." Gloria pushed among the papers on her desk. "I've got the schedule here somewhere. I think the unit's going out the second week in November. They want to get the interviews with the Navy people and the crew after the first fifteen-day trial." She gave up looking, and said, "I snuck a look at the budget. You wouldn't *believe* it!"

"Sure I would," Lynne said. "Anyway, Ned is hinting we can get to work right away, once the budget comes down."

"You know I've been dying to do it. I've got a file six inches thick with research stuff. *And*," she said excitedly, "I've got a fantastic lead! Remember Judy Jones, the singer? She was really big maybe ten years ago. Had this kind of catchy whine to her voice, remember?"

"Vaguely."

"I checked her out and she'd be willing to talk about what happened to her, the court case, the whole thing."

"Did she lose?"

"Yes and no. The case got a lot of attention. The guy only got a suspended sentence. I called MCA, got her number and phoned her up. I figured, what the hell, right? Anyway, she's willing. It'd be a hell of a piece if we could use her."

"Have you got clippings on the trial?"

"Naturally." Gloria grinned as she opened the top drawer of her desk and brought out a thick file folder. "Read it and weep," she said, presenting the file to Lynne. "Boy, I hope Dianna's got her stories straight. I've gone up and down on this damned thing so many times I'm afraid to let myself believe little Neddy's actually going to send it upstairs."

"Is he in? Did you notice?"

"He's in. He came bouncing in after a three-hour lunch about ten minutes ago. I saw him come in, didn't see him go out again. Dianna's here. She's in her cozy lair reading the latest crop of letters and making loud noises."

"I'll see her after I see Ned." Lynne rose, picking up her coffee.

"Oh, by the way. In case you're interested, it just came in over the wire that some guy from Caltech, and another guy from Harvard, and some Japanese scientist won the Nobel Prize in Physics. Another guy from Harvard won the chemistry prize. Big day for Harvard. They sent Harvey right up to Boston with a unit so they can slot an item for Sunday's broadcast."

"Where's everybody else?" Lynne asked.

"Mort's out with Greg shooting a bunch of interviews with guys from the Newspaper Guild, doing a follow-up on the *Times* strike. Don's home with the 'flu. Frank's out with a unit at the Fair grounds, doing a retrospective on New York's wonderful World's Fair and its closing. Let's see. Who else? I told you about Harvey. Tom went with Frank. George and Ken are closeted somewhere working up a joint proposal for a Berkeley segment. I don't know where Art is. I think one of his kids is sick. And Norm's on location in D.C. covering the open hearings on the Klan. Me, I'm up to my chubby little buttocks in this Sealab crap."

Lynne laughed. "I'll do my best to rescue you," she said, heading through the desks toward Ned's office. "Is he on the phone?" she asked Sue, his secretary.

"Naturally. You want to see him?" Lynne nodded and Sue said, "I'll give you a shout when he's off."

Lynne thanked her and went back to her office. Donna, the secretary she, Greg, and Tom shared, poked her head around the door to say, "Hi. Anything need doing?"

"Could you get me some FAX forms?"

"No problem. Anything else?"

"I'll probably have a few letters before you leave."

"Okay. You want coffee? You've got coffee. I'll get you the stuff." She moved to go then came back. "Dianna's looking for you."

"Thanks."

The phone rang.

"Sue says you want to talk. C'mon in," Ned said and hung up.

Carrying her coffee and cigarettes, her handbag safely stowed in the bottom drawer of her desk, she went to Ned's office. Sue waved her in with a smile.

Ned sat, his hands flat on the desk and his chair tipped precariously backward, as if he was ready to leap up at a signal and go running out of the office. He hadn't changed much since the days when they'd both been production assistants. In all the years she'd known him, he'd always had an aura of unapproachability, despite his frequent smiles, quick and earnest manner of speaking, his seeming enthusiasm—when the situation warranted it—and his habit of looking people squarely in the eyes when he spoke to them. Regardless of his apparent bonhomie, Ned wasn't available. Lynne couldn't help feeling that behind the rather small but ever-sincere brown eyes there were wells of contempt for everyone, including Keith, the executive producer, and the board of directors, the head of the network, everyone.

She and Ned were roughly the same age, but Ned seemed years older due to a carefully cultivated work-worn expression, and the loss of much of his hair. They had never been friends, yet Ned consistently treated her with an annoying familiarity, as if they shared a lengthy history of intimate friendship that extended all the way back to the day he'd first arrived at work. Lynne could effortlessly recall the impression he'd made upon her that day, of a young man crammed full of opportunism and ruthlessness that was disguised thinly by a layer of Uriah Heepishness that had him bowing and scraping to anyone he thought might see his potential and be in a position to assist his upward climb. He'd been an obsequious and oily young man with a talent for successfully accusing others of mistakes he'd made himself. The only difference between that young man of fifteen years ago and the man seated now behind the desk was the display of nearly palpable pleasure he took in wielding his power. Lynne had never liked him and no one else claimed to. Yet Ned was always surrounded by associate-producers sweet-talking as they presented their latest proposals. Ned was wined and dined and given expensive gifts at Christmas by everyone from production assistants to some impressively-placed politicians. He had his eye on Keith's job, as executive producer, and there was little doubt in anyone's mind that it was nothing more than a matter of time before he found a way to get it.

"What's on your mind?" he asked, indicating she should sit down.

His office, unlike any of the others on the floor, had been expensively decorated and furnished, with floor to ceiling draperies, thick carpeting, a low-slung teak desk and matching chair, limited-edition prints on the walls, several not very comfortable upholstered armchairs, and a teak bar with a drop-leaf front that opened to reveal Rosenthal stemware in varying shapes and sizes and a good stock of the best liquors.

The previous producer, whom Ned had ousted through a series of dirty tricks and subtly-selected words whispered into the right ears, had actually worked in this office. Clark Lucey had been a dedicated, if forgivably befuddled man who'd been responsible for the creation of "Up to the Minute." It was he who'd hired Mort and Harvey, the original hosts; he who'd argued with the men upstairs for the program format, insisting that there were intelligent viewers out there who'd appreciate the program. He'd been a man with vision. It had only taken Ned six years to get Clark's job. Happily, Clark hadn't suffered. His reputation miraculously still intact after Ned's careful campaign to rid the show of him, Clark had gone on to become executive producer at another network, where he'd stayed, putting out superior products, until his death two years earlier. Lynne had learned more from Clark than from anyone else with whom she'd ever worked, about budget proposals, about how to put together a good unit, about how to edit a segment so that it had not only continuity but impact. He'd been a patient, scholarly man who'd never been too busy to encourage someone he felt had potential.

Since Ned had taken over the job, he'd hired and fired, promoted and demoted with a vengeance, rarely considering the good of the show or its image, but with an eye firmly fixed on the ratings. Ned knew the value of controversy and dissension, and created both with near genius. The "Up to the Minute" employees were no longer the friendly, united group Lynne had joined sixteen years before as a secretary. Ned had managed to stir up an atmosphere of rampant mistrust and suspicion, with the result that the turnover in staff in recent years was formidable. Production assistants who'd been repeatedly overlooked for promotion left regularly to accept producing jobs with other stations. The people he chose to promote almost always wound up making grave errors in judgment that resulted in their being fired. Of the original employees, only Harvey and Mort remained as hosts, and only Greg and Tom, as associates. She and Dianna had both been on staff when Clark was producer, Dianna as a part-time interviewer and Lynne as a production assistant. Julie had been there, and so had Gloria who should, by rights, have been one of the associates by now. Ned consistently overlooked Gloria. His reasoning seemed eminently clear: there was already one woman producing and directing segments. Any more would represent something too close to a power base for Ned's comfort.

"I understand," she said, setting her coffee on the polished edge of his desk, "that you're sending my outline up to Keith."

"I'm working on it," he said with typical evasiveness. He was famous for never giving a straight answer.

"Either you're working on it, or you're doing it. Which?" she asked with a smile.

"It's gone upstairs. You know I can't approve this one on my own, Lynne. It's too touchy a subject."

"May I go ahead and put my unit together?"

"Why not? Get your FAX in to me with a budget proposal." He turned briefly to look out the window. "Sure," he said, facing her again. "I assume you've got your subjects, your locations."

"We're working on it," she answered, taking some small pleasure in using his figure of speech.

"When d'you want to go with it?" he asked, looking at several folders neatly stacked to one side of his desk.

"Right away. Next week. As soon as possible."

"Right," he said distractedly. His eyes fixed on her as if he were coming to a decision. She disliked the feeling she had of being on a slide under a microscope. The only times she felt unattractive and too aware of her faults were those occasions when the full weight of Ned's attention fell on her. "Yeah," he said. "Get it done and in the can. Take a look at this"—he held up a folder—"and let me know what you think of it."

"What is it?"

"Antiwar stuff. It's going to be big. There's word there's going to be a lot more demonstrating. I'd like to get a Negro angle too. Maybe get a unit out to L.A., talk to some people in Watts, maybe get some Detroit footage too. Berkeley's hot."

"That's two different assignments," she said.

"Yeah, but the whole thing's west coast, except for Detroit. We'll have to talk." This was, Lynne knew, his way of dismissing her. She was to go off with the researcher's file, read it, and come up with one or more proposals. If Gloria hadn't told her that George and Ken were working up a proposal on Berkeley, Lynne might have been excited at the prospect of having an opportunity to work on such an important piece. Now she was simply mystified, trying to understand Ned's latest game strategy. She couldn't help feeling that even though she was purportedly going to be allowed to do the rape segment, she was being given a pacifier to suck on.

"I'll get back to you," she said and left with the file, remembering only when she was at the door to Dianna's office that she'd left her half-empty coffee cup on the edge of Ned's desk. She hoped it left a white ring on the perfect teak finish.

"What did he say?" Dianna asked, beckoning Lynne in.

"It would seem we're getting approval."

"I told you that!" Dianna snapped. "What's that?" She pointed at the file under Lynne's arm.

"I'm not sure. I think it constitutes a ploy."

Dianna's eyebrows rose questioningly.

"It doesn't merit discussion," Lynne said. "I'm going to go ahead with the paperwork. And I've got a subject to preinterview, not to mention reviewing the file Gloria's prepared. I'll be here half the night. What are you up to?"

"They're letting me rebut some viewers' letters this week. Ned's got a new format idea he's trying out. He's allocated two minutes at the bottom of the show. He's talking about expanding it into a regular segment, having me and somebody else—somebody new—take opposing viewpoints on the same subject and having a little war on the air. Cute."

"It's not a bad idea," Lynne said consideringly. "It could be interesting."

"Right. Well, he's starting out this week by *allowing* me to respond to the vicious letter of my choice. You should read this shit!" She picked up a handful of letters and waved them in the air.

"So tell him you don't want to do it."

"You know better than that," Dianna said tiredly. "You don't argue with the boy wonder. You do as you're told or you join the ranks of the unemployed and pick up your government check once a week."

Lynne looked at the woman seated opposite, thinking Dianna was beginning to show definite signs of battle fatigue, deepening lines around her eyes and mouth, a certain tremor in her hands. She remembered the call from Dianna that had come one morning, about three months after Alec's death. In her peremptory fashion, Dianna had declared, "We'll have lunch today. I want to talk to you."

Taken offguard—she and Dianna had never been close, but they'd never been enemies either—Lynne had agreed. They'd met at a small French restaurant in the east Fifties and even before the waiter had brought their menus, Dianna had sailed into what was obviously a prepared speech.

"You're overdoing it," Dianna had stated. "I've been watching you the last few months and you're starting to look glazed. You can't make your job take the place of everything else."

"Glazed?"

"Just listen!" Dianna had said impatiently. "You can't *do* what you're trying to do. You're knocking yourself out, working up proposals on this, that, and every other goddamned thing, shooting miles more footage on segments than anyone could possibly need or use. I know what's happening, but I'd bet my life you don't. It's just a goddamned TV show, Lynne. Even *I* know that. You used to know it. But since Alec died you've forgotten."

Lynne had stared at her, for a moment fascinated by the pebbly quality of Dianna's skin under the substantial layer of pancake makeup she always wore. Then the words seemed to penetrate and she wondered if Dianna were delivering some sort of ultimatum.

"You're doing it again!" Dianna had said sharply, tapping her long, bright, red-painted fingernails on the back of Lynne's hand. "You need a vacation; you need to back away. Maybe you need a new job. I don't know. You just can't spend your every waking hour in the office, working on the show. For chrissake, some of the proposals you've been concocting are so convoluted I don't even understand them. It's a lucky thing I've got an in with Sue and I've been able to get her to let me have a look at the stuff before it goes in to Ned, and save you from making a total asshole

of yourself. Not to mention seeing your job go right down
the toilet. It's as if you're trying to find out why Alec did
what he did by looking for answers in the research material.
Proposing segments on British Hospices and crap like that,
educating people to deal with death. That's not where it's
written. Listen!'' she said in a softer tone, her eyes probing
Lynne's so that Lynne became aware all at once of how
vulnerable Dianna was. Behind the almost impenetrable
wall of her defiant and angry intelligence, Dianna was simply another woman, a too-tall, self-conscious woman who
dressed and behaved in a fashion designed to direct attention away from the stigma of her height. She had succeeded
so well in recreating her own image that the general view of
her was almost what she wished it to be. But the close to
begging way she was asking Lynne to listen brought into
reality the fact that it wasn't what Dianna was saying that
was so important but rather that it was Dianna who was
saying it.

''Why do you care?'' Lynne had asked, rather awed by
this new view of the woman.

''Don't be a horse's ass!'' Dianna had scowled, her fingers scrabbling to light a cigarette. ''You're a damned good
producer and someday you're going to get a crack at doing
some worthwhile segments. Without you, I wouldn't have
any chance at all. They let you do the things Greg and Tom
and the others wouldn't touch with a barge-pole, the segments on women we manage to sneak in every once in a
while, the segments that have a halfway human touch to
them. But you're starting to get like those morons who write
in wanting to have it confirmed that there really is an Atlan-
tis, or that there really are little green people with superior
intellects living on other planets who drop onto earth every
so often just to keep tabs on us. They think that because
Mort, with his God-help-us sky-high credibility, or Don
with his boyish sincerity, do the commentary on a segment
about UFOs or mysterious asteroids that they're in touch
with information the public never gets a crack at. You're
looking for answers and you think you're going to find them
by spending every waking hour working on some new and
different proposal.''

The waiter arrived and, cowed by Dianna's tone and obvious irascibility, silently slid the menus onto the table and retreated without bothering to take their drink order. Peripherally, Lynne watched him take up his post at a polite distance, where he waited for a gesture to bring him back to the table. Lynne had thought it was remarkable the effect Dianna had on people.

"Jesus Christ!" Dianna had exclaimed, seeing Lynne's attention wandering. "Will you for chrissake pay attention?"

"Sorry." Lynne returned her eyes to Dianna's.

"Take a vacation. Do something, but ease off!" Dianna had said carefully. "If you don't, you're going to wind up minus a job, and find yourself in a straitjacket, bouncing around in a little rubber room."

"Why do you care?" Lynne had asked again, fascinated by Dianna's ferocious adamancy.

"What the hell does it matter why I care?" Dianna had said, waggling her fingers at the waiter. "The point is somebody's got to tell you and since it's obvious no one else is going to, I designated myself. Don't get paranoid on me and start thinking I'm trying to do anything but what I'm saying. Go book yourself a cruise or some goddamned thing, but get yourself out of the office for a while before you go crazy." She'd paused and looked hard at Lynne, then turned to the waiter dutifully standing at attention at her side. "A double Cutty, neat, water on the side." She looked again at Lynne and said, "Make that two." The waiter went off. Dianna took a hard drag on her cigarette, then put it out. "I hate advice," she'd said angrily, "all that 'womanly' bullshit of commiserating and leaning. And here I am doing it. Christ! As of Monday, you're on two weeks' vacation. I went ahead and set it up with Ned because, knowing you, in the condition you're in, you'd never do it, and I don't want to watch you have a breakdown, or see you lose your job." She paused and then said, "Okay?"

"Yes, okay," Lynne had replied.

"Well, thank Christ for that!" Dianna had sighed. "I'm glad you're going to be reasonable. I can't stand these women who cry and make a goddamned fuss over everything.''

After the lunch, which had consisted of Dianna's drinking both the double Scotches, and Lynne's consumption of a whole wheat roll and the waters-on-the-side Dianna had not used, Dianna had escaped. She'd gone hurrying off up Lexington as if she fully expected Lynne to go running after her, announcing she'd changed her mind.

Lynne had taken the two weeks to go househunting. The result was the cottage near Pear Tree Point, and her return to work in a considerably calmer state.

''What're you smirking at?'' Dianna wanted to know now, interrupting Lynne's reverie.

''Sorry.''

''Who have you got in mind for the unit?''

''I want Frank for sound. He'll be sympathetic. And so will Dave.''

''Dave? Dave Grushen? You must be cracking up. He'd be about as sympathetic as Madame Defarge.''

''His daughter was raped and badly beaten last year. We've talked about it. He's even willing to let us talk to her.''

''Oh!'' Dianna sat back in her chair, folding her arms under her breasts.

''I've got to go.'' Lynne stood. ''I want to get the paperwork done. And I've got this''—she held up the file—''to read. Ned's playing games again.''

By eleven-thirty that night, when she'd finished the Facilities and Production Request form, along with the budget proposal, and had read her way through Gloria's file and the one Ned had given her, she was both exhausted and confused. Not where Gloria's file or her own segment were concerned, but by Ned's giving her the file at all. There wasn't the remotest possibility she'd ever be allowed to do a segment on the material contained in it. Not that she wouldn't have liked to. She was morally outraged by the facts and figures in the file. It galled her to think that Johnson might actually get passage of an appropriations bill for

$119.3 billion, $46.9 billion of which would go to defense, while only $3.38 billion might go for foreign aid. It further galled her to read that Defense Secretary McNamara had, in April, estimated the cost to the U.S. of the war in Vietnam at $1.5 billion annually, with economic aid at $300 million, food and agricultural supplies at $70 million, military assistance at $330 million, and the cost of U.S. forces at $800 million. In July, Johnson had announced that the forces actually in Vietnam would be increased from seventy-five thousand to one hundred twenty-five thousand, and that the draft would be doubled from seventeen thousand to thirty-five thousand a month. Just a week earlier, on the fifteenth and sixteenth of October, demonstrations against U.S. involvement had been held across the city; these were followed by a series of rallies and petitions supporting U.S. policies. Yet nobody seemed to understand or want to know about the Vietnamese position in all this, or that the supposed threat of communism was entirely in the minds of the U.S. government.

Ned was quite right, of course. The demonstrations were bound to proliferate as the antiwar campaigns took hold. But she wasn't going to give him the satisfaction of playing a new game with her by dangling such a choice carrot—one so hopelessly forever out of her reach—in front of her nose. She swiveled around to her typewriter, tore a memo sheet from the pad on her desk and typed a note to him saying that she'd read the file and felt that her personal views would critically interfere with any proposal she might write. Therefore she wanted to thank him for allowing her to see the file but, regretfully, she had to decline. Let him figure that one out! She left the note and the file on his blotter, then pushed the day's mail and some expense forms into her briefcase and left the office.

The drive back to Connecticut would relax her. She'd have a drink, then a good long sleep. Tomorrow, she'd preinterview Judy Jones and Dave Grushen's daughter, and put together some notes and clippings for Dianna to work with.

As always, when striding through the damp, dimly-lit

underground garage, she felt menaced by the ranks of silent cars, the numberless shadowy areas where someone might stand concealed, waiting to spring out at her. For years the tenants of the building—Associated Television being the primary one—as well as the people who rented these parking spots, had been asking the building management to install more and brighter lighting down here. But nothing had ever been done. No one had suffered any mishap here, either, it was true. Nevertheless, Lynne couldn't avoid feeling a whispery sensation of danger. There were odd noises; the sound of water gurgling through large overhead pipes, sudden startling creaks, and what might have been sighs; the noises made by recently parked cars whose engines cracked and pinged as the metal cooled. Every noise caused her to jump inwardly. She rushed along the main aisle, the clatter of her heels echoing on the concrete.

Once inside the car with the doors locked and the motor warming, she exhaled slowly and opened her bag for a cigarette. Her heart was racing and she was annoyed with herself for being overimaginative, for endowing an empty, locked garage with a population of potential rapists and muggers. Yet the fear was very real, and one, she was sure, every woman felt at some point or another. All the more reason to do the segment. Every time she had to come alone down into this garage her determination to publicly air the subject was renewed.

The car's headlights illuminated the low-ceilinged garage as she drove through and hit the remote control device to send the heavy double-width door on its slow upward trip. Before the door had fully opened, she gunned the motor and shot up the ramp to street level. Once out on the street she felt immediately safer, as if she'd been disinterred, despite the fact that the streets were unusually deserted for twelve-thirty on a Wednesday night. The crosstown bus on Fifty-seventh swayed eastward; a few taxis cruised in its wake. She fiddled with the radio, found a station with classical music, and headed toward the FDR Drive.

Ross had said he'd try to call today but he hadn't. She was disappointed. He'd probably been busy; or perhaps he was clever, someone who dangled the bait of a promise to try to call, knowing full well he had no intention of doing it. He wasn't like that, she decided. He was different, and she liked him. He'd have a reason for not calling.

As she left the Bruckner for the turnpike she sat up straighter and narrowed her eyes as the overhead lights abruptly ended. It seemed an especially dark night and objects in the distance and on the periphery of the highway took on bizarre forms. From several hundred yards away she thought she saw a man standing near one of the off-ramps, only to approach and see it was an exit sign.

She arrived home to discover she'd forgotten to leave on the outside lights, so she had to grope her way along the path in the dark to the back door and fumble her key into the lock. As she got the mud-room door open she heard a loud screech and the sudden frenetic rustling of the bushes near the rear of the cottage. Shakily, she turned to look, listening, and heard the rapid patter of animal feet as something—perhaps a raccoon—pursued some smaller creature through the garden.

A glass of Scotch in hand, she sat down in the rocker wondering why she felt so jumpy. It hadn't bothered her so far, living alone. Was she going to start imagining all sorts of things here, the way she did in the underground garage? She was probably just about to get her period. Her nerves seemed to move closer to the surface of her skin for about eight or nine days out of every month. She let her head rest against the back of the rocker and sipped her drink, listening to the wind whistling hollowly in the fireplace chimney. The telephone rang. Who could be calling at this time of the morning? She let it ring three times before picking up the receiver.

"I thought you'd probably still be up," Ross said. "You weren't sleeping, were you?"

Relieved, she laughed. "No. I just got in."

"I wanted to call during the day but I didn't get a chance. I've been calling every half hour for the last few hours. I've been thinking about you all day."

"Why?" she asked bluntly. It sounded like a well-rehearsed line.

"I'm not in the habit of finding myself preoccupied with a woman. It bothered me."

"You're preoccupied with me?"

"I was today."

"I see. Should I be flattered?"

"I honestly don't know. You've got a good telephone voice, throaty and low."

His voice, she thought, belonged to a much younger man. It was one that contained a lot of hope, even optimism. "You don't sound like you," she said, knowing at once he'd misinterpret her words.

"Who do I sound like?"

"You, but young. You've got a young voice."

He laughed so loudly that she had to hold the receiver slightly away from her ear. "There's something," he said after a moment, "about late night telephone conversations. Have you ever thought about it?"

"They have a confessional quality. I think people tell all their secrets late at night."

"That's probably true. I feel fairly irrational at the moment. It's the end of a very long day and I felt like giving in to the impulse to call you. You're not annoyed, are you?"

"Not at all. I was just sitting here having a drink before I go to bed."

"If you don't like little cocktail parties and clubby gatherings, what *do* you like?"

"Oh, I don't know," she sighed. "I'm not up to enumerating my preferences in pastimes right at the moment. I've also had a pretty long day."

"Sorry. Look, I'll let you go. I'm looking forward to Saturday night."

"Don't anticipate too much," she cautioned. "I meant what I said. I'm not looking and I'm not ready."

"You're working on the assumption that my interest in you is solely sexual, and it isn't."

"Perhaps," she said slowly, "mine is."

He laughed again. "You're incredible!" he chortled.

"No," she corrected him. "I told you: I'm being truthful. I haven't yet arrived at the point where I can reconcile my thoughts with my actions."

"Well, you've got nothing to worry about. I'm not going to pressure you—about anything." He paused once more and she heard him lighting a cigarette. "I just enjoy your company."

"Do you see a lot of women?" she asked, filled with Scotch-given courage.

"Christ, no!" he answered quickly. "I see people from time to time, but a lot, no. Nothing even remotely like that. Do you see a lot of men?"

"Fewer and fewer. I'm considering giving them up," she said lightly.

"Well, don't do it yet. Enjoy your drink and have a good sleep. I'll see you Saturday."

She hung up and stared straight ahead, oddly able to hear a replay of their conversation, as if the words were tangible and hung, dipping and bobbing, in the air before her. He had called her after all. Be careful, be very careful, she warned herself. It was no good to have expectations—of people, of situations, of anything. Once you acquired expectations, the burden of fulfilling them fell to other people, and somehow it never worked out. It was best to expect nothing, then you could never be disappointed.

❖ Six ❖

JUDY JONES WAS a surprise. Lynne didn't know what she'd been expecting, but it certainly hadn't been this cheerful woman on the other end of the line. Judy seemed so in control not only of herself but of her memories of the rape that Lynne had to wonder aloud how, in fact, the experience had affected her.

"Oh, I know," Judy said confidently. "I sound too healthy, too normal. Isn't that it? I think people expect me to get hysterical all over again every time I talk about it. The thing is I've already done all my crying, and I've dealt with most of my anger. Now I'm angry for all the other girls and women who've been through it too.

"Look, don't worry," she said. "Come with your crew. I'll give you a good interview. We can't really get into it on the telephone. I know your problem, and I know you're afraid that maybe I'm too glib, maybe it's just a cover-up. I'm not covering anything. It's taken me a few years, but I've managed to deal with it. Now I want to do what I can so that people understand that it's not something women provoke, that it's not their fault. I don't care who the woman is; I don't care if she's fast and loose or if she's a nun. She has a right to say what happens to her body. And no guy has the right to violate that."

Reassured, Lynne said, "We'd like to shoot the interview toward the end of the week after next. I'm waiting for some last-minute things to be cleared and then I can give you a specific time. For now, could we tentatively set it up for that Friday?"

97

"Let me check my book. Hold on a minute." Judy put down the receiver, and Lynne sat, waiting. She still had to call Beth Grushen. Beth was at least fifteen years younger than Judy. If she was even a quarter as communicative, they'd have a hell of a segment, with two women of different generations, and Dianna, of another generation still. There'd be a lot of built-in contrast. Lynne just hoped Dianna wouldn't come on too strong. She'd have to prime her, warn Dianna to go gently. The last thing anyone wanted was to have Dianna appear unsympathetic.

"Friday when?" Judy asked, coming back on the line.

"Evening would be best. Then we could take our time. I'd like to make sure we get all the footage we can. You do understand that it'll be edited down. The entire segment will only run sixteen minutes, give or take a few seconds, and along with you we've got another woman, and two professionals who deal regularly with victims."

"I've got it. What time?"

"Let's say eight, for the moment."

"Fine."

"We'll be in touch with you early in the week to confirm. I'm looking forward to meeting you. And thank you for agreeing."

"It's important," Judy said simply.

After the call, Lynne got up to walk around the office, putting her thoughts in order. She'd made notes during her conversation with Judy, and she'd picked up several more points she wanted Dianna to cover in the actual interview. Once she'd spoken to Beth, she'd revise the questions, then get them to Donna for typing. Dianna had already reviewed the preliminary questions; they'd gone over all the possible angles, with Dianna contributing a list of the questions she wanted to ask, as well as her suggestions for commentary. Lynne had decided they'd do the commentary voice-over after the filming. Once the film was edited and in the can, she and Dianna would sit down together and plan the inserts and how they'd be slotted against Dianna's live in-studio introduction and closing.

She didn't know why precisely, but her enthusiasm for

this project seemed to rise and fall very arbitrarily from one hour to the next. She could only conclude that the two years between her original concept and its ultimate acceptance had taken their toll. So much had happened in those two years. Kennedy had been assassinated and Johnson had taken over. American involvement in Vietnam continued to grow, and was arousing violent, and opposing, reactions in people. Women had begun to make demands as people with equal rights. Martin Luther King had won the Nobel Peace Prize. Gracie Allen had died and so had Herbert Hoover. Johnson had been reelected. Eddie Cantor had died and so had Cole Porter. There'd been a critical water shortage in New York. Malcolm X and T. S. Eliot had both died. King and more than three thousand people had marched from Selma to Montgomery, demonstrating for equal civil rights. The first commercial communications satellite, Early Bird, had been placed in orbit. Stan Laurel and Shirley Jackson had died, and so had Alec. The Houston Astrodome had opened. Horowitz had given his first concert in twelve years. And Alec had died, almost two years ago. Alec. There were no organized demonstrations or marches or protests whereby the people who got left behind might group together to air their feelings.

She sat back down behind her desk and reached for the telephone.

Beth had a little girl's voice, high and small, but unexpectedly strong.

"My Dad said you'd be calling. I've thought it over and I want to do it."

"Do you think you'll be able to talk about what happened to you?"

"You're not going to ask for details, are you? I mean, you know, stuff like that?"

"Nothing like that."

"Well, that's okay then."

"Dianna will ask you about your feelings then, and now, a little bit about how the attack took place—the circumstances, about your injuries, and about what happened after."

"Sure. When d'you want to do it?"

"I'd like to schedule it for a week from Thursday, in the evening, if that's all right. I know you go to school. How would eight o'clock be?"

"That would be fine."

"Either Gloria, my production assistant, or I will call to confirm the time at the beginning of the week."

"And my Dad's going to be the camera-man?"

"That's right."

There was a thoughtful pause and then Beth said, "Does my Mom have to be in on it? I mean when we do the interview."

"Not if you don't want her to be."

"Well, I don't know. She gets so upset, you know."

"We'll leave that entirely up to you, Beth. Whatever you're comfortable with. It's important that you feel comfortable."

"Thanks. I guess you understand."

Lynne hung up and turned to look out through her office door. Gloria was at her desk, setting up appointments with the psychiatrist and the police officer who'd consented to interviews. Since all their subjects, except for Judy, were unavailable during the day, most of the filming would take place on the Thursday and Friday, and on the weekend. By the following Monday, the film would go to the house lab for processing and, with luck, by the end of that week, Lynne would be able to get started on the editing. A month from start to finish.

She got up carrying her notes and left the office. Gloria was just putting down the telephone. Lynne went toward her desk, pulled over a chair and sat down to wait while Gloria finished jotting something down.

"We're all set on my end," Gloria told her. "The cop's going to get hate mail for the next thousand years. He's one of these sweethearts who believes women get what they ask for, and he's hot to say it publicly. The psychiatrist's kind of strange but I think he'll be okay. I mean, he's got all kinds of whacked-out ideas on why men rape, but he's supportive on the women's side and he's worked with a lot of victims with pretty good results. I've just got a few more things to add and then I'll have my stuff finished for you to look at."

"Great! Get it in to me as soon as you can. I want to get everything in to Donna for typing."

"Sure." Gloria leaned on her hand and looked at Lynne. "Has Keith sent down the budget yet?"

"Not yet. Look, I'm going home in a little while. I won't be coming in tomorrow. I want to work on the script at home. Call if you need me for anything."

"Okey-dokey." Gloria turned to look at the papers covering her desk. "I'll have this stuff on your desk in half an hour."

"Have you seen Dianna?" Lynne stopped to ask.

"She came in about half an hour ago, hung up her coat, went into Baby Neddy's office and has been in there ever since. D'you suppose they're doing it on the floor?"

Lynne laughed. "What a terrible thing to say!" she exclaimed.

"Yeah! I'm a b-a-a-a-d girl."

Lynne patted her affectionately on the head and cut through the desks, stopping to tell Donna, "I'll have everything ready for you before I leave, in about half an hour. I'm just waiting for Gloria to pencil in her revisions. In the meantime, you could get started on this." She put her notes on Donna's desk. "Send it up to me by messenger tomorrow whenever it's done. Okay?"

"No problem. I'll get right on it."

Lynne thanked her and returned to her office. She sat down, lit a cigarette and looked briefly out the window. She'd work at home all day tomorrow and Saturday. Saturday night she'd be seeing Ross again. The thought gave her a pleasant lift.

"I've changed my mind," Ned was saying.

"About what?"

"I was thinking I'd drop by your place later this afternoon, have a little visit."

"I don't think so," Dianna said. "You decided to end it; let's keep it that way."

He smiled and tilted farther back in his chair. "I should be able to get there by four-thirty."

"It's not a good idea," Dianna said. "You had the right idea when you called it off. You were right about that." The words felt like chunks of broken glass in her mouth. He'd put an end to the affair and it still galled her, but she had no desire to start up again with him, so she was willing to pander to his ego if necessary, and allow him to think he had displayed wisdom in his initial decision.

He was still smiling, and about to speak when the telephone rang. He picked up and at once underwent a fascinating transformation, from the smiling, cocky, I've-got-you-by-the-balls manipulator to the gushing, eager, I'd-never-harm-a-hair-on-anyone's-head young producer. It was evident that this was going to be a long call, and Dianna had no desire to sit and listen, or to witness the almost visible calculations Ned was making. She got up to go, and Ned's eyes fixed on her. He pushed back his shirt cuff and pointed to the face of his watch. He intended to be at her place at four-thirty. Defeated and angry, she returned to her office where she paced up and down trying to think how best to handle the situation.

The simplest thing, of course, was for her not to be home when he came. But if he showed up and she wasn't there, he'd be furious, and she was afraid to risk incurring his anger. "God damn it!" she whispered, pausing to light a cigarette. She leaned against the wall smoking the cigarette, trying to see some way out of the corner he'd so neatly moved her into. It was her own damned fault. She should never have allowed it to begin. Now he could call the affair off, or start it again, depending on his mood, and unless she wanted to get herself fired, there wasn't a hell of a lot she could do about the situation. Her contract didn't mean spit, in view of Ned's recognized ability to find useful technicalities with which to oust people in his personal disfavor. He'd done it before. Look at what he'd done to old Clark, making subtle comments about Clark's loosening grip on the associates, about Clark's lack of good judgment in what should and shouldn't be aired, about Clark's association with certain female employees. All lies, all told with an innocent air, passed along as hearsay rather than as evidence manufactured entirely by Ned himself. No. Were she to go to Bloomingdale's, say, and not be home for Ned, she could, in very short order, find herself paid off on her contract, and out looking for a new job, trailing behind her a string of savage rumors that would make it difficult, if not impossible, for her to find one. She wanted to kill him.

Lynne was still here. She'd seen her talking to Donna as she'd left Ned's office. She could suggest going for a drink, maybe dinner. Legitimate business. They could talk over next week's shoot. But that might put Lynne in jeopardy, too. Ned's venom had been known to spread. Hadn't he gone after half Clark's associate producers and fired them? Ned had cleaned shop like someone out of a horror movie. For several months, everywhere one turned there'd been another person clearing out his desk, packing papers and personal items into a cardboard box from the deli down the street.

"Damn it!" she said and crushed out her cigarette in the ashtray on the bookcase. She was trapped. She was going to have to be home, waiting for Ned when he came. All right. She had to be there, but she'd be fully dressed and waiting to tell him what he could do with his latest on-again off-again sport. She wasn't going to put up with this. Who the hell did he think he was? She marched to her desk, snatched up the receiver, and dialed Ned's extension. Susan answered.

"Is he still on the goddamned phone?" Dianna demanded.

"He just picked up on another call. You want me to give him a message?"

"Yes!" She stopped, considering what to say. "No! Never mind!" She slammed down the phone and resumed her pacing. There was nothing, *nothing* she could say or do. She reached for the phone and dialed Lynne's number.

"What are you up to?" she asked Lynne.

"I'm just about to leave. Why?"

"Nothing. Never mind."

"Did you want to see me about something?"

"It's not important. I'll talk to you tomorrow."

"I won't be in. I want to work on the breakdown, get the script in order."

"It doesn't matter," Dianna said. "I'll talk to you Monday."

"We've got everyone lined up for the week after next—Beth Grushen for Thursday night, Judy Jones Friday night; Saturday the psychiatrist, and Sunday the pro-rape policeman." Lynne gave a small, sharp laugh to indicate what she thought of the policeman and his views. "Donna will have everything for you by tomorrow afternoon."

"Fine." Dianna hung up and stood gazing at her desk top feeling abandoned. Sensing someone in the doorway, she looked up.

"What's the matter?" Lynne asked, in her coat, and carrying her briefcase.

Dianna shook her head.

"We could go downstairs for a drink," Lynne offered. "I've got the time."

Dianna looked at her, at the solicitous expression on Lynne's face, and thought, You're okay. You really would be willing to change your plans and take me down for a drink, to sit and listen while I poured my problems into your ear.

"It isn't important," Dianna said again. "If I've got a gripe with the script or any of the questions I'll call you at home."

"Are you sure? Come have a drink," Lynne coaxed.

"If I have one," she said wryly. "I'll have six. And I can't. I've got to be somewhere by four-thirty. Go on! Scram!" She managed to return Lynne's smile. "It's just been one of those days."

Lynne hesitated, sensing something very wrong. But if Dianna wasn't willing to discuss it, Lynne certainly couldn't force her.

"I'll see you Monday," Dianna said, making a pretense of gathering together her things.

"Take it easy," Lynne said and, reluctantly, left.

Dianna watched her go, then exhaled slowly and began in earnest gathering her coat and bag, various papers. She'd gone past being angry. What was the point? She'd go home and be there, waiting. She couldn't beat Ned, not this time.

❖ *Seven* ❖

NED SAT BEHIND his desk, the office door closed, and read through Lynne's paperwork. He smiled and swiveled his seat around to reposition himself in front of the typewriter that sat on a white metal stand to the left of his desk. First a bit of careful erasing, then he rolled the FAX into his typewriter and made several small changes. The budget required but one small alteration. Everything completed, he laid the pages on his desk and studied them. Satisfied, he reached for the telephone and got through to Keith's secretary.

"I've got some stuff that needs immediate approval," he told her.

"Let me check." She went off the line for a minute or two.

He waited patiently, the receiver held slightly away from his ear, his eyes on his handiwork. He felt good, better than good. He felt strong and in control, masterful. Things were going to work out beautifully. He just wished he'd thought of this sooner.

Keith's secretary came back on the line to say, "He'll see you now if you come right up."

"I'm on my way," he said cheerfully, and hung up. He placed the papers in a tan manila folder, tucked the folder under his arm and headed toward the elevators. Keith's office was two floors up, on the executive level, positioned just three doors down from the chairman's. Between Keith's and the chairman's were the offices of the president and vice-president. All the suites on this floor were large, individually furnished in styles reflecting the tastes of the occupants, and had private bathrooms. The chairman occupied the corner suite which had a sweeping two-sided view of the city. Ned had only been inside that office three or four times. He knew Keith's office very well. It was painted white; the furniture was upholstered in black glove leather; his desk was white lacquer. The carpet and the matting of three framed posters were all a deep burgundy color.

The secretary waved Ned on, and he knocked and entered, smiling.

"Hope I'm not catching you at a bad time," Ned said, moving over the thick pile carpet. "We need an approval on this right away." He actually didn't care whether or not it was a bad time for Keith. He found Keith, with his elegantly understated custom-made clothes and old school ways, a nitpicking pain in the ass who, unfortunately, happened to be highly placed in the network. But not so securely positioned, Ned thought, that he couldn't be ousted. That would take time, though. Right now, Ned had to deal with Lynne Craig.

He slid the file across the desk to Keith, explaining, "It's a last minute decision."

"Sit down," Keith said quietly, looking up at Ned for a moment before turning his attention to the folder. He deeply disliked Ned, despite Ned's success in hiking the show's ratings. Everything about the man ran against the things Keith had been brought up to believe in. He was underhanded, conniving, an opportunist of unparalleled degree; he lacked breeding, sensitivity, and tact, but he was one of the most successful producers in the employ of the network. Therefore, Keith had to swallow his dislike and regularly deal with him, approving the budgets for "Up to the Minute," sitting in on the production meetings, and even socializing with him—to a minimal degree. Keith had, for years now, been waiting to catch Ned red-handed in one of his acts of sabotage, and so paid far more attention to the goings-on for "Up to the Minute" than he did for any other of the shows under his aegis. Keith wanted to believe that it was only a matter of time before Ned's cockiness trapped him into going too far, pushing just too hard. Then, Keith would have the satisfaction of a lifetime in sending Ned permanently on his way. So far, Ned's caution had saved him. But one of these days, Keith thought . . .

Ned had no choice but to seat himself on one of the sofas situated a fair distance from the desk. He hated the furniture arrangement in this office. It automatically put him at a disadvantage by removing him from the immediate arena of Keith's attention. Unless Keith were to get up and join him in the seating area, Ned would have to sit and wait, like some goddamned secretary, until Keith elected to take notice of him. He crossed his legs and folded his hands comfortably in his lap, striving to look casual. He watched covertly as Keith opened the folder with his long-fingered, manicured hands, then read the contents, his chin resting on the back of one hand, his elbow propped on the desk. Ned looked at his watch. Twenty to four. Keith wouldn't take long, and Ned would be able to get over to Dianna's place by four-thirty. He was eager to see her, and it confused him. What had started out as a challenge had evolved into an obsession. His attempt to call off the affair had resulted in his spending hours each night at home stalking the silent rooms of his sleeping household while he tried to comprehend his fascination with this woman, a fascination that had rendered him dissatisfied with every other area of his personal life. He knew she was anything but fond of him. Yet she made love as if nothing else in the world mattered but his being there with her. Even on those occasions when she declared she didn't want to go to bed with him he was able to change her mind with his caresses, thereby disproving her declarations. He was irresistibly drawn to her accessibility, to the acquiescent girl he saw in her. He was convinced no one had ever seen Dianna in quite the way he did: someone who, when naked, was far more than merely without clothes. In removing her garments she set aside the elements of her day-to-day personality that made her seem like such a bitch. She became eager and uncertain and somehow helpless, and this view of her nagged at his attention in private moments until she was almost all he could think of.

The frightening truth seemed to be that he'd somehow managed to fall in love with her. The fact that she scarcely seemed able to tolerate him, let alone reciprocate his never-stated feelings, had no effect on his captivation with her. He would have to keep on seeing her, being with her, making love to her until he could regain the control he'd lost in becoming emotionally involved. He could never allow her, or anyone else, to know the extent to which he'd accidentally become fixated. That would be dangerous on too many levels. He had impulses that were beginning to worry him: he found himself wanting to buy her gifts, rewards for those glimpses of the girl beneath the woman; he wanted to call her at odd hours of the night simply to hear the sleepy sound of her voice; he wanted, wanted. . . . He had to content himself with arriving at her apartment with bottles of the twelve-year-old Scotch she liked when he'd have preferred to enclose her long, pale neck in a heavy gold chain he'd seen at Tiffany's. He'd have liked to take her into her bathroom, sit her down and carefully, gently remove her makeup so that he might finally see who she really was, and tell her what the sight of her face and the touch of her meant to him. He wanted to praise her lavishly. Instead, he was risking getting her fired as a result of those papers now on Keith's desk. If that happened, he'd see to it she got another job, a better one. He'd already put out a few subtle feelers, and interest was strong. He knew she had no idea how successfully he'd built her public image. She'd have no problem landing another job. She'd be scared and angry, though, were she to lose her place on "Up to the Minute." He liked the idea of reassuring her.

What the hell was he doing? he wondered, recrossing his legs. He risked blowing everything he'd worked so long and hard for if he let himself get too tied up with Dianna. He tried to tell himself she was just another lay, another pushy broad who'd ruthlessly use him given half a chance, but it wasn't the truth. It might have started out that way but right now, were circumstances to allow it, he'd be willing to divorce goddamned Janet and *marry* Dianna. And to hell with those two whining brats who were perpetually glued to the fucking TV set. Let Janet have them! He'd take on Dianna. It didn't matter a goddamned bit to him that Dianna was older than he was. He could make her one of the biggest names in television.

He looked over at Keith who was reading his way through the FAX and the budget, appearing totally preoccupied with the task. Stupid bastard! Ned thought. Paying all the attention in the world to a couple of forms, as if they mattered, as if he'd be able to spot irregularities. Keith wouldn't notice a thing. He'd assume the corrections were typing errors.

He didn't dislike Keith; he merely found him too slow, too attached to the old ways of doing things. That was the trouble with most of the people around here: they couldn't move; they couldn't grab an idea and run with it. Instead, everything had to be proposed, discussed, analyzed, budgeted. By the time a concept had been through this process, it resembled raw meat on a tray in a butcher's shop; all the life and excitement gone. What they needed around here were people with ideas, and the personal momentum required to turn those ideas into something tangible and marketable. But Keith and the others were always so busy fussing and worrying about this, that, and the other goddamned thing that most of the good, high-powered ideas that arrived on their desks simply died there from atrophy.

He looked away from Keith and glanced again at his watch. Ten minutes Keith had been sitting there, reviewing the damned paperwork as if it were the Guttenberg Bible. If he took very much longer, Ned would be late getting over to Dianna's place. Being late getting there would mean being late home which, in turn, would mean bitchy, recriminating silence from Janet and sullen silence as usual from those two listless little buggers he could scarcely believe were his children. What the hell was going on with kids today? As a kid himself, he'd been forever on the move, racing around on his bike, out with friends, playing baseball, or going over to the rink to ice-skate. There'd always been something going on that he'd been a part of. Brad and Jennifer never got off their asses. The minute they came off the school bus they headed for the television set in the den and sat there, not two feet from the screen, their eyes unblinking and mouths slightly opened. During the commercials they got up lethargically to get a bag of potato chips or some Twinkies from the kitchen and only moved with energy when they thought the commercials might be ending and they were running the risk of missing some part of their show. It was always "their show" or "my show." They had personal attachments, proprietary claims on what was offered for viewing. It struck him as both ironic and meaningful that he should work in the very medium that had turned the brains of both his kids to absorbent mush. They could sing or recite every commercial that had been made during their lifetimes; they could dish out verbatim entire half-hours of sit-com dialogue; they could recreate almost anything they'd ever seen on the tube, but they scarcely knew how to read and their schoolwork was always only just above the passing mark. If they went to a friend's house, they watched more television. They rarely played, and if they did, Jennifer and her friends got out Barbie dolls and re-enacted TV shows using the dolls. Brad and his friends favored war games, using tanks and trucks and soldiers. They were like little old people, displaying eagerness only when it came to discussing some show they'd all seen. Then they erupted into enthusiastic babble, endlessly repeating their favorite moments and lines. Ned thought if he had to hear the neutral nasal voices of the Cleaver family one more time, he'd go straight out of his mind. Perfect June, just and manly Ward, cutely teenage Wally and the obnoxious Theodore "Beaver" were a family that could only have been created in the mind of someone who had a family precisely like Ned's. As a cleverly-planned revenge, the writer had foisted the Cleaver family on the American public in order to firmly establish in the minds of millions of kids an ideal of family life that could never possibly exist. The Nelsons, "Father Knows Best," the Cleavers, "I Remember Mama"—all shows about perfect people who never got constipated, never shouted, never had hemorrhoids or headaches or bad periods or dried-out dinners that had waited too long in the oven for Dad to get home from the city. The goddamned shows made money because little buggers all over the country wanted to believe that every other family but theirs lived these perfect, untroubled lives.

"It looks all right," Keith said, interrupting Ned's interior polemic.

Ned got up and approached the desk, daunted by the flawless sheen of the lacquer finish: not a fingerprint or a smudge visible on its surface. "I thought it did," he concurred, gazing into Keith's ear. It was as clean and finely formed, as hairless and translucent as a baby's. How the hell did a guy in his late forties come to have ears like an infant? Keith's almost pretty handsomeness never failed to intrigue Ned. Had it not been for the in-person evidence of Keith's absolutely gorgeous wife and five perfectly bland children, Ned would have sworn the guy was queer. But the way Barbara hung on the man, smiling up at him with adoring eyes, Ned had to believe Keith was managing to keep his wife well satisfied. What with, though? Ned had to wonder. Probably money, he decided. Guys like Keith had a way of presenting their women with little blue boxes from Tiffany's containing gifts of such a conspicuously expensive nature that a woman would be a fool to complain.

Keith, aware of Ned's scrutiny, and mildly irked by the small man's proximity, initialed the various papers, closed the file, then sat with his hand atop the folder, his eyes homing in on Ned. Ned waited, knowing Keith was putting together something he wanted to say. For a moment, Ned was nearly overcome by a desire to pry open Keith's jaws and rip the words from his throat. It drove him crazy to have to hang around waiting for the momentous thoughts to take shape and then be delivered from Keith's mouth. In the time it took him to express one thought, Ned could have dictated three letters, taken a leak, and made a couple of phone calls.

"When's the shoot?" Keith asked, privately savoring Ned's impatience. Ned was altogether too abrupt, always in too much of a hurry for Keith's liking. Caution had no part of Ned's nature, and it might one day prove to be his undoing. At least Keith devoutly hoped so. He missed Clark's studied, scholarly approach to his work. Clark had been a man of conscience and intellect. Keith knew perfectly well that Ned had engineered Clark's dismissal; what he couldn't be sure of was precisely how Ned had managed to accomplish it.

"Within the next two weeks," Ned answered.

Keith nodded slowly, drawing his nostrils together. Ned reeked of cologne. Obviously no one had ever explained to Ned that a little subtlety—in all matters—went a long way.

"Lynne's got the unit put together. Chuck's unit-managering. Dianna's going to do the interviews. Everything's all set."

"What's the rush?" Keith asked, sensing something amiss in all this urgency.

"It's hot," Ned said simply.

Keith looked down at the folder as if surprised to see it still resting on the desk beneath his hand. He picked it up and held it out to Ned. "Is it scheduled for an air-date yet?"

"I've got it down to discuss at the production meeting next Wednesday. We'll throw it around, see where it'll fit in."

Keith nodded, his eyes now apparently on something only he could see on the corner of his desk. Ned wanted to grab the folder and get the hell out of there, but he knew better. There was more Keith wanted to say. With luck, Ned thought, it wouldn't take him more than ten minutes to say it. Then Ned would be able to get the hell out of there and be on his way to Dianna's.

"I understood George and Ken were at work on a segment," Keith said at last, closely observing Ned's reactions.

"That's right," Ned answered, feeling pinpricks of alarm. Maybe Keith was more observant than Ned had credited. "A whole different thing." He smiled and folded his arms across his chest. Keith watched him, suspicious of the change of heart indicated by the papers contained in the file. What, he wondered, had made Ned decide, after all this time, to allow Lynne a chance at a major segment on a hot issue? It didn't seem possible that Ned's well-known aversion to Lynne as a female associate could have so suddenly dissipated.

"I'm glad," Keith said, "you're giving Lynne this opportunity. We've been discussing her recently. It's time she had more of a fair share of the bigger items."

"Exactly!" Ned agreed, more and more alarmed. Why the hell had he altered the forms? If this blew up in his face, it'd be all over. It was too late to do anything about it, though. He'd taken it this far, he'd just have to see it through. Keith's eyes remained on him for so long that Ned was sure Keith could feel the sudden heat radiating from his body. Was the bastard playing games? Ned decided to extricate himself. He pushed back his sleeve and looked at his watch, and with a smile, said, "I've got a four-thirty appointment. If we're all squared away here . . . ?"

"I've scheduled a meeting for Thursday next week. Lunch, in the dining room."

"I'll make a note of it." Ned started for the door. "Anything in particular?"

"Twelve-thirty," Keith said in his softly-modulated voice, speaking so quietly the words might have come from a ventriloquist hidden behind the desk.

"Right!" Ned got the door opened, and escaped.

As he rode down in the elevator he wondered if the summons to lunch on Thursday had some special significance. The upstairs gang probably just wanted to congratulate him again on the latest Nielsen ratings. They liked to give the production boys lunch in the executive dining room every so often. Ned smiled, feeling secure. They'd all sit around while the dining room staff fell on top of themselves bowing and scraping, replacing the ashtrays every time someone put out a cigarette. The food would be mediocre and bland, the service oppressively correct, and the conversation around the table would be terse and cryptic. There'd be plenty of self-congratulatory laughter while the air grew thick with smoke from expensive cigars, and smoked salmon shriveled on the plates awaiting some signal from the chairman that it was time to attend to the tedious but necessary process of eating.

He locked the folder in the top drawer of his desk—he'd have Sue make the copies and file everything on Monday— got his things and left.

He had the cab stop at the liquor store a block from the apartment. He ran in, bought a quart of Glenlivet, and ran back to the cab. As he waited for Dianna to buzz him into the lobby he wondered if he shouldn't have given in to the impulse and bought that necklace for her at Tiffany's. No. The Scotch was enough. At least he wasn't one of those assholes who came to a woman's place and drank all her booze. He always brought a bottle.

"You're losing weight," he noted, pressing the palm of his hand against her hipbone.

She wanted to say that it was because he had a way of killing her appetite, but said nothing. She'd promised herself she wouldn't go to bed with him, yet here she was, well after the fact, naked, hungry, and tired, wondering how he'd managed to do it to her again. She let her head sink deep in the pillows hoping he wouldn't stay much longer. She had some research reading to do, as well as a huge stack of letters to go through, to decide which one she'd respond to on Sunday's show.

"It's a stinking idea," she said, turning to reach for her glass.

"What is?"

"Having me respond on air to one of the letters. What're you trying to do to me?"

"Hey, listen! It's one of the hottest goddamned ideas we've come up with. Those two minutes will put you on the map for good. It's a hell of a chance for you. Are you crazy or what?"

"A chance to make a complete fool of myself."

"Bullshit, Dianna! They'll love it!"

"Sure," she said sourly.

"Trust me. It'll become a regular feature."

"I see. Once a week the humiliation of Dianna Ferguson

will be a regular occurrence on 'Up to the Minute.' It ought to hike the ratings to the sky.''

"You're getting paranoid!" he accused. "Where the hell d'you get humiliation? It's a chance to respond however the hell you want. You think the guy who wrote the letter's an asshole, here's your shot to say so."

"Forget I mentioned it," she said, draining the glass.

"Hate to do it, but I've got to go," he said. "I'll miss my train." Instead of moving to get dressed, he turned toward her, capturing her nipple between the tips of two fingers.

"I thought someone had seen us together," she said. "I thought you'd been warned off seeing me."

He sat up, found his socks on the floor and began pulling them on. "Maybe I don't like to do what I'm told."

"You know what?" she said, pouring herself another drink. "I don't think anybody saw anything, Neddy. I think this is some kind of new game you've decided to play. And you know what else? I'm getting tired of you and your games." She felt herself poised on the edge of a dangerous decision, but the Scotch and her fatigue propelled her forward. "I don't want you to come here again, Ned," she said, her heartbeat speeding up.

"Bullshit!" He turned to grin at her. "You love it!"

His words caused a small fuse to take light inside her chest. "Don't come here again!" she repeated. "You want to find some way to get me fired, fine. Go ahead and do it! I'm fed up with this whole thing. I'm not some goddamned call girl. You think a bottle of Scotch buys you something. Well, it doesn't buy you shit! I'm too old for this kind of garbage. I'm tired of having you come and go, calling the shots. I don't know who the hell you think you are, and I don't care." She kept her voice low, as she tried to contain the dynamite that threatened to go off inside her chest. She was trembling now from the effort.

Stunned into silence, he quickly finished dressing, then came around to sit on her side of the bed. "It was a mistake calling it off," he said, groping for the set of words he could speak that would make her change her mind. "Okay, I did lie about somebody seeing us. It's just that it was starting to get a little heavy. I've been thinking a lot about you . . . us.''

She stared at him, unwilling to believe him. "You've been thinking about me? Are you trying to be funny? You've never thought of anybody in your entire life but yourself.''

"That's business," he argued.

"Go home, would you?" She turned on her side, away from him, praying he'd go before the explosion took place. At this point in time she didn't care what the consequences of her sending him away for good might be, but later, in a few hours or by tomorrow, she knew she'd be caring a lot.

He stared at her naked back in disbelief. He'd never dreamed she'd take the initiative and get rid of him. He'd been so sure of her, of how he thought she was.

"We've got to talk about this," he said, looking at his watch. "I'm going to miss my train." He got up. "I'll call you tomorrow and we'll talk.''

She whirled around and half sat up, leaning toward him on her hands. "*Don't call me! And don't come back here!*" she shouted, her face contorting. "You're a goddamned menace, you know that? I'd rather masturbate for the rest of my life than have to put up with you! Go home," she said, lowering her voice. "I'm not one of these sniveling women who'll do anything to get laid! I'm not some dumb fuck! I was around long before you and I'll be around long after you. You go back to your wheeling and dealing, moving people around like goddamned Monopoly cards, but leave me the hell alone! And if you think you can get me fired, then go ahead and try! But I'll make you sorry you were ever born! Go home!''

He went down the hall to the living room to get his coat and briefcase. He felt very hurt, and innocent of any crime. He simply couldn't understand what had caused her to turn so violently against him. He stood by the front door for more than a minute debating going back to try to explain himself. If he stayed any longer, he'd miss his train. Then he'd have to listen to Janet bitching and moaning about how his being late had screwed up her plans. Shit! Goddamned women! His anger, healthy and righteous, began to spurt through him. He opened the door, slammed it furiously behind him, and stomped down the hall toward the elevator.

She gulped down her drink, poured another with unsteady hands, and sat back reviewing that final scene. Idle threats. There was little if anything she could do to retaliate, should Ned take action to get her fired. He had power, God damn it, and those idiots upstairs listened to him.

She drank herself to sleep and awakened just after two with a sick headache and what felt like a residual ache in her chest, caused, she was sure, from the tremendous effort of containing her rage at Ned. She poured herself a hefty drink before reaching for the telephone.

He answered on the fifth ring, and groaned at the sound of her voice. She talked quickly, trying to make him understand, the words hurtling out of her mouth like living things escaping a fire. He listened. He was actually listening. It made her feel infinitely better. She rushed on, trying to unravel her convoluted thoughts and feelings, her anger with Ned, and her fear. She began to cry helplessly, her voice ranging into uncontrolled upper levels as her throat started to close on the tumultuous surge of words and emotions. It was quite some time before she realized that the connection had been broken. At some point during her outpouring, he'd gently put down the receiver. Since it was she who'd placed the call, her line remained connected to his, so there was no dial tone when he hung up. There was only the hollow black cup into which she had fruitlessly poured her liquid tears.

The receiver resting in her lap, she held her glass with both hands and stared into the depths of the bedroom. She finished the drink and poured another, her eyes absorbing the negative details of the black-on-black nightscape as the frenzied projections in her mind gradually slowed. After a time, she staggered into the bathroom and paused to study her image in the mirror. Her vision blurred, she thought she looked better than might have been expected. She opened the medicine cabinet, took two sleeping pills with a cupped hand full of water, then made her way back to the bedroom, feeling her way along the walls. Upon final review, she decided she was pleased with the way she'd handled Ned. She settled down to sleep only to realize she'd left the bathroom light on, and the water running in the sink. People were supposed to be conserving water, she reminded herself, but a marvelous lassitude was spreading through her limbs and she didn't want to move. Fuck it! she thought, and plunged back into sleep.

❖ *Eight* ❖

HE COULD HAVE arranged to unload the wood later in the day but John chose to make the delivery early Saturday morning. He liked to work first thing in the day when the air had a fresh taste and he could feel the healthy pull of his muscles. He could let his body attend to the work while his mind was free to follow narrative leads; he could get entire chapters written in his head. It was the same when he went out for a run. Usually he chose to go just after dawn, but he hadn't been running much lately. For one thing it had been too wet, and for another he'd been getting up an hour earlier, at five, in order to get in an hour or two of work on the book before setting out for whatever jobs he'd lined up for the day. The yardwork in town was just about over for the season. Until the snow started things would be pretty quiet—the occasional delivery of wood, some small carpentry or electrical jobs, a night here and there delivering pizza for Joe.

While he stacked the wood he worked over the details of the next chapter, trying out the dialogue, getting scenes prewritten in his head so that when he finally got to the typewriter it would all flow out. He couldn't work the way he knew a lot of writers did, with index cards, the whole book plotted out. That would've spoiled the pleasure for him, the delight of discovering that characters he'd created had wills of their own, and desires that took them off in completely unexpected directions. He'd begun with an idea of where he wanted the book to go but by the halfway point

121

he'd discovered that Abie and Snow intended to go somewhere else, and he was eager to arrive at the end in order to know their ultimate destination.

It was funny how writing had taken him over. He'd never done well in comp. classes in school; he'd been distressed by his inability to create anything of interest out of how he'd spent his summer vacation, by his failure to find appropriate words with which to describe sunsets, or the most interesting character he'd ever met. He'd always kept a journal so he could jot down his thoughts; by reviewing what he wrote he was able to determine how he felt about things. Putting his thoughts into written words gave him some perspective not only on his feelings but on the people around him. Most of the time he felt distanced, separated from others by his lack of skill with small talk and by his failure to appreciate the artful badinage his college friends had substituted for communication. He'd have liked to join in, to be a part of a large, cheerful group always going off somewhere. But he felt different, as if a small spotlight constantly held him in its uncomfortable glow and no matter how hard he tried to fit in, no matter how he struggled to lose the feeling of being years and years older than his classmates, he couldn't rid himself of that light that relentlessly showed up his differences.

By his senior year he was spending an hour or two each night on his journal, making notes on his perceptions, describing people he saw, even creating brief stories out of minor incidents that took place on campus. He did a piece on the college's mystery vehicle, an ancient Volkswagen van whose original color was impossible to determine. The body, from the bottom up, was in an advanced state of corrosion, with massive rusted areas, like lace-work, halfway up the sides. Across the driver's side, someone had written in spray paint RUST NEVER SLEEPS. No one seemed to know who owned the van but it was always parked on campus, always able to elicit smiles. Feeling bold one afternoon, John had submitted his piece on the van to the editor of the college newspaper. To John's amazement, they'd accepted it and for a few days following its appearance in print people had approached to congratulate him while John, flushed and uncertain, mumbled thank-yous. Even the success of the piece failed to help him bridge the gap. He continued to write but resigned himself to the reality that he'd never be the life and soul of any party, that he'd never master the art of inconsequential chit-chat, and that he really didn't mind these failures. He'd discovered that he wanted to write and he carried this knowledge with him like invisible armor; it gave him strength and independence, and it gave him the courage to become friends with Lizzie, who'd majored in journalism and was one of the editors on the campus paper. She, too, was distanced, and he recognized it, although in her case it wasn't all that obvious. She was pretty, and had exquisite long, silken brown hair; she was a little on the heavy side, both physically and intellectually, but she was interested and honest and he liked her. They were able to discuss things from their mutual distances, and weren't bothered by their inability to make closer contact. Their meetings usually involved food of one kind or another, since Lizzie was invariably hungry, and while they ate, they'd talk urgently, exchanging ideas and opinions. Since graduating, Lizzie had taken a reporting job on the Stamford *Advocate* and had her mind set on one day moving to New York to work for the *Times*. From there, she hoped eventually to end up as a foreign correspondent. Lizzie's talk, lately, included more and more observations on the prospects of living in Manhattan and the likelihood of her attaining sufficient background to impress the people who hired and fired at the *Times*.

He worked steadily, unloading the wood from the back of the pickup, stacking it neatly, symmetrically. He liked to give all his energy to whatever he did. He knew that when he finished and stood back to look, he'd feel satisfied seeing that all the logs were perfectly aligned. He intensely disliked sloppy workmanship. It was a quality he liked to think he'd inherited from his mother. The truth was it was a direct legacy from his father. If he and his father could have been a bit closer, been able to talk a bit more effortlessly, John wouldn't, he knew, have felt so resentful about the old man's insistence on trying to direct John's life. Living over a pizza parlor and doing odd jobs to support himself was, in his father's words, ". . . a daily slap in the face." He still tried to talk John into getting himself outfitted at Brooks Brothers and showing up in town at the office, ready to go to work learning how to buy and sell on the Market. It was John's idea of living death. His mother understood his feelings, but the issue had become so major that John stayed away from the house altogether these days, unless his father was out of town on a business trip. Then he and his mother would, like conspirators, get together and bring each other up to date on their lives. He admired his mother, but it was funny how he could only seem to see her as a character in a novel—one so perfectly and thoroughly detailed in his mind that from time to time he found himself sitting back and watching her, too, from a distance instead of entering into the heart of things with her.

He glanced over at the cottage thinking about Lynne Craig, realizing that he didn't feel distanced from her. Was it possible, he wondered, that he'd found another person who wasn't making full-time contact with the world? Was it possible that this woman, for all her generosity and appeal, had as much trouble connecting as he did?

She was awakened by the sound of the truck pulling into the driveway, and remembered that the wood was to be delivered today. She gazed at the vaulted ceiling for several moments then turned to look at the clock. Seven-thirty. Knowing how early it was made her feel tired. She'd gone to bed just after two, planning to sleep until at least ten. She would, she decided, go back to sleep, and turned on her side, dragging the bedclothes over her head. He'd have to be paid; she'd have to get up, write him a check. Shivering in the morning cold of the room, she sat up and pulled on her robe.

Dressed in a pair of jeans and an old sweatshirt, she got the coffee started, thinking about Ross. He was outside her life. Her involvement with him, whatever it was to be, would be extracurricular, separate. She breathed deeply, slowly, sorting things out. Two years was a long time to have lived without anyone whose touch she desired.

She turned to the interior of the cottage and was pleased by the early morning sun streaming in through the windows. Slabs of light slanted across the furniture to lie carpetlike on the polished wide-board floors. The light seemed to penetrate her, thawing her inside, easing the tightness.

She dropped two slices of whole wheat bread into the toaster and stood warming her hands while she waited. Her brain seemed to slide into neutral and rest there as she ate standing near the living room window, watching the young man—what was his name? Grace. John Grace—stack the wood. He worked like an exquisite machine. Her eyes shifted and she looked at the garden. The last of the leaves had dropped and lay twitching on the damp grass. The wind sent some of them skittering over the driveway and out of sight. The light was stark, cold-looking, unlike summer sun which seemed weighted, full and heavy with heat. It might be a good day to walk down to the point for a stroll along the beach. Her experience of late fall and early winter walks there reminded her that the beach would be damp and chilly, the sand dark and wet, the flag flapping noisily on the flagpole, the surf choppy and gray. The fishy sea-smell would be powerful at low tide and the tide-line would be clotted with countless tiny polished stones and broken shells, ragged clumps of seaweed, bits of styrofoam and paper: the remnants of fast-food takeout meals. The previous winter she'd gone several times to walk along the snow-encrusted sand, watching the yellowed ice rim of the shoreline. For some reason she felt both closer to Alec at these times and also acutely conscious of his absence.

As so often happened, she wished now she could turn to discover him sitting on the rocker by the fireplace, reading the *Wall Street Journal* from front to back, circling items of interest in red pencil. She let her eyes fall on the empty chair, then raised the mug to her mouth to find she'd finished her coffee. She was pouring some more when John knocked at the back door. He looked so young, she thought; he couldn't possibly be more than twenty.

"I've got your check," she told him. "God, it's cold! You must be frozen. Would you like some coffee?"

"That'd be great," he said with a smile that touched her with its completeness. "Could I wash up?"

"Sure. Help yourself. You remember where it is?"

He went through to the bathroom, quickly washed his hands, then returned to the kitchen. He felt both bold and timid, exuberant and wary.

"You take cream and sugar, don't you?" she asked, holding a mug out to him. He gave her another smile and once more she was touched.

"You got a good memory," he said, accepting the coffee.

"Are you a student?"

"Not any more. I graduated four years ago."

"Really! You don't look that old."

"I'm twenty-six."

"You don't look it."

"Sure I do," he said easily.

"Well, maybe you do," she conceded. "I always used to be the youngest," she said, a little wistfully. "Now everyone looks young to me."

"You're not that old."

He was again wearing that wonderfully earnest expression.

"I'm forty," she said, wondering why she would admit that so readily. She knew women who'd have to be tortured before they'd confess their ages.

"You don't look it," he said appraisingly. "I'd have guessed thirty-two."

"What was your major?" she asked. "Have you had breakfast?"

"I've already eaten, thanks. I majored in political science."

She smiled widely. "Thinking of going into politics?"

He laughed. "Oh, never. I just wanted to understand the mechanics of it all, but it was a total waste of time. Well, maybe not total, but a waste. I'm trying to write."

"Are you? What? Fiction, non-fiction?"

"Fiction."

The telephone rang. She said, "Excuse me," and moved to pick up the kitchen extension.

"Come to dinner tonight," Amy said imperiously.

"And good morning to you, too," Lynne responded, smiling.

"Good morning. Come to dinner. I haven't seen you in weeks, months!"

"You saw me two weeks ago. And I can't. I've got plans this evening."

While she spoke on the telephone, John watched her. When he heard her mention her plans for the evening, he was glad he hadn't asked her out as he'd intended. Maybe, though, she'd be willing . . . some other evening . . .

"Hell!" Amy was saying. "I just knew you would, and I felt like seeing you. I had this vision of a nice relaxed evening, some good conversation. D'you know what I hate most about being divorced? Weekends alone. What plans?"

"A date," Lynne answered, glancing over to see John looking awkward, as if he wished he didn't have to be there to overhear this conversation. "Dinner. Nothing special."

"Something wrong?" Amy asked. "You sound a little off."

"I've got someone here."

"Oh?"

"Not what you think," Lynne said curtly.

"Well, I won't keep you then."

"Look, let's do it one night this week. You know I'd like to see you."

"This week stinks, except for tonight and tomorrow. Maybe next Sunday?"

"I'll call you and we'll make plans. Everything all right?"

"Just swell. The usual crap: letters from the kids pleading for money and complaining about the world in general. You know how they are: they think they've discovered reality; they've got an inside track and we're just a bunch of feeble idiots who don't know a thing. They're so damned arrogant. It really stuns me when they are. . . ."

Lynne looked at John and smiled, with a gesture apologizing for being so long on the phone. John gestured back, pointing toward the door, indicating he'd leave if she preferred it. She reached out and took hold of his wrist, then returned her attention to Amy.

". . . Lucinda's threatening to drop out and go live in Colorado for a year, and Tim wants to switch from premed to economics. I refuse to get involved anymore. Let them figure it out for themselves."

John looked down at her hand on his wrist. It was long and wide, cool, strong. After a few seconds she released him, but he could still feel the pressure of her fingers. He was pleased she wanted him to stay.

". . . anyway, I've got to run. I've got to get to the supermarket and then to Bloomingdale's in the city. All my sheets are starting to disintegrate in the washer. You know what I'd like?"

"What?" Lynne asked, wondering why Amy could never pick up on cue and cut short a call. She turned to look for her cigarettes, found them at the far end of the counter, and lit one. It was awful to keep John standing there. She turned to smile at him again and raised her shoulders apologetically.

"I'd like to leave town for about a year," Amy declared, "and come back when it's all over. Call me!"

"Next week," Lynne promised and put down the receiver. "I'm sorry. My sister. She never knows when to cut things short. More coffee?"

"I don't want to hold you up."

"You're not. More coffee?"

"Okay, sure. Thanks."

She refilled his cup, saying, "Tell me about your writing."

"Are you in publishing?"

"Television. I'm an associate producer with 'Up to the Minute.'"

"Rottenmouth Dianna Ferguson," he said, then paused. "Maybe I shouldn't say that."

"*Rottenmouth*? Is that what you think of her?"

"You're probably best friends," he said, wishing he hadn't just blurted that out.

"Not quite," she said.

"That's a relief. I was about to step over to the sink, pick up that knife there, and start hacking away at my wrists."

She laughed. "I don't think that'll be necessary. You may not like her, but she makes for good television. She knows her job and she's a first-rate journalist."

"Maybe, if you like blood-letting in public. She makes my teeth hurt. I don't mind the guys so much. I mean I don't watch the show all that often, except when I'm visiting my folks or something. My Dad's addicted to the program. He says it's the only worthwhile thing on the tube."

"What do you write?" she asked again.

He sighed. "I'm working on a novel. I've been at it for two years, more than that."

"Is it good?"

"I think maybe. If I ever get it finished I'll know for sure. Have you ever thought of putting a skylight up there?" He indicated the ceiling.

"A skylight?" She looked up. "No."

"You'd get great light, even on bad days, and it'd be a lot warmer during the day, save you money on heating."

"That's a good idea. It's never even occurred to me."

"Would you be interested in going out?" he asked. "I mean, I thought if you weren't doing anything . . . tomorrow night, maybe . . . or sometime . . ."

She turned slowly. "Tomorrow night?"

"We could have something to eat. I mean, if you're interested."

"How much d'you think it would cost to put in a skylight?"

"Depends on how big you wanted it, if you wanted safety glass or regular."

"Safety glass, I would think."

"Maybe around a hundred, a hundred and fifty."

What was he after? she wondered, examining his light features, his round brown eyes. She could tell that it had taken a lot of his courage to extend the invitation. Her initial instinct was to turn him down politely, as she'd so quickly turned down Amy. She'd have to call Amy back and tell her she was free tomorrow afternoon and could stop by, maybe for lunch. Why was she so quick to refuse all offers? She enjoyed looking at this young man to such an extent that the idea of being free to study him for a few hours over a meal seemed appealing. His directness and his lack of complication contrasted sharply to the people she knew in the city; it was a little like being offered a glass of fresh cool spring water after subsisting for years on hard liquor. For a few seconds she had an almost overwhelming desire to put her arms around him. He was reminding her of how horribly painful it was to be young.

"What time?" she asked.

"What time? Tomorrow, you mean?"

"That's right. What time?" She wished she knew what to say that would ease his obvious discomfort.

"Seven? You really want to?"

"Seven will be fine. Do you have a car?"

"Just the truck. I . . . You really want to?"

"Pick me up at seven and we'll go in my car. How's that?"

"Fine, great. Well!" He put his mug down and looked over at the back door. He felt as if he'd just been punched in the stomach. "I guess I'd better be going. I, uh, I'll be here at seven tomorrow."

"Good."

"Okay. Well, I'll be going then." He hurried to the back door, opened it, then turned back, his expression one of complete bewilderment. "You're sure?"

"I'm positive. I'll see you tomorrow."

Looking stunned, he closed the back door and walked toward the truck. She remained leaning against the counter, watching him go, wondering why she'd accepted his invitation. She was almost old enough to be his mother. What would people think, seeing the two of them together? Hell! she thought, people could think what they wanted. It was a perfectly innocent outing. They were only going out for dinner, nothing more. He was a sweet young man, eager and sincere. There was no harm to spending a few hours with him. No harm at all.

He drove back toward Rowayton in a state of shock. She'd actually agreed to go out with him. He couldn't believe it. He felt suddenly filled with energy, as if his skin was all at once too small, too tight to contain his body.

❖ *Nine* ❖

IN HER DREAM the telephone rang. She knew it was Alec calling, that he was only allowed to let the phone ring once at her end. She knew she had to get to the telephone, but she couldn't move. She lay trapped on her back like some helplessly beached sea creature, unable to do more than twist ineffectually, straining to attain a mobility that was beyond her evolvement. She could do no more than lie there, struggling inside herself for the strength to move, while the telephone went unanswered and Alec was lost to her forever.

Then there was a shift and, with the perfect logic dreams seem to have, she was outside the cottage, standing in the driveway, watching in fascination as plant life in the form of rapacious, thick-leaved vines quickly enclosed the walls of the house, sealed the windows and doors, even the chimney. Within minutes the place was nothing more than an oddly shaped mound, a rounded outcropping that might tempt children to play King of the Castle. She felt no sadness at the loss of her home, only a strange sense of rightness to this transformation. She stood for quite some time watching the way the wind ruffled the luxuriant growth of leaves. Then she climbed into Alec's old BMW and drove away. She hadn't waited to warm the engine. Alec would be annoyed, but that couldn't be helped. He'd understand once she told him what had happened to the cottage.

She awakened at twelve-thirty with a headache, annoyed with herself for having failed to set the alarm. She'd intended to sleep for two hours at most after John had left; instead she'd wasted the entire morning, thereby falling behind on work she'd planned to do both on the script when it was delivered and in preparing her expenses for the month. She hated to waste time. It was undoubtedly a habit acquired from her mother. Mary Conners had been a woman afflicted by something that went far beyond the Puritan work ethic. It was an ingrained conviction that idleness not only stunted one's personal growth but also contributed to the increasingly shoddy way in which things were done in general. A basic tendency toward laziness was responsible for products that fell apart after being used once; it was what lay behind cars with chronic mechanical problems, and clothing that came apart at the seams. Lack of pride went hand in hand with inertia. Therefore even when at rest she'd been busy with something, knitting cardigans for Amy's children, mending aged linen sheets and tablecloths, working crossword puzzles, reading, or out canvassing on behalf of some political candidate. After spending the first seventeen years of her life with this woman, it didn't surprise Lynne to find she'd inherited many of her mother's habits and beliefs. What did bring her up short was the constant realization of how utterly unaffected Amy was. Lynne had always found it easier, more sensible to go along with their mother and her ideas. Amy had rebelled, not in overt, active fashion but in small, almost senseless ways. Lynne could recall dozens of conversations with her older sister, trying to convince her of the harmlessness of going along. "It won't kill you," Lynne had said far too often as a teenager. "Maybe not touching your face or leaning on your hand does keep you from getting wrinkles; maybe a well-groomed woman doesn't go around with her hair down. She's only trying to *help*. Just go along with her. It'll make life so much easier."

Amy had refused to give in; she was someone who constantly made life more difficult for herself than it needed to be. Which was probably why, despite words of counsel from the entire family, she'd gone ahead and married the first man who asked her, only to find herself left ten years later with two small children and a list of grievances that would have taken days to recite, had anyone given her that opportunity. It was why Amy could never find anything when she went to look for it, and why, at the age of forty-eight, she too often resembled a raddled beatnik with her badly-cut gray-blond hair, outsized jeans, and men's shirts. But perhaps it was also why Amy was immediate in her affections, caring, supportive and generous. Lynne herself was more like their mother: reserved, cautious, a hoarder of emotions, someone who refused to be controlled by her feelings. I can control this, she often thought, and exerted all the will she could muster in order to effect that control.

She set the bedroom to rights, collected her materials, and went to the kitchen to make a fresh pot of coffee. Then she settled at her desk and began sorting out a month's worth of receipts—for parking, for gas, for lunches and dinners in the city, for calls made on her home telephone. The meals receipts were always easy. American Express kindly supplied her with additional copies of her charges, just in case she'd misplaced the ones given by the restaurants. But she rarely remembered to ask for parking, gas, and toll receipts; nor did she clock her mileage as staff were always being asked to do. Memos pertaining to the expense accounts circulated through the office with sickening regularity, directed downstairs by Keith who took budgeting—right down the line—with lethal seriousness. He didn't look like the kind of man who'd be capable of nit picking to the extent he did. Keith was very tall, almost six-and-a-half-feet, with beautifully silvered hair and small, almost pretty features. He dressed exquisitely in suits of subtle grays and tans that served to point up his surprisingly rosy skin and silver hair. He was a graduate of the Harvard Business School; he spoke softly, smiled frequently, and had been known to hound people to distraction with his endless memos, all pertaining to personal accounting. In reality, his job overlapped with that of the comptroller, and as a matter of form, Keith often added the comptroller's name to his memos. It was a courtesy to his associate. Keith, despite his fanaticism on money matters, was a fair-minded man.

Lynne regularly wondered how Ned had managed to so bamboozle Keith that Keith actually believed Ned was working along the same lines, with the same principles in mind, as Keith. It said something about Ned's talent for performing convincingly, but Lynne couldn't help feeling that one of these days Ned would find himself called to account for too many acts of sabotage. If for no other reason than to vindicate Clark, Lynne hoped to be around long enough to see Ned take that one disastrous step too far.

The month's accounts finally totaled and signed, she was feeling a bit better. She'd be able to work on the script, if it ever arrived, and the lists of questions to be used for each of the subjects. All the preproduction work became mild drudgery at some point; it was inevitable, after reviewing questions half a dozen times in order to ascertain that no vital point had been missed. Always, just prior to a shoot, Lynne was impatient, ready to get on with the job instead of fussing over costs. Keith, of course, demanded from all the associates far more accurate budget proposals than she believed any other station, except O & Os, those locally owned and operated ones, might request. They were smaller outfits, with considerably less staff, and considerably less interference from upstairs; they also had a lot less impact, as their audiences, being local, were smaller. To be associated with a network show—even the fourth-ranking network—meant large-scale recognition, although she could think of several former associates who'd gladly gone out to smaller stations after a dose of Ned's politics.

At three o'clock, the messenger came. She put the package down on her desk and stood stretching, a little dizzy from three cups of coffee and half a pack of cigarettes. The room was hazy with smoke and she opened the window to let in some fresh air. She remained by the window, revived by the crisp air, thinking about the evening to come. Something was bound to happen tonight; it was inevitable. And why had she accepted John's invitation? What was she doing? She let her forehead come to rest against the glass, absorbing the cold shock.

She was getting what she'd wanted: the opportunity to do

her segment after all this time. Why, she wondered, couldn't she feel as enthusiastic as she should have? Because, she answered herself, she didn't believe it would happen. Nothing felt right; everything was slightly off-kilter. She wasn't excited because, in her bones, she knew she was going to be conned. But by whom, and for what reason, she didn't know.

Did it really matter anymore? she wondered.

She had, for the last two years, worked harder than ever before; perhaps because if she risked stopping for any length of time she might discover that with Alec's death she'd lost her impetus. His long-suffering acceptance of her career had impelled her to keep the career going. They had been, she saw, engaged in a silent but ongoing battle over her career. It frightened her to think that by taking his life Alec might just have won.

Ross played two sets of tennis with the other three regulars at the indoor club, begged off the usual beers and bullshit session afterward and returned home just past four. After getting cleaned up, he settled in the Eames chair in the den to get some work done. There were half a dozen financial reports, including profit and loss statements and long-term projects, on companies the corporation was considering taking over. How, he wondered, setting aside the first two reports, had the corporation wandered so far afield? When had it been decided, and by whom, that the corporate interest would turn toward, for example, the manufacture of sporting equipment? Maybe the scouts were getting a little cocky. Or maybe he was losing track of the day-to-day politicking. He reached for the telephone.

"Have you seen these reports?" he asked Fielding, who'd taken over three years earlier as president when Ross had agreed to be bumped upstairs.

"I've seen them."

"When the hell did we become interested in hockey pucks?"

"There's some interest," Fielding said guardedly.

"Who by?" Ross wanted to know. "I haven't heard a

goddamned word about the acquisition of Ace Sports or Fabco Manufacturing, not to mention Clyde Engineering, Bonnie Fay Limited, or the rest of them.'' As he spoke, he shuffled through the reports then dumped them on the floor. "Bonnie Fay!" he snorted.

Fielding laughed. "Hell of a name," he said, in a good old-boy tone. "But a hell of an outfit. They're pulling down almost two million net annually. We could probably hike that to three mil, maybe four in eighteen months."

"What for, George?"

"Why not, Ross? We're in business to make money."

"Maybe I'm getting old but it's a hell of a long stretch of the imagination from tool and die to Bonnie Fay Limited. What the hell *is* Bonnie Fay anyway? It's a terrific report but I'll be buggered if I can figure out what they're selling."

"Cosmetics, Ross," Fielding said patiently. "Door to door. It's a good, solid little company."

Ross listened to George swing into a sales pitch that would have done any Fuller Brush man proud, thinking that maybe the time had finally come to exercise his stock options and retire. If the corporation could make such quantum leaps in considering acquisitions in no way related to its business then perhaps it was time for him to quit. The corporation seemed to have grown into an immense, indiscriminate glutton, gorging itself on anything and everything. "I have the feeling," he interrupted George, "that one of these days in the not too distant future we're going to start receiving calls from the anti-trust boys."

"Your imagination's working overtime. We're not in violation of any laws."

"Okay, George," Ross sighed. "Never mind. Who scouted Bonnie Fay, by the way?"

"Harrison. A very bright young man. He's earmarked to go up."

"Harrison," Ross repeated, trying to put a face to the name. He couldn't. "We'll talk on Monday," he said and hung up. He stared at the documents littering the floor. Bonnie Fay, Harrison, subrosa field-trips. He had the uneasy feeling that things had gone beyond any individual's power to control them.

"Jesus!" he exclaimed softly, sinking into his chair.

"You look wonderful," Ross said, returning his attention to the road ahead.

Automatically, she replied, "Thank you," wondering if he was the sort of man programmed to compliment women in order to make them feel good.

"You don't believe me."

"Oh, I do," she said, looking at his manicured hands on the steering wheel. His hands looked strong, flexible. She liked the size and shape of them.

"No. You think I complimented you as a matter of form."

"That's true."

"Well, you're wrong. You happen to look lovely and I wanted to tell you so. Are you suspicious of everyone?"

"I'm not suspicious. I'm just . . ."

"What?" he asked, removing one hand from the wheel, allowing it to rest on his thigh.

"Maybe I'm jaded. I've heard all the lines in the past two years, every one of them."

"And now you've got all men catagorized. Fairstone's the complimentary type. File under *C*."

She laughed softly, becoming increasingly nervous, and not really quite sure why. "You win that round."

"Nevertheless," he persisted, "you think I'm insincere."

"I honestly don't know," she admitted, somewhat fatigued by the verbal sparring. "Soon we'll be having those mornings when you wake up and everything's frozen. I lost my power several times last winter."

"Years back we had no power for six days. Ella made light of it the first day, cooking hotdogs and baked beans in the fireplace, all of us in sleeping bags in the living room. By the afternoon of the second day it wasn't fun anymore. I said to hell with it and we all piled into the car and drove into the city to stay at the St. Regis until the power was turned back on.

"We had to throw out everything in the freezer, and of course we had a burst pipe. The boys had a whale of a time, running up and down the corridors in the hotel, but Ella . . ." He trailed off, then started again. "She was already ill then, but we didn't know it. It must've been three months later she started having all the tests. She lasted another three years, though. Nobody thought she would, but she did."

"Cancer?"

He nodded. "They took out most of her stomach, part of her intestines. I didn't think she'd make it past the surgery, but she was a scrapper, Ella." He spoke of his late wife in respectful tones. Lynne stared at him for a moment, intrigued to have this viewing of the man who got left behind. His feelings, at least on the surface, seemed to parallel closely her own.

"This is it!" he announced and she looked through the window at his house. It was magnificently eccentric, constructed of light-colored stone, with pillars and archways, and statuary in the front garden.

"How long have you lived here?" she asked, noting the mullioned windows, the slate roof, and old-fashioned chimneys. It was a house with an inbuilt sense of humor.

"Almost five years. I bought the place after Ella died. I really didn't want to stay on in the old house."

The foyer had a fine, gray slate floor and was built in a semicircle off of which led a number of doors and corridors. Directly opposite the front door was a huge, round window, beneath and in front of which sat an immense Kentia palm, spotlit from above.

"It's a wonderful house," she said. "Whoever built it had a strong sense of whimsy."

"Are you sincere?" he asked with a laugh. "You're too serious. How hungry are you? Would you like a drink first, or a tour of the house?"

"A drink and a tour," she answered, startled when he took hold of her hand. It seemed an innocent enough gesture, even childlike: someone showing a new friend his territory. They'd done things like that as children, she and Amy. She could remember dragging a new second-grade friend over the threshold, pushing in through the screen door so that it closed with a smart slap behind them. She could recall the pride—both in her friend and in her home and family—as she'd led the child through the house to the kitchen where her mother and Margery, the cook, had been preparing dinner; she could see herself and her friend carefully carrying glasses of milk and a plate of cookies up the stairs to Lynne's room. Was Ross right? she asked herself. Had she grown suspicious? It upset her to think that he might be right.

Mrs. Wain, the housekeeper he'd spoken of, was a small, thin woman who was standing near the sink smoking a cigarette and drinking what looked to be a large Scotch and water. Ross introduced them and Lynne shook hands with the woman whose grip was as firm and dry as Ross's.

"How long have we got?" Ross asked the woman, heading across the kitchen to the bar beside the serving hatch.

"Everything's ready. All you've got to do is set the oven at three fifty and put the food in. Mike's coming for me any minute now."

"Mike," Ross explained to Lynne, "is Peggy's son. Peggy spends Sundays with them up in Waterbury."

"Is that where you're from?" Lynne asked her.

Mrs. Wain laughed and leaned her hip against the counter, taking a hefty swallow of her drink. "Dublin," she answered. "Nineteen-forty. I run off to London and took up with a Yank in the RAF. We come over after the war and lived in Boston two years. Two years, two babies, and he took himself off one night and that's the last we saw of him."

"Don't let her get started," Ross said, handing Lynne a glass of white wine. "She'll tell you her entire life story. Why don't you have a sip of that and then I'll show you the house."

"What did you do then?" Lynne asked Mrs. Wain, all at once afraid of finding herself alone in the house with Ross. He looked too solid, too appealing with his well-shaped hands, his effortless smile, his closely-shaven face. She could scarcely look at him without feeling an internal reaction.

"Went to work," the woman replied, "into service. Not much else I could do, with two babies."

"It must have been hard," Lynne sympathized.

"Wasn't easy," Mrs. Wain said, "but we managed."

A car horn sounded outside. "There's my Mike," Mrs. Wain said. She finished her drink, crushed out her cigarette and gathered up her coat and bag. "Don't let the food cook too long," she reminded Ross. "Half an hour at most."

"Have a good weekend," he said indulgently, smiling, his arm curving around Lynne's shoulders.

The front door opened and closed, and Mrs. Wain was gone. Lynne was having trouble breathing.

"Let's have our tour," Ross said, taking the wine glass from her, and setting it down on the counter. "It's not a practical house," he said, directing the way back through the foyer and up the staircase tucked to the left of the front door. "The stairways are too wide in some places, too narrow in others. I did a lot of the decorating myself," he admitted sheepishly, as if his pleasure in decorating reduced him in status. He smiled at her and again took hold of her hand.

He showed her the boys' bedrooms and then continued to the far end of the corridor where he opened the door and waited for her to catch up. She walked slowly toward him, thinking how nice he looked in gray slacks, a white shirt, and white V-necked cashmere sweater. He looked grown-up and calm, someone in control. She stepped into the room, turned and found herself in his arms, being held against the warmth of his wide chest. She wasn't sure who initiated the move, but she found the strength and weight of his arms comforting. Two years, she thought; two years since Alec had died, since she'd made love. Two years of brief, insignificant contact; contact with sisterly flesh, with the unwanted, quickly rejected hands of strangers; no access, no desire. Yet she wanted this man. She was curious and, she felt, grotesquely eager. She was filled with need, quaking with her inability to contain it. She knew she either had to break away from him or remain and allow the next inevitable step to happen.

"We don't have to," Ross murmured, stroking her hair.

"I told you I'd want to," she responded, waiting for him to kiss her, to touch her. She could scarcely see; Ross hadn't had a chance to turn on the lights.

"You also said you weren't ready."

"It doesn't matter." She lifted her head and looked at him in the darkness, willing him to proceed, to kiss her, to make the first contact.

"You're the first woman I've invited here," he said, wanting her to understand that he hadn't planned this; it hadn't been his intention to seduce her.

"I understand," she said truthfully, aware of his hands moving up her back.

While he lay sleeping, she crept around the room gathering up her clothes. She needed air, and time to think. In the kitchen she found some paper and pencil and wrote a note which she left on top of the casserole where she was sure he'd find it. Then she retrieved her coat from the living room and quietly let herself out.

She hurried up the driveway feeling dislocated and sad, even criminal. Why was she running away? The night was cold. She was hungry. For a moment or two she was strongly tempted to turn and go back, but it would be the wrong thing to do. She needed time alone to decide how she felt. During those long minutes when Ross's arms had held her and his body pressed in against hers, she'd experienced a sensation akin to terror. It wasn't at all the way she'd hoped it would be. He'd been slow, and gentle, a tender lover, but her feelings seemed to have deserted her. She'd been unable to lose her awareness of the mechanics of what was happening, couldn't lose herself to sensation. Now, walking toward home, she felt swollen with unreleased tension. Her thighs ached and her mouth felt bruised. She wondered if the time would ever come when she'd be ready to share herself fully again.

John worked all afternoon. He rewrote one chapter and completed an entirely new one. Pleased with his progress, he took a break and sat on the floor with a cup of tea thinking about how he'd asked Lynne Craig out. He wondered why she'd accepted. She didn't strike him as someone who dished out charity. Maybe she liked him. He wanted to think so. She had such a lonely look to her, the look of someone who didn't bother to cook regular meals for herself, who spent her time alone surrounded by silence. It had to be rough, being a single woman in a town like Darien where everybody was married and had kids, where everyone was ready to be transferred at a moment's notice. The turnover was getting bigger all the time. It seemed lately as if people stayed just long enough to get the furniture in place, the pictures on the walls, and then the moving van came and they were off to Denver, or Houston, or San Jose. It wasn't his idea of a way to live.

She was actually going to go out with him. He'd take her to dinner and then, if she were in the mood, they could go to a movie. Or maybe they'd just have a long dinner and talk. It felt like forever since he'd really talked to anybody, except for Lizzie. And lately, Lizzie had been getting a little eager. It turned him off. Her eagerness struck him as sad. He wished she'd find somebody else to fix on so that the two of them could continue being friends. He preferred to sit in bed at night and turn himself on with a copy of *Playboy* rather than make love with someone he didn't really want.

It had been a long time since he'd made love, not since his senior year when he'd been dating Joanna. He'd been halfway in love with Joanna, but she'd been marriage-minded and that had made him nervous. They'd broken up at the end of the year and she'd married another guy six months later. He'd seen her one afternoon in a bookstore in Norwalk. He'd gone to check out the new paperbacks, and Joanna had been there, with a baby in a stroller. She'd looked embarrassed, as if he'd caught her stealing. The entire time they'd talked she'd kept casting guilty looks at the baby. Finally, she'd put down the two books she'd been holding, and left the store. That had been three years ago. He hadn't seen her again. He almost never thought of her but, oddly, he did think about her baby. The kid would be pretty big now, running around and getting into everything. He liked kids, except for his nephew, Luther. They were so goddamned funny. Joanna's kid had been cute, with one of those tiny little noses, and round, fat cheeks.

He decided he'd go downstairs for a pizza. Maybe Joe would take time out to keep him company while he ate.

By the time she arrived home she was angry with herself, able to think of dozens of reasons why she should have stayed with Ross. For one thing, he'd wake up to find himself alone, and be upset. In all likelihood, the first thing he'd do would be to telephone. She wasn't up to talking to him, and she was hungry. Without bothering to go inside the cottage, she climbed into the BMW. She wanted to go someplace where she could sit in a booth and eat in relative peace and quiet, without feeling she was being watched by pitying crowds of couples.

She drove along the back roads to Rowayton. When she saw the pizza parlor with its invitingly near-empty parking lot, she pulled in. The place had a homey, New York kind of look to it with a neon beer sign and several sadly bedraggled plants hanging above it in the window. She pushed inside to be welcomed by a warm blast of doughy-smelling air. Aside from four people in a corner booth and two men at a table near the service counter, the place was deserted. She started for a small table near the window when someone called her name. She turned to see John getting to his feet, smiling and waving.

"Hey, hi! Come and sit with us," he invited, coming over to her.

She allowed him to take her by the arm and lead her across the restaurant.

"This is Joe," John said happily, "my landlord and good friend."

Beaming, Joe jumped up to shake Lynne's hand. "Sit down, sit down," he urged.

John took Lynne's coat to hang it up, then returned to sit between her and Joe, smiling happily. "Did you come to

eat? I mean, I've got a big pizza working and you could
share it if you like.''

"I'd love to," she answered, wondering why she felt
rejuvenated simply by the sight of John. It seemed to happen every time she saw him. Just being near him made her
feel lighter, less weighted by her years of living, of working, of contending with too many problems.

"You wanna coffee or a beer maybe?" Joe offered, on
his feet and leaning on the edge of the table, impressed by
the good looks of John's ladyfriend.

"A beer would be fine," she said, warming at once to the
small, round-faced man who smiled approvingly and hurried off to get the beer.

"I don't mean to be nosy or anything," John said, "but
weren't you supposed to be going out tonight?"

"I went. It . . . ended early."

"Oh." He closed the matchbook and watched her exhale
a thick stream of smoke. He shook his head and said, "I've
never seen you in here before," and then laughed loudly,
tilting his chair back, his hands holding the rim of the table.
"Boy! What a line!"

"I've never been in here before," she said, wishing he
hadn't referred, however indirectly, to Ross. He was probably trying to reach her by telephone at that very moment,
and she wasn't there to take the call. "You live here?" she
asked.

"Upstairs."

"Have you been working on your book?" She wanted to
steer the conversation into safely neutral territory.

"I got an entire chapter done today," he said excitedly.
"It's been forever since I actually did an entire chapter in
one go."

"Maybe it won't take you too long to get it finished."

He righted his chair and looked for a moment at his
hands. "On a quiet night like this, I can get a lot of work
done. But usually"—he looked around the restaurant—"it's
really busy, with the jukebox blaring, people coming and
going. Tonight's a weird night for a Saturday. It'll probably
get busy around eleven."

Joe returned with the beer and a glass which he went to the trouble of wiping on his apron before setting it down with careful ceremony. Lynne thanked him, then seeing he intended to go, said, "Join us. Don't let me drive you away."

"Okay." Joe resumed his seat. He folded his arms on the table and gazed at her with frank appreciation. "So," he said, with a smile that revealed all his teeth, "you're John's friend, huh?"

She looked over at John who seemed temporarily suspended, as if her answer to this question was of major importance.

"That's right," she said after a moment, returning her eyes to Joe. "I'm John's friend."

❖ *Ten* ❖

"AT HOME, every Sunday in the afternoon you go to the park, see all your friends, have an ice. This stuff they got here, they call it 'Italian ice.' Pah! Garbage. And shoes, huh? You wanna paira beautiful shoes, with leather soft like the insida your hand, you get from Italy. Shoes you want to wear, not this plastic stuff, they call it leather.

"Me, I believed you come to America and pick up gold from the streets." Joe laughed hugely and scratched his ear. "What you pick up is dogshit, huh? You excuse my bad language," he said to Lynne. "I work nine years a waiter in New York to save enough to put the down payment on this place. Don't look like nothin' much, but you wait. One of these days I have a nice place, serve good Neapolitan food, no more a this pizza. Pizza." He made a face, sighed, then asked Lynne, "You want another beer?"

"No, thank you."

"Some coffee," Joe offered. "We all have some coffee, huh?"

"That would be good."

"You, too, huh, Johnnie?"

"Sure, great. You want a hand?"

"No, you stay, you sit with your friend." Joe stacked the plates on the empty pizza tray and carried them back to the kitchen.

"He's a good guy," John told Lynne.

"He seems like a very nice man," she agreed.

"They're saving up to remodel this place. They've got

the plans all drawn, new tables and everything picked out. They hope to get it started next spring.''

"I like the place the way it is," she said, looking around at the old-fashioned booths, the worn linoleum floor. "It has charm; it reminds me of places I knew in New York years ago, places we'd go after work for what they advertised as 'home-cooked meals.'" She laughed softly, remembering how she and Alec used to settle into those booths as if returning home. There'd been something so familiar and reassuring about the split leatherette, the scarred tabletops, the thick white coffee mugs and rich-tasting coffee drawn from immense urns, slabs of apple pie. "There was a place we used to go to, called Burton's Bar and Grill. We'd meet there, Alec and I, almost every day after work. We'd sit for hours over coffee and a piece of pie or a sandwich and no one ever bothered us. We had so much to talk about. Later on, it was as if we spoke in code, giving each other messages, but never talking the way we did at the beginning." She looked down at the table, wondering why she was saying all this.

"It's like that a lot," John said surprisingly. "When you start out, there's all this curiosity about the other person, wanting to know what they think about things, how they feel; do they think and feel the same way you do. Then, after a while, when you think you know the way their minds work, you sort of stop bothering to find out if you're right. A lot gets taken for granted that way."

"I don't think we took each other for granted," she said consideringly. "But maybe we did. Maybe that's what happens to people when they live together for a long time. Sometimes I used to look at Alec and wonder what had happened to all the *excitement*. We used to be so eager to be together, to talk; we had so many things to tell each other. I suppose part of it has to do with being young, although Alec wasn't all that young. He was six years older than me."

Joe returned with the coffee just as the door opened and a large group of people came in, noisily grouping themselves around two tables they pulled together. Joe went off for menus. John leaned on his elbows on the table watching Lynne pick up her cup. "Go on," he said.

She shook her head. "I wasn't going to say more."

"Do you mind if I ask what happened?"

"Alec died. Two years ago."

"Oh. That's really too bad. I'm sorry."

He did look sorry, she thought, and wondered why he'd care.

"I ask a lot of questions," he explained. "I think it's writer's curiosity, but it could be that I'm just plain curious. If I get out of line, tell me."

"You're not out of line."

"You never know with people," he said soberly. "You ask a question and it turns out you're prying, digging into something they don't want to talk about. I've had that happen. Then you get nervous about saying anything at all."

"That happens to everyone. We've had people we're interviewing clam up because Dianna hit a sore spot."

"Tell me about her," he asked. "What's she really like? I've got this whole picture in my head about what she's like off the tube."

"What's your picture?" she asked, amused.

"Oh, let's see." He tilted his chair back and chewed on his lower lip for a moment. "She's divorced, and getting big alimony. She lives in an apartment on Fifth Avenue, a big place that's pretty messy but looks okay on the surface. She's a zippy dresser but her clothes never look quite right, as if they need cleaning, maybe. She's tough, and hard, and would run you over if you got in her way. She thinks that because she's on network television she's a big gun. She probably eats little people for breakfast."

She laughed appreciatively.

"Am I anywhere near right?" he asked.

"Dianna is divorced and she does get alimony, but she's got two daughters in college and I honestly don't think her salary's all that huge. I know for a fact she isn't paid anywhere near what Mort and Harvey, for example, are paid. She has an apartment on Central Park West, but I don't know what it's like inside. I've never been there. She's certainly not a 'zippy dresser.' God! That's marvelous! She's of the old school that believes being tall is a disaster, so she always wears flat-heeled shoes, or ones with tiny heels, and very understated clothes to minimize her height. She's almost five-ten, you know. People are always surprised, meeting her in person. TV has a way of reducing people, you know, of distorting them, so that you can't really be sure what you're seeing. She has never been known to step outside her apartment door without a full face of makeup, but, really, she's not as bad as you might like to think. She's very bright, and she can be quite kind.''

"She probably is bright. I mean, she manages to keep people watching.''

"That's a lot harder than you might think.''

"I can bet it's hard. I wasn't putting her down. Not her ability, I mean.''

"I didn't think you were. You're very concerned about being misinterpreted, aren't you?''

"I guess I am. Words are important; what you say, how you say it.''

She glanced at her watch and he felt a surge of disappointment. She was going to leave and he didn't want her to go yet.

"It's early,'' he said.

"I thought it was at least eleven, but it's only nine-thirty.''

"Does that mean you'll stay and have another coffee? Or we could go up to my place. I've got some wine.''

If she had stayed with Ross they'd have just now been finishing dinner. Ross would have been attentive, even loving. But she'd run away, like a startled schoolgirl, frightened of facing the consequences of her own actions. She'd behaved like a fool. Now she was feeling faintly menaced by a young man's invitation to go to his apartment and have a glass of wine. For a few seconds, she was again filled with rage at Alec for taking his life and leaving her alone to cope with situations and with people who, at times, seemed incomprehensible. After her unsettling and disappointing encounter with Ross, and in view of John's invitation to go upstairs, she couldn't help wondering if she hadn't made the biggest mistake of her life in moving away from the city in a doomed effort to escape the suffocating weight of memories associated with Alec. She'd left none of it behind; she'd simply relocated, redistributed the memories, and reaped an entire new crop of additional problems.

"I just thought we could talk some more," John said, sensing her reservations. "I didn't have anything else in mind."

"I know that."

"That's the second time I've seen you go off that way," he said.

"What way?"

"You go—distant, I guess. You did it that first day when I worked on your yard."

"I did?"

"It's all right, though. I mean, I guess it's pretty rough getting over something like that."

"Like what?"

"Your husband dying."

"Sometimes, you know, it's as if he never existed at all. Other times, it's as if he's playing some scary game: he's around but won't show himself. It makes me furious, as if I'm supposed to keep on looking for him, keep on playing until he decides it's time the game can end." John was nodding as she spoke, and she wondered how it was possible for him to seem so almost unbearably young at moments and so consolingly wise at others.

"My little brother Kenny died when I was fourteen," he said. "He drowned. I still can't really believe it. He was only ten. I did artificial respiration on him for hours. Nobody could make me stop. I couldn't believe that he wasn't going to start breathing again any second. I know what you mean. Boy! We're getting into some heavy stuff. Would you like to come up?"

"All right. But only for a little while. I've got a lot of work to do."

"Great!" He got up and went to get her coat. "Don't worry about the tab," he explained. "I've got an arrangement with Joe."

"At least let me leave a tip."

"Joe's feelings would be hurt."

She closed her handbag and stood to allow him to help her on with her coat. He was most mannerly, deferential. It gave her an odd feeling, as if she were his elderly aunt, or even his mother. She waved goodbye to Joe and followed John out of the restaurant.

The moment she walked through the apartment door she knew it was going to be all right. She was greatly amused and charmed by his efforts to personalize the place. Reminiscent of L'il Abner he'd painted a black crescent moon on the bathroom door. Diagonally criss-crossing the bedroom door he'd nailed two boards: condemned. In black paint he'd written construction-site graffiti on the door to compound the effect: Danger! Blasting site; Death is nature's way of telling you to slow down; Stand well back!

She laughed, exclaiming, ''You've got a wonderful sense of humor!''

''I just went with the general theme of the place. It was in pretty terrible shape when I moved in. Joe didn't really want to rent it; he used this as a storage area. But I begged,'' he admitted with a grin. ''I'm a terrific beggar when I have to be. I guess he felt sorry for me, and I convinced him the sixty a month would beef up his renovation fund. Come and sit down. I'll get the wine.''

He went to the kitchen and she continued to stand, looking around. Two sawhorses supporting an unpainted door served as his desk, atop which stood a Smith-Corona portable typewriter and several tidy stacks of paper. An ancient kitchen chair, minus several of its spine struts stood before the desk. The seating area consisted of half a dozen enormous pillows covered with printed Indian cotton. An expensive-looking hi-fi system was set out on bricks, and two fair-sized speakers served as tables either side of the heaped pillows. On the wall were a number of posters Scotch-taped into place.

''I got the posters from the book store,'' he explained, ''and some from Joe. People are always coming in, asking him to put stuff in his windows. He lets me go through, take what I want. Please sit down.''

She shrugged off her coat, folded it in half and placed it

on the floor before lowering herself into the pillows. With effortless grace he sank down beside her, all the while keeping hold of a half-gallon jug of Gallo Chablis Blanc and two glasses. He filled the glasses, and gave her one, then jumped up.

"I forgot! D'you like music? I've got a new record. Would you like to hear it?"

She nodded, took a sip of the wine and sat back, watching him slide an album from its jacket and, with exquisite care, clean it before setting it on the turntable. He paused a moment to adjust the controls, then returned to the pillows.

She let her head fall back and gazed at the ceiling as the first bars of music emerged from the speakers. He'd covered the light fixture with an oriental umbrella of deep blue-colored paper. It soothed the light and cast a pleasantly muted glow over the room. "I like the music. What is it?" she asked.

"Jacques Loussier."

"It's wonderful."

"I don't usually go in for classical stuff. I mean, heavily classical. But his Bach is so easy."

"I rarely get a chance to listen to music anymore. It seems I'm always reading or away on location on a shoot."

"What did he do, your husband?"

"Oh, God," she sighed. "He was a businessman. He started out right from college in the training program of a corporation and worked his way up the ladder for twelve years, until what he called the 'corporate mentality' started to get to him. He decided to go into business for himself, as an advertising consultant. Actually, as an advertising marketing consultant. He advised businesses where they could place their advertising most profitably, and he played liaison between publications and advertisers. It would have worked out if he hadn't allowed his initial success to delude him. He rented an entire suite of offices, hired a lot more staff than he needed; then he had to scramble for clients to keep the whole thing afloat. He kept it up for four years, until, one by one, the staff had to go, and then the offices. Even then it might have been all right, but he'd somehow got caught up in his own momentum. He was running himself into the ground to pay off the backlog of debts he'd accumulated, and at the same time trying to build up his clientele. I offered to help.'' She looked at John searchingly, as if seeking an understanding she doubted he could extend. ''I had my salary and a small amount of money I inherited when my father died.'' She shook her head and looked down at her glass. ''He wouldn't hear of it. Well.'' She took a deep breath and went on. ''On the surface things were fairly much as they'd always been. We had the co-op; we entertained regularly; we went out once or twice a week. He kept on assuring me everything was all right, that we could afford all that.

''I came home from work one night and he was dead; he'd taken sleeping pills. There was no note, nothing. He'd just done it and I was supposed to make sense of it. And in a way, I could. Alec was very rigid in most of his thinking, with strict ideas about the way things should be done. Since he'd always been this way, it was what I expected of him. So I didn't mind. I mean, he was a man who never in his life owned or wore a pair of jeans. He always chose to go on vacation to places where you dressed for dinner. It was his heritage, I suppose. His father had been exactly the same way. What I'm trying to say is that he maintained the lifestyle we'd had, even though things were falling apart. That was why I was so shocked. . . . Later, when I talked to his lawyer and saw his will, I was livid because he'd known for quite some time what he planned to do. He'd arranged it so that I wouldn't be left with the business debts he'd been unable to pay off. He'd planned his death exactly the way he'd planned our lives, somehow managing to exclude me while at the same time including me.''

''My dad's a lot like that. The fathers of my friends are like that. Benevolent despots.''

''That's awful!'' she said, looking appalled.

''I don't mean they're bad people,'' he qualified, ''because they're not. I could never say my father's a bad man. *He* thinks he's doing everything exactly right. I guess it's okay for someone like my mother because it's what she grew up believing she should expect.''

"In a way, I suppose I did, too. Benevolent despots. It sounds so awful."

"Maybe I put it a little too strongly. I'm crazy about words, remember." He smiled encouragingly at her. "Anyway, it couldn't have been all that bad, or you wouldn't have stayed married for . . . how long?"

"Seventeen years."

"See? You wouldn't have stuck with it."

"I loved him," she said simply.

"I love my dad. I just can't live with him. Let me ask you something. If you met Alec today, would it be the same?"

"Do you mean would I fall in love with him and stay married for seventeen years? I don't know. Perhaps not. I know a lot now I didn't know then; things have changed."

"You feel guilty," he said incisively.

"Of course I do. Alec suffered to maintain what he believed in. You have to admire that."

"I don't know that I admire it, but I respect it."

"All right," she said angrily. "It's the same thing."

"No, it isn't. There are all sorts of things I respect that I don't admire at all. I respect and admire Martin Luther King. I respect Lyndon Johnson but I don't admire him."

She sat silently, absorbing the impact of what he'd said. Her chest ached; she wanted to cry. It seemed critically unfair that this young man should, with his words and his perception, force her to feel so disloyal to someone she'd loved. Yet she couldn't avoid the truth: were she to meet Alec now, she doubted she'd fall in love with him.

"You're upset," he said quietly. "I guess maybe I shouldn't have said any of that."

"No. You're right to say what you think. It's just that I haven't really talked about Alec since it happened. It doesn't feel . . ." She shrugged, unable to describe the mix of disloyalty and anger she felt.

"But it's better to talk about it, don't you think?"

"You're very young. The young discuss everything. Then the young grow older and become middle-aged people like me who think a great deal but say very little." She gulped the last of her wine and put down the glass. "I've got to go."

"I hope it's not because you're angry."

"Not with you," she said, reaching for her coat. "With myself. I keep finding more and more pockets, things to think about that I've been avoiding."

"Is it still all right for tomorrow night?"

"Seven o'clock."

He watched her put on her coat. She seemed quite small suddenly, even frail. She looked older, as if their conversation had robbed her of years.

"I don't get to talk very often," he said. "I mean . . ."

"I know." She held up her hand as if to stop him physically. "Neither do I. I didn't intend to insult you by calling you young. I'm tired," she said, looking and sounding it. "Thank you for the pizza and the wine."

"I'll walk you to your car."

They went down the stairs and out into the parking lot. The restaurant had filled up. Through the steamed-over front window, John could see people moving about inside. He'd go in and give Joe a hand after Lynne left. He turned to look at her, seeing that she had the door unlocked and was prepared to climb inside. On impulse he touched his hand to her cheek. Her skin was soft and cool. "Don't be upset," he said. "It's only words."

"No. It's more than that. But it's all right."

She got in and fastened her seat belt.

"How come you always do that?" he asked.

"The seat belt? I was in a car crash once." She put the car into gear and drove off. He turned and went into the restaurant.

She drove, still able to feel his hand upon her cheek. She felt faintly disgusted with herself, moved by the touch of a young man's hand on her face while the evidence of her earlier activities with another man lay sticky on her thighs.

❖ *Eleven* ❖

"You look wonderful, absolutely wonderful!" Amy declared.

Amy's mouth smiled, her arms embraced, but her tone of surprise and the expression in her eyes contradicted the warmth.

"How are you?" Lynne asked, following her sister into the sunny kitchen.

"Oh me," Amy sighed. "The same as ever: hurrying to go nowhere. Would you like some wine?" She looked at her wristwatch. "It's early, but what the hell! Want some?"

"Sure. That would be fine."

"I've only got white. It's not bad though." She hefted a half-gallon bottle of Gallo Chablis Blanc from the refrigerator and Lynne stared at the bottle, the sight of it returning her to the previous evening at John's apartment.

"Let's go sit in the living room," Amy said, handing her sister a glass of wine. "Kitchens depress me." She walked away and Lynne had no choice but to go after her. She studied Amy's figure, squared-off and matronly, feeling as if this weren't her sister but some woman she was meeting for the first time. Amy's manner was conscientiously off-hand, a studied display of nonchalance, even disdain.

"Sit down, relax," Amy invited, flopping heavily onto the sofa. She turned to watch Lynne arrange herself on the sofa, following the movement of her sister's arm as she set down her wineglass. "God, you're so thin! How the hell d'you do it?"

"We always have this conversation." Lynne smiled, glancing around the room. Amy had made an effort to tidy up. She was, and quite proudly admitted to being, a lamentably uncaring housekeeper. There were always moisture rings on the tables, scattered newspapers, streamers of dust drifting from the ceiling on heated air that rose from peeling, white-painted radiators.

"I really need to lose weight." Amy looked down at her legs, then at her feet which were propped on the coffee table. "I'll go to my grave needing to lose weight. Wine okay?"

"Fine." Lynne was trying to locate her sense of family feeling, her fondness for this woman. "Have you heard from the kids again? How are they?"

"Let's not talk about them," she said unhappily. "Motherhood's the biggest fraud of them all, after marriage. I can't get over the way you look!" She leaned against the back of the sofa, studying Lynne assessingly.

Lynne looked at her sister, their eyes moving over one another in somehow ritualistic fashion. Amy was an attractive woman, but her skin had the leathery look of someone who spent too much time in the sun; her eyes and mouth were enclosed by many fine wrinkles, giving her a prematurely aged appearance. Her hair, more gray than blond, had been cropped too short, exposing too much of her neck, ears, and forehead. She was wearing a red plaid man's sport shirt with the sleeves rolled up and baggy jeans, white tennis socks with green stripes around the cuffs, and sneakers. She looked like a cook in a logging camp, Lynne thought, then at once felt bad. She laid her hand on Amy's arm, stroking the warm solid flesh above the wrist. She longed to be able to talk, to tell her sister about the feelings she had for a man fourteen years her junior, about her ambivalence toward a very nice man she'd made love to then run away from.

"You look a little tired," Amy said at last. "Let me go check the salad mold. It should be set by now." She got up and went out to the kitchen.

Lynne sat with her elbows on her knees, contemplating

the glass of wine she didn't really want to drink. It wasn't yet noon. What she really wanted was a second cup of coffee, but she knew Amy would offer her a cup of instant and she didn't want instant coffee.

"We'll eat in about ten minutes," Amy said, returning. "Okay?"

"Sure. Fine."

"Who is it?" Amy asked, taking a large swallow of wine.

"Who is who?"

"You told me when I called you were going out last night. Who was it?"

"Oh! Ross."

"Ross asked you out?"

"We've gone out a couple of times." Lynne tried to sound offhand.

"Are you interested in him?"

"Amy, I don't know. I've seen the man twice."

"You know something?" Amy asked.

"What?"

"I haven't slept with anyone for six years."

"Really?"

"Really. My friend Muffy talked me into going to this get-together at the United Church. Everyone there was either widowed or divorced. It was kind of interesting, all things considered. Anyway, we split up into little groups to have a discussion. I forget what the exact topic was, something to do with how your children should or shouldn't react to the new person in your life. It doesn't matter. The point is I met this man and we wound up going out for drinks after the meeting. I got absolutely stinko and brought him home. The kids were away that weekend. I think they were with their father. It wasn't bad," she said reflectively. "He was a good ten years younger than me, just divorced. I even had my period and he didn't mind. I felt pretty optimistic, thinking maybe I'd finally met someone. He left and I didn't hear from him for three weeks. Then he called at eleven o'clock one night asking if he could come over. He wanted to get laid. I told him where he could put it, and that was that. My last time.''

''You never told me,'' Lynne said.

''We don't see each other all that often. Anyway, it's not the sort of thing I like to talk about.''

''I'm sorry.''

''I love you,'' Amy said. ''I wish we saw each other more often. I don't see you for weeks on end and I think about you, worry about you, and I build a case for calling you up, getting you to come over so we can be together. But I tell myself you're busy, you don't have the kind of time I've got. So I let it ride. Finally, when I don't hear from you, I tell myself I'd better check in, see how things are going. So I call you and you're busy, or you're behind on your work and then I feel embarrassed for calling. Christ! I wish things could be the way they used to be. I wish things could be the way they've never been. I don't know. You and Alec used to drop by. Remember? You'd be out for a Sunday drive, or on your way back from visiting Mother and you'd show up at the front door. It used to give me such a charge. Can you beat that?''

''I feel the same way sometimes. But there's no time anymore, not the way there used to be.''

''I know that. Lately, you know, the real estate people have been calling a lot.''

''Why?''

''Checking in to see if I'd like to sell the house. I've lived here for twenty-three years. I love this goddamned house. My kids were born here; I feel safe here. It's all I've got that's mine. Shit! This is turning into a bitching session. I didn't mean to say any of that.''

''If you need money . . .'' Lynne began.

''That wasn't what I was talking about. Ignore me. It's just menopausal self-pity. Come give me a hug.''

She opened her arms and Lynne surrendered herself to Amy's embrace. She couldn't imagine how Amy had to feel, living untouched for so long. Why did they feel incomplete without a man in their lives?

''It shouldn't matter,'' she said, disengaging herself gently. ''It bothers me that it does.''

"What?" Amy asked, lost.

"Men. Why do we do it, counting off the months and years since we made love, since we spent time with a man who wanted us? Why do we do it?"

"Every year I care a little less. I find things to do, and I've got friends. But you're young."

"So are you," Lynne argued. "Forty-eight isn't old."

"Not to me, not to you maybe. But to all the men out there getting rid of their wives so they can take up with their twenty-two-year-old secretaries, forty-eight is over the goddamned hill."

"It's crazy," Lynne stated.

"Yeah," Amy sighed, and then laughed loudly, once more gathering her younger sister into her embrace. "You're so damned skinny. I can feel all your bones. You're like a little bird." She rested her cheek against the top of Lynne's head. "You should've had kids, sweetheart. It would've done you good. I bitch about mine, but they're the best thing that ever happened to me. They make me feel I'm not a total failure."

"Alec didn't . . ."

"I know all about Alec's dids and didn'ts. Don't canonize him because he's dead," Amy warned. "Let's go eat before this gets really depressing."

As they were headed into the kitchen, Lynne asked, "How old do you feel?"

Without a pause, Amy answered, "About eighteen. You?"

"About the same."

"Christ!" Amy exclaimed. They both laughed.

John drove by the cottage on the off chance she might be there, but the car wasn't in the driveway. He was let down. He felt they had a lot to talk about; he also believed that it was somehow important to his book that he spend time with Lynne. In some way the futures of Abie and Snow, as well as his own, were tied up with this woman.

He told himself he was being stupid, creating all kinds of mystical excuses for not getting down to work. Yet he felt as if his life was inextricably involved with Abie's and

Snow's: none of them could proceed until John dealt with the matter of his feelings for Lynne. He was being a creep, hanging around her place, expecting something from her. He didn't have the right to expect anything.

He drove back to Rowayton, parked the pickup at the rear of the restaurant and got out to stand looking up at the sky, gray and miserable and full of winter. As he went up the stairs he told himself he was becoming fixated on this woman and it wasn't healthy. Maybe, he thought, this was how assassins worked: they found a candidate and then become so totally obsessed with that person that in the end the only satisfaction they could get would come through taking that person's life in order that no one else could have it, not even that person.

He sat on the floor pillows and ate some soup right from the pot, his eyes on the window and the dark sky beyond. Periodically he looked either at his watch or at the telephone. At last, the soup gone, he got up and went to peer into the closet at his meager collection of clothes. Several sets of overalls, a couple of pairs of Levis, half a dozen work shirts, three good shirts, two decent pairs of slacks, a sports jacket and one tie. He hated ties, always felt as if he were being slowly strangled when he had to wear one. He'd wear the tie tonight, along with the tan cords, the white shirt, and the herringbone tweed jacket. His only good shoes were loafers; they'd have to do.

As he shaved, his hair drying into tight curls, he considered how disturbed Lynne had been the previous evening. He probably shouldn't have said all that about the difference between respect and admiration, but he couldn't have lied. If you started out saying the things you thought people wanted to hear, you ended up with nothing.

He was sorry she'd got upset, but he couldn't have done it any other way. He wanted to hear real things, true things, and he believed Lynne was like that too.

He was dressed and ready too early. Running his finger around the inside of his too-tight collar, he sat down at the desk to reread the half dozen pages he'd written that morning. He had almost an hour. If he kept going he might get the chapter finished. He hated to leave in midthought. Continuity was his biggest problem.

He rolled in a fresh page, stared at the wall for a minute or two, then began. It was working; he found himself sliding contentedly, purposefully into what he thought of as "the bubble." When he worked, the world ceased to exist; only Abie and Snow and their lives had reality, and that reality became his. He fitted himself into position, in a mental chair where he could oversee the characters and their actions and record the proceedings. It seemed an almost too pleasurable occupation to him, especially at those times when the words gushed onto the paper, so quickly he could barely keep up with them. Abie and Snow were working their way toward the climax of their story and John wanted to know how it would end. He suspected what the ending would be, but he wasn't sure. The book had taken entirely different turns from the ones he'd imagined.

When he paused to look at his watch, he saw, with a jolt, that it was five to seven. He was going to be late. In a panic—he hated being late, for anything—he grabbed his keys and took off. Once in the truck, he was furious with himself for not stopping to phone and explain that he'd lost track of the time.

He pulled into her driveway at twelve minutes past seven and raced up to the door, his apologies prepared all in a string. She came to the door with her coat on and he felt ill with embarrassment.

"I'm really sorry. I hate keeping people waiting. I was halfway here when I realized I should've stopped to call you, to say I was going to be late. I was working and ran overtime. I'm really sorry."

"It's all right," she said, holding out the keys to the BMW. "You're only a few minutes late."

"I can't stand it when people are late. If I'm waiting and somebody doesn't show up, I always think they're dead."

She laughed, fighting a strong desire to touch him, to assure him no harm had been done. She looked at his fine, freshly-shaved face and his clear brown eyes and found him not only beautiful but wonderfully unsophisticated. She still held the keys and finally he took them from her.

"You trust me to drive?" he asked.

"Sure."

"I'll be very careful. Wait just a minute and I'll move the truck." He ran down the steps, climbed into the cab, backed the truck out into the road then pulled it up alongside the BMW. Once they were inside the car, he followed her example in fastening his safety belt. Then he got the car started and reversed into the road.

"It's a beautiful car," he said as they headed toward the turnpike. "What year?"

"Sixty-three. Alec had one. I mean, I got used to driving it. I traded in the old one when I moved here and bought this one."

"I don't know if I'd trust somebody else to drive it, if I had a car like this."

"It's not my time to die yet," she said, looking out the window.

"Why do you say things like that?" he asked.

"It's the truth. I'll know when it's my time. And it's not now, not with you today."

"You said you were in an accident. What happened?"

"It happened when I was at college. There were four of us in the car. Two of the girls died. I was lucky. Ever since then I've always worn my seat belt. How's your book coming along?" she asked, changing the subject. She sometimes still dreamed of the accident, of Betsy Wilkins turning to smile at her as the car came through the intersection.

"I'm getting near the end. It's kind of scary."

"Why?"

"Because once it's finished, it won't be mine anymore."

"I've never heard a writer say that before."

"Fiction's different from nonfiction. The investment's different. Nonfiction is facts. The material's all there; all you have to do is put it into some kind of order. I mean, there's skill involved and all that, but it's not the same as creating entirely new people, creating your own material."

"And why isn't it yours once it's finished?"

"Then it's a piece of property to be sold. It belongs to the agent, if you have one, and to the editor, if a publisher wants to buy it. Everybody has little pieces of it. It's never yours again in the same way."

"It might be interesting to do a segment on you," she said, thinking aloud.

He shook his head vigorously. "No way. If I ever had to try to deal with that lady I'd probably never be able to write again."

"Dianna's not as cruel as you seem to think." She was about to go on to say that one of the male hosts could just as easily do the interview, but John hurried to respond.

"Sure she is. She'd ask me things like: What makes you think you've got anything to say? Or, Why do you think you've got any talent? Those're the sort of things she says to people. I couldn't handle it."

He was probably right. Given that this imaginary interview were to take place with Dianna, she would ask those questions and they would appear cruel. "She and the others, Mort and Harvey, Don and Frank, they can only point up what a person is, or isn't. They can't destroy."

"They can damage," he argued.

"Don't you think you could defend yourself?"

"Sure I could," he answered readily. "The thing is: Why should I have to? I'm not going to apologize to anyone for doing something I believe in."

"You're right," she said, noticing that it was beginning to rain. "God! We spend a lot of time doing that, don't we?"

"I used to. I don't anymore. I mean, I'll apologize if I'm wrong, or I'm late, or something like that. But I won't say I'm sorry for being alive, for being me, for trying to do some work I believe in." He found the control and turned on the windshield wipers.

"No," she said slowly, "people should never do that." She lit a cigarette, thinking about Ross. He hadn't called. Or perhaps he had but she hadn't been home. At some point he'd catch up with her; they'd have to talk.

"Boy! It's really starting to come down." He eased back on the accelerator, slowing down to fifty, then to forty-five.

"You know," she said, "Dianna was very kind to me after Alec died. It's funny how time's divided now: Everything either happened before, or after Alec died."

John didn't comment. She let her head fall back against the seat. Daring to look at him she felt an anxious flutter in her chest, and a renewal of her desire to touch him. As if her limbs had a will of their own, her hand reached out to touch the firm line of his jaw where it met his chin.

He was so preoccupied with trying to drive that he was only distantly aware of her touch. The rain washed in sheets down the windshield; the visibility had turned poor. Trees lining the highway whipped back and forth in the gusting wind. Lynne sat up and reached over to turn on the defrosters.

"Perhaps we should pull over and wait this out," she suggested, wondering how he could see at all to drive. He'd slowed to forty but it still seemed rather fast for the conditions.

He was about to answer, already removing his foot from the accelerator when, ahead of them, the traffic seemed to go berserk. Two cars, both in the process of changing lanes, sideswiped and lurched apart. The cars immediately behind them slammed on their brakes, swerving to avoid the two that had hit, but were too late. Spotting an opening, John spun the wheel hard and pulled over onto the shoulder, coasting to a stop as more cars plowed into those ahead. The scream of brakes could barely be heard beneath the thundering downpour, as half a dozen more cars—the drivers seeing the pileup too late—applied their brakes, spinning their steering wheels in an effort to avoid the others.

It seemed to last forever. Lynne wanted to look away, but couldn't, and watched the two original cars get struck by at least five others before the traffic finally came to a halt. Automobiles were strewn all over the road. People were getting out of their cars, trying to see what had happened.

Her heart hammering, Lynne watched as a woman slowly emerged from one of the two original cars to collide. Covered with blood, she stood shakily, her hand held to her face. Then she turned and tried to get the badly-dented back door open. Lynne put her hand on the door, her eyes still on the woman. They couldn't just sit here and watch. "Drive down the shoulder to the exit," she told John, as she opened the door. "Find a phone and call for the police, some ambulances." Reaching over the back seat, she grabbed the blanket and umbrella she kept in the car, then got out and began to run toward the woman who was still trying to get the rear door of her car open.

John sat for a moment then shifted into first and raced forward, headed for the off-ramp. As he passed the car, and the woman tugging feebly at the door, he saw what Lynne had: two children pounding at the window with their small hands, their faces contorted as they screamed.

Other people joined Lynne as she ran between the cars. Two men fell in beside her and together they hurried through the rain, toward the woman who was losing strength. One of the men put his arm around the woman and directed her to the side of the road. The other man set to work on the door. Placing her blanket and umbrella on the front seat, Lynne crawled onto the glass-strewn seat and glanced briefly at the driver who lay slumped over the wheel, his face hidden from view. The two children were screaming shrilly.

"Come here!" Lynne ordered, reaching over the seat for the child nearest, a small boy of three or four whose face was dark with blood. Her authoritative tone momentarily quieted both children. The boy, sobbing, held out his arms. "You'll be all right," she told him more quietly. "Stand on the back seat and I'll lift you out." He did as he was told and she managed to lift him over the seat. The man, meanwhile, had succeeded in opening the back door and took the second child out of the car, carrying her off toward the side of the road.

The child heavy in her arms, she bent to retrieve the blanket and umbrella, clumsily wrapping the boy in the blanket before carrying him to the side of the road where she settled him in her lap while she got the umbrella open.

The rain had washed away some of the blood so that she could see the lips of two alarmingly deep gashes that ran across his mouth and chin. Blood oozed thickly dark, welling up in the wounds and spilling over. She should have thought to grab the first-aid kit from her glove compartment. Then she might have been able, at least temporarily, to do something more concrete than sit helplessly on her knees with the child in her lap, looking about and waiting for the ambulances to arrive. Why hadn't the police, the ambulances come yet? She smoothed the wet hair back from the boy's face and curved herself protectingly over him, whispering, "You'll be all right, dear. Don't be afraid." She glanced around every few seconds. Injured people seemed to be everywhere, some lying in the road, others by the roadside, still others standing, dazed, beside their smashed-up cars. There was shattered glass and pieces of chrome everywhere, and cars, pointing in half a dozen directions, clogged the road. In the distance, cars were backed up for miles; rows of headlights stretched seemingly into infinity.

She looked down again at the boy, trying to shelter both of them from the rain beneath the too-small umbrella. His eyes, round and unblinking, gazed up at her. She stroked his head, whispering over and over again, "It's all right. It's all right." The lower half of his face and his neck were black-looking with blood, and he was trembling violently. She wrapped the blanket more tightly around him, hearing sirens at last. She lifted her head to see a state police cruiser coming up the shoulder, followed by several ambulances and wreckers, all with roof lights revolving and sirens slicing the night. The din was tumultuous.

"People are coming to help," she told the boy. "It won't be long now."

His large eyes searched her face. She found his hand—tiny and very cold—and held it, as she continued to smooth his forehead. Even with the injuries, his features stained with blood, he was a beautiful child, with a neatly-shaped head and thick dark hair. She drew him closer, opening her coat and closing it around his blanket-wrapped body. Again, she looked up to see what was going on.

Several people were dead. The body—Lynne assumed it was the boy's father—of a man she'd seen slumped over the wheel was placed on a stretcher and put in the back of an ambulance. Two people from the second car were also placed on stretchers, their faces covered over, and removed. At least half a dozen people who were still mobile were assisted into the backs of ambulances. At last, a rain-coated attendant, his face and hair streaming, came over to Lynne. He unwrapped the blanket to listen to the child's heart; he briefly studied the two severe facial wounds then told Lynne, "I'll get someone over here in a minute or two with a stretcher." Throughout all this, the child remained unmoving, staring up at Lynne, his eyes clinging to her even while the attendant examined his face. She felt a profound attachment to this child, and desperately wanted him out of the rain and on his way to the hospital. She closed the blankets around him again, and drew him back inside her coat, then looked around to see that the wreckers were already starting to remove some of the cars, clearing a lane so that the backed-up traffic could start moving. Red flares had been placed here and there, and police officers were taking statements from witnesses.

Finally, two attendants came and carefully lifted the child out of her lap and onto a stretcher. With difficulty, Lynne got to her feet, her eyes still on the boy. She made an effort to smile at him—she was certain she merely looked grotesque, but she smiled nonetheless—and said, "Don't be afraid. They'll look after you."

"You the mother?" one of the attendants asked her.

"No. The mother's over there." She turned to look at the roadside only to see that the woman was gone. "She was there. They must have taken her in one of the ambulances."

"We'll find her," the attendant said confidently, and wheeled the child away.

Lynne walked to the shoulder and looked about for John. She couldn't see him, but she did notice, for the first time, the dozens of people lined up behind the guardrail at the edge of the highway, watching the scene.

Chilled, her blouse and skirt saturated with blood and rain, she wrapped her arms around herself, standing hunched under the umbrella, and studied the crowd of watchers. Two teenagers, smiling, were drinking a Coke, sharing the bottle back and forth. One man was smoking a cigarette which he kept cupped in his hand, his head moving back and forth—as if he were at a tennis match—following the progress of the wreckers, the police, the ambulance attendants. Someone touched Lynne on the shoulder and she turned, expecting to see John. It was the man who'd taken the other child from the car. "How was the boy?" he asked warmly, their joint efforts in this tragedy briefly uniting them as friends.

"He'll be fine, just some bad cuts."

"The girl's all right, too. The parents are both dead. Awful business," he said sadly. "You want to get out of this rain. You're soaked through."

"I will. I'm waiting for my friend to come back with the car."

He patted her on the shoulder and continued on his way to his car. She watched him open the door of a white Cadillac and climb inside. The interior roof light illuminated a well-dressed, fur-coated woman who turned to say something to him. Then the interior light went off. Lynne stood shivering, wondering where John had managed to get to. She felt as if she'd been out in the rain for hours, as if she'd held that little boy for half a lifetime, but when she looked at her watch she saw it had only been about forty minutes. One lane of traffic was slowly moving past; people in the cars craned to look at the remaining wrecks. The crowd standing behind the guardrail continued its vigil, small groups discussing what they thought had caused the accident.

She turned away to see John running toward her along the shoulder. He, too, was drenched.

"Come on!" he called, signaling to her. "I've got the car at the bottom of the ramp."

She started toward him, her sodden high heels making it difficult to walk very quickly. He draped his arm around her shoulder, steadying her as they moved down the ramp toward the BMW whose flashers were going, casting blood-red pulse beats on the wet roadway.

Once inside the car, she found her bag and lit a cigarette, still shivering. He'd left the heaters and defrosters going full-blast so the car was very hot inside.

"Are you okay?" he asked.

"I will be. I need a drink."

"You still want to go out to dinner?" He looked highly surprised.

"If I went home now, I'd be up most of the night, replaying the whole thing, editing it, silently adding a commentary track, a voice-over."

"Sure. Okay."

She unbuttoned her coat to let her clothes dry a bit.

"Your outfit's ruined," he said regretfully, glancing over.

"It doesn't matter," she said distractedly. She was thinking of Betsy Wilkins and Sandy Butler, both dead in the car, and herself sitting in the road with her head bent to her knees, fighting down waves of nausea, while beside her Abby Scott stood sobbing noisily, openmouthed, urine running down her legs.

❖ *Twelve* ❖

Ross TURNED HIS pencil from end to end over and over as he listened to Harrison, the scout, outline the background of Bonnie Fay Limited. He'd done his homework, Ross thought, suppressing a yawn. Harrison was a comer, with an eye to rising fast in the corporation. He was intelligent, thorough, the perfect corporation type: St. Paul's and Yale, good solid family background; he shopped at Brooks Brothers for his clothes, was undoubtedly married to a leggy, tennis-playing, Radcliffe or Vassar or Sarah Lawrence young woman with whom he probably had one and a half children; he most likely lived in Westchester, Tuxedo Park, or maybe Tarrytown, and had had help from both his family and his in-laws in putting together the down payment on the four bedroom, two bath, fairly new colonial with a family room that young men like Harrison believed was good for their image: nothing too artsy or rustic, just a good, solid house that would hold him and his aspirations.

Jesus! Ross thought, bored. When had people started to appear so predictable to him? Five, six years. One of the reasons he was attracted to Lynne was her lack of predictability, her independence. She threw him at every turn, and he enjoyed the challenge of a direct, articulate woman who wasn't living by anyone's pattern but her own. He was concerned at having been unable to reach her the day before, and hoped she hadn't been upset by what had happened. If he hadn't fallen asleep, things would probably have been all right.

George Fielding stood up to take over from Harrison, a sheaf of papers in his hand. George was an older, more finely-honed version of Harrison. George lived in a five bedroom, three bathroom mock Tudor in Riverside. He and his wife had two children. His wife was a wicked tennis player, always on the winners' lists at the club, always in the lineup to receive some trophy or another. George himself was ideal Brooks Brothers material, although he favored school and club ties somewhat more than might have been acceptable had he not been president of the corporation. Since he was president, he'd set a trend, and in the course of the past year and a half, the men in the company had taken to appearing in their old school ties.

George was solemnly intoning the virtues of Bonnie Fay and suddenly Ross had had enough. He put his pencil down on the slick surface of the immense boardroom table and simply walked out. Several heads turned but Ross kept going. They'd assume he was going to take a leak, until he failed to return. Then there'd be whispered discussions as to why Ross had left, if it was an indication of dissatisfaction on his part with the proposed acquisition of Bonnie Fay. The discussions would be purely a matter of form, a mild display of professional paranoia, because Ross had very little input as chairman of the board. He couldn't yea or nay with the rest of them, although he could effect a veto if a vote came to a stalemate. It wouldn't come to that, though. Bonnie Fay, he thought wryly, was as good as had. For a moment, he had a mental image of a plumpish, middle-aged woman, comely and flushing, as a clutch of rapacious board members spread her naked on the gleaming boardroom table. You're fucked, Bonnie Fay, he thought, smiling as he strolled along the thickly-carpeted corridors back to his office.

Brad jumped up as Ross entered, looking confused.

"Is it over already?"

"Relax," Ross said, still smiling. "They'll be in there for at least another two hours, diddling poor Bonnie Fay."

Brad smiled. "They're going ahead?"

"They certainly are." Ross perched on the edge of

Brad's desk. "Bonnie's about to get herself royally reamed and they'll pay her in stock, stock options, promises. If she makes any fuss at all, she'll soon discover that she's given away control of her company, and that she'd be just as wise to lay back and enjoy it because there's not a goddamned thing she can do. Jesus! Does it make any sense to you?"

"Honest answer?" Brad asked, offering Ross a cigarette.

"No, thanks. I'd love to hear an honest answer."

"It's ridiculous," Brad said in a much lowered voice. "I mean, getting into cosmetics. They can't justify it."

"I think," Ross said judiciously, "they've gone way past the point of caring about justification."

Brad gave him a smile of complicity.

"Let's go eat," Ross said.

"Great! Oh, listen! I've finished the rundown on the Craig file. Zip. She's as clean as a whistle. I checked with Associated T.V. and she's legit, been there for years, has a good, solid rep. And that's about it. I left the file on your desk."

"I'll have a look at it after lunch," Ross said, feeling guilty at having subjected Lynne's life to a stranger's inspection. "C'mon, I'll put you on the expense account as a relative of Bonnie Fay's."

Laughing, the two men headed for the elevators.

Lunch was a pleasant interlude, but by the time Ross had been back in his office half an hour, he felt restless again. Fielding had called to ask why Ross had left the meeting and Ross had fabricated a story about an appointment. Satisfied with the lie, Fielding had let it go. Ross was disappointed that Fielding was so readily mollified, and a little alarmed to realize that the corporation's activities bored him more every day. The large and little intrigues, the headhunting, the raiding of young men from other companies, the scouting of new acquisitions, the slow rape-in-progress of Bonnie Fay all seemed like nothing more than highly complex yet basically meaningless games played by a group of men fixated on standards of doubtful significance. The only man around who appeared to be firmly grounded in reality was Brad, and he wouldn't stick with the corporation long. For a moment he envied Brad, envied him his youth, his integrity, his proud disinterest in company politics, and his refusal to engage in them.

There'd been a time when he'd been like Brad. He'd been young and strong and idealistic, but that had been before the insidious corporate disease of power-lust had begun gnawing away at him. He looked around his office, his gaze coming to rest on the photograph of Ella and the boys. Why were things so complicated now? These days there was such a plethora of logistics attached to even the simplest of endeavors that half the joy of entering into any act was lost in attending to minor details.

"You're out of your time," Ella had once told him. "You want to live a life of truth and simplicity in an era when those things are all but unattainable. You'll have to go on compromising to the end, Ross, because all the knights are dead and the Round Table's long-since been chopped up for firewood. It's not possible to have high ideals and maintain an ironclad integrity when you're surrounded by people who're motivated entirely by a desire for money and power."

"I could always quit," he'd countered.

"You won't, though," she'd said sagely. "There's too much of a challenge there and you've always loved a challenge. You'll go on believing you can summon up the latent honor in these men, because you refuse to accept the truth, which is that they simply don't have any honor."

What she'd said distressed him then; it distressed him more now because time had proved her right. His honor had been compromised repeatedly in the better interests of the corporation. But it was his desire to retrieve his honor somehow, and not a search for that same quality in the men around him, that had made him stick with the job. He'd attempted to explain this to Ella, admitting this and many other truths about himself, during those last months of her life when their conversations had had a keenness and purity that could only have been generated by their knowledge of her imminent death.

He had never, through all the years of their marriage,

thought that she would die. He'd always assumed it would be he who would die first. It was not until the truth of her death was absolutely unavoidable that he attempted to deal with how he felt about continuing on into the future without her. It was not until she had the last and fatal relapse that he understood what a tremendous emotional investment he'd had in her. He'd never thought she'd die, and not in that way, with the flesh disappearing from beneath her skin so that the skin fell against her bones in lifeless folds and her face altered so that he'd had to keep staring at her, trying to recognize the woman he'd fallen in love with thirty years earlier. When she'd died at last, he'd mourned the loss of her as his confidante and supporter, his most cherished friend.

His eyes left the photograph and he swiveled in his chair to look out the window. Another bleak, colorless day; depressing weather. He thought of himself as a summer man, a sailor, someone who came fully to life in the sun. Winter was a time to hide away somewhere deep and dry, not a time to be caught up with mergers and acquisitions and the highly visible ambition of young men.

He was fed up with sitting in his expensively-decorated cell. He got up, grabbed his coat, opened the door and walked to the outer office where Brad sat with an open file in front of him, making notes on a ruled pad.

"I'm leaving," Ross told him. "Anything urgent crops up you can reach me at home later this evening."

"What about your afternoon appointments?" Brad asked, pulling over the diary.

"Get Janet to reschedule them. There's nothing important."

"Okay." Brad put down his pen and reached for the telephone.

"I'll see you in the morning," Ross said, on his way out the door.

He sat in the near-empty smoker with an unlit cigarette between his fingers. He closed his eyes and saw himself in West Palm Beach, standing on the dock at some marina, gazing proudly at a thirty-five foot sailboat with glaringly fresh white paint and gleaming brass fittings. Before him the ocean stretched temptingly into infinity. He wore comfortably loose shorts and a shirt; on his feet were nicely broken-in Docksiders. His head was bare to a sun that shone beneficently from a cloudless sky. The picture was so clear, so real that he felt himself lifting in anticipation of the salt spray against his face. This was his alternative, more tempting, more satisfying than anything he could conceive of. And he'd do it. But first he wanted to talk to Lynne.

"Am I catching you at a bad time?" he asked.

"No, not at all." She glanced over at the open door to her office. "How are you?"

"A little miffed with myself because of the other night."

"But why?" she asked, taken aback. "You didn't do anything wrong."

"It was pretty crude of me to go to sleep that way. I'm not surprised you left."

"That wasn't why I left, Ross. Your going to sleep had nothing to do with it. It had to do with me, not with you. Are you in town?"

"I'm at home. I left early. We're in the middle of a new acquisition. I don't have the stomach for these things anymore. I'm thinking long and hard right now about taking early retirement."

"What would you do?"

"Go to Florida, buy a boat, find a place to live."

"Really?" She smiled. "And you wouldn't be bored?"

"Not half as bored as I am commuting into the office every day, to sit in the board room listening to my colleagues gloat over the blood from the latest kill. I'd be a hell of a lot happier just sailing around in the sunshine."

"Where would you sail to?"

"South to the Caribbean, down the coast of South America. Anywhere, everywhere."

"It sounds idyllic."

"Are you staying late in the city tonight? I was hoping you might like to have dinner with me."

"Could I call you right back?"

"Sure."

She hung up and sat for a moment, thinking. Then she went out into the central area. Gloria was sitting at her desk with her hands placed flat on its surface, glaring at a sheet of Teletype.

"These idiots from the Klan!" Gloria exclaimed. "Naturally they're all pleading the Fifth. What the hell did anyone expect?"

"Would you do me a favor?" Lynne asked.

"What?"

"I've been waiting all day for Ned to pass along the budget. God knows what he's done with it, but I promised we'd confirm today on the dates and times for the shoot. Will you call Judy Jones and Beth Grushen and confirm next Thursday and Friday nights?"

"Okay. I don't mind. You don't think there'll be any problem, do you? I mean, about the budget."

"He said he'd sent it up to Keith."

"Okay. I'll get on it."

"Thank you."

Lynne returned to her office and dialed Dianna's number.

"It's Lynne. Look, something's come up and I've got to get back to Connecticut right away. Gloria's working on the confirmations."

"Oforchrissake!" Dianna snapped. "Gloria couldn't run with two other people in a one-legged relay race. What the hell's going on?"

"It's only some phone calls," Lynne said calmly. "What are you so angry about?"

"I wanted to go over some things with you."

"We'll do it tomorrow."

"Tomorrow's no good." Dianna sounded most unlike herself. "I'm going to have to put everything on hold for a few days. I won't be in tomorrow and Wednesday's out. I've got the production meeting for Sunday's show in the afternoon and I've got to put some kind of script together so I can give them my clever out-cue and all the rest of it."

"If there's a problem, we can talk, you know, Dianna."

"Don't go turning typically female on me, Craig," Dianna cautioned. "I count on you, you know." Why did she always talk to Lynne in this tough-guy fashion? She wished she'd never started, but since she had, she couldn't suddenly stop now.

"Dianna, what's happening? What's wrong?"

"Everything, anything. Take your pick."

"Then let's talk about it."

"What about your emergency in Connecticut?"

"It can sit on hold for another hour. Anyway, I'm still waiting for Ned to bring in the budget. He's taking his time, and I don't like it."

"I'm leaving now myself," Dianna said abruptly. "I'm not going to stick around to see little Neddy. I'll see you when I see you."

Lynne had to take a moment to catch her breath, and sat back wondering what was disturbing Dianna, and why she was going to so much trouble in order to have dinner with Ross. She was doing it because she felt guilty about running out on him, guilty about finding John as attractive as she did, guilty about not pursuing Dianna and insisting they sit down and talk about whatever was upsetting her; guilty, guilty. "Christ!" she said aloud, and reached for the telephone.

Ross picked up on the first ring.

"Could you make it for seven?" she asked.

"I'll be there on the dot."

"All right. I'll see you then."

They chatted easily throughout the meal. Saturday evening wasn't mentioned. When the coffee came, Ross leaned on the table, saying, "Have you noticed how complicated everything is nowadays? Maybe I'm wrong, but it seems as if things used to be a hell of a lot simpler. I like you, Lynne. You're a bright, beautiful woman. I enjoy your company. It doesn't have to be anything more than two people enjoying each other's company, if that's the way you'd like it to be. But I'd like us to go on seeing each other."

"Something's happened, hasn't it?" she asked.

"Why do you say that?"

"You're—different. I'm not sure I can explain it."

"I made the decision today. Riding home on the train, it occurred to me that I've had enough. It's time to do the things I really want to do. And what I want is to get away from the corporation, away from this part of the country. I want to be out in the sun, on the water, with a boat. I want to feel that I'm living my life according to my choices and not the way I'm expected to."

"So you're going to retire and go away."

"That's right."

"Where?" she asked. "When?" She hadn't expected this announcement, nor the sharp, attendant sense of loss that it inspired.

"Soon," he said. "If you wanted to, you could come with me. No strings."

"Ross, we don't even know each other."

"We know as much as we need. I'd take care of you."

"I wish," she said cautiously, "that I was someone who could just say yes. Part of me wants to. It's a very appealing offer. I like you, too, you know. Very much. How soon do you think you'll go?"

"It'll take me a good month or more to wrap things up at the office. I have no idea how long it'll take to sell the house. But with luck, I could be on my way before the first of the year."

As he talked, unraveling his plans, she recalled the feeling she used to have saying goodbye to Alec when he was about to leave on one of his business trips. They'd stand in the small foyer of the co-op, talking; Alec would promise to call from Dallas or Kansas City or wherever he was going. Then they'd embrace, Alec would pick up his overnighter and his briefcase, and go. Always, after the door closed, she'd feel bereft, as if he'd just left her life permanently. They were, she understood in retrospect, small foretastes of the ultimate, ongoing bereavement. Now it was about to happen again, with Ross, and she didn't want him to go, but to tell him that would be to admit to a degree of caring she wasn't certain she felt.

"We'll see one another before you go," she said.

"A lot, I hope. I'm going to work awfully damned hard at convincing you to come with me."

"I used to think Alec would always be there to look after me," she said softly, looking at Ross's strong, long-fingered hands. "We never talked about death, or insurance, any of that. He died and almost all I've thought about since is how much I depended on him, and for so many things. I've had to learn how to depend on me, to learn that my well-being hinges solely on myself."

"There's no reason," he said understandingly, "why you couldn't find yourself another job with a TV station in Florida."

"It's not just the job, Ross. It's the whole way of life I've established. One half of me really likes it. The other half wants to go back to being looked after. I think the half of me that likes the independence and the self-reliance is the stronger half."

"Think about it," he said. "I don't want to change anything you're happy with."

When he dropped her off, she took the initiative and kissed him on the mouth. Her sense of panic was still there, but not quite so strongly. He held her hand for a moment, then released her. "I'm in love with you," he said. "Just think about it. All right?"

"I will."

"Thanks for coming out. I know you had to do some fancy fiddling to arrange it."

She got out of the car and stood in the driveway watching his taillights disappear down the road. He was going to leave, and she would miss him. She already missed him, well in advance of his going. Was she crazy to turn him down? It was the offer of a lonely man who scarcely knew her. Yet he claimed to be in love with her. Maybe he found her familiar, as she did him. There was a real comfort to be derived from someone whose background and lifestyle were so similar to her own, someone whose frames of reference coincided with hers. Unquestionably, there was security and warmth in that.

❖ *Thirteen* ❖

SHE WALKED UP the stairs of the porch, startled to find John sitting on his haunches beside the front door. He said "Hi," and unwound himself to stand awkwardly, looking at her from beneath slightly lowered lashes so that he appeared younger than his years.

"How long have you been sitting out here?" she asked, pleased to see him, yet annoyed that he'd sit in the cold waiting. Her annoyance was compounded by the fact that he had to have not only seen Ross but seen her kissing him as well.

"Not long. I knew it was one of your nights in the city and I thought I'd, uhm, take a run and . . . here I am. I just wanted to say hi."

He had to be thoroughly chilled, dressed as he was in shorts and a sweatshirt. "You must be freezing," she said, looking for a moment at his long muscular legs. "Come on in. I'll make you some coffee, then I'll drive you home."

"You're mad," he said, shaking his head. "I'll just go on home. I only thought . . ."

"I'm not mad," she said, the sharpness of her tone belying that. Why was she being so hateful, so cruel? "It does seem a little crazy, though, that you'd sit out here in the cold, waiting when you didn't even know if I was coming home tonight." She was compounding the cruelty. "There are times," she tried to explain, "when I spend the night in the city and come home in the morning."

"It's just that we didn't really talk the other night, at

185

dinner, I mean, and I'm starting a job in a couple of days so I'll be tied up for a while. . . ."

She got the door open, reached inside to turn on the lights, then said, "Come in. What kind of a job? A full-time one?"

Hesitantly he stepped inside. "A construction job, for a friend of mine who's a contractor. It's just for three days."

"I'll put on the coffee," she announced and headed for the kitchen.

He followed her, continuing to explain. "I guess it sounds pretty stupid. I mean, I wasn't really hanging around waiting for you, or watching, or anything like that."

"What would be stupid is if you took a full-time job. Then you wouldn't be able to work on your book."

"I've got almost a year left before I get to that point. Of going after a full-time job, I mean." He felt more idiotic by the minute and wished he'd never given in to the impulse to come here. She was pissed off, and he couldn't blame her. What could she think, coming home to find him parked on her porch, waiting like a sentry or something? "Listen, you don't have to bother with that," he said, indicating the coffee pot. "I don't want to tie you up. You probably want to go to bed. I mean, I know you've had a long day and the last thing you needed was to come home and find some asshole sitting in the dark on your porch."

"You don't want coffee," she said flatly. "In that case, I'll have a drink." She turned off the kitchen light and walked past him into the living room where she shrugged off her coat and poured some Scotch into a glass. She turned to see he was still standing near the kitchen door, his eyes tracking her every movement, his attitude one of defeat. She positioned herself half a room's length away from him and raised the glass to her mouth. In spite of herself she wanted to touch him again. He was the most wonderfully unsullied person she'd met in years. She wished it were possible to capture all she liked about him, to capture the young man himself; to hold him perfectly contained and ever accessible within the invisible, barless cage of her thoughts. She wanted, she realized with a jolt, to lie skin to skin with him and have him touch her with his broad, work-ravaged hands.

For just a moment, as she realized this and looked at him, time seemed suspended. She experienced a sudden, very clear insight into the size of the world and their minuscule positions on it. It was an insight that filled her with an ineffable sadness, overwhelming and complete. Nothing was of any consequence, and the best of anyone's efforts could only amount to very little. Why then worry about anything? Why seek success, or power, or even long-term companionship? None of it had meaning. It would be infinitely easier to succumb to the potential pleasures of the present than to concern oneself with the past or future. She felt, then, completely sympathetic to this beautiful young man who stood, so lost and bewildered, as if waiting for her to direct him. That was it! She was going to have to direct him. She was staggered, and frightened. Never in her life had she had to be aggressive with a man, to instigate actions. But if she wanted this man, she'd have to make clear her desire, because he was someone who would never risk approaching her, except in friendship. His fear of rejection was as strong as his attraction to her.

Acutely, almost painfully aware of her every movement, she set down her Scotch and extended her hand. "Come here," she said, her voice gone thick.

He came across the room and took hold of her hand, which was soft and very cool. He gazed at her hand, holding it in both of his own, examining first her palm and then the back, fascinated by the thin skin, the tracings of veins, the narrow girth of her wrist. His fingers followed the length of hers; he touched each of her long, unpainted fingernails, then, helplessly, he stood with her hand enveloped in his, speechless with the desire to examine every part of her with the same meticulous care. She entranced him; her pale skin and slippery-looking hair, her long, slim body all seemed to have been designed specifically for his enchantment. He swallowed and managed to look into her eyes.

She watched him examine her hand, felt each tentative touch register as if it were a musical note. His touch was exquisite, piercing. And if, she thought, he could respond in such intense fashion to the offer of her hand, how might he react to the offer of her entire body? The imagined pleasure, she reasoned, was bound to surpass the reality.

"Why do you doubt yourself?" she asked in that same thickened voice.

"Nobody wants to come across a fool." His voice, too, sounded more dense. "Maybe it's because I get myself into things, get too involved . . . I don't know. I don't know what you think of me, I mean, what you think I am . . ."

"What do you think of me?" she asked, curious.

"You? I think you're . . . are you asking me honestly?" She nodded.

If he risked saying what he thought, she might laugh at him. But what did he have to lose? Everything, he told himself. So did she, though. If she was willing to risk hearing what he had to say, surely he ought to face up to that. "I think . . ." He stopped, chewing for a moment on his lower lip. "I think you're generous, and kind. Sad, and lonely in a way. A little scared. I've got this feeling we could talk, maybe forever, and never run out of things to say."

"And?" she prompted.

"And uh . . . whew!" He laughed nervously. "I uh . . ." He looked around the room and then back at her. "I really want to stay," he said at last.

"Why?"

"Why? If I answer that you'll think it's just, you know . . ." He shrugged.

"It's just sexual?"

"That, and maybe that I'm some kind of opportunist. I don't want you to think I'm something I'm not."

"You don't know what I think of you," she said reasonably.

"No," he agreed. "I don't, not altogether. I know you think I'm just a kid, but I'm not. I'm twenty-six. Most of my friends are married already; they've even got kids. Oh, shit!" He released her hand and again looked anxiously around the room.

She drank down the Scotch in one swallow. It took her breath away so that she shuddered as she set down the empty glass. Straightening, she threw back her shoulders before walking across the room to fold open the shutters, first on one side of the bedroom and then on the other. He remained motionless, watching.

The doors opened, she stood near the foot of the bed and began to undo the buttons of her blouse.

He was electrified by the realization that she was going to undress in front of him; she was going to make love with him. And here he was all sweaty and grubby from running. He couldn't bring himself even to think of approaching her. He cleared his throat and said, "Would you mind . . . could I take a shower? I've been running . . ."

With her shirt hanging open to reveal a lacy white brassiere, she walked over to open the bathroom door. "Help yourself," she said. "I'll get you a towel." She went to the closet and reached inside for a fresh towel. She gave it to him and he closed himself in the bathroom.

Once he was out of sight, she lost her momentum. She sat down on the end of the bed and pushed off her shoes, threatened by depression, her brain conjuring up squalid, sordid images: Older woman seduces younger man, exercising her power over him. What power, though? She had none. She sat in her stockinged feet hearing the water go on in the shower. What was she doing? If she sat there any longer, she'd call the whole thing off. And she didn't want to stop now.

She stood up, threw off her clothes, then went to the bathroom door, testing the knob. He'd left it unlocked. Taking a deep breath, she switched off the light, opened the door and stepped inside. John made a surprised sound when the light went off, then was silent, as if awaiting an explanation. She slipped past the shower curtain and stepped close to him under the water. The spill of light from the bedroom allowed them to see one another.

He felt as if he were dreaming, that this was the most superb dream of his life. He took the soapy washcloth and began to wash her, first her arms, right down to her fingertips, and then her shoulders and neck. After relathering the cloth, he drew it over her breasts, learning the shape of her body through the fabric, feeling the response in the pit of his stomach. Gently, he scrubbed down the length of her belly, then knelt to lift her foot onto his knee and washed the outside of her leg. His heart was beating heavily, almost painfully, as he started on the inside of her foot and worked his way slowly up the length of her leg. He looked up to see that she'd braced herself against the wall with her hand, and was watching him intently. He eased her foot down and lifted the other one. At last he stood again and turned her by the shoulders to wash her back, drawing the cloth across her tapering waist and down over her buttocks. Finally he turned her again and carefully washed her face. She rinsed off and then silently took the cloth and bar of soap from him, and began to bathe him. There was something primitive, she thought, and yet wholly appropriate in this introduction to each other's bodies. He was solidly built, and just a little plump in the belly, but perfectly beautiful. She abandoned the washcloth in order to apply the soap to his body with her hands. Everywhere she touched him she could feel the muscles gather and clench beneath the surface of his skin. In response, her own muscles tightened, like hundreds of fine wires drawing taut. She wound her fingers into his hair and let her body align itself to his, the stream of water blurring her vision.

He wrapped his arms around her slick body and closed his eyes to more fully receive the impact of her small breasts and long thighs pressed against him. Like a blind man, he ran his fingers over her face, tracing the outline of her mouth, investigating the fullness of her lower lip. He kissed her, startled and utterly aroused by the heat of her mouth and its avidity; her fingers wound more tightly into his hair and he could feel his body coiling inside, like a giant spring.

She moved to turn off the water. The shower curtain rings clattered as she shoved back the curtain and handed him a towel. She dried herself quickly, dropped the towel on the floor and went into the bedroom to throw back the bed-clothes.

When they lay down together, she sighed deeply, elated by the contact and by his weight. Her hands traveled over him in profound gratification. She could, she thought, sustain herself for months, even years, on this encounter.

He sat up and began to explore her body in the way he'd examined her hands, lingering over her breasts, her arms, hips, and thighs. Rapt, she examined him in like fashion, finding this exercise almost too pleasurable to bear. As he proceeded with his delicate inspection, his most cautious touch stirring her further, she had an increasing desire to savage him, to sink her teeth deeply into his flesh until he cried out in pain, to dig her fingernails into the most tender parts of his body, to lock him, snakelike, to her groin and writhe upon him until he was lifeless.

She freed herself and sat upon him, thrusting her body down over his, then rested, considering the sensations. His hands settled on her hips and he moved slightly, the motion recording itself everywhere inside her. Her knees tight against his hips, she bent to kiss him, her body commencing a wild ride. She managed to maintain an awareness of him despite her frenzied need to bring the ride to completion. She heard his breathing change, felt it in the heaving of his chest against hers; he gasped and she accelerated the forward pitching of her pelvis, rapidly approaching a satisfaction that promised to be cataclysmic. He'd wound his arms tightly across her lower back and was lifting to assist her. She went rigid, her lips just touching his, and let him complete it for her. Her eyes clamped shut, paralyzed with pleasure, the breath left her lungs in a long, low groan.

She had no desire to move, but her body, where exposed to the air, was cold. As she was about to retrieve the bedclothes, John bent to pick them up and covered her. Then he climbed back into the bed and drew her over against his chest.

"I know what you're thinking," he said, "but you're wrong."

"What is it I'm thinking?" she asked drowsily.

"You think this is all I wanted, but it's not true. I really love you. I knew it when you went to help those kids in the car.'' He spoke with that earnestness she found so poignant.

She wanted to speak, couldn't, heard herself laugh, then found herself crying. She thought of Ross, didn't want to think of him, and pushed him out of her mind. She remembered her frustrating call to Greenwich Hospital, asking about the condition of the little boy whose name she didn't know. The operator had put her through to the emergency room and, luckily, the nurse on duty remembered the accident as well as the victims. She'd found the name of the child and his room number on the index and was able to report, ''He's doing just fine. He's being discharged today.'' Ronald Volken and his sister had both been discharged. Lynne had asked to whom and the nurse said, ''I wouldn't know that, I'm afraid.'' And that was the end of it. Except that it wasn't, because at random moments she thought of the silent, staring child and of how inadequate she'd felt trying to shelter and warm him.

''You're so young,'' she said, aware again of John, and tightening her hold on him. It would have required hours for her to expand on all the implications those three words contained for her.

''I knew you'd say that,'' he said calmly. ''And you're wrong about that, too. Is it okay if I stay?''

She blotted her eyes on the edge of the pillow case. ''It's okay,'' she said, grateful he'd chosen not to comment on her tears. ''I don't know what I'm doing, but it's okay.'' She couldn't let him leave yet. She wanted this entire night, every hour of it.

''You do know,'' he said consolingly, confidently. ''It'll just take you a while to accept it.'' He stroked her still-damp hair, feeling that all the segments of his life had suddenly welded together. He wasn't the same as he'd been before; he'd never again be the same. He'd found someone to love and it gave him certainty and self-assurance. He no longer had any doubts; he could be positive for both of them, if it was needed. He knew, too, that he'd be able to finish the novel now; it was meant to be finished because it belonged to that part of his life that had come before Lynne.

His future had just been altered and he felt a keen sense of optimism, of boundless hope. If his present could deliver to him something so remarkable as this woman, the potential of his future was limitless. He might do absolutely anything.

"I'll drive you home in the morning," she offered. Morning seemed very far off in the distance, a point in space that might not ever reach them in this lifetime.

"You don't have to do that. It'll only take me half an hour to run back to Rowayton. I like to run in the early morning."

This was an accident, she thought, not really listening to what he said; a lovely accident. She shouldn't have allowed it to happen, but she wasn't sorry. Still, she'd have to face the consequences. He was already making declarations of love and while, at this moment, she felt she cared for him, she knew positively that they had no future together.

"Don't worry," he said, smothering a yawn. "I'll take care of you."

"Don't go too quickly," she cautioned. "You're getting too far ahead."

"People worry too much," he observed, resting his large, warm hand on her shoulder. "You worry too much."

She wanted to say: I have a great deal to worry about. I'm forty and you're twenty-six. I've had a career almost half of my life. Daily I have to contend with people and their political doings, their ambition, and their opportunism; people you'd undoubtedly be repelled by because of their dishonesty. But I understand them; I'm one of them. I've got my own streak of ambition. It just doesn't happen to flow the same course as the others' do. Your mother's probably just a few years older than I am. Your friends would make all kinds of unpleasant remarks if they saw us together, and so would mine. I remember the war, and Benny Goodman, Glen Miller, and VJ Day. You think the world began about the time you were born. "Go to sleep," she said softly, her thoughts already turning toward the shooting schedule, the subjects, the questions, camera angles and voice-overs.

"I won't wake you when I leave. And I'll call you during the day. All right?"

"Of course it's all right."

"I feel terrific," he said, stretching so that his bones cracked. "Fantastic! You look so nice now, with your hair all soft and your face all smooth. You have a really beautiful body."

She laughed and put her hand over his mouth. "I have a forty-year-old body with a lot of mileage on it. You don't have to compliment me just because we've made love."

"That's not why," he protested.

"That *is* why," she argued. "You may not think so, but it is."

He looked into her eyes for a long moment, then said, "I'd be proud to be seen anywhere with you. I know you think it'd bother me, what people would say. It'd bother *you*, but I wouldn't care."

He was going to go on talking, and force her to think about all the things she wanted to reserve for a later date. "Let's not discuss it anymore," she said, stroking his chest, then drawing his mouth down to hers, bending her leg over his hip. Morning was still a long way off.

She fell asleep finally to dream she was seated on a chair in a blindingly white room. On a slab of elevated white marble Ross lay beneath a white sheet. His chest rose and fell irregularly. She watched him closely, afraid he might stop breathing. A door opened somewhere behind her and she tried to turn to see what was happening, but she couldn't move. She looked down at her hands. They were unfettered, resting, apparently freely, on the arms of the white chair. Yet she couldn't move. She ordered herself to stand up, but nothing happened. She heard a small pattering noise and turned her eyes as far to the right as they would go. A white cat walked toward her. She followed its slow, lithe progress, then gasped in fear as the cat brushed itself back and forth against her immobilized legs. The cat seemed to be taunting her, as if it knew she was incapable of movement. Only her eyes had mobility. She opened her mouth, wanting to shoo the cat away, but no sound emerged. When she looked down again at herself she was naked, her flesh pale and puckered with cold. Remembering Ross, she looked over to see that his heart now sat upon his chest, pumping visibly, blood spurting into the air with each contraction. As his heart continued to pump, Ross seemed to shrink. It's the loss of blood, she told herself, the cat now between her calves and peering up at her with alarmingly human green eyes. Rising onto its rear legs, the animal placed its paws on her knees and pushed with amazing strength, parting her thighs. Terrified, she tried to draw her legs closed, but she still couldn't move. The cap leaped gracefully onto her lap, its claws nipping lightly at her flesh, turned itself around and began, with its rough tongue, to lick her. The sensation was painful yet monstrously pleasurable. Her muscles were shrieking in protest, but she couldn't dislodge the animal. It continued to draw its tongue back and forth, lapping at her. She looked at Ross who was shrinking more and more quickly, the blood still spurting from the disconnected veins and arteries. She was very wet. The cat was bringing her to orgasm. It was obscene, hateful. She strained, longing to scream, to move, to get to Ross, and put his heart back inside his chest. Her muscles were contracting involuntarily. The cat's fur tickled her thighs and belly maddeningly. Ross's chest rose and fell, but very slightly. The cat's tongue flicked against her again, again. She opened her mouth, her eyes rolling back in her head, and prayed to scream, to move. At last, at the very instant her body was convulsed, her physical self was returned to her. She screamed, "ROSSSSS!" and threw the cat from her lap and ran toward the marble slab. Her body weakened from the ongoing spasm, she ran weak-legged toward the slab, but for every step she took the slab moved that much farther away. She stopped running and stood, her arms wrapped tightly around herself, watching in horror as the white cat leapt up on the slab, opened wide its jaws, and in one motion swallowed the dripping heart. The instant the heart disappeared into the cat's mouth, the body on the slab began to dwindle. In just seconds it had vanished. When she looked again at the cat, it was in the process of transforming itself. In two or three seconds little Ronald Volken, his gashed face dripping dark blood, stood upon the slab holding his arms out to her. She took several steps toward the child but before she'd managed to cover even half the distance, the figure began to change again. Ronald's body lost its dimensions and began a shuddering expansion that went on until it was John standing naked upon the slab, his mouth forming the words, I love you. She bowed her head and wept, her bare feet numbed with cold from the slick icy floor.

She willed herself to wake up. John slept peacefully on the far side of the bed. Shakily, she lit a cigarette, then reached for her robe. She went to sit in the living room, staring out the window at the empty road that traveled past the front of the cottage. After a time, she turned on a small reading light and went for the script and her notes.

❖ *Fourteen* ❖

DIANNA WAS VERY angry. Her reasons were like numerous discordant songs being played simultaneously. Bob's check was three weeks late and so was her period; Trudy had announced she planned to drop out of college, just three months prior to graduation; her anger was overlapping from her private life into the show and she couldn't seem to stop herself; she'd lost nine pounds and her clothes looked like hell, even her shoes felt loose; her mink coat—once her symbol of accomplishment—was disintegrating, splitting at the seams, and she couldn't afford to buy a new one; she was still waiting for Ned to retaliate in some fashion, but so far he'd said and done nothing. On top of everything else, she'd just learned her apartment building was going to go co-operative. The present tenants had ninety days either to purchase their apartments or to vacate. She didn't want to move; she wanted to buy the goddamned apartment and be done with it. The price was right; she simply didn't have enough money, and the banks were unwilling to give her a big enough mortgage because she was divorced and planned to carry the mortgage on her own. If she laid out all her available cash, she'd still have a monthly payment she couldn't possibly meet. She needed another ten thousand in cash to put against the down payment. Then, at least, the banks would be happy and she'd have a mortgage payment she could handle. The problem was that no one she knew had that kind of money to lend, except Bob, and he couldn't even keep up with his stinking alimony payments. She felt like murdering somebody, anybody. Her anger was general; it included everyone.

She was on her way to meet Bob for lunch. She would not, as he undoubtedly expected, make a fuss about the lateness of this month's check. She planned, instead, to approach him for a loan, or a buy-out. If he'd give her the ten thousand she needed, she'd sign off on the alimony payments. He'd be ahead of the game if he agreed. If he refused to go for that idea, she'd ask him for a loan. She wanted and needed that money. She'd lived in the apartment for sixteen years and would never be able to find anything comparable for the price, even if she had any idea where to begin to look. Bob simply had to agree.

As she headed across town toward the restaurant where they were to meet, she told herself to calm down, to get herself under control. In her present state, were Bob to show even the slightest sign of refusing to go along with her proposition, she might actually kill him. She'd spent the last seventeen years fighting with the son of a bitch, over everything. He'd never made any effort to spend time with the girls after he left, yet when the time had come he'd believed he ought to have a say in which colleges the girls would attend. In the end, it had been the girls who'd won out. Who the hell, they'd wanted to know, was Bob anyway, to ignore them for years and then come along, throwing his weight around, trying to tell them where to go to school when he didn't even know them or what they were interested in? Collectively, Dianna and the girls had told him to butt out, and that had been the end of it. Until the matter of their tuition, which was his responsibility, arose. He'd dribbled payments here and there, until both schools got after Dianna to pay up or remove the girls. Dianna had taken him to court. He'd paid up.

She could feel anger mounting as she considered Bob's past behavior. The bastard wasn't going to help her. Why should he? Never mind the logic of being free of alimony payments. He'd refuse in order to punish her for all the years he'd already had to pay. He'd refuse. She realized her fists were clenched, and told herself to relax, cool down. He might not say no.

It seemed unbelievable to her that three years of marriage to this man had resulted in seventeen years of misery. She still didn't know why he'd left in the first place. She'd thought they were happy. They'd entertained a lot, made love a lot; they'd had two little girls less than a year apart. He'd claimed he found her beautiful; she'd loved him. A too-tall girl, with wiry red hair, skinny legs and big breasts, she'd lived on a euphoric plane for three years, unable to believe her good fortune in having someone like Bob claim to love her. Then, with no warning, he'd said he was leaving, and a week later he was gone. He'd walked out on her and two babies aged five months and fifteen months. At twenty-seven, she'd been the unemployed mother of two, with no special skills, but a Master's degree in English from Columbia, and no income until the lawyers could come to some agreement. Leaving the kids with her mother, she'd gone out to try to get herself a job and wound up the production assistant on a radio show, thanks to an old college friend who'd worked her way into the upper echelons of the station. From P.A. on the show to producer of a late-night tabloid-type panel show, and finally to host of that same show had taken her four years. From there she'd moved to "Up to the Minute"—a calculated risk at less pay, but higher visibility—and she'd been fighting her way upward ever since. She'd played the power games with the best of them, having taken what she considered a crash course in those skills during her brief-lived marriage to Bob. She'd watched him, listened to him, saw how he'd altered face and voice to suit given situations, and she'd learned.

The marriage, though, had screwed everything up. She might have married again, had it not been for the fact that she'd have lost her combined alimony and child support, and had it not been for the fact that her marriage to Bob had destroyed her capacity for trusting people. She could never, afterward, be certain that she wasn't out with another Bob who was sporting a face and voice designed solely to suck her in. She'd needed the contact, however, so she'd had herself fitted with an IUD, and she'd taken to meeting the men on their terms: she'd drink the drinks and make the small talk, she'd eat the meal and allow the progressive advancement of little liberties, she'd drink just a few too many, and then she'd go off somewhere with the man of the moment to work off her tensions. Over the years, she'd come to see men as worthy only of her contempt—until Ned, who'd somehow managed to gain the upper hand.

Bob was sure to ask what she'd been doing with her salary for all these years and she'd have to keep her anger in check while she patiently explained to him the facts of her life, and how little her salary really was, what with rising costs, rent increases, and all the rest of it. She'd been able to save almost nine thousand dollars, roughly five hundred a year. She thought it was just shy of a miracle that she'd managed to save anything at all. Twenty years before, her savings would have been considered substantial, but these days the money had about half the value.

The damned man was going to refuse. She could feel it in her bones. She felt achy and overheated. And why the hell was she walking? she wondered, taking stock of her surroundings. It was a lousy, cold day and she was still twenty blocks away from the restaurant. If she didn't grab a cab or take the subway, she'd be late, and that would guarantee Bob's refusal to help. Why did he have to be such a bastard? She stepped over to the curb and scanned the street, trying to spot a taxi. The traffic was heavy, and all the cabs seemed full. She saw a free cab at last and raised her arm. The taxi swerved in to the curb. She opened the door, stated her destination and sat back for the ride, reviewing what she planned to say to Bob. Unbuttoning her coat, she fanned herself, hoping she wasn't coming down with something. She felt rotten.

Lynne arrived at the office in the middle of the afternoon on Wednesday with a container of coffee and a doughnut from Chock full o' Nuts and set them down on her desk while she hung up her coat. She felt energized, ready for anything. She'd have Gloria call to reconfirm the various shooting appointments, then review all the material prior to actually going out on location.

She checked her phone messages, made several calls,

finished her coffee and doughnut, then got out the file for the segment.

Gloria appeared in the doorway, asking, "Have you seen Dragon Lady yet?"

"Not yet."

Gloria looked at her watch. "Great! She's got a production meeting in ten minutes and she hasn't shown up."

"Call the apartment. Maybe she's lost track of the time."

"I tried ten minutes ago. I can't believe she's just going to skip a production meeting."

"She'll be here," Lynne said.

"Not before she gives everyone ulcers."

"She'll *be* here," Lynne repeated with a smile.

The meeting was held without Dianna. Gloria made several more calls to the apartment without success. Lynne insisted that Dianna would show up at some point, and she'd have an explanation for why she'd missed the meeting. Gloria returned to her desk unconvinced. Lynne couldn't see any cause to become seriously alarmed by Dianna's failure to attend the meeting. It wasn't typical of her, but since Lynne knew just how important her career was to Dianna, it wasn't likely she'd miss a meeting without a damned good reason. Lynne did wonder how those involved in the meeting were taking Dianna's absence. Undoubtedly Ned would be angry and make a fuss, especially since Dianna's rebuttal segment was due to be introduced on Sunday's show. There'd be another meeting on Saturday, though, just in case any last-minute changes were to be introduced into the rundown, and they'd be able to cover Dianna's segment then.

Lynne tried to work but her thoughts kept sliding toward John, and when they did, she could feel herself beginning to smile. Annoyed by this girlish lightheadedness, she kept checking herself. She'd had a night she knew she'd remember, but it was wrong to hope that it could be more. She hated the idea of finding herself at age fifty with a man of thirty-six who'd be embarrassed to be seen with her in public.

She was aware of the meeting breaking up. There was a

sudden increase in volume of the activities in the outer office and Greg and Tom walked past her door on the way to Greg's office. She was about to get up to go for a fresh cup of coffee when her telephone rang.

"You're going on location a week from tomorrow, right?" Ned asked abruptly.

"That's right."

"And Dianna's slated for the interviews, right?"

"That's right."

"D'you have any idea why she'd suddenly decide to start skipping production meetings?" he barked.

"I'm not Dianna's keeper, Ned," she said quietly. "Something must have come up, some emergency."

There was a brief pause, and then he said, "Shit!" He sounded worried.

"What's the matter?" she asked.

For the first time in his life, Ned wished he had a confidant, someone to whom he could express his concern. Dianna's failure to show up meant something, he was convinced. He couldn't rid himself of the idea that by missing the meeting she'd been making a loud statement directed solely at him. What he couldn't decide was whether or not Dianna could actually do him any damage. He wanted to talk—to almost anyone—but he'd started certain things in motion, and were he to confide suddenly in Lynne it might, afterward, look pretty damned peculiar. "Never mind," he said, abrupt again. "If you hear from her, get her to call me."

"Certainly," she said, and hung up.

She sat looking at the telephone for a long moment then got up and walked over to Gloria's desk.

"Want to go out to dinner?" she asked.

"Sounds great! I want to get the hell out of here. Are you ready for the latest?" she asked, snatching her coat from the standing rack near her desk.

"What?" Lynne asked.

"Dianna's ex called half an hour ago. Fuming! Wanted to know where 'that bitch' was and why she'd kept him waiting over an hour in some restaurant. They were supposed to be having lunch,'' she explained, poking at the elevator call button. ''How the hell am *I* supposed to know where she is? I'm just one of the P.A.s, not her personal secretary. I even called her stupid hairdresser, just in case she was having a touch-up on her roots today and forgot minor little things like lunch with her ex and a silly old production meeting. I swear to God I'll *kill* her tomorrow when she comes in.'' Gloria stomped out of the elevator and got halfway across the lobby before she realized she didn't know where they were going. ''Where d'you want to eat?'' she asked.

''What're you in the mood for?''

''Nothing serious. Seven or eight martinis.''

Lynne laughed and put her arm around the younger woman, directing her out onto the sidewalk. ''Why don't we go over to the China Dream? I wouldn't mind some fried rice and barbecued ribs. Will you eat something?''

''Oh, probably. You know me. I can never resist food. Lon says I'm turning into a whale.''

''Charming.''

''Yeah, I thought so. It's nervous tension. If I wasn't driven crazy all day long, I wouldn't want to eat. But between Dianna and Uncle Neddy and morons like Greg Waldren who think you can research a segment, get it timed, and do a script breakdown in twenty minutes, forget it. By the time I'm thirty-five I'll weigh six hundred pounds and be the world's fattest P.A. They're sure as hell never going to let me go any higher. How come you're working?''

''I got a call from Myra, everyone's favorite publicist. She's got an author she thinks would be the basis of a good segment. She sent the book over and it does look interesting.''

''What's it about?''

''The end of the world as we know it.''

''You're kidding!''

''No. It's plausible. He's predicting that within twenty years interest rates'll hit more than twenty percent, and inflation will go as high as thirteen or fourteen percent. Cheery stuff like that.''

"Jesus!" Gloria sighed, as they followed the hostess to a table at the rear of the dimly-lit restaurant. "That's all we need: bread at two dollars a loaf, eggs for six bucks a dozen, two thousand a month for a bachelor in Hell's Kitchen. It sounds like post World War One Germany, with wheelbarrows full of deutsche marks worth about a buck and a half."

Settled with their drinks, Lynne sat back, as if with newly-clarified vision, looking at Gloria. Even with the additional weight she'd gained, Gloria was very pretty, with long, thick blue-black hair, warm olive skin, and almost oriental-shaped deep brown eyes. Her skin was exquisite, with a natural flush in the cheeks. She was very fond of Gloria, and believed Gloria would make a good producer.

"Seriously," Gloria said, looking up from the menu, "what d'you think she's up to?"

"I don't know. It might have something to do with one of the girls. They seem to get themselves in a lot of trouble. Last year Trudy was suspended for three months for violating curfew God knows how many times, and getting drunk. They'd have thrown her out if Dianna hadn't gone to see the dean. The year before that, Tricia got herself pregnant. She has her hands full with those two."

"What happened to the baby?"

"I don't know. I think she had it and gave it up for adoption."

"I could never do that," Gloria said. "Boy, what I wouldn't give to see old Dianna on her knees, begging—for anything."

"You don't know what you'll do until it's your kids."

"You're not going to get any sympathy out of me."

"Okay." Lynne smiled. "I'll give up. Want to share?"

"Definitely. Shrimps in lobster sauce?"

"Good. Egg foo yong?"

"With egg rolls, pork fried rice, and ribs."

They ordered. Lynne lit a cigarette, took a swallow of her Scotch, and glanced at her watch. Six-thirty. John would be home by now. "I've got to make a quick call," she told Gloria. "If the waiter comes, order, will you?"

"Take your time. You know what this place is like. It'll

be days before Charlie Chan shuffles over here. The four waiters in this place share a brain, for God's sake!''

Laughing, Lynne headed for the ladies' room where there was a telephone. John wasn't home. On impulse, she asked the operator to try Ross's number. He answered almost immediately.

"I'm not sure why I'm calling," she said.

"I don't care why. I'm glad. How are you? Are you in the city?"

"I'm working late, getting some things done before we go on location next week. How are you?"

"Oh, good. I've given in my resignation. The wheels are rolling. I can't say anyone was especially surprised, but I feel like a kid who's being let out of school early."

"You sound it."

"I feel great. I don't know why I waited so long. I should've done this years ago." He paused, then asked, "Is something wrong, Lynne?"

"I don't really know. Dianna didn't show up today for a production meeting. It's not like her. It's got us all on edge."

"She doesn't usually do this sort of thing?"

"Never."

"I don't suppose there's anything I can do?"

"I wish there were. I'd better go. I just wanted to talk to someone who wasn't involved."

"I'm glad you called. You're sure there's nothing I can do?"

"If I think of anything, I'll call you."

"I'll be here."

She hung up and returned to the table.

After dinner, considerably calmed by two martinis and a lot of food, Gloria commented, "I can see myself turning into one of those women who carry a flask, having a snort on the subway on my way home, or whipping into the john for a quick belt."

Lynne didn't respond. It suddenly struck her that if Dianna failed to show up by tomorrow, the entire segment would have to be scrapped. While she'd been anticipating that something would go wrong, she'd never imagined that it would be Dianna who'd be responsible, however indirectly, for it happening.

"I'm going to try her number again," Gloria said, as if reading Lynne's thoughts. She returned moments later to say, "There's still no answer at her place. Oh! I just had a sickening thought. What the hell do we do if she's gone missing on us? And why are you being so calm?"

"I'm hardly calm. I've just been thinking the same thing."

"I've got this sick feeling something's happened to her," Gloria said softly.

"I'm sure she'll be in tomorrow," Lynne said, despite her feeling that they were discussing an already dead issue. It was, she suspected, merely a matter of time, and formalities, but the shoot was as good as canceled. Was it possible, she wondered disloyally, that Dianna and Ned had cooked something up between them? No. She discarded the idea at once. Dianna would never sabotage her, Lynne decided. So what did all this mean?

❖ Fifteen ❖

DIANNA FELT SHE was going to die. At first she'd thought they'd let her go once they'd finished with her. But as the hours passed and there was no indication they were going to release her, she began to think about death. Actually, she hoped she would die. It would be a relief. Even breathing was painful, the simple act of drawing air into her lungs. She couldn't seem to see: focusing was difficult. One eye felt peculiar, as if it was half shut, so that everything she saw was through a dark red haze. She touched her tongue to her teeth and closed her eyes. She couldn't believe that this was how it was all going to end. The girls would be all right, though. They were old enough to fend for themselves. They were probably going crazy at the office, wondering where she was. They'd be trying the apartment every five minutes; they'd probably even call Bob, if he hadn't already called the office in a rage, demanding to talk to her.

It was odd, but she didn't care much about what was happening at the office, or with the show. She cared about Lynne, about letting her down when she knew how much this segment meant to Lynne. But Lynne would cope somehow. She always would, when it came down to it. Lynne was all right. . . . She was probably going to die and she'd never even told Lynne she liked her. They should have been friends. The rest of them, though, and the job, too, now appeared meaningless to her. All the panic, the drama, the self-importance seemed grossly out of proportion. A few minutes of air-time out of an entire week and people—

people like Ned—were willing to do any rotten goddamned thing they had to in order to achieve and then maintain a stranglehold on that access to the public attention. Why the hell, she wondered, had she struggled so long and so hard for something so *stupid*? Stupid! It all struck her as ridiculous: the production meetings, the quiet battles taking place neverendingly for credit for this or that, the gigantic egos at war.

She started to cry again. It hurt. Her left hand had no feeling in it. She wet her lips, then swallowed. She could hear them talking but couldn't distinguish what was being said. Her back ached, her chest felt crushed. She wished she could move, but if she remained completely motionless, they might leave her alone. She wanted, more than anything, ever, in her life, to become invisible in order to be left alone. She wanted to die; she wanted to be saved. She felt suspended, caught midway between a desire to return to a life growing daily more tedious, and a longing to escape altogether, leave all the trouble behind. She thought of her months of sexual antics with Ned, and froze an image of the two of them in her mind. She enlarged the frame, then excised herself from the image so that only Ned was there, in outsized, exacting focus. She gazed and gazed at his features, and all at once something slid into place in her mind. She felt, almost physically, an understanding pull itself together, and studied Ned on her inner screen, quietly astounded by her personal revelation. No one in a thousand years, not a million, would ever have believed her, but she finally understood that Ned was in love with her. Why could she see and understand it with such lucidity now when the knowledge was of utterly no use to her? Yet it did please, and even console, her. She contemplated Ned in the light of her new comprehension, her body relaxing somewhat beneath its weight of pain. It was distinctly as if the pain were an exterior thing, an object that had been applied to her body, beneath which she lay helpless. If she remained absolutely still and tried to concentrate on other things, the density of the pain seemed diminished. Ned. It was astonishing. She smiled inside herself, the fingers of her right hand curling reflexively.

He'd played game after game, leaving, backtracking; games where he'd believed himself the master; games wherein power ceased to be an issue because he'd involved himself—willingly or unwillingly, it was irrelevant—and power was useful only as an objective, as a goal. Once it was attained, those who had sought and won it were compelled to acknowledge that they were just as alone as they'd been at the outset of their quest; they were still, and would be forever, sequestered with the empty company of those they liked least: themselves. Ned's climb toward power had been halted because something inside him had acknowledged a caring for a person that superseded his caring for success. Poor Ned, she thought affectionately. She doubted he'd ever thought about any of this, let alone understood it.

Had she not been entrapped, victimized by the ceaseless pain, she might never have thought about it herself. But time had become surpassingly elastic now; it bulged, allowing her to fill it with proliferating concepts as she struggled to keep her attention from haphazardly meandering back toward the dangerous realms of the body's shock.

She was thirsty, and wet her lips again, thinking, drifting.

Gloria leaned urgently toward Lynne asking, "What're you going to do?"

Lynne took a deep breath and said, "I don't know." It was, of course, a lie. She did know, had always known what would have to be done. What distressed her, causing her stomach to clench and unclench, was the question of Dianna's whereabouts. It was now after seven and obvious that Dianna wasn't going to arrive. "We'll scrap it," she said in a neutral tone. "You tell the crew, then call the policeman and the psychiatrist. I'll call the women."

"Let me make the calls," Gloria volunteered, knowing in advance the annoyance she'd have to deal with. People were always upset at being bumped off a show, for whatever reasons. "Why should you have to be the heavy?" she said. "I'll do it."

"Thank you." Lynne put her hand on Gloria's arm. Their eyes held for a few seconds, then Gloria's face relaxed into a resigned mask and without another word she turned and went back to her desk. Lynne continued to stand where she was, trying to cope with the conflicting emotions she felt. She might, under other circumstances, have been angry with Dianna, but her present anger was insubstantial and outweighed by her genuine and rapidly increasing fear for Dianna's well-being. What the hell did it matter anyway? she asked herself, leaning against the wall, staring out at the central area where a P.A. sat at a desk, a sheaf of Teletype printouts spread before her, a cup of coffee close at hand. She'd felt defeated about the project since the afternoon of Dianna's call saying she'd managed to convince Ned to pass the thing on for budgeting. Dianna's disappearance simply placed punctuation and italics on her defeat. Maybe she should have been embittered, but her perspectives seemed to have undergone radical changes recently. Things were no longer so clearly defined, or even so worthy of pursuit as they'd been. She wanted something now that her career couldn't provide; yet she was anything but clear as to the specifics of her desire.

After they'd finished the last of the calls, they drove in Lynne's car to Dianna's building where they managed to convince the super to let them in, although he insisted on staying with them while they were in the apartment.

They went from room to room checking. The place was charmingly done, with a lot of chintz and many tall, healthy-looking plants; it was spotless, and had an ominously vacant air. Lynne scribbled a note she doubted Dianna would ever see and left it in the telephone dial. She and Gloria thanked the super and went down to the lobby where they stood, trying to decide what to do next.

"I think we should go to the nearest police station and report her as a missing person," Lynne said.

"This is getting scary," Gloria said shakily. "I'm starting to get really worried about her."

"She went out yesterday with her mink coat and her handbag, and she went out before dark because she'd have left some lights on otherwise."

"How d'you know that?" Gloria asked, impressed.

"First, she didn't pick up this morning's paper, and, second, she told me once she hates coming home to a dark apartment. She always leaves lights on."

"I wouldn't have believed she could be that human," Gloria said, then looked ashamed. "I shouldn't talk that way."

"She's not dead yet. Come on. We'll find the nearest police station and then I'll drive you home. I can't think of anything else to do."

"Wait a minute! Don't you have to be related or something to file a report like that?"

"My God! I think you're right. We'd better get in touch with her ex. We don't want to upset her daughters. You've got his number, haven't you?"

"It's back at the office," Gloria groaned.

They drove back. The night doorman chuckled when he saw them coming. "Working late?" he asked. "Or did you forget something, girls?" He pushed the register toward them. Lynne signed in.

"Yeah!" Gloria snapped. "Our douche kits, you asshole! We can't work our corner without them!" She strode off toward the elevators.

Laughing, Lynne hurried after her.

"He's such a cretin!" Gloria carped as they rode up in the elevator. "You call the ex, okay? I'd rather take my flak from people I know. Dianna's ex is so goddamned hostile. I'll go round up some coffee."

An hour later, having dropped Gloria off home in the Bronx, Lynne was on her way to Connecticut. Dianna's ex had been angry about the call. Keeping a lid on her temper, Lynne had explained the situation, concluding, "It's been more than twenty-four hours, which I believe is the time limit. Please do it! Just to humor me, all right? In all the years I've known her, Dianna's never done anything remotely like this. She would never run the risk of putting her job on the line this way."

Grudgingly, he'd agreed to file a report.

Exhausted, Lynne had then reluctantly, but importantly,

put in a call to Ned at his home. He'd sounded atypically upset and asked several times if she and Gloria had checked Dianna's apartment. Upon being reassured that they'd gone there in person, Ned had sighed heavily, and said, "I'd better arrange a sub for Sunday's show, I guess. I can't leave these things to the last minute."

"Something's happened to her," Lynne had said.

"Shit!" he'd exclaimed tiredly, so that his voice seemed to echo. She'd almost been able to picture the darkened house at his back. "I'll talk to you in the morning." He paused, then added, "Thanks for letting me know. I'm sorry about your shoot. Maybe we can reschedule, with someone else."

"I don't think so," she'd said quietly. "We'll talk in the morning."

It was now almost midnight and Lynne wanted nothing more than a long Scotch and time away from this problem. The armholes both of her shirt and her suit jacket were drenched with perspiration, probably ruined.

Instead of leaving the turnpike at her exit she drove on to the next one. She found herself parked in Ross's driveway and sat staring at the house, soothed by its beautifully eccentric facade, wondering what automatic device had taken over to direct her here. Never mind, she told herself. It had been the right thing to do. Ross, with his nearly-achieved freedom, represented a kind of sanity and serenity she craved just now. She removed her hands from the steering wheel and let them rest in her lap. The car idled almost silently. She readjusted the heat levers and opened the window slightly then looked again at the house. It was sad, she thought, that Ross couldn't take this house with him; sad that houses, unlike people, weren't portable.

After a few minutes she put the shift into reverse and was about to back out of the driveway when the exterior lights went on and the front door opened. Ross, in his robe, appeared in the doorway. When she saw him, she turned off the ignition and got out to stand with her hand on the car door.

He came down the steps and walked toward her, his

hands in the pockets of the robe. "I had a feeling you might stop by," he said, stopping several feet away. "Would you like to come in for a nightcap?"

"I'd love it," she said gratefully. "Dianna's gone missing. We've had to scrap the shoot."

"I'm sorry," he said simply.

"It's turning into a nightmare," she said, allowing him to take her coat. "I'm convinced something's happened to Dianna."

"Brandy?"

"I'd prefer Scotch, if you have it."

"I have it. How would you like it?"

"Neat."

"Fine. Come in. Sit down." She followed him into the living room where a fire was going in the grate. She sank down into the deep sofa, her eyes drawn to the fire. On the floor near the fireplace were a number of files, some open, and several sheets of paper covered with handwriting. She watched Ross returning with her drink and thought how grown-up, how relaxed he seemed. He had years of experience in dealing with crises behind him; this knowledge eased her. He was someone who would, without the need for undue explanations, understand her problems.

"Were you working?" she asked as he gave her the drink.

"Clearing things up," he explained, sitting in the armchair opposite. "Details," he said with a fatigued air. "You can't get away altogether clear." He looked over at the files and papers for a moment, then back at her. "You look tired. It's been a long night."

She nodded, feeling the Scotch begin to send its warmth outward from her stomach.

"I listed the house today," he went on. "It's unbelievable how much it's appreciated in five years. Are you hungry? I am. Would you like something to eat?"

"If you're going to have something, I wouldn't mind. I'm not keeping you up, am I?"

"No." He smiled and shook his head. "Come on. Let's go see what's in the refrigerator."

Drink in hand, she walked with him to the kitchen. He opened the refrigerator door and peered inside. "There's leftover roast chicken. We could have bacon and eggs. There's half a crab quiche. Mrs. Wain makes superb quiche."

"Let's have it."

"Hot or cold? I could put it in the oven."

"Cold will be fine."

He got two forks and some napkins and they sat at the round wooden table in the kitchen and ate the quiche out of the pan.

"It's delicious," she said, washing down the last of the food with a swallow of Scotch. "How are you going to live without her to do your cooking?"

"Well now," he said, pouring himself a glass of milk. "That's an interesting point. I told her my plans, and she asked a lot of questions. She's a hell of a talker once you get her started, as you may have noticed. Anyway, she said she thought it'd be a good idea to move to Florida."

"You mean she's willing to go with you? What about her son, and her weekend visits?"

"She'll make monthly visits. I'm willing to foot the bill. The plan is, I'm going down over Christmas to find a place. You're welcome to come along."

She laughed softly, relaxed by the food and the drink and his company. "You're not going to give up, are you?"

"Nope. I know a good thing when I see one."

"Good," she said. "Don't give up!"

"Would you like to go back to the living room?"

"I'm happy right here."

"Okay." He finished his milk, then sat with his legs extended, looking down the length of the kitchen. "Funny thing about houses," he mused. "They're only as real to you as the people who've lived in them. I won't miss this place. I'm the only one in the family who's spent any time here. The last house, though, that was a wrench. For weeks after it was sold, I'd come off the train, get in the car, and be halfway home before I remembered I didn't live there anymore. I've never really felt as if I lived here. It was kind of fun fixing it up, but once it was done I lost all interest. This house needs people in here who love it.''

"Have you told your sons about the move?" she asked.

"Last night. They said, 'That's nice, Dad.' That sort of thing. They've got their own lives." He turned to look at her a little sadly. "It's hard realizing they've already been turned loose when you're just getting used to the idea that you can't keep them forever. What d'you think'll happen if Dianna doesn't turn up?"

"I don't know. I'm trying not to think about it."

"How about some chocolate pie?" he suggested. "There's some left."

"What about your diet, your potential paunch?" she teased.

"Screw it! You want some?"

"Sounds great. I don't know why I'm so hungry. I had a big dinner."

"Tension, pressure," he said knowingly. "The only times I'm really hungry are when everything's hitting the fan." He got the pie from the refrigerator, took two fresh forks from a drawer and returned to the table. "This is fun," he said, as they attacked the pie. "It's been years since I raided the 'fridge in the middle of the night."

"Me, too," she said, her mouth full of creamy chocolate.

"If you don't feel like driving home, you can stay here. There's all kinds of empty bedrooms."

"I'm going to have to go. I've got a lot of calls to make, things to do in the morning."

"You're more than welcome to stay." He reached into the pocket of his robe and took out a pack of cigarettes. Lighting one, he asked, "What do you want for yourself, Lynne?"

"Want how?"

"For your life, your future. What would you like?"

"I don't know."

"Tell me," he urged. "I'm interested."

"I have two entirely different sets of dreams," she began, wondering if he'd understand. "In one set, I have someone who provides everything I need. In the other set, I provide everything I need.''

"Go on," he encouraged her. "Elaborate."

"I can't tell you what I want," she said truthfully. "I'm not sure I know. What I want changes depending on who I'm with." She looked at her watch. "I'd better go. It's after two."

"Would it interest you to know I have what I suspect are two identical sets of dreams?"

"Really?"

"Really. In one set, I'm utterly free, in a way I've never actually been. I have my boat and I'm entirely self-sufficient. I sail where I want to, when I want to. I'm above, or beyond, needing anything more than the basic elements of sun, sea, and my own good health.

"In my other dreams, I'm with someone who's good company, with whom the time I pass is well spent. We're at ease with each other; we make no unreasonable demands; we have an understanding. And together we enjoy the sun and the sea and each other's good health.''

"What's the conflict?" she asked. "Is there one?"

"Between the two dreams? Oh sure," he said. "The conflict is inherent in the second set of dreams, because I'm not convinced two people can live together without some kind of conflict. It seems to generate itself. Little things people do that irritate the other person.''

"It's more than that," she said. "It's a question of dependency. I don't ever again want to be dependent the way I was on Alec.''

"But you never would be, would you?" he said reasonably. "You've had that experience, and it's changed you. You're not likely to enter into any situation with the same expectations.''

"That's true," she said thoughtfully. "Look, I really have to go.''

He walked with her to the door. "I'm glad you came."

"So am I." She put her arms around him and rested her head on his shoulder, once again deriving comfort from his proximity.

"If you think I can help," he said, "call me. Call me anyway." He smiled engagingly. "I like the sound of your voice, and I like what you have to say. If you don't call me, I'll call you."

She hugged him close for a moment, then hurried to her car. She arrived back at the cottage to discover John's truck parked at the top of her driveway, and to one side, so that there was ample room for the BMW. She walked slowly, calmly down the length of the drive to the front of the house where John sat curled up against the front door, asleep. He seemed, she thought, like an enormous parcel left behind by a bemused postman. Smiling, she made her way up the steps and bent to place her hand on his arm. He came awake with a start.

"Come inside," she said. "It's very cold out here."

He got to his feet, asking, "What time is it?"

"Late." She got the door open and waited for him to enter. "Almost two-thirty."

"Two-thirty." He rubbed his face with both hands. "How long were you asleep out there?"

"A couple of hours," he admitted sheepishly.

She wanted to ask him not to make a habit of sitting out in the cold waiting for her, but it didn't seem the right time. Instead, she said, "Would you like something hot to drink?"

"No, that's okay. You go ahead, though. I mean, don't let me hold you back. I'll just head on home." He stood watching her remove her coat, thinking she was going to get really pissed off with him if he started hanging around her front porch waiting for her to come home nights.

She looked at the sweet perfection of his features and felt something inside her expand exquisitely. "Why don't you get into bed?" she suggested, her heart tripping giddily. "I want to take a quick shower." When he failed to move, she smiled and said, "Go on. It's all right. There's no point in going home now. You've got to be up in a few hours, don't you?"

He nodded uncertainly.

"We're not going to make a habit of this," she said, still smiling as she moved toward him.

"I don't want you to think . . ." he began.

"Ssshh." Her hand on his arm, she turned him in the direction of the bedroom. "Go ahead. I'll be five minutes."

While she was in the shower, she imagined herself emerging to find him once more soundly sleeping. She envied him his gift for sleep, his ability to fall so effortlessly into it. Her own sleep seemed, more and more, to be fraught with indecipherable or bewildering messages sent from one part of her brain to another as if her consciousness were compartmentalized and highly specialized, sending memos from one section to another.

He was awake, sitting against the headboard, waiting for her.

In darkness, she fitted herself to his body, at once overcome by that same near-violent desire for him that had seemingly controlled her actions on the previous occasion. Her body all too apparently had intentions of which she was unaware, for it was more than ready to engage in the fierce, silent tussle that was their lovemaking. They labored together in urgent, mutual need until, very quickly, it was ended. After a time, still without words, they separated.

Her dream was a complex, tangled scenario involving both John and Ross. She was, at one point, in the center of a vast bed, flanked by the two men. Somehow she was a human fence separating the two men; she was also a catalyst. Through her Ross and John were able to coalesce. Caringly, she accepted both men into her body. She lay above John gazing into his beautiful face, while Ross's arms and warm body held her securely from behind; armor at the gate. Her body sexually elastic, she contained them both effortlessly, deriving cataclysmic pleasure from their ministrations and from the innate knowledge of their love for her.

He awakened her at dawn. In a state halfway between waking and sleeping, she held her body open to him. He seemed immense, incredibly potent, and she wondered if she mightn't be dreaming after all. His tenderly determined motion stirred her sensitized flesh, while her brain floated languidly. Then her brain seemed to drift away altogether and she clung, dependently vulnerable, yet confident of their extraordinary ability to satisfy each other. He stroked and kissed her, propelling her into the heart of frenzy. Then he was gone, the front door closed quietly, and she turned, plunging into feathery, substanceless clouds.

❖ *Sixteen* ❖

FIRST THING IN the morning, knowing she was risking Bob Ferguson's considerable wrath, she put in a call to his office.

"What is it?" he asked brusquely.

"Have you heard from Dianna?"

"No, I have not heard from her. And yes, I did file with the police. I gave them your number, so if there's any news they'll call you. Which means you can stop hounding me. I really don't give a damn anymore. Understand?"

"You're a heartless bastard, aren't you! Dianna certainly didn't exaggerate on that score!"

"Look," he said, sounding worn out. "I've had it. Okay? I've been paying Dianna off for *seventeen* years. I've had to put up with her drunken telephone calls at two and three in the morning. She's harassed two women I happened to be in love with. She wrecked my second marriage and she's wrecked our daughters. They won't even *talk* to me! What you fail to understand is that I've paid my dues and then some, and I am not going to keep on paying them. *Please*, give me a break and let me get some work done, will you?"

"I'm sorry," Lynne said, "but she is missing, and she is the mother of your children. I thought you might be concerned."

"I was concerned enough to go to the police station last night. I can't do anything more right now, can I?"

"No, I don't suppose you can."

"Okay. So if and when she turns up, we'll all climb back aboard the merry-go-round and start again. She's probably finally managed to drink herself into oblivion. It wouldn't surprise me. In the meantime, do me a favor. Spare me your observations on my character, and your phone calls. I'm sure you're a very nice woman, and I know you're worried. But I've gone as far as I can go. Okay?"

"All right. Thank you." Lynne hung up. Talk of drunken middle-of-the-night phone calls altered her image of Dianna, but rather than creating a harsher picture, this information rendered Dianna someone even more in need of sympathy. Lynne didn't for a moment believe Dianna would ever allow anything to push her so far out of control that she'd be remiss about tending to her obligations.

She got up and went out to the central area to get herself some coffee. Her telephone was ringing as she returned to her office and she rushed to answer it, hoping that it would be some news of Dianna. It was Keith, not his secretary, but Keith himself.

"Could I see you?" he asked.

"Certainly. When?"

"Would you mind coming up now?"

"Not at all. I'll be right there." Leaving her coffee on the desk, she got her handbag from the bottom drawer and made her way to the elevators. When Keith himself requested your presence it had to be important. Perhaps he had information about Dianna.

It was mostly darkness. Long periods of time passed and then it seemed she awakened. She wasn't sure if she was actually awake; it was more that the darkness altered. There was a glow of light that penetrated her eyelids. When she was aware of it, she believed she was awake. People touched her, moved her, did things that were monstrously painful, but she couldn't be sure if the sensation of movement was real or imagined. She'd traveled into a state beyond pain—out from under that mountain of agonized sensation—to a region where her body had ceased to exist except as an entity somewhere beneath her head. At one point the voices had been very near, then followed a lengthy silence and she'd had that sensation of being moved, but she couldn't be sure. Distantly, she heard the sounds of traffic, and once, the whine of a siren. Then the light was extinguished and her eyes floated freely, bobbing against the darkness. Perhaps this was death. It didn't seem possible that this insensate state could be the culmination of one's life. If it were indeed death, undoubtedly this was hell. She couldn't conceive of a god so unfair as to create a heaven comprised of bodiless, sightless, speechless beings. No, it had to be hell. If she was dead, though, why could she hear the sounds of traffic and sirens? It didn't make sense. Was she possibly caught in limbo, hanging between life as she'd known it and her ultimate resting place? Maybe she'd lost her mind.

She thought her mouth might be open. It felt as if air were being towed, like some weighty solid object, in and out of her lungs. She must be breathing, she reasoned; therefore, she couldn't be dead. When, she wondered, did death come? Did everyone spend some period of time in this suspended state before finally being released? Was this purgatory? Had she lived so evil a life that it couldn't be decided where she was to spend eternity? She hadn't been evil. No, she hadn't. She'd done her best, with what she'd been given. And surely purgatory was the place where people like Lynne lived when someone they loved died. What else could her condition have been called?

She remembered Aunt Gussie telling her, when she was quite a little girl, that there was good in all people. She could remember it well. Her Aunt Gussie, considered unfortunately too tall, and gauntly thin with it, her red hair shot with gold, her long nervous hands always fluttering, as if with lives of their own, in the air before her; Aunt Gussie had sat in the white-painted wicker rocker on the porch, teaching the child Dianna how to tat, displaying limitless patience as she repeatedly unraveled the tangled, graying white thread. Sometimes, Gussie had told her, you had to look very hard to find the good in some people because they wanted to resist it. Gussie's high, clear, youthful voice had woven, like the threads, in intricate, patterned knots as she'd leaned over to correct another of the little girl's errors.

She could see her aunt so clearly, even the printed cotton dress she wore that fell from her shoulders to below her knees in almost a straight line. Her long, bare arms were freckled and, Dianna could see in the afternoon sun, covered with fine, red-gold hairs. The woman and the child sat on the porch, working and talking, their voices barely audible beneath the thick, overhanging shade trees and the hot heavy air ripe with the scent of newly-cut grass and flowers and Gussie's lilac eau de cologne.

She remembered Bob standing at the apartment door with his suitcases. He was saying the words again, making the statement that had defied her comprehension for all these years. "You're never going to come out," he was saying, "because that would take a kind of courage you don't have. You'll go on hiding behind that tough pose until the person in there is nothing but ashes and the pose will have become the person. You don't understand a goddamned thing I'm saying, do you?"

She remembered shaking her head back and forth, back and forth, this one time admitting her failure to understand, his words more tangled than her tatting efforts as a child. Why was he doing this, leaving her, when she loved him so much? Her love for him was a vast desert she was destined to wander in thirst for the rest of her life because she was not his final choice but simply the first of many choices.

There were women who'd slept beside him, women whose voices had answered hello when all she'd wanted and needed was to hear the sound of his voice, to have him explain what he'd meant. How many? Three, no four. He'd married two of them. He was still married to the last one, five or six years now. They had a little boy. He'd answered the telephone one evening when she'd called, needing to talk to Bob, just to hear the sound of his voice and know he was still alive in the world. Each call to him was a source of shame and anguish, continued abuse she voluntarily heaped upon herself for her singular failure to love sufficiently, or well.

At first she'd thought she had the wrong number because she'd known nothing of any child. But she'd thought to say, "Could I speak to your daddy?" and the little boy had dropped the receiver and gone running off, calling, "Daddy! There's a lady wants to talk to you." How long ago had that been? Not so very long, she didn't think, judging by the still lingering sense of betrayal that child's existence had generated within her. The boy was a half-brother to Tricia and Trudy. They didn't even know they had a brother. She should have told them. The idea that she hadn't made her want to weep, but the very thought of shedding tears, the concept of it seemed to rise beyond her grasp. Mentally, she stood with her hand outheld, reaching too late to take hold of too many things now, possibly, forever out of reach. Was this hell after all? Purgatory? Lynne had lived there for a time.

She remembered taking Lynne to lunch because she cared about Lynne and she'd seemed to be having some kind of quiet breakdown. Lynne's husband, that Alec, he'd killed himself. She'd watched Lynne sink, altering visibly, and had wondered why, when Alec had been the kind of tight-assed guy Dianna had never liked. A tight-assed, dictatorial kind of guy, he'd been telling Lynne what to do and how to do it for years, pissed off by his wife's career and her success, and jealous of it too. Then he'd killed himself and Lynne had been like someone drowning in air. She'd gone around taking tiny sips of air, as if she'd been afraid of getting drunk, or of overloading her lungs. Top-heavy, she might have fallen, facefirst to the ground and never been able to get up again. She'd gone to live in some nightmare place inside her head and Dianna had watched it happen, had watched while Lynne spent more and more time in her office, just staring into space, sometimes for hours. Beautiful Lynne, with her honest-to-god natural blond hair and helpless eyes, had been sliding away, and Dianna couldn't stand seeing it happen. So she'd said, "Come to lunch," playing the tough guy the way she always did with Lynne because she never wanted Lynne to know how much she liked her, how much she admired her. She'd said, "Come to lunch,'' and Lynne had come. Dianna had been frightened by how much she cared about this thin, tormented woman who could, at times, be stronger than any man Dianna had ever known, with more stick-to-itiveness, more guts than most men, willing to go the distance for something she believed in, without ever considering selling any part of herself to get it. Not like Dianna who'd sold parts of herself to so many men, like shares in some nonexistent corporation; not like Dianna who could never trust her own abilities but preferred to deal in the time-honored fashion, in currency readily accepted.

Dianna had laid it out, telling Lynne just what she could see happening, and it had been like talking to someone at the far end of a long tunnel, shouting to make herself heard. But Lynne had heard, finally, and her eyes had clicked into focus so that for the first time in months she'd looked alive. She'd badly wanted to ask Lynne why she'd gone to live in purgatory over the death of a man like Alec, a man who'd planned their lives into oblivion, a man who'd never applauded either the best or the least of his wife's efforts, but rather, had challenged and disputed every step of the way. They'd fought without words over Lynne's career, but Lynne had won.

Yet Alec had killed himself, and Lynne had become disattached, like the little tab on a zipper; disattached and useless; an appendage prematurely severed. Dianna had been so scared by her feelings for the woman that she'd said what she'd had to say, tossed down a couple of drinks, and then ran away.

Now, floating in her darkened space, she wished she'd admitted to Lynne that she felt as if she loved her, that more than anyone else alive she admired Lynne for keeping the parts of herself intact instead of selling them off in order to climb. Lynne was the only person who'd really care about this strange business that was happening to her. She wished Lynne would find her, would come.

The secretary motioned to her to go right in. Lynne knocked and entered Keith's office, surprised to see Ned seated in one of the armchairs. Upon seeing her, Keith stood up from the sofa and smiled, extending his arm as he said, "Come in. Come sit down, Lynne."

There was a tray on the coffee table bearing a silver coffee service. "Will you have some coffee?" Keith asked, as Lynne settled herself in the armchair opposite Ned's.

"Thank you," she said, studying Ned's expression. He looked odd, as if he was afraid, and being unaccustomed to fear, didn't quite know how to mask it. He kept his eyes averted from her.

Keith handed her a cup then sat down. "Help yourself to cream and sugar. Any news yet on Dianna?" he asked.

This wasn't about Dianna, she realized. But what then? "Her former husband has filed a missing persons report," she told him, her eyes returning briefly to Ned who steadfastly refused to look at her.

"I understand you've scrapped the shoot," Keith said, the words sounding outrageous coming from him. He was someone unsuited to the use of jargon of any kind. Without fail, each time he used technical euphemisms, Lynne felt jarred. She wondered why he tried, why he didn't simply say, You've cancelled your production plans.

"I prefer not to go ahead without Dianna." She took a sip of the coffee.

"It was my understanding," he said slowly, "that this shoot was to be part of the Berkeley segment."

She stared at him, mystified.

"How is this going to affect your scheduling?" he asked Ned, who, Lynne now saw, seemed to be having difficulty breathing. Without awaiting an answer, Keith turned back to Lynne. "Of course you can reschedule, work around the immediate problem."

"I don't think I want to do that," she said, certain now they were talking at cross-purposes. "I spent two years requesting permission to do the piece. Dianna's been an integral part of it from the beginning. I couldn't possibly do it without her." She trailed off, seeing that Keith was once again staring at Ned.

"It would seem we have a bit of confusion here, Ned,"

Keith said mildly. "Originally, it was planned we'd discuss this over lunch," he explained, including Lynne, "but with Dianna's disappearance and the subsequent scrapping of Lynne's shoot, I think we're going to have to talk about it now. Ned," he said to Lynne, as if Ned weren't in the room, "for reasons known only to himself, made several changes on your proposal. That's why I asked you to join us. I thought we could both hear the explanation and save some time." He turned expectantly to Ned, prepared for a major confrontation. He knew there wasn't enough here to take in to the executive offices; he hoped to embarrass Ned, to force him—even if only once—to admit to his wrongdoing. It would be a minor satisfaction, but Keith was willing to be content with that.

For several seconds Ned stared at the older man. He was finding it hard to concentrate. He'd been up most of the night calling all the hospitals to see if Dianna might not have been admitted somewhere. He was exhausted and so worried he couldn't seem to function. He emitted a long sigh and sank back into the chair. "I didn't think you'd pick up on it," he said.

Keith hadn't expected this. He'd imagined Ned would try to lie his way out of the situation. Regarding the man now with open interest, he said, "Go on."

Lynne lit a cigarette and leaned forward with her elbows on her knees, closely watching the interaction between the two men. She might as well not have been there. They seemed completely unaware of her.

For the first time, Ned looked at Lynne. "I changed your FAX."

"Why?" Lynne asked quietly, fearful of breaking this strange mood.

"Why?" he repeated. "Who the hell knows anymore? It's academic anyway. You can't do the shoot because nobody knows where Dianna is. The whole thing's a bust. So what d'you want?" he asked Keith. "You can't go anywhere with this, and you know it." Ned pushed up out of the chair and made his way to the door. "I'm going home. Do whatever you want, but try to take this in to the big boys and they'll laugh you right out of town." He walked out.

There was silence for several moments and then Keith said, "I wasn't expecting him to admit it. I wanted you to know what was going on," he said. "It's not worth ten cents to either of us, but there you are." He shook his head. "There are times when I think this is an exciting business. Not very often anymore," he qualified. "But every once in a while we air a segment on "Up to the Minute," or put together a special that's perfect in its own right. Then I feel good about passing up . . . other opportunities to work in television. Most of the time it's a matter of dealing with money, with personalities, with ratings and surveys and prime-time advertisers and a lot of people who think they know something about television but who don't know a thing about it. It's a thankless job, this one," he said, with a deprecating little smile. "I honestly can't imagine why Ned wants it."

"Why do *you* want it?" she asked, intrigued.

He smiled, relaxing. "I wake up every morning asking myself that very question. I might ask the same of you."

"I used to know." She returned his smile, then grew thoughtful. "Now I think it's a habit, one I'm getting a little tired of. What I don't understand is why Ned just changed the game the way he did."

They both looked toward the door, as if Ned might still be standing there.

"What will happen?" she asked. For a few seconds, she ran through a little scenario. Keith would turn to her and say, "If you want his job, it's yours." She'd stare at him in surprise, pleased, and say, "I'm going to have to think about it." She'd ask how much time she had and Keith would say, "Very little." Of course the terms would have to be worked out, a new contract negotiated. In conclusion, he'd add something to the effect that Ned's contract wasn't going to be renewed, that it had been planned all along that she'd be offered Ned's job. She'd confess her surprise, and Keith would say, "We may seem as if we don't know what's going on downstairs, but let me assure you that we do."

"It's a file and forget situation," Keith said, with an expression that clearly indicated his dissatisfaction.

"I see. So why include me?"

"I wanted you to be aware of it."

"I see," she said again, not seeing at all.

"I am sorry about your segment being scrapped," he said, "but Ned knew I'd never give it approval."

Suddenly, she did see, and her chest was constricted with anger. These two men had just played out a little charade, and she'd been invited along in order to be made to understand once and for all precisely where the power lay in the organization. Ned had put her through the paces like a little puppy, and she'd played good doggie right to the end. "You knew my request wasn't for a segment on Berkeley," she said, her voice rich with controlled anger. "Why did you approve the budget?"

"I had no choice," he said simply. "I wanted you to go ahead and get it done. Then, when the time came, I'd have the ammunition I needed—those doctored forms and the film—to present as evidence. I thought Ned had finally made his major gaffe, and I'd been lucky enough to catch him. Unfortunately, you happened to get caught in the crossfire."

"Why tell me you're sorry my segment had to be scrapped?" she asked. "Why say all of that when you've known all along I was out on a wild goose chase?"

"I'm sorry," he said, "because I dislike using people, and you would have been used. I myself would have used you just to see Ned fall flat on his face."

"So I was lucky enough to be the ammunition in your private little war. That's very flattering."

"It's the business," he said, with a small smile.

"And you love it," she accused. He winced. A direct hit. She wasn't sorry.

"You're due for review," he said. "Your contract comes up for renewal in January, doesn't it?"

"That's right," she responded, feeling emboldened, uncaring. If he wanted to tell her right now they wouldn't be renewing her, that was fine. She just didn't give a damn.

"You can relax about it," he said.

"Well, thank you." She was, she understood, being dismissed.

They shook hands and she left the office, feeling shaky with disbelief at what had just transpired. So much for her little fantasy.

Gloria hurried over as Lynne returned, to say, "What's going on? Little Neddy came through about half an hour ago, made a couple of phone calls and then took off for parts unknown like his pants were on fire. You were there? What's going on?"

Lynne looked at her watch. "Let's have lunch, and we'll talk."

"I've got a couple of things to wrap up. Half an hour?"

"Fine."

"D'you ever see Moon Doggie?" Gloria asked.

"Sure I have. The silent giant who stands around midtown all rigged out like a viking, in a red suit and a hat with horns."

"This one time," Gloria said, "I came charging out of the subway, racing up the steps, and ran right into him. It was like hitting a brick wall. I looked up and up—he must be over seven feet tall, for God's sake—and he never even seemed to notice me. There's this other guy, too. D'you ever see this one? He's always on Madison, around lunchtime, in the mid-Forties. He's kind of a scrawny guy, wears a mustache and has this trench coat. On his back, he's got framed pictures of himself all beat up, and a framed letter, too. I've never gone close enough to read it, but I think he wants people to beat up on him or something. He gives me the willies. The weird thing about the guy is he's so ordinary-looking. I mean, he dresses all right, and he's clean. D'you ever see him?"

"I don't think so."

"Weird," Gloria said with a shudder. "Walking around with pictures on his back, showing him all beat up and bloody. He's got this backpack. Yeah, the pictures are on the backpack. Maybe he carries his whips and chains in it."

"Cheery conversation," Lynne observed.

"Yeah." Gloria looked down at the table. "Lon thinks she's dead. He says she has to be. He thinks she's lying dead somewhere, raped and murdered."

"Don't," Lynne protested. "Don't say it, don't even think it."

"Maybe we'll never find out what happened to her."

"Maybe not."

"You think she's dead, too, don't you?"

"No!" Lynne said strongly. "I don't think that. Shall we order?"

"I'm not really hungry. I've lost five pounds in five days. All this business has killed off my appetite. I mean, every time I start to feel hungry, I think about what could've happened to Dianna and I don't feel like eating anymore. I even dreamed about her last night, but I can't remember what it was about. I just remember her being in it."

Lynne had stopped listening. She was going back over the session in Keith's office, and filling with anger. For a moment, she longed for time to fritter away, to spend pampering herself, doing anything but what she was doing.

"Hey!" Gloria said. "Where have you gone off to?"

"Sorry. I was just thinking."

"What about?"

"Nothing relevant." Lynne lit a cigarette and turned to look out the restaurant window. It was snowing.

Following her gaze, Gloria said, "Oh, great! It's snowing. I hate driving in the snow, and naturally I brought the car in today, had to fight Lon for it. He thinks it diminishes his prestige to ride the subway. Now I wish I hadn't brought the damned thing into town. It's coming down like crazy. Are you in love?" she abruptly switched subjects. "Or has suave Uncle Keith suggested a dirty weekend somewhere discreetly out of town?"

Lynne laughed loudly.

"It's that funny, huh?" Gloria grinned.

"My sister accused me of the same thing a month or so ago, of being in love. Why is that the first thing women always think of?"

"Well, are you? You're so straitlaced," Gloria accused. "It's okay to be in love, you know, if that's what's happening. What *is* happening? It's getting hard here to keep from asking direct questions. My subtlety's starting to crack."

"I'm not in love," she said, and then wondered if that was the truth. "I am seeing someone, though. Actually, I'm seeing two someones."

"Well, aren't you something!" Gloria said admiringly. "Not one, but two. So, tell me. What're they like?"

It was very interesting, Lynne thought, that Gloria was more excited by the prospect of learning about Lynne's love-life than she would have been about hearing something pertaining to work, to the show. "One is a lot younger," she said cautiously, wishing she'd said nothing.

"How much is a lot?"

"Fourteen years."

Gloria emitted a low whistle. "What about the other guy? I take it he's the right age and everything."

"The right age," Lynne said. "Yes, he is."

"So, you've got this one guy who's too young and another guy who's just right—this sounds like Goldilocks with the porridge. We'll leave Uncle Keith and the dirty weekend out of it for the moment. I'll just bet you don't know which one you like more."

"Something like that."

"Amazing! You're the last person on earth I'd've ever thought would have two guys going at the same time. Let's order, okay? My appetite's coming back." She picked up the menu, then lowered it. "You look ticked off. Am I out of line? Or did something big go on upstairs?"

"What would you say," Lynne said, looking closely at her, "if I told you Keith offered me Ned's job?"

"What would I say? I'd say never in this world. That didn't happen, did it?"

"No, it didn't happen."

"Boy! You really had me going for a second there. So what *did* happen?"

"You should be producing, Gloria. You should've been producing a long time now."

"One of these days." Gloria shrugged philosophically.

"Would you fight for it?"

"What for? There's no chance. Look what . . ." She stopped suddenly.

"What were you going to say?"

"It's nothing."

"No, tell me."

"All right. Look what they do to you, the way they let you have a good shot one time, then, the next time, just to keep you humble, they hit you with a piece of crap. You're okay. You can handle it. Me, I'd go upstairs with a gun and shoot the bastards. And I'd start with Ned. You're going to get mad at me."

"No, I'm not. It's the truth."

"Jesus, Lynne! What's happening to. you? What is it, eight years now? At least eight years, and it's the first time we've ever had a really personal conversation."

"Maybe," Lynne said slowly, "I'm changing."

"Maybe you are," Gloria agreed. "Are you going to tell me what went on upstairs?"

"Not much. Ned fiddled with my forms, changed them to look like I was going to be shooting part of the Berkeley segment. Keith caught it, but he was going to let it go through and pretend he didn't know. Then, when the film was in the can—he never for a moment even considered airing the segment—he was going to use it for ammunition to get Ned axed."

"Oh, shit," Gloria murmured. Then, red in the face, she exploded. "*See*! See what I mean? I wouldn't put up with that garbage. But look at you! Calm and collected. I'd *kill* the bastards."

"I'm not calm and collected," Lynne corrected her. "I'm just trying to decide which way I'm going to go." She looked again through the window at the snow. "My contract is supposedly going to be renewed. It sounds like a reward, doesn't it?" she asked, facing Gloria again.

"You going to go for it?"

"Sometimes," Lynne said, "I think the best place to be doesn't exist."

"It's in here." Gloria pointed her index finger at her temple. "It's all in here."

"I'm going to play it by ear for the next few days."

"I detect hints of mutiny," Gloria said.

"It's possible," Lynne admitted.

"You're not going to renew, are you?"

"I don't honestly know. I've got to think about it."

Gloria shook her head and turned to look for the waitress.

✦ *Seventeen* ✦

ROSS DEBATED INVITING Lynne to accompany him to dinner at the Whitings. He'd been promising to come for months and now that the date had arrived and he could no longer put it off, he viewed the evening ahead as he might a movie he'd seen half a dozen times before. He was fond of Buffy, an old school friend, and his wife, Jinks. But he knew in advance precisely how the evening would go.

Buffy and Jinks were alarmingly predictable, filled with an insatiable appetite for information about people from their pasts. It seemed to be their only interest, their only real sustenance in recent years. Buffy was very thin, florid-faced, as keen a boating man as Ross; a man who went to the liquor store the way most women went to the supermarket, emerging with cartons heavy with half-gallons of vodka, or Scotch, or gin, whose consumption occupied the primary portion of his and his wife's days. Buffy had opted for early retirement several years before and the onerous chore of filling suddenly empty days had quickly taken its toll. While they'd both been fairly heavy drinkers in their younger days, Buffy's business involvement and Jinks's activities with various volunteer groups had forced them to keep a limit on their consumption. With the need to remain sober gone, they had, like giddy children, embarked upon an apparently carefree lifestyle that revolved, in the summer, around their boat and, in the winter, around their enjoyment of their half-dozen pure-bred dogs.

Jinks was a bleached blond, with the hard look of a

237

predator. She was big-breasted, thick through the middle and exceptionally thin in the arms and legs. Jinks in a one-piece bathing suit looked like a Cubist drawing, disproportionately large in the head and torso, her limbs added as hasty afterthoughts. Her voice, which had always been deep, had with the recent years of hard drinking, descended to a rusty, booming baritone.

It would be a deadly evening, with oft-repeated reminiscences barely breaking the vast echoey silence of the many uninhabited rooms of their immense house on the Sound in Riverside. Their half-dozen dogs would rush here and there, streaking through the living room to thrust their snouts into Ross's crotch until he could no longer keep silent. Then he'd say, ''Would you mind . . . ?'' and with a show both of concern and disdain, Jinks would coo, talking babytalk to the obese and utterly demented animals, and herd them into the pen she'd created for them out of the sun room. They would then yelp and bark for the remainder of the evening. Jinks would return, puffing and red-faced, to freshen her martini, or highball, or screwdriver, and settle back into the conversation with a flourish, having remembered, while penning the dogs, three or four other people from whom they'd lately heard, or about whom she'd been wondering. At ten or ten-thirty, Buffy would gently remind his wife about dinner, and Jinks would rise to totter out to the kitchen on her spindly legs to tell the cook it was time to serve the meal.

Some fifteen or twenty minutes thereafter, the three of them would make their way to the table in the dusty, rarely used dining room and the cook would present the meal. Ross, in despair and ravenously hungry by now, would heap food on his plate, his mood much lightened, only to turn to see Jinks sitting with minuscule portions, if any, on her plate, and Buffy with his plate altogether empty, the two of them eagerly watching Ross prepare to eat, as if he were a new pet they'd acquired.

Feeling self-conscious, yet unwilling to surrender to it, Ross would eat the meal, every so often looking up to see that while he'd consumed half his food, Jinks had taken perhaps three tiny bites. Buffy would be sitting with his elbows on the table, gazing forlornly into space as if wondering how he might put an end to the destructive sameness of their days.

No, Ross decided. It would be unfair to subject Lynne to an evening like that. If the prospect of spending time with these old friends bothered him, then Lynne would be dismayed, to say the least, by a viewing of the Whitings at home.

He was in the process of wrapping things up, honoring all the invitations he'd deferred for too long, seeing old friends he mightn't have occasion to see again. A funereal process, it would not be kind to inflict any part of it on someone he cared for as much as he cared for Lynne.

With the project scrapped and nothing in the immediate offing, she could have remained at home, but Lynne chose to go into the city to the office each day. She had the purely arbitrary feeling that if she were to learn of Dianna's whereabouts, the information would come to her at the office. She also wanted to go through her desk and filing cabinets.

She spent two days discarding outdated project outlines, and throwing out old correspondence and files. Her filing cabinet finally cleared, she sat down at her desk to gaze out the window. Each time the telephone rang, she hurried to answer, hoping for news of Dianna. When on her third and now idle morning at the office the telephone rang, she was surprised to hear Ned's voice.

"I'd like to talk to you. Could you make it for lunch today?"

"Well, I . . ." she hesitated. She really wasn't in the mood.

"Look, it's not business," he jumped in. "I just want to talk to you."

"All right," she agreed, and at once heard the note of relief in his voice as he named a restaurant in the east Thirties. They set a time and she put down the receiver, wondering what he could possibly have to say to her.

She arrived early, but Ned was already there. He stood

quickly to hold her chair, then seated himself again saying, "Thanks a lot for coming. I hoped you would."

He looked nervous and strangely fragile, as if he were trying to contain a thought or an emotion so immense that it threatened to blow apart his body. His hands had a slight tremor as he reached for the water glass and sipped from it. His small dark eyes met hers then slid away and, abruptly, as if remembering they were in a public eating place and that certain procedures were to be followed, he made a waving gesture to summon the waiter. He appeared so distraught that for the first time Lynne not only felt sorry for him, she actually felt a delicate sprouting of fondness. She found it close to impossible to relate this Ned to the boldly manipulative tyrant who'd so blatantly attempted to use her for purposes which still remained unexplained.

"Let's order," he said. "Would you like a drink? Let's have drinks and then we'll order. Or would you rather order now?"

"Have a drink," she said. "You look as if you need one."

He cast a grateful look at her, then turned to the waiter. "I'll have a vodka and tonic, hold the tonic."

Lynne laughed and Ned again turned to look at her, obviously failing to see the humor in what he'd said. A second later, he smiled tentatively then looked down at his clasped hands on the table as Lynne asked for coffee. The waiter left and Lynne sat waiting to hear what Ned would say.

"It's all gone crazy," he said, still gazing at the interwoven fingers of his hands. "First I thought I didn't give a shit. I was going to call the shots because things were getting too—involved. So I called it off altogether. But as soon as I did that I wanted things to be back the way they were. I went home and I couldn't stand the house. The kids drove me crazy. All they ever do is watch television— 'Flipper' and 'I Dream of Jeannie' and 'Get Smart'—until I could lose my mind. And my wife," he looked beseechingly at Lynne, "my wife's this featherbrain, this suburban dodo whose whole life is running to PTA meetings and chauffeuring the kids around and shopping for clothes and talking half the day and night on the phone to her featherbrain friends. Jesus Christ!'' He unclenched his hands and ran one haphazardly over his thinning hair. ''I'm sweating, for God's sake! I'm a nervous goddamned wreck. Have you got a cigarette?''

She opened her bag and placed her cigarettes and lighter on the table. Ned fumbled one out of the pack but couldn't manage to make the lighter function. Silently, Lynne took it from him and held the flame to his cigarette. He took a hard drag, exhaled tremulously, then said, ''Thanks. Jesus!'' He looked furtively around the restaurant. ''You probably find this funny.'' He studied her cautiously as if fearful she'd confirm this.

''Nothing's funny,'' she said flatly.

He gave a bitter-sounding laugh to indicate his agreement. ''That's the goddamned truth.'' He wet his lips, took another drag on the cigarette then hurried on with what he wanted to say. ''I pressured her,'' he admitted shamefacedly. ''I did. I used everything, throwing my weight around. The thing is, I didn't know how I felt. I wasn't sure. I mean, she's older and all the rest of it and it was kind of a power thing, I guess. I don't know. At first, it was this big challenge. You know? Could I get to her? Then, it got to be important. I couldn't break it off; I wanted to keep it going. But she did, she broke it off. I couldn't believe it. I thought she could tell how I felt. It had to show, you know, by the way we were together. But it didn't show, or maybe she knew and didn't care.

''I moved out of the house last week. I've got a room at the Algonquin. I figured I'd start getting things organized now, so the two of us could get together, sit down someplace neutral and talk about it. I could get a divorce and we'd get married. Then she doesn't show up for the production meeting, and nobody can find her.'' He shook his head again and fixed his eyes expectantly on Lynne.

''You're talking about Dianna,'' she said.

''Jesus! Right! Dianna. I can't even *talk* anymore. I figured you knew, that you'd know what the hell I was talking about. That was what I thought the meeting with goddamned

Keith was going to be about. I thought . . . because you're friends, maybe she'd talked to you, told you about it.''

"And I'd be able to tell you how she felt about you," Lynne offered.

"Something like that. Right."

"Dianna's never discussed you with me. Not ever, Ned."

He looked crushed, shattered.

The waiter arrived with Lynne's coffee and Ned's vodka. After he'd gone, Lynne said, "Why did you do it?"

"Shit! It doesn't matter now."

"Of course it matters," she said patiently. "You were trying to do something. And Keith was trying to do something else. I know what Keith was doing. What I'd like to understand is what you thought you'd accomplish."

"I was going to sneak it through, right under his nose."

"What?"

"I knew he'd never approve the goddamned segment. Haven't I always told you that? So I threw a different title on it figuring he'd pass it on. But he picked up on it. I was trying to get it through for you."

"What was the point?" she asked. "He'd never have allowed it to be aired."

"I had some plans I was working on. I *tried* to get you a shot."

It was becoming too convoluted to pursue further. "You've left your family," she said, "and you want to marry Dianna. You invited me here because you thought I might know where she is."

"Do you?" he interrupted.

Was he having a breakdown? she wondered. "I don't *know* where she is. Ned, you're not thinking clearly. If you were, you'd realize that whatever had happened between the two of you, Dianna would never intentionally do anything this drastic. You thought this was some sort of romantic ploy, didn't you?"

"I hoped you'd know where she was," he said again.

"Well, I don't. Considering what you tried to do to me, I really shouldn't be here at all."

He looked decidedly ill now, his face shiny with perspiration. "I wasn't going after you," he said, then took a gulp of his drink.

"Oh, for Christ's sake, Ned," she sighed. "You're a liar. You've been trying to get rid of me for years. What the *hell* is the point of sitting here lying about it now?"

"You don't fit in," he said. "And you're so goddamned judgmental, always after me to let you do something *significant*. It's television, not Sunday School."

"I'm probably better qualified to understand what television is than you. You wouldn't know the difference between editing tape and a can of film. I've spent *years* learning what I know. You've spent years pushing people around for the sake of your own importance. Please don't presume to lecture me on my place. You're hardly in a position, at the moment, to criticize me. I've certainly never stepped on anyone else's face in order to get something I wanted. All this *garbage*," she said hotly, "this self-indulgent crap I've had to listen to from you and Keith. I'm so *tired* of men like you, people like you.

"Even," she said, "if Dianna and I were close confiding friends—which we aren't—and this was some sort of ploy on her part, you'd be the very last person in the world I'd admit it too. The trouble with you, Ned, is you think that everybody else is just like you, that we're all as underhanded and ruthless as you are. But we're not. I think you think Dianna's like you. She isn't. For all of her veneer, Dianna's someone with loyalty and sensitivity. That takes her light years away from your level, Ned. Which is probably why when I do find out where she is, you'll be one of the last people to know, and positively the first person who'll be refused if you try to see her. Does that answer your question?"

"You don't understand . . ." he began.

"I most definitely *do* understand," she said coolly. "Try another route."

"Where the hell d'you get off, talking to me this way?"

"It's your party and you invited me. You know what I think? I think you should go home to your 'featherbrain.' At least she's willing to put up with you. There might be other women, if you want to spend the time looking for them. But I can guarantee you Dianna wouldn't be willing. This is unbelievable!'' she said, looking for a moment at the ceiling before returning her eyes to him. ''First you try to get me fired—and I don't give a damn about your convoluted, supposed reasons why—then you expect me to be sympathetic because you want a woman who doesn't want you.'' She returned her cigarettes and lighter to her handbag and pushed her chair back from the table. ''There's four or five weeks left to my contract,'' she said. ''You can play emperor for another few days, and that's all, because I intend to work out my contract, period. I don't like you; I've never liked you. I can't name *anyone* who does like you. Certainly *you* don't like you. You don't have the right to expect people to offer sympathy. If you want to send me out on another quickie dogwork assignment before my contract's up, that's fine. Otherwise, I'm going to put in my time at the office until Dianna turns up.'' She stood up and carefully returned her chair to the table. ''There's one last thing,'' she said, leaning toward him over the back of the chair. ''Give Gloria my job.'' She watched his eyes widen and his mouth open, and hurried on. ''She deserves it and she's damned good. If you don't give her the promotion, I'm going to find some way to use this little conversation to do you just as much harm as I can. You see, Ned.'' She smiled. ''I'm really not Sunday School material. And when it comes down to it, I can be just as aggressive and nasty as you.''

Outside, she flagged down a taxi and went back uptown to pick up the BMW. She wanted to go home.

At four that afternoon the telephone rang. Lynne jumped up to answer thinking it might be Ross, or John.

''Is that Lynne Craig?'' an unfamiliar voice asked.

''That's right.''

''This is Sergeant Leo Gold with the Twelfth Precinct. We've got you down here to call with regard to a missing persons report on Dianna Ferguson.''

"Have you found her?"

"We have a Jane Doe at Bellevue who matches the description. She may not be Mrs. Ferguson. Would you be willing to come in and make an identification?"

"Is she dead?"

"No, ma'am, but she's in critical condition."

"Of course I'll come. Where?"

She jotted down the information then snatched up her coat, bag, and keys and ran out to the car. It wasn't until she was on the turnpike going through the Greenwich toll that the words "critical condition" registered. What was she about to see? She hadn't thought to ask how the woman had come to be at Bellevue. She should have called Bob, but it was too late now. If it was Dianna, she'd call him from the hospital. Then he could call the girls.

Just before Pelham she looked into her rearview mirror to see a man in a brown car waving at her. It took her several seconds to realize he was a policeman in an unmarked car and that he was signaling her to pull over. She drove onto the shoulder and rolled down her window. The officer took his time getting out of his car and checking her license plate number before approaching.

"You were doing seventy-eight miles an hour, Miss. Could I see your driver's license and registration please?"

"Look, I just got a call from a Sergeant Gold of the Manhattan police, asking me to come to Bellevue right away to identify someone. She's on the critical list. And why the hell are you cruising the highway in an unmarked car? You're not even state police. You're what?" She glared at his badge, trying to read what it said. "Pelham? For God's sake! Is the town that desperate for money? There must've been a dozen cars that *passed* me in the inside *and* outside lanes and you have to pick me? I want your badge number," she cried, reaching for her purse to get something to write on. "I produce for a national TV show in New York that has thirty or forty million viewers. I'm sure they'd be fascinated to learn how local police have taken to the interstate highways to harass drivers."

Throughout this explosion, the expression on the officer's

face slowly altered from one of arrogant superiority to one of reluctance and doubt.

"Now, hold on just a minute," he began.

"Not *this* time!" she insisted, furious now. "You've held me up, cost me time. If that woman *dies*, I'll be coming after you with a lawsuit that'll put you out of business for good." With that, she checked the traffic, floored the accelerator and sailed back into the stream of traffic. She looked into the rearview mirror to see the policeman standing watching her. After a moment, he turned and walked back to his car. She kept checking to see if he was following, but he left the highway at the next exit.

She was directed to a ward where a nurse, upon hearing Lynne's explanation as to why she was there, showed her to a curtained-off bed at the far end. As they went along, the nurse whispered, "The officer went for coffee. He said if you came while he was gone, would you please wait."

Lynne nodded, unable to breathe deeply in this place. The illness-redolent air made her feel ill. The nurse pulled aside the curtain and waited while Lynne stepped forward to look at the woman on the bed. Lynne wanted badly to sit down. She pushed out through the curtains and left the ward for a waiting room a short distance down the hall. She sat and lowered her head to her knees, fighting nausea.

"Miss Craig?" a voice asked.

Without moving, she answered that she was.

"Are you all right?"

"I will be, in a minute."

"I'm Leo Gold."

She heard him sit down in the chair beside her.

"Is there anything I can get you?"

"No, thank you. I'll be all right."

"Take your time."

She heard him lighting a cigarette, and breathed in the smoke gladly; it disguised the death smell that still lingered in her nostrils.

"Is it Mrs. Ferguson?" he asked quietly.

"No." She straightened and turned to look at him. He appeared to be very young, John's age, with empathetic blue eyes and a prematurely aged expression. "What do we do now?" she asked.

"We keep looking." He tapped the ash from his cigarette into the ashtray on the table to his left.

"How hard are you going to try?" she asked, dry mouthed, skeptical.

"As hard as we're able. It's an easy city to get lost in."

"Dianna isn't someone who'd intentionally get lost."

"I'm sorry you had to go through this. The description did seem to fit. It's rarely ever as easy as that, though."

"Will I be called every time you find someone who fits Dianna's description?"

"Probably."

"Well," she sighed. "I suppose that's the only way you can do it."

"That's about the size of it," he said. "Think you'll be up to it?"

"I'm going to have to be. Her former husband isn't willing to do it."

"What about her kids? I read in the report she has two grown daughters."

"I don't even know yet if he's told them Dianna's missing." She looked around the stark, deserted waiting room. "I guess I'll go home."

"Might as well. We'll be in touch."

After telephoning Gloria at home to tell her of the false alarm, she left the hospital and made her way to the parking lot. She had to turn off the car radio; she found the cheery voice of the announcer irksome. In a cocoon of silence, she drove home.

John was sitting on the front steps when she arrived. She watched him get to his feet as she climbed out of the car. Gladdened as she was by the sight of him, she wished he hadn't come. She didn't feel like talking, and wondered if he planned on staying the evening.

He thought she looked tired, and there was an aura of anger about her. It was the first time he'd seen her look unattractive. Her face seemed closed, completely without animation; her eyes looked smaller, and there were smudges of darkness beneath them. He said, "Hi," and waited, trying to gauge her mood.

"I had to go into the city to identify a woman they thought might be Dianna."

"Is she missing?" he asked.

"Yes."

"Was it her?"

"No." She got the door open and turned to see he was still in the same spot on the steps. "Come in."

"I don't think you're in the mood for company," he said quietly. "I'll just head on home."

"Come in and we'll talk about it," she said.

She walked inside and slouched on the sofa, still in her coat. He sat in the rocker, careful not to disturb the books and notes stacked on the floor nearby.

"Would you like me to get you a drink?" he asked, sitting on the very edge of the chair. "You look as if you could use one."

"That would be wonderful."

"Scotch, right?"

"That's right."

"Ice? Water?"

"Just some ice, please."

He got ice from the refrigerator, dropped the cubes in a glass, then added a liberal amount of Scotch. After handing her the glass, he returned to perch on the edge of the rocker, asking, "What's happened?"

"Nobody knows. She just disappeared almost a week ago." She paused to take a sip of the drink. "This whole business is making me reevaluate my feelings, about a lot of things."

For a moment he felt afraid, unsure what she meant. He stared at her, suddenly seeing written in the wearied lines of her face an answer to the question he hadn't asked. Right then, seeing and listening to her, he knew that no matter how much he cared about her, no matter what he might do to convince her, they were not going forward into a shared future. There was a gulf between them that he couldn't possibly bridge. Disappointment filled him inside like something solid.

"So," he said, "where did you have to go?"

"Bellevue." She closed her eyes, again seeing the woman in the bed. A tall woman, who did indeed have red hair, but bore no resemblance to Dianna, she'd been hooked up to a battery of machines, all of them making noise of some sort, each monitoring some aspect of the woman's bodily functions. Tubes in her arms, in her throat, down her nose; needles and gauges and levers and pulleys, and a noxious odor. "The poor woman was dying," she said, opening her eyes, "and no one even knows who she is."

"Are you hungry?" he asked. "I could make something. You could relax, take a nap or a shower or something while I fixed some food."

"I think I'd prefer to spend the evening alone, if you wouldn't mind. It's sweet of you, but I'm just not up to talking; I wouldn't be fit company. It's been a dreadful week."

His feelings were hurt, she saw. It made her feel cruel. "Don't be hurt," she said benignly. "It has nothing to do with you. There's no one I'd want to see right now." Even as she said the words she knew it wasn't the truth; she could have seen Ross at that moment and he'd have understood perfectly. Without the application of any sort of pressure, he'd have been able to deal with her mood as well as with the situation. He wouldn't have placed her in a position where even the slightest decision had to be made. Rather than asking if he could do this or that for her, he'd simply do it, knowing the things that required doing.

"It's okay," he said, forcing a smile as he made his way to the door. "I'll call you . . . later."

"Thank you for offering, about the dinner." She kissed him lightly on the mouth then opened the door. His youth, his eagerness, his many desires—stated and unstated—constituted a major pressure. "Have you got your truck?" she remembered to ask. "Could I give you a ride home?"

"I'm parked just up the road. Take it easy and I'll call you." He went off down the steps and started up the road.

She closed the door and took off her coat, then stood staring tiredly into the living room. Why did he have to be so damned sensitive? Why did he have to take it personally?

She was worried and enervated; it had nothing to do with him, yet she knew he believed he was being rejected. It simply added to her fatigue knowing she had to cope with his sensitivity, his fear of rejection, as well as everything else. She went to the telephone.

"I just wanted you to know," she told Ross, "that nothing's changed. I had to make a trip in to Bellevue today, but it wasn't Dianna." She wasn't yet ready to tell anyone about her conversation with Ned, and her resignation.

"How are you?" he asked, sounding warm and concerned.

"Ready for a hot bath and oblivion." She laughed grimly.

"Then, go to it. I'll phone you tomorrow. Are you going in to the city?"

"I'm going to take some time off."

"Well, good. I'll talk to you in the morning."

She hung up and carried her drink with her into the bathroom where she got the bath filling. Then she sat on the side of the tub and sipped at her drink, feeling eased. Ross knew, he understood. It reduced her anxiety about John.

She dreamed she was standing under the shower when the curtain was suddenly pulled back and Ned was there, brandishing a knife. Before he had a chance to speak or move, her hand shot to the hot water faucet, she snatched the hand shower from its holder, and directed the spray of scalding water at him. The knife clattered on the tiles as he screamed, turning, and ran. Leaping from the tub, she ran after him, shrieking, and chased him out the rear door which she slammed shut and locked. She stood, wet and naked, panting, whispering, "Coward, coward, coward!"

❖ *Eighteen* ❖

JOHN SAT DOWN and tried to think of whom he could call. He wanted to be with someone, wanted not to be alone with his feelings. There had to be someone, he reasoned, he could call up and go see. There was his mother, but he was unwilling to run the risk of encountering his father—even if only on the telephone. There was Cathy, but even if he'd been willing to drive all the way over there, he wasn't sure he was up to the sight and sound of his sister, wafting through the house in something cleverly voluminous, to hide the weight she'd gained when pregnant with Luther seven years before, and hadn't managed to lose yet, discussing the latest diet she thought she might try, or some new nutty philosophy. Cathy seemed to have some sort of hotline that kept her informed of the newest cults and crazes. John thought she was looking for an answer, and hoped to find it in slim, soft-covered books published by obscure presses in California. While there were occasions when he was able, with amusement and tolerance, to sit and listen to Cathy expound on her readings, this wasn't one of them. Just the idea of seeing her hover by the stove as she prepared a pot of herbal tea while her listless voice made random dents in the air around her—speculative, lengthy streams of thought having to do with the problems of society and their likely solutions—made him feel logy.

There was always Lizzie but she was likely to misinterpret his call as a sign of a kind of attention he didn't want to pay her. He merely wanted to sit with someone in companionable silence, perhaps at a movie. He didn't want to have to consider the state of the world and the problems Negroes and women were having—to hear Lizzie, or Cathy, tell it, women were like a newly-emerging third-world nation—nor did he wish to hear Lizzie rattle on about her ambitions, her plans for the future.

He could always go downstairs, sit with Joe and Gina, have a couple of beers and some pizza. Joe, though, would want to talk; he'd ask about Lynne, and John wasn't up to that, either.

He'd made an ass of himself, pursuing a woman who obviously couldn't see him as anything more than someone too young. He wasn't young, though; he never had been. Maybe his life was delusional, his goals and ambitions unachievable. If Dianna had ever had a chance to ask him why he thought he had anything new or different to say, he'd have been unable to answer. His writing, his desire to write, was based on an interior, never-spoken conviction that he saw and heard things *differently*. The things he perceived seemed not to be the things other people he knew saw and heard, or if they did, paid no special attention to. Up until now he'd believed these were his tools, a part of his ability to recognize the commonplace and elevate it to a point of significance. Surely the small moments, the almost inconsequential seeming events shaped the world and the people in it? And if you pointed out these things, if you highlighted them in series to illustrate how truly consequential they were, didn't the very fact of your recognition of these elements place you on a separate plane? Could the truth be that he was deluded, like people who went religious and got saved?

He felt bereft, almost violated. He sat hugging his manuscript to his chest, his eyes scanning the walls, his thoughts coiled around this woman he'd touched and held and tasted. They'd shared something so privileged; they'd been naked together. He'd been allowed to see her without guard, to witness the arching, convulsive evidence of her passion. There was no part of her he hadn't seen and caressed. She had allowed him to join with her; she had voluntarily joined, juxtaposing her body to his in heat and secret silence. And now she no longer wanted him. She was actively denying the attraction, scalding and unavoidable, that existed between them. He wanted to scream, to beat his head and fists against the wall in protest.

He'd suffered through down periods before, but nothing as dark and tainted with injustice as this. The world as he knew it seemed all at once an ugly place, populated by people given to misjudging. He tried to imagine a place where he might escape to, without concern for anything but his writing, somewhere to live. He couldn't. He was rooted to this squalid apartment, to this little town and the few friends he had here. His knowledge, his understanding, the very core of his identity had all sprung from here. Nevertheless, he wished with everything in him he could just get into the truck with his few belongings and drive away to somewhere new, some place entirely free of anything that might have associations with Lynne.

He'd fallen in love with a woman who simply could not see him as he was, nor could she see what he was offering her, how eager he was to demonstrate in any way, every way, his love for her. There existed between them now an unsurmountable barrier constructed of her extreme reservations.

Well, he wouldn't go back. He'd leave her alone. He knew how she felt, knew she thought of herself as a kind of vampire, some not entirely human creature sucking the youth out of his veins. He didn't want anyone to feel that way, and he didn't want her to feel that way, in particular, about him.

Still, there ought to have been some way he could make her see that he knew how she felt, and that she was completely wrong. He felt defeated, wanting to believe his powers of persuasion—after all, words were supposedly his tools, his strength—were sufficiently strong to enlighten her to the error of her thinking; yet knowing that nothing he could possibly say or do or put down on paper in the form, say, of a letter would alter the situation. You couldn't force someone to change—not her personality or her thinking.

The desire had to come from the person herself. And who was he, he demanded of himself, to wish or hope or think that anyone would find him so worthy and inspirational that she'd seek to change in order to evolve a more perfect relationship? Why should she do that? What right did he have even to consider attempting to alter her attitude? He had no rights, and no power. Increasingly depressed, he could do no more than admit that he was going to have to learn to live with this failure, this loss.

Well, he'd learn. He could do that. But he knew he'd never again feel about any woman the way he felt about Lynne. It would be impossible to duplicate the galvanizing pleasure he'd derived simply from the touch of her hand.

"Let's go for a walk on the beach," Ross suggested. "It's the perfect day for it. Unless you were planning to go into the city."

"I can go in later this afternoon. I only want to check the mail . . . I really don't have to go in at all, but it's been a few days, and until Dianna turns up, I can't help feeling I should. I'd love to go for a walk." They'd been talking daily on the telephone, but it had been close to a week since she'd seen him. It would be good to be with him.

"I'll pick you up in half an hour," he said, and hung up.

"I like the beach in winter," he said, gazing out at the horizon. The Sound waters were choppy today, a harsh white-gray. "It fits in with a melancholy mood I get every so often."

"I know," she said. "My first winter in the cottage I spent hours sitting on a bench at Pear Tree Point. I'd sit there staring at the water until my ears ached and the last of the dog-walkers had gone. Then I'd go home and sit in the living room staring at the walls. Nothing made very much sense."

"And that's changed?"

"Not much. The more I think I understand, the less I realize I know."

She could see the sailor in Ross today. He wore a pair of

baggy, wide-wale gray cords, and a navy pea jacket. He kept his hands jammed deep into his jacket pockets as they walked. Regularly he turned to look out at the water, his profile strong and thoughtful. She could readily picture him at the wheel of a boat, keeping watch on the skyline. Ross seemed, even at his most relaxed moments, to be in control. But no one, she reasoned, could enjoy exercising a constant vigilance, being always in control.

"D'you have moments when you wish someone else would hold the world for you?" she asked.

"Frequently," he answered without hesitation. "It's funny, but there are a lot of things they never tell you—whoever 'they' are. They never tell you that having kids means you're a parent for twenty-four hours a day, seven days a week, for the rest of your life. They never tell you that someone you love will die and leave you to try to understand why. They never tell you you'll get fed up with things, with your career, with being the provider, the one everybody depends on. They never tell you you'll change, you'll lose interest, you'll want something different from what you have.

"When I was a kid, I was taught to understand that I was going to have to grow up to become *responsible*. And that's the way I did it. I never minded. Not really. It was the way things were meant to be. But since Ella died, I've started minding about all kinds of things. There are times when I'd like someone else to field the calls, to deal with the movers and shakers—those self-important pains in the ass who think their sweat smells like perfume . . . I don't know. It's a luxury most men can't afford. If I don't do the job, it won't get done. Or some young eager beaver will sneak up on me and not only do the job but do it better."

"The curse of competent people," she said, "is that less competent people depend on them."

"You're competent," he observed.

"Would you change it at all?"

"Nope. Most of it I actually like. Would you change?"

"I don't know," she answered. "I'm thinking about it."

He withdrew one hand from his pocket and took hold of her hand. "D'you really have to go into the city today?"

"Not really, but I will. I'm putting in my time."

"You don't seem all that pleased about it."

"I don't know anymore how I feel." She told him of the meeting with Keith, and then about the one with Ned, carefully omitting mention of her resignation.

"Typical," he said, when she'd finished.

"That's all?" she asked. "Just typical?"

"It's the way things get done."

"You don't like it any more than I do," she said.

"That's why I'm getting out. Are you upset about having to cancel your segment?"

"Two years ago, I'd have been heartbroken. Now . . ." She shrugged and looked down at the wet sand. "It just makes me tired," she said, absorbing the feel of his hand around hers. "I think even just a couple of months ago the whole business would have upset me."

"What changes that now?"

"I'm not sure." What changed everything, she thought, was the knowledge that she was able to talk about it to this man who could, effortlessly, put things into perspective for her. But he'd soon be leaving. Reminding herself of this she felt suddenly unsteady.

"Are you interested in lunch?" he asked. "There's a nice little place in Greenwich."

She wondered if he'd again ask her to go with him to Florida. Until this moment she hadn't realized how important that invitation was. It represented an alternative, an option she might exercise.

As if reading her thoughts, he tugged on her hand and, with a grin, said, "I'm starting to freeze. Let's have lunch and I'll work some more at persuading you to come to West Palm with me."

"I'll let you do that." She returned his smile.

"It passes the time," he said lightly. "I'm not giving up yet."

"Good," she said. "Don't."

"Am I making a dent?"

"I don't know. But I like being asked."

When Lynne arrived at the office, Ned's secretary came hurrying in to say, "He's been trying to reach you. He wants to talk to you."

"Dianna?" Lynne asked her.

"Haven't heard a thing."

"Okay, thanks. I'll be along in a minute."

The Ned who sat behind his desk bore no relationship to the Ned who'd met her last week in the restaurant. She knew at once from his demeanor and the way he fussed with several thick files on his desk that his brief lapse had ended. He selected a file and held it out to her.

"Have a look at the research and tell me what you think of this," he told her.

"I'll take it home tonight." She turned to go. He called her back.

"Close the door for a minute and sit down."

She did as he asked.

"About the other day," he began. "I'd appreciate it . . ."

"I'm not going to tell anyone about you and Dianna," she interrupted.

"Thanks. I'd appreciate that." He crossed his arms over his chest and tilted back his chair. He studied her assessingly and she found herself becoming annoyed.

"Is there something else you want to talk about?" she asked.

"I've decided not to take you up on what you said."

"Meaning what?"

"I want you to renew. And I'm not about to push Gloria up into your slot. She can't cut it."

This was unexpected. She sat back in the chair and crossed her legs, opening her bag for a cigarette. "Are you, by any chance, saying I'm too good to lose?"

He shrugged. "If you want to take it that way."

"Why the sudden change of heart? A week ago, I was only qualified for teaching Sunday School."

"A week ago, I didn't know you could go nine rounds."

He brought his chair upright and folded his arms on the desk, leaning toward her. "I've talked to Keith. They're willing to negotiate a new contract. I've got something in mind."

"What?"

"I'd like to try you in Dianna's spot."

"You're out of your mind!" she declared. "I don't want it."

"You'd do a damned good job. You're sharp, and you're a good-looking woman. People like you."

"What do my looks have to do with anything?" she wanted to know. "I'm not an on-camera person. I'm a producer, for God's sake."

"You'd get a hell of a lot more attention."

"I don't *want* attention. Why are you doing this?"

"Because I know what sells."

"I am not for sale."

"I know," he said, all seriousness. "That's what I like about you."

She couldn't keep up with the changes he seemed capable of making. Like the shifting of negatives in a developing pan, he seemed to emerge in a different form with each slight alteration of light.

"You ought to think about it," he said.

"I have no intention of thinking about it. And what about Dianna?"

"Dianna will be taken care of."

"How?"

"It'll be taken care of."

She remembered the file on her lap and looked down at it. "Do you really want me to have a look at this?"

"Are you going to renew?"

"As what?" she asked hotly.

"Whatever. If you're smart, you'll make the swing over."

"I guess I'm not very smart. I don't want any of it." She placed the file on the corner of his desk and walked to the door. "Your 'love,'" she said, "is a fairly frightening thing, if what you're doing to Dianna is any indication."

"You don't *know* my plans for Dianna," he argued.

"I don't want to know. Everything still stands. And that includes what I said about Gloria." She turned and left.

Back in her own office, with a cup of coffee she'd stopped for along the way, she looked out the window, watching the sky go dark, and wondered why she was there. There was nothing to be accomplished. She drank the coffee and smoked a cigarette, thinking things through. It surprised her to think that so much had happened that it felt as if months had passed since her first official date with Ross. It had only been about five weeks. In just over a month changes of a radical nature had taken place. And where was Dianna?

Below, the streets were thick with traffic. The lights in buildings all around looked deceptively warm. The taxis and buses and automobiles moved up the avenue; endless pairs of lights, red and white, traveled along the rutted pavement: people going home. It was time, she decided, to go home herself.

She'd managed to miss the early rush. As she walked through the underground garage, she felt a pang about John. She'd sent him away that night, and he'd taken it badly, completely misunderstanding her mood and her needs. He hadn't called for days now. God! Why had she ever given in to her impulse to touch him? Never had she had an equivalent desire to hold and caress someone, to impale herself on a pinnacle of flesh and allow the pleasure inherent in that act to obliviate every other consideration. The net result was that she'd done damage, something it had never been her intention to do.

She was about to open the car door when she heard footsteps running, echoing noisily. Was something at last about to happen to her down here in this damp, eerie place? She fumbled to get the key into the car lock, frightened. The footsteps rushed closer and she whirled about, prepared, if she had to, to use the keys—quickly thrust between the fingers of her right hand—as a weapon.

It was Gloria. "Thank God I caught you." She huffed, coming to a halt with her hand on the fender of Lynne's car as she caught her breath. "That Sergeant Gold called again. He thinks this time it's Dianna. I told him I'd come with you."

"Where?" Lynne tried to breathe deeply, waiting for the fearful rattling in her chest to subside.

"Bellevue." Gloria fanned herself with her hand. "I'm so out of condition," she complained "Can't even run a block."

"Bellevue again," Lynne said, removing the keys from between her fingers. They had left deep red impressions on her flesh.

"Again?" Gloria looked confused. "Is that where you went last time?"

"The whole hospital must be filled with unidentified people."

"They send everybody there," Gloria wheezed, pressing her hand against her chest. "I think I'm having a heart attack."

"You're too young," Lynne said, getting the car door open finally.

"Not according to Lon. According to him, I'm a prime candidate. I'm hypertensive, overweight, and overemotional. He thinks it's just a matter of time. He'll probably cash in my insurance and marry some skinny kid with big tits."

Lynne thought of that red-haired woman and the intimidating tubes and wires and machines, and the death smell thick in the air all around her. How many times, she wondered, would she have to travel downtown to this hospital to study the ravaged faces of women who might be Dianna? How many more times would she be able to do it? Not many, she thought.

"Are you okay?" she asked Gloria.

"I'm okay."

The two of them got in the car. Without bothering to wait for the engine to warm—Alec's voice a nagging intrusion on the urgency she felt—she shifted into first and drove toward the exit ramp. The double-width door lumbered upward, and then they were out on the street.

"Is this one alive or dead?" Lynne asked nervously, her previous trip to the hospital still too fresh in her mind.

"Alive."

"What did he tell you?"

"He said that this woman had a stroke on the street. Naturally, everybody thought she was drunk, so she was ignored. Finally, someone had the wits and courage to check and see that she was ill. By that time, according to the Sergeant, she'd been picked clean, handbag, coat, the whole thing. So she had no I.D. Anyway, they took her to Bellevue and she had a heart attack while they were examining her in the emergency room."

"My God!" Lynne said softly. "Is she critical?"

"We don't know for sure it's Dianna."

"It is. I know it."

Gloria stared at her, then looked at Lynne's hands on the steering wheel.

"Where are your rings?" she asked.

Lynne glanced down at her hands. "I must've forgotten to put them on when I left the house this morning."

"Oh!"

"Nothing symbolic." Lynne smiled over at her.

"You look a little funny, kind of green around the mouth."

"I'm tired."

"I'm not surprised. Boy! This is some creepy neighborhood."

"It's not beautiful, is it," Lynne agreed. "I'm glad you could come with me. Did you call Lon?"

"Didn't have time. I thought I'd call from the hospital. You know something?"

"What?"

"I hope it is Dianna. I mean, she's always given me a rough time, and she can be the world's biggest bitch when she wants to be, which is most of the time, but I don't want her dead. I'm sort of used to her. And in a funny way, I even kind of like her. You really like her, don't you?"

"I really do," Lynne responded.

"Maybe she's different with you," Gloria said generously.

Leo Gold was waiting for them in the lobby. Lynne introduced Gloria and then they started toward the Coronary Care Unit.

"I'm afraid you won't be able to come in," Gold told Gloria.

"Oh, that's okay. I don't really want to. I'll wait out here and call home."

Filled with dread, Lynne allowed the sergeant to take her by the arm and direct her silently through the unit.

"I hope this is the last time you've got to go through this," he said in a whisper. "I know it's rough."

Unable to speak, Lynne nodded. Her heart was thudding slowly, heavily.

"Over here," he said, and Lynne turned, her heart giving a massive leap as she broke away from him to hurry toward the bed.

"Dianna!" she cried.

Tactfully, Gold kept his distance, watching as Lynne put out her hand to stroke the wildly disheveled hair framing the woman's face. After a moment he turned and left the unit, in search of Gloria.

Trembling with relief and shock, Lynne watched Dianna's head turn toward her. A grimace twisted her face and she lifted her hand. Lynne took hold of her hand, and tried to smile. Dianna uttered some unintelligible sounds, and Lynne was horrified to realize that not only was the grimace intended to be a smile but that Dianna couldn't speak coherently. The impact hit her in the pit of her stomach and in her knees. She looked around, spotted a chair, and pulled it over beside the bed.

"It's going to be all right," she said, again taking firm hold of Dianna's cold hand. "I'll stay with you now."

❖ *Nineteen* ❖

SERGEANT GOLD GAVE Gloria a lift back to the office to pick up her car. Lynne remained beside Dianna's bed. She had to struggle not to cry. Dianna seemed so old, her face and body ravaged by her illness. Gray showed at the roots of her tangled hair, and no one had bothered to clean her face so her eyes were black-rimmed with mascara, and the rouge she'd applied more than a week before sat blotchy and surprising upon her cheeks. On her wrist was an identification bracelet with the name "Jane Doe." After staring at the bracelet for quite some time, Lynne carefully removed it, withdrew the slip of paper and printed Dianna's name on the back. Then she replaced the bracelet, feeling better.

Throughout all this, Dianna's eyes followed her every movement.

"I couldn't stand that another moment," Lynne told her. "I've put your name on it."

Dianna lowered her eyelids to signify she understood.

Lynne leaned in closer, still holding Dianna's hand tightly to say, "I've always been your friend; I've always cared. D'you remember that day you called me up and said 'Come to lunch'? We went out and at one point I looked at you and I thought, She really cares. It wasn't what you said that made the difference, Dianna; it was the fact that you cared that got through to me. Up until that time I thought you simply suffered me, that I was a competent annoyance you had no choice but to contend with. But that day at lunch, when I sat and watched you toss off those two double

Scotches." Lynne smiled. "I knew you were involved, whether you wanted to be or not. I've always appreciated the effort you made, always liked you."

Bob was wrong, Dianna thought, suddenly understanding the remark he'd made in the doorway as he was leaving seventeen years earlier. It wasn't that she couldn't come out, but rather that other people failed to *see*. Lynne had seen, though, and she'd recognized the caring, even if it was ineptly handled. She tried to tell Lynne some of this, but the sound of her own garbled, meaningless words frustrated and maddened her. She turned her head away, ashamed to have Lynne see her weeping, and in this place.

Lynne sat until her back was aching and Dianna's hoarse, guttural attempts at speech tapered off and she fell into a deathlike sleep. It was almost three A.M. Lynne stood up and slowly walked out of the unit. There was a ladies' room down the hall and she pushed inside, the bright lights near-blinding after the dimness of the unit. All at once the last of her energy drained away and she leaned against the wall feeling sick. Letting her handbag drop, she sat down on the floor and bent her head to her knees, breathing deeply and slowly, until the nausea receded. She sat for several minutes longer, then got up and went to the row of sinks to wash her hands and face. She straightened her clothing, ran her hand over her hair, lit a cigarette, and went out into the corridor in search of a telephone.

She didn't give Bob Ferguson a chance to say anything more than hello.

"We've found Dianna," she told him. "She's had a stroke as well as a heart attack. She's in very bad shape. They let me stay with her. Look," she said impatiently, "I don't care what kind of problems she's given you in the past. She needs help now. I've been here for hours and I've got to go home and get some sleep. Will you *please* come down here and stay with her just for a little while? I think you should be the one to call Trudy and Tricia, and Ned, too. God! I don't mean to sound this way. . . . The thing of it is . . ." She had to stop and swallow back tears. "The thing is," she began again, "she can't *talk*. The stroke affected her speech."

"Oh, Jesus!" He sounded genuinely upset. "What time is it?"

"Just after three. I know you don't want to be involved . . ."

"Listen, it's all right. I'll be down in half an hour. Will you be there?"

"I'm sorry. I've got to go home. I'm exhausted and I honestly don't feel very well."

"Don't worry about it. Give me a number where I can reach you later."

She gave him the Connecticut number, then said, "She looks so . . . I just want to warn you."

"I'm on my way."

"Thank you," she said gratefully.

"No, thank *you*. I know I've been a bastard, but I honestly had no idea . . . I'll check with you later."

She hung up and went out to the car. It was a dark, moonless night, and very cold. She was too tired even to be afraid of finding herself out on the street alone. She got the car started and sat waiting for it to warm up, trying to deal with the feeling she had that although Dianna was still alive, to all intents and purposes she was dead. What would Dianna do? How would she live? She couldn't even make herself understood. The grief Lynne felt was overpowering. She pictured Dianna lying on the street while scavengers stripped her of her handbag and coat, leaving her to die. She felt a murderous rage.

"God damn it!" she cried, pounding her fist on the steering wheel. "Damn it!"

She lit a fresh cigarette and started driving.

The house was dark. She got out of the car and walked, on shaky legs, to the front door. She rang the bell and waited, hoping it would be Ross and not Mrs. Wain who came to the door. It was Mrs. Wain.

"I've got to see Ross," Lynne said.

"Come in, come in," Mrs. Wain urged, positive Lynne had been in some sort of accident. Her face was bloodless, her eyes stark. "I'll go wake him."

"No, don't!" Lynne said quickly. "I'll go up."

"I could make some coffee."

"Please, go back to bed. I'm terribly sorry to get you up."

To her great surprise, the small woman put her arms around Lynne and gave her a hug. "There now," she crooned. "Whatever it is, it'll get taken care of."

"Thank you," Lynne said thickly, and made her way toward the stairs.

She opened the door, able to make out Ross's outline in the bed. On tiptoe, she went across the room and, still in her coat, lay down beside him. She breathed in the fragrance of his aftershave; the smooth regularity of his breathing was almost as comforting as the weight of his arms would have been. She placed her cold hand on his cheek and he started.

"It's me," she whispered. "I didn't mean to frighten you."

His arm came around her as he tried to wake up.

"We found Dianna," she explained.

He twisted around to look at the dial on the illuminated bedside clock. "You've been up half the night," he said, turning back to her. "Your hands are freezing. Did you just get back from the city?"

"Could I just lie here?" she asked. "I didn't want to go home."

"At least take off your coat and get under the blankets."

"I don't want to move."

"I can put you to bed in one of the boys' rooms."

"Don't get up." She stayed him with her hand. "I don't want to go anywhere. She had a stroke and a massive heart attack. She looked so dreadful, Ross, and she can't speak. I wanted to do something for her and there was nothing I could do. I sat there for hours, holding her hand, telling her everything was going to be all right. But it isn't going to be all right."

"What can I do for *you*?" he asked.

"I don't know. I'm getting used to you, Ross. I'm starting to count on you being here."

"Is that bad?"

"It feels as if it might be, and I don't know why I feel that way. You haven't done anything to make me feel that way."

"I like it that you come here," he said inadequately. "Most nights I'm hoping you'll show up."

"Why?"

"It pleases me that of all the places you could go, you choose to come here, to me. It means something."

"I don't have many places to go," she disagreed.

"There's Amy."

"Amy can't make love to me. Amy can't fill the gaps, or understand the things you can."

"But we . . . It wasn't good."

"It was me, not you. I suddenly realized, looking at you, then looking at myself in your mirror, that I wasn't young anymore, and it frightened me." Her eyes had become accustomed to the dark now and she could see him more clearly. She moved a little closer to him. "I didn't want to admit to myself that I was middle-aged, not when I didn't feel that way inside, even though I've never had any problem saying the years out loud, in words." She paused, then said, "I've been seeing someone else, as well as you."

"I know. I saw him."

"You *saw* him?"

"That night I dropped you off. I saw him sitting on the porch, waiting for you."

"But what did you think? Why didn't you say anything?"

"I didn't think anything, if you want to know the truth. Maybe I've lost my pride or something. Whatever. I saw him and thought, Well, she's a beautiful woman. Why wouldn't she have other men interested in her?"

"He's very young."

"I thought he was."

"I made love with him."

"What do you want me to say to that, Lynne? I don't own you. I don't even have a lease on you." He laughed softly. "Sorry," he apologized. "I realize it's not the time for jokes."

"Maybe it is. I never again want to go through anything like these past weeks."

"Let me take your coat off," he said, sitting up.

"Please don't put the light on. It hurts my eyes."

He reached over in the dark, undid the buttons and got her coat off. Then he pulled off her shoes and sat on his haunches chafing her feet as he had her hands. "You're like ice," he said, briskly kneading her feet. "Are you . . . involved with him?"

"You look very nice in your pajamas, very nice. I can't be involved with him. I'm too old. It isn't fair to him."

"But you want to be. You're in love with him."

"I may be in love with you."

"You can't force it."

"I'm not forcing it. Your Mrs. Wain was so kind when I came to the door. Oh, hell!" Tears filled her eyes. She went silent, her chest heaving.

He lay down and gathered her into his arms. "You're too damned honest," he said, tenderly stroking her back. "You didn't have to tell me any of that. I don't mind especially that you did. I think it makes me like you more. But don't get yourself so worked up. *Are* you in love with him, Lynne?"

She shook her head. "It was probably tactless of me to tell you, but I hated having the feeling that I was sneaking back and forth between the two of you. Make love to me, Ross."

"You're worn out," he said solicitously.

"I'm exhausted and wide awake. Hasn't that ever happened to you?"

"More times than I care to count."

"Then you understand." She touched his face with her newly-warmed hands. Her fingers found his lips. He caught hold of her hand and kissed her fingertips. "It means more and more to me, that you understand." She drew in her breath, pressing closer to him. "I'm choosing you, Ross. While I was driving up here, I was trying to think of what I could possibly do for Dianna, and I think I've got an idea. I'm going to give her my house to live in. It's paid for. She could stay there and go to Stamford or Norwalk for therapy or whatever would have to be done. I'm sure she's got some savings. I want to do something for her."

"And what about you? Where will you live?"

"With you. I'll go with you."

"What about your career? Have you thought this through?"

"I've had enough. I can't take any more. It doesn't mean enough to me; it's not worth the infighting, the plotting; being used by one man to try to oust some other man. My reasons aren't any different from yours. No different at all. Is the invitation still good?"

"Absolutely."

"Then I accept. Make love to me." She kissed him, then slipped off the bed to undress. Cold, she slid beneath the bedclothes and waited while he removed his pajamas. When his warm body came close to her, she wound her arms around him, kissing him again, familiar now with the shape and feel of his mouth, secure in that familiarity.

She was immediately so totally involved in sensation that she was able to ignore the mechanics and allow herself to feel. In her heightened awareness, she responded to the gentle insistence of his hands and mouth, to the warm resiliency of his skin, to the swelling of his flesh against hers.

He wondered briefly if he shouldn't feel angry or upset after all at her disclosures, but the truth was he didn't care. This was no clumsy, accidental encounter like the first time. This time she was here because she chose to be, because she wanted him. He caressed her breasts, putting his mouth to her nipples; he drew his fingers down the length of her arms, across the soft mound of her belly. He explored the satiny sleekness of her inner thighs, elated to find her wet. Her legs parted readily and he bent to put his mouth to her, feeling her responses under his hands. She quivered, her head arching back and for a moment he gazed at her taut body, awed by her receptiveness.

"I love that," she told him. It was something that Alec had rarely done for her, something he'd only do when he'd had a lot to drink. "I love it," she said, spreading herself until the tendons in her thighs threatened to snap, "love it."

She had to stop him finally. "I want to wait. Come here, come up here," she murmured, reaching for him. He sucked in his breath, galvanized with pleasure as she ran her tongue down his thigh while her hand, and then her mouth, encircled him.

"You taste very sweet," she whispered drunkenly, as he sat in the center of the bed and she lowered herself into his lap. She locked him to her with her arms and legs, her mouth against his. His hands cupping her buttocks, they rocked slowly, strands of her hair caught in their mouths.

"I don't give a damn about anything else," he said, his hands directing her. "If you'll come with me, it's all I want."

"Ssshhh," she whispered, covering his mouth with her hand. "There's something more I have to tell you. It may change your mind."

"Nothing's going to change my mind," he insisted.

"This might. It's most likely the worst time in the world to pick to tell you, but I feel so close to you right now. I'm going to come. Please don't move for a minute. Just stay still; wait for me." She drew her hands up and down his broad back. "I might be wrong. I might be. It's possible I'm overwrought and imagining things.

"Alec never wanted children. I used to think I did. There were all sorts of things I used to think I wanted that Alec didn't want. He killed himself."

"I know that."

"How do you know that?"

"Tell me whatever it is, then I'll make my confession." He lowered his head to kiss her shoulder, then rested his cheek briefly against her arm before straightening. "You're so tight. Like a young girl. You feel wonderful."

"God! Please don't move. I feel as if my skin's going to split and I'll come pouring out. He killed himself and I was so ashamed. Somehow it felt like my fault. I know it wasn't, but I couldn't help feeling that way, that something in me was to blame. It's only been in the past few months that I've started to stop feeling that way. Alec, Alec. What I want to say . . . I never even thought about it, about taking some sort of precautions. Alec was the one to do it. I never liked it. There was always that moment when he stopped and put it on and it would be ruined for me every time. I

hated the feel of it, hated having to stop for that. He insisted
it was his responsibility to protect me, and I accepted that. It
wasn't the truth, though, Ross.

"I used to dream I was pregnant, huge with it, bursting. I
gave birth so many times in my dreams. It was quite pain-
less. I was so immense; I simply split open at the vagina and
there was a child. I was so happy in those dreams. Amy's
forever telling me I would have made a good mother. It's
like a perpetual accusation, as if I failed as a woman because Alec didn't want children and I went along with that.
Now I'm forty. In a few months I'll be forty-one. God! I'm
stalling, talking all around it."

"You think you're pregnant," he guessed.

"It's far too soon, I know. But I forgot, you see. With
you, and then—I'm sorry—with John. I simply, honestly
didn't think about it. All those years, seventeen years with
Alec, I never had to think about it. He was the only man I'd
ever slept with, and it wasn't until the last year or so before
he died that I enjoyed it at all. People would say I was
simpleminded or something, that I'm too intelligent to forget something so important. But none of it was planned, not
with you and not with John. Now I think I'm pregnant. I've
been feeling so ill the past few days. Maybe it's all this
business about Dianna and my being so worried about her,
wondering what could have happened to her. I haven't been
sleeping . . ."

"It doesn't matter . . ."

"No, wait. I thought about so many things, driving
home. I thought about giving Dianna the house, making
sure she was all right. And then I had to consider being
pregnant, what it would mean. If I am, I don't know whose
baby it is. I've got enough money for a while, and I'll still
own the cottage, just in case I want to come back someday.

"I'm so damned *old* to be having a baby. So many things
could go wrong; it's very risky. But I'd like to have one. If
I'm not pregnant, I'm going to be so damned disappointed.
I wouldn't care what people thought, not about that. I'd care
what they thought of me being with John, my being so
much older. But having a baby, I wouldn't give a damn

what people had to say about that. I don't know what else
there is. You're a parent, a father, surely you understand
that.''

"Of course I do.''

"How,'' she remembered to ask, "did you know about
Alec?''

"This is where the score gets evened out. I had you
investigated. I'm sorry, but I did.''

"Why, though? Did you think I was some kind of industrial spy or something?''

"It was the last straw,'' he said, "the last stinking straw.
Here was someone I was interested in and what was the first
thing I did? I had Brad, my assistant, run the standard
check. It disgusted me. Your file was one of the ones I was
burning the other night when you came by. Does that upset
you?''

"It's the confessional hour of the morning,'' she said,
easing back with him so that she now lay atop him. "I don't
care about it. Screw it! I'm so stupefied I can hardly think.
Let's see how we look to one another in a few hours' time. I
can't talk anymore. I'm going to come. I'm not ready . . .''
She went rigid and he moved beneath her, holding her as
tremors shook her body and left her liquidly pliant.

After a minute or so, she resumed the ride, wanting him
to know an equal pleasure. There was a moment when she
felt him draw back into himself, a moment of inner stillness
they shared when she knew they had finally, importantly,
made contact.

❖ *Twenty* ❖

"I KNOW WHY you're calling."

"Do you?" she asked. "Why am I calling?"

"You've decided we shouldn't see each other anymore."

"I thought you might like to come over so we could talk."

"Talk about not seeing each other anymore," he said.

"There are things I'd like to explain. . . . John, this really isn't a conversation we should be having on the telephone."

"Sure it is," he said. "I understand."

"I'm not at all convinced of that."

"I *do*," he insisted. "You've made a totally unilateral decision. I don't have any part in it. It's okay, though. I really do understand."

How could he, she wondered when she wasn't at all sure she did? "Come have coffee, and let's talk about this. I don't like the idea of leaving it this way."

"*You* don't understand," he said, betraying emotion for the first time. "I can't do that. I don't want to come over there. I'm not judging you. I don't blame you. I'd probably do the same thing if our positions were reversed. But they're not reversed and I don't want to sit and pretend I agree with you. If there was some way I could change what's happening, change your mind, I'd do it. But I can't. How can I? You've made up your mind, and nothing I can say or do will change it."

He was right, she thought. She was merely attempting to

273

extend a courtesy, and it was something he neither wanted nor needed.

"I'm sorry," she said sadly. "I don't know if you'll believe me, but I am truly sorry. It was never my intention . . ."

"I believe you," he cut in. "Are you going to marry him?"

"I'm moving to Florida."

"Are you going to get married?"

"I don't know. . . . Yes, probably."

All his prior restraint seemed to dissolve suddenly and he asked, "Why?" in a tone filled with pain and confusion. "*Why*?"

"I can't answer that," she said in a low voice. "It wouldn't be fair to either of you."

"You don't love him. You love me. I know you do. You do!"

"John, please don't force me to a point where I have to say things that you'll find hurtful."

"You'd be lying!" he accused. "I know the truth. Well, listen," he paused to clear his throat, regretting his outburst. "I hope it all works out. I've got to go now. Joe's waiting for me to deliver some pizza. Thanks a lot for calling." The connection was broken.

She sat trying to think if there might have been some other way she could have done it, but couldn't think of any. She'd been truthful; she'd dealt honestly with him. She did wish, though, that he'd allowed her to explain in person. She was sure the entire exchange could have been accomplished far more gracefully, and with a more successful understanding on both sides. She felt guilty.

She got up and went for her coat, deciding that perhaps he'd been right after all not to come there. The two of them in one small place was potentially dangerous. Desires had a way of getting out of hand; instincts better left undiscovered had a way of surging to the surface.

Dianna looked worse. Daily she seemed to shrink, and despite the fact that the therapist had had some success and

Dianna was now able to make herself understood a bit, she didn't seem to be progressing as she should have. She held out her hand eagerly, curling her fingers tightly around Lynne's hand. Lynne sat in the chair beside the bed and unbuttoned her coat, trying for the smile she usually maintained here. It didn't want to come. She started to tell Dianna about her plans, and she felt distinctly as if she were about to abandon this helpless woman.

Dianna, however, seemed glad and squeezed Lynne's hand several times, nodding her head to indicate her approval.

Lynne sighed and said, "I'm glad you understand. I won't be going for a month or so. By then you'll be out of here." She looked around the stark hospital room into which Dianna had been moved the previous week. "Will you please think about my offer?"

I wish I could speak, or even write, Dianna thought, miserably frustrated. So many things she might have said to this woman, her friend. A hundred things, a thousand things. She might have said: I'll never leave this room, and I don't care anymore whether or not I do. But you, I'm happy about you. Go live in Florida with your man, he sounds like a decent guy; he'd better be good to you. You deserve someone to be good to you.

They sat silently, holding hands, each of them wishing Dianna could speak. Lynne had gone the day before to visit her gynecologist in Greenwich, a bluff, hearty man who'd processed her like a chicken inspector. She'd dutifully spread herself on the examining table, her heels in the cold metal stirrups, and stared up at the mobile dangling overhead while he'd checked her inside and out. Closing her mind to the sudden discomfort—how was it she managed every time to forget the pain of having a speculum expand inside her?—she'd concentrated on the reason for this visit. She'd come away from his overcrowded office with gooey underwear and a prescription in her bag for antinausea tablets, a sample bottle of multiple vitamin tablets, and a sense of jubilation. All the tests had been positive.

Now she debated telling Dianna this final bit of news.

"I want to tell you something," she said, stroking the back of Dianna's hand. She searched Dianna's eyes—alert and inquisitive—and smiled finally as she'd been unable to do at the outset of this visit. "I'm going to have a baby. Only Ross and Amy know. But I wanted to tell you. I'm so . . . When I'm sixty, this child will be nineteen. It's a little scary, but I want to do it. I'm happy about it. I don't . . ." She had to stop, wet her lips, and start again. "I don't know whose baby it is." She took a deep breath and studied Dianna's face, awaiting a reaction. Dianna's eyes slid away, her eyelids slowly lowered. After a moment, she opened her eyes again and gave Lynne's hand another squeeze.

"I wish to God we could talk," Lynne said fervently. "All these years and we've never talked the way we should have, the way I should have. It's as much my fault as anyone's.

"I know about Ned. He told me. He claims he wants to marry you."

Dianna emitted a sound that could only be interpreted as laughter.

"That's what I thought," Lynne said. "It's what I told him."

"Good!" Dianna got out distinctly.

"Get better!" Lynne spoke emphatically. "These one-sided conversations are murder."

Dianna nodded in agreement, still trying to decide how she felt about Lynne's announcement of her pregnancy. "If it makes you happy," she tried to say, "I'm happy for you." She could tell Lynne didn't understand what she was attempting to say. Her frustration rushed back and she freed her hand impatiently to describe an arc in the air over her own belly, nodding her approval.

Weakened by this small effort, Dianna returned her hand to Lynne's and closed her eyes. Lynne sat on at the bedside waiting until her friend would be sufficiently restored in strength to continue their odd, lopsided conversation.

It was a cold day, but very sunny. The sun glinted off ice-bound trees; the silence was broken only by the occasional snàp and tinkle as a cone of ice fell to the ground, and the creak of sagging overhead wires weighted by ice. The fir trees nearby swayed slowly, turning with the wind. The minister's voice was very low, solemn.

There were perhaps thirty people all told. Lynne turned to look at Gloria who was gazing downward, a tissue in her gloved fist held against her nose. Ned, looking distraught, stood a polite distance from Keith who held his hands clasped in front of him, listening intently to the minister's words. Half a dozen others from the office were present— Harvey and Mort, Don and Frank. Gus was there. So were Bob Ferguson and his two daughters, Tricia and Trudy. Tricia, the elder, looked so much like Dianna that Lynne's eyes were repeatedly drawn to her. She was very tall, with long, lustrous red hair, pale freckled skin, and angry green eyes. Unlike her mother, who'd lived trying to draw attention away from her height, Tricia flaunted it, wearing boots with heels that were at least four inches high. The younger sister, Trudy, was small and dark and strongly resembled her father, with light brown hair, deeply set gray eyes, and tiny, childlike features. The two girls stood slightly apart from their father who stared at the coffin fixedly. From moment to moment Tricia tossed her hair back over her shoulders with a disdainful twist of her head. Each time, Trudy glanced over with an expression that plainly stated her dislike for her older sister.

Bob Ferguson looked at Lynne, nodded in recognition— they'd encountered each other several times at the hospital—then turned toward his older daughter who'd yet again tossed back her vivid hair. Lynne looked at the others assembled. She failed to recognize half the people, and wondered who they were. It didn't really matter.

The brief service at the funeral chapel had been critically overattended. The chapel had been completely filled and the overflow had spilled into the foyer and up the stairs; people had been packed tightly right to the door. Lynne had found a seat at the rear of the foyer and had sat studying the faces of those assembled while she'd strained to hear the eulogies. She'd had the oddest sense of dislocation being there, one among dozens publicly mourning this woman. Who, she'd wondered, had actually known Dianna? She herself had some small idea of the private woman, but she could never have claimed that she'd known her.

It had been an unusual assemblage, familiar faces here and there: Billy Rose and Ed Wynn seated side by side several rows ahead; Gertrude Berg and Dean Acheson also side by side; all in a row sat Henry Luce, Mischa Elman, and Langston Hughes; Hubert Humphrey and Nelson Rockefeller were positioned very near the front of the chapel; standing near the door were Dan Duryea and Franchot Tone; and talking quietly together in whispered tones were John O'Hara, Ogden Nash, and Bennett Cerf.

Some of these and other celebrities present had been subjects of "Up to the Minute" segments, but the majority had no connection to the show. Lynne had to wonder at Dianna's evident popularity. It seemed she'd been known to a large, most diverse population. Everywhere in the chapel were faces that, due to constant exposure, seemed personally familiar.

With Keith elegantly directing the proceedings as if this were a hot new program that would be aired to phenomenal ratings and he need do no more than present the stars without undue embellishment, half a dozen men and women made their way to the front of the chapel to speak of the Dianna they'd known. It seemed to Lynne as if not one but half a dozen different women were being eulogized.

Clifton Webb, frail and tearful, was quietly eloquent in describing his one encounter with Dianna, some years before, when—no mention that this had been a bit of moonlighting on Dianna's part—she'd done an interview with him for another network. He spoke of her interest and enthusiasm, her kindness and intelligence.

Adam Clayton Powell, his charm an almost palpable entity, spoke at length of Dianna's efforts on behalf of women and of the Negro people; his words creating an image of a Dianna as someone vitally concerned with the simultaneously strengthening causes both of women and of Negroes.

Dorothy Parker, just a little drunk, and not entirely steady on her feet, managed to imply that Dianna had, in her youth, been no less than an integral part of the famous "round table" group that had hung out at the Algonquin in better days. Lynne had to wonder if the woman had actually ever known Dianna, if she hadn't mistaken Dianna for someone else she'd once known. Certainly none of her references sounded remotely like the Dianna Lynne had come to know.

Gypsy Rose Lee, the subject of another moonlighted interview for yet another network, spoke lispingly but feelingly of Dianna as someone with sensitivity and integrity, someone who was a credit to all women. Lynne scarcely heard the words; she was captivated by the glittering jewels adorning the tall, attractive woman. And by this point, Lynne was automatically discounting the majority of what was being said about Dianna because little, if any, of it rang true.

David Sarnoff commended Dianna for the quality of her work, and for her perseverance in a field dominated by men; he declared he was saddened that someone who'd contributed so much to the quality and expansion of broadcast journalism should be struck down in her prime.

Woody Guthrie sang several songs and most people spontaneously joined in. Lynne opened her mouth but could get no sound out. She felt too removed from what was happening, and unable to decide whether all this was in perfect taste, or a deplorable display of contrived after-the-fact admiration.

Only Ned had seemed real, wearing grief and bewilderment upon his face. He hadn't appeared either to see anyone or to hear the words they spoke. Lynne's eyes had been drawn repeatedly to him, drawn to the evidence of his caring. She recognized the truth of his mourning; she shared it.

The majority of people had left after the service and only this depleted group had volunteered to make the trip to the cemetery.

It was over finally and the group began to disperse. Lynne started toward her car, with Gloria at her side.

"Will you stay in touch?" Gloria asked.

"Of course I will."

"People always say that, but they never do."

"No, I will," Lynne assured her. "Perhaps you and Lon will come visit sometime. I've yet to meet the mysterious Lon."

"Sure," Gloria said dispiritedly. "Sometime."

"I'd better be going. I'm due at my sister's."

They embraced, then separated.

"I'm going to miss you," Gloria said tearfully, her eyes red rimmed.

"I'll miss you. But you'll be so busy, you won't have time to think about anything."

"I've got you to thank for it, haven't I?"

"Not at all. They finally just recognized that they had someone they ought to be using."

"You'll let me know your address, okay?"

"I will stay in touch," Lynne promised firmly.

"It feels like the end of the goddamned world!" Gloria protested. "Take care of yourself, okay?"

"You, too."

Lynne got into the BMW, fastened her seat belt. The engine was completely cold; it was slow turning over. She hadn't bothered winterizing it, but thought now that perhaps she should have. She rolled down her window to say, "Don't stand around out here. You'll freeze."

"I'm going." Gloria turned reluctantly and started along the icy road to her car.

Lynne shifted into first and pulled out. Ahead of her was a limousine bearing Bob Ferguson and his daughters away. She could see their three heads through the rear window of the limousine. They didn't seem to be speaking. At the gates, the elongated black Cadillac turned left toward the city. Lynne turned right, headed for the access road that would eventually take her to the Hutchinson, and then to the thruway.

Everything was ended. Dianna was dead and in the ground. Gloria had moved up to fill Lynne's slot on the show, and Lynne had, for more than two weeks, been free—as she'd once thought she'd like to be—to fritter away time. Except that her time had been spent sorting and packing, making preparations.

The roads were messy with slush, the shoulders treacherously slick. She drove with the windshield wipers going, several times ducking involuntarily as passing trucks sent sheets of brown slush smashing into the windshield. She was to spend the night with Amy and then start off first thing in the morning for Florida. Ross had left three days earlier, to drive down with Mrs. Wain. He'd booked hotel rooms for the three of them, where they'd stay until they found a house. The contents of the cottage had been packed and put into storage. She'd listed the cottage with a real estate office in Darien just two days earlier, on the afternoon of Dianna's death, and it had been sold within twenty-four hours to a young man who taught English at the high school. The only thing that worried her was the distance she was about to place between herself and Amy. They'd never lived more than a hundred miles apart. Amy, however, was being philosophical, delighted Lynne had decided to go with Ross to Florida.

"He's a nice man," Amy had commented. "He's old enough to know who he is and what he wants."

This observation had struck Lynne as singularly appropriate.

As for Lynne's several weeks of tense anticipation, Amy had scoffed, "You're way too old to be breeding. But I'm happy if you're happy."

She had been happy, but Dianna's death had temporarily put an end to her optimism. For the first time since Alec's death, she'd wept in anguish for many hours. She'd wanted Dianna to live, despite the evidence of her failing health. She'd wanted the two of them to continue the process—however belated it had been in commencing—of getting to know one another. It had been dreamwork on her part, she now admitted. Dianna had lasted weeks longer than the doctors had expected she would, in view of her condition upon admission to the hospital.

Ross had only been gone a few days, yet she missed him. In a very short time, he'd managed to become her anchor.

He was someone to whom she could always return, certain of a warm welcome. He could, in his calm, sensible way, restore order to her thoughts and feelings. He did all this and more for her and asked nothing in return but her company, something she found it effortlessly easy to give him. Because he harbored no expectations of her, it pleased her to give to him time, thoughts, small gifts. She derived an increasing satisfaction from the privilege he accorded her of giving.

As for John, it was possible that the child she was going to bear was his. Ross had insisted, "The child is *yours*, in the last analysis. You have my word it will never be an issue between us." It might become an issue someday, though, which was why she was waiting until the child was born before accepting Ross as her husband.

She turned off at the Greenwich exit and made her way through town toward Amy's house. The snow's frozen surface was invitingly unbroken. She recalled how, as children, she and Amy had rushed out of doors in their snowsuits to climb the frozen swells and leap repeatedly through the ice-crusted surface to the powdery snow beneath, their laughter visible as frozen clouds.

The gracious homes she passed were adorned discreetly with lights and a variety of wreaths. She couldn't imagine what sort of Christmas spirit palm trees and balmy weather might inspire. Mrs. Wain would be spending the holiday in Waterbury with her family, leaving Ross and Lynne to fend for themselves.

"We'll have a turkey with the works," he said. "And you'll get to meet the boys. They're all coming."

"I'm not much of a cook," she'd warned him.

"You'll be the navigator." He'd laughed. "I plan to do the whole thing myself. It can't be that hard. There's not a hell of a lot of intelligence needed to put a turkey in the oven. The creamed onions and chestnut stuffing might be a whole other story." He talked on about his culinary projects and she'd sat with a weak Scotch and water, smiling, watching and listening as he'd sorted through the last of his papers, consigning the majority to the fire, reserving certain others which he placed carefully to one side. In a pair of old jeans and a Harvard sweatshirt, with ancient ragged sneakers on his feet, he'd seemed younger, energized.

It occurred to her now, as she drove the glassy, winding road, that Ross in many ways was more youthful than John. It was his lack of staidness and resignation, and his capacity for enthusiasm that made the difference.

Oh why, she suddenly, impatiently, demanded of herself, did she persist with these odious comparisons? John was fire and Ross was food. There was no question of which was most necessary in her life. Ross was sustenance, constancy, wisdom, and caring; he was acceptance, experience, and understanding.

She passed a house that was beautifully decorated. Several saplings near the front door had been hung with blue and white fairy lights, and a row of red velvet bows on a ribbon graced the front door. She started to smile, thought of Dianna, and felt her throat close.

She pulled into Amy's driveway and sat for a few minutes studying the house as the sadness subsided.

Amy met her at the front door saying, "I was beginning to get worried. I thought you'd be back sooner."

"The roads were bad."

Amy hugged her, her face hot against Lynne's cold cheek.

"Ross just called. He wanted to let you know they've arrived safely. He said he'll call back later tonight. Are you all right? How did it go? I've got coffee made." Amy went off toward the kitchen, her words trailing behind her.

Lynne stopped on the threshold to look back at the street, silent and snowbound in the dusk. It wouldn't have surprised her to see John standing at the foot of the driveway. She'd liked his unexpected visits; she'd liked the beautiful look of him, the sight and feel of him, and his earnestness. It would take her and Ross some time to arrive at a physical understanding that would match the one they had emotionally, intellectually. They might never arrive at a physical match comparable to the one she'd made with John. As lovers they'd been perfectly attuned. Perfectly. But there'd been little, if anything, to say when the heat ebbed. And that was the time when she and Ross seemed to have the most to say to one another.

She closed the door and saw that, in her absence, Amy had placed Christmas decorations in the front hall, and had given the place a thorough cleaning. The wood surfaces gleamed darkly, and there was an aromatic fire going in the fireplace. Candles in freshly-polished brass candlesticks stood at either end of the mantelpiece.

With a smile she hung away her coat, then stood for a moment with her hands pressed flat to her belly. Of course she couldn't feel anything; it was too soon.

"What're you doing?" Amy called from the kitchen.

"I'm coming," Lynne answered. She'd have a cup of coffee with Amy. Dinner was already underway. In a few hours, Ross would call. His younger man's voice would engage her entirely for five or ten minutes. Then she'd sleep the boundless, depthless sleep of recent times. And in the morning, she'd put her overnight bag on the back seat of the car, then head toward the turnpike, and Ross.

INTERLUDE
July 1966

❖❖❖❖❖❖❖❖

❖ *Twenty-one* ❖

SHE FELT WONDERFULLY well, despite the bulk of her belly and the frequent little thrusts and jabs the baby made as if to remind her of its presence. She sat, with her hand shaping a small protrusion at her left side, trying to decide if it was a hand or a foot that pushed against the gentle pressure of her palm. Absently, she turned to look at the water, then at the sky. She'd picked up from Ross the habit of periodically checking the conditions. There was a slight swell, but the sky, aside from a puffy cloud here and there, was clear and a deep blue.

Ross was at the wheel, guiding the boat on a course for Grand Bahama Island. That morning, they'd decided on the spur of the moment to make the short trip over to the island to spend the night. They planned to get up early tomorrow and have a look around West End, then have a picnic lunch on one of the beaches. In the afternoon, they'd make their way back to West Palm Beach. With the baby due in another two weeks, it was the last chance they'd have for at least a month to make one of these impromptu trips.

Settled in the lee of the foredeck, buttressed by heaps of brightly colored, canvas-covered pillows, Lynne reached for the novel she'd been reading, made drowsy as always by the lift and fall of the boat. They were, by her estimate, about a third of the way to the island. She positioned the book against the mound of her belly and tried to find her way back into *The Fixer*.

The swell, Ross noticed, was increasing. He checked his

readings. They were right on course. Another forty minutes or so and they'd be putting in at the marina at Grand Bahama Hotel. He'd stayed there several times, primarily because of their marina facility. It was a sprawling place, comprised of a number of different-sized whitewashed buildings spread over the hotel's property which took up the entire east end of the island. The rooms and service were only adequate, but the Turtle Walk restaurant served surprisingly good food. It was a huge place, with about fifteen hundred rooms, and offered guests almost everything from skeet shooting to scuba lessons. There was a good stretch of white sand beach but most of the guests preferred to use one of the two pools, since it was known that sharks often prowled in the near offshore waters. The last time they'd stayed at the hotel, some months earlier, he'd been unable to sleep. Checking to see that Lynne was sleeping soundly, he'd dressed and taken a walk down to the pier, thinking to watch the sunrise.

To the right of the pier was an aquarium of sorts, enclosed by mesh wire, that housed a number of large-sized tropical fish. During the day families often came to study the fish, watching as they swam indolently within the enclosure.

As Ross had walked along the pier, approaching the aquarium, he'd become aware of thrashing sounds, and had stopped to listen, straining to see in the near-dark. He'd moved closer and saw that the waters were roiling within the enclosure, as if the fish within were darting about frantically. He couldn't clearly see the shark, but rather sensed its presence on the far side of the enclosure. There was silence for a moment, then a tremendous splash, and Ross realized that the shark had somehow managed to hurl itself past the protective wire and into the enclosed area. Now the waters seethed; the fish becoming crazed as the shark moved among them.

Except for the lapping of the water, there was suddenly silence again and Ross, both alarmed and fascinated, had stood very still, watching the water within the enclosure turn dark with blood. It all lasted perhaps three or four minutes. Then there was another splash, and the silence continued. In the deep red light of dawn, he'd moved to the edge of the pier to gaze down into the aquarium. The bloodied surface of the water was already calming, but the smell of blood and fish was very strong. Within minutes, the outgoing tide had cleansed the water and the enclosure was silent and still. He'd turned to face the horizon and sat down on the rough wood of the pier to watch the sun come up. To his left lay a large pile of conch shells, robbed of their hosts, that had been set out to dry in the sun for a few days. They'd been only haphazardly cleaned and their smell was foul. Any pleasure he might have taken in the sight of the sun pushing slowly over the edge of the horizon had been destroyed. He sat a minute or two longer and then, chilled, he'd made his way back to the room. He'd never again risked swimming from the beach and had discouraged Lynne from it, too. On their last visit they'd sat on the beach in the lounge chairs the hotel provided, but they'd bathed in the larger of the two pools.

He checked his readings again, then looked up at the sky. The clouds were collecting, the sky becoming overcast. The weather was capable of making swift and utterly unanticipated changes, despite the forecasts. Earlier, when he'd phoned in to get the conditions, he'd been told the day was expected to remain clear with scattered clouds. Now it seemed obvious they were in for some weather. Had he been alone, he wouldn't have minded. But Lynne hadn't yet been subjected to the vagaries of sudden squalls and this was hardly the best time to have her experience one.

He looked over to see that she'd fallen asleep. The book had slipped from her hand and lay face-up on the deck, the growing wind fanning the pages. She seemed quite comfortable, sheltered by the pillows. He wouldn't disturb her. Perhaps they'd make it to port before the weather broke.

The swell was all at once higher, the boat dipping more deeply into the troughs, the waves breaking far up the prow. The sky was quickly going gray, the clouds closing off the sun. "Damn it!" he whispered, holding the wheel firmly to stay on course.

She curled more into the pillows, resting on her side with her knees drawn up: her habitual position for sleep in the past two months. Ross watched her briefly, then returned his attention to the charts. With the increasing turbulence, the compass needle swung wildly from side to side, forcing him to guess at their position. He believed they were still on course but it was hard to tell. When the first heavy drops began to fall, he called out, thinking to wake her, but she didn't seem to hear his voice over the noise of the wind and waves. He called louder.

They were on a train, going through snow-covered mountains. There were holes in the roof of the compartment that admitted the melting snow. It dropped maddeningly on the heads of the passengers. She opened the newspaper she'd been reading and held it over her head to protect herself. Ross appeared at the far end of the compartment and called to her. She moved to rise, but couldn't. She looked down at herself to see, with horror, that her bared belly—like some critically malformed Siamese twin—was shuddering, its naked surface pleating, accordionlike, with sudden pain. Wildly, she looked around to see that the other passengers were staring at her in disgust. She tried to cover herself with the newspaper, to hide from public view the immense growth. Ross had her clothes and was holding them aloft, signaling to her as he called her name. Again she attempted to move, but couldn't. She looked helplessly at Ross who was trying to push his way through the glowering crowd to get to her. She longed to shield herself, to cloak her hideous nakedness, but all she had was the sopping newspaper that had, she noticed, left streaks of black on her arms and breasts, belly and thighs. Her belly drew itself up again, smoothly distended, and remained motionless. She closed her eyes and waited for Ross to reach her with her clothes. The melting snow continued to drip ceaselessly on her head.

The rolling motion of the train was constant as it shot around curves, descending the mountain. When she opened her eyes again, Dianna was seated by her side, berating her for appearing in front of an audience in her deplorable condition. "You promised me you were going to have it seen to!'' Dianna accused in a hiss. ''You were supposed to stay as you were. How could you *do* this?''

Mutely Lynne told her, ''I wanted this. It's not what it seems. There's a child, a baby inside. You'll see. You'll see.''

Scoffing, Dianna turned away. The train roared into a tunnel; they were in total darkness, then emerged into glaring daylight. Dianna was gone. Ross was still at the end of the compartment, clutching her clothes. He apologized with his eyes, with the impotent lift of his shoulders. He shook his head, indicating the mass of people crowded between them. He called to her to cover herself with the newspaper.

''I can't!'' she cried out to him. ''The words are coming off on me!'' She couldn't explain. Each lead, the headlines, some of the photographs had imprinted themselves on her flesh where they'd made contact. And the words burned, like small needles tattooing indelibly their disasters into her flesh. Everything that adhered to her, each news item branded into her skin, represented a failure—hers, the world's. She would never be able to cleanse herself of the stains. ''I can't!'' she cried again, willing him to understand.

Her hair was sopping; water trickled down her neck and shoulders, ran itchily into her eyes and down her nose. The mound pleated itself again, paining her terribly. It was working to disattach itself. Already some of the edges had loosened and raw flesh, pink and vulnerable, showed beneath. She held her hands to the freed edges, trying to keep the entire mass attached, but another pair of hands was working against hers, in an effort to tear free the mass. She looked up to see that the hands belonged to John. He refused to look at her but worked steadily, shifting the mass from side to side with an expression of fiercely determined concentration.

Suddenly, she froze the frame and listened to her own voice say, ''This is a bad dream. You can wake up.'' Her dream self seemed to want to dispute this and argued, as her fingers scrabbled to close the now gaping edges of her flesh. ''You can wake up,'' she told herself. She took a final look at John's rage-distorted features, then pushed upward toward the surface, leaving behind the compartment filled with gaping eyes and pointing fingers as she heaved into a brief blackness before opening her eyes.

It was raining. She sat up with some difficulty, realizing at once that they'd been caught in a storm. She looked over to see Ross signaling to her. She got to her knees, clutching the rail and, fighting for balance, succeeded in getting to her feet. The small distance she would have to travel between the prow and the cabin seemed to have stretched into miles. The boat was rolling from side to side, then plunging into the deepening troughs between the waves. Water washed over the sides. The pillows, freed from her weight, began to float across the deck, ironic squares of color, moving farther as each new wave sent more water onto the deck.

Clinging to the rail she began to inch her way along the port side toward the cabin. At one moment the boat seemed to be suspended in midair. Then it crashed into the next wave, causing her legs to jar upward in their sockets. She fought to remain upright, dragging herself another few steps. A low pain stopped her, and she hung onto the slippery rail, waiting until it passed, her face stinging from the slap of the salt spray.

Watching, Ross knew she wasn't going to make it unaided to the shelter and relative safety of the cabin. He tied off the wheel, and stepped out on deck. He was at once struck by the wind and rain and driven back several feet. Suddenly furious—he was damned if the two of them would die this way—he stiffened his body, resisting the wind, got a handhold on the rail and made some progress toward her. She was still hanging precariously over the rail, her head bent. Her thin cotton dress was plastered to her body. The water washed over her bare feet. Her shoes were floating with the pillows.

Finally, he reached her and put his hand on her arm. Her skin was very cold.

"Hold on to me!" he shouted. "I'll get you into the cabin."

Wordlessly, she allowed him to free her hand from the

rail and fit it around his belt. Satisfied she had a good grip on his midsection, he started back toward the cabin. At that moment, the boat floundered, hovering again in midair before crashing down into the next trough. They both fell to their knees, but managed to keep hold of each other.

It occurred to Lynne then that they might die in this storm, be washed overboard, or capsize with the boat. Yet, strangely, she wasn't afraid. Her grip on Ross's belt secure, she struggled to her feet while he assisted with his free hand. She had the irrational idea that if they could just make it back to the cabin they'd be safe. They were halfway there, moving like elderly cripples against the force of the wind and driving rain.

Ross extended his arm. It waved wildly as he sought something to hold onto. The boat bucked, tossing them back against the rail. Her back hit the rail and the pain was sharply piercing, like a needle penetrating the base of her spine. She cried out, the sound swallowed by the ravening mouth of the wind. On the next try, Ross managed to gain purchase on the cabin door and with a heave pulled both of them inside.

"You've got to get into some dry clothes," he said, quickly throwing open one of the lockers to unearth her overnight bag. He set the bag on the closed lid of the locker then found some towels in the head and gave them to her, both of them lurching within the confines of the cabin as the boat leaned perilously first to one side, then the other. "I've got to figure out where we are," he said. "Can you manage?"

She nodded, distracted, holding the towels with one hand, steadying herself with the other. The pain of her collision with the rail had receded to a dull ache in her spine, but the other pain, the one low in her belly, returned, capturing her attention. She shivered, turned inward to the pain, waiting for it to pass. It was over in a few seconds. She caught her breath, unbuttoned her dress and let it fall in a wet heap, to which she added her underpants and brassiere. She began to towel dry one-handedly, fearful she would fall and do some damage to the baby. She got most of the wetness out of her hair, and bent to open the suitcase when her insides seemed to yawn expansively. It was a peculiar feeling, almost pleasant, followed by a sudden relief-giving gush of fluid down her thighs.

Ross turned to see her staring at what he thought was a puddle of water at her feet. "What's wrong?" he asked, accustomed to the sight of her swollen breasts and belly, yet perpetually fascinated by the changes her body had undergone these past months. Ella had rarely allowed him to see her nude in the advanced stages of her pregnancies. She'd believed herself deformed, unattractive. Lynne had willingly, delightedly exclaiming over the changes, sharing with him the sensations and her reactions.

"I'm in labor," she said almost inaudibly, surprised and a little frightened. "My water just broke."

He couldn't say anything for a moment. Then, "But it's too soon."

She straightened and smiled at him. "It's definitely too soon, according to Dr. Francis. But not according to this baby."

"What the hell . . . ?" he began and trailed off, turning back to the wheel, with new urgency attempting to determine how far off course they might be.

"It's all right," she reassured him. "The contractions aren't very close together. We'll have time to get to a doctor once we land."

"We're off course," he told her, and watched the understanding displace her smile. "Frankly, I don't know where we are. We could still be on course, but I can't tell. I knew I should buy that radar installation."

"Would that have helped?" she asked, looking now in her suitcase, trying to find something suitable to put on. He didn't answer and she turned to see him fighting the wheel. She pulled a pair of outsized cotton drawstring trousers from the bag and a sweater, then dried her feet before grappling with the clothes. Once dressed, her shivering subsided and she felt better.

"I'll go down to the galley and make some coffee," she offered, sitting on the locker lid and, with difficulty, tying the laces on her sneakers.

"Stay topside!" he warned. "Everything'll be bouncing around down there. There's coffee left in the thermos, if you want some."

"I don't want any," she said, making her way—like climbing the side of a very steep hill—toward him. With one hand braced on the rim of the control panel and one arm around his waist she tried to see out through the window, which the wipers were working ineffectually to clear. The water, like some enraged, living thing, flayed the boat. "What's going to happen?" she asked.

"With luck, it'll blow past fairly soon. With luck, we're still on course and will be at the island in about twenty minutes. I can't get an accurate reading off this damned thing." He wrapped his hand around the compass as if prepared to rip it from its moorings. "Are you all right?" he asked, concerned.

"For the moment." She smiled again, and smoothed the wet hair back from his face. "I have complete confidence in you," she said. "I'll get out of your way."

She stumbled back to the rear of the cabin, to the lockers, unearthed a blanket, wrapped it around her shoulders, and wedged herself into a corner, seated tailor-fashion atop the lockers. Through the porthole she watched the water dip toward them, then away. She hung onto the brass frame of the porthole to steady herself as the boat tossed about. She was relatively comfortable in this position, with the bulk of her belly cushioned by her thighs. It was seven minutes before the next contraction came. She stroked the taut, rippling flesh as the pain peaked and ebbed. There was always the radio, she told herself, if things became really bad. And she did have confidence in Ross. He'd steer them through this safely.

The ceaseless motion was nauseating. She shut her eyes and concentrated on trying to breathe with the rise and fall of the boat, breathing out slowly as they rode the crests of the waves, breathing in in the troughs. It helped. She made an effort to remember the chapters on delivery she'd read in the half dozen books Dr. Francis had recommended she get from the library. The baby's head, she knew, was working itself into position at her cervix. She'd begin to dilate sometime soon. Ross would be able to discern the degree of dilation if she told him what to feel for. She doubted he'd be squeamish. After all, he'd displayed great interest in her changing body throughout the pregnancy. It seemed unlikely he'd suddenly lose that interest now. But what if there were complications? Dr. Francis had said all along that she'd have a normal delivery, that there'd be no problems. Those things weren't always possible to predict, though. No, there'd be no complications. If they had to, she and Ross could deliver this baby. They might have to. She opened her eyes. Ross remained at the wheel, his back very straight, his entire demeanor one of alertness. She closed her eyes again and tried once more to pick up on the rhythm of her breathing. Her position was no longer quite so comfortable. Perhaps if she opened one of the lockers and lined it with the pillows and the Mae Wests she'd be able to lie down. That way she'd run no risk of toppling off the locker in the event she fell asleep.

On second thought, she decided it would be wise if both of them wore Mae Wests. She got two from the lockers and, a second time, made the uphill climb to help Ross into the vest. "Just in case," she told him with a smile. She got into a vest herself, then working slowly, steadily, she untied the cushions covering the locker tops, cleared one of the lockers—stowing the contents in the other lockers—and lined the interior space with the cushions. She climbed into the locker and lay back, using one of the Mae Wests as a pillow. She could still see Ross, and she felt far more secure. With the blanket tucked around her she closed her eyes as another contraction—was it slightly stronger than the previous ones?—fixed her attention.

Ross looked over his shoulder, at first unable to see her. He hoped she hadn't gone below. It was the worst place to be in a storm. Then he saw the open lid of the locker and her hair, light against the bright orange of the life vest. He smiled automatically, thinking she was damned clever to find herself such a sensible place in which to rest. His smile quickly fading, he faced forward once more, glancing at his watch. They were now long overdue in port. He fiddled with the radio, hoping for an updated weather reading.

* * *

It was two hours before the storm passed. As soon as Ross felt it safe, he tied off the wheel, removed his Mae West, and went to check on Lynne. Her face was flushed and damp, and she looked tired.

"They're about three minutes apart now. Do you know where we are?" she asked.

"We're way off course, about fifteen knots from a small group of islands—sandpits, really—just north of Grand Bahama. There's nothing there, but we can put in. I could try for Grand Bahama but I don't know if we've got the time. Do you want to try for it?"

"How long d'you think it would take?"

"A couple of hours."

"I don't think we've got a couple of hours," she said, pushing herself to a sitting position inside the locker. "It depends on whether or not I'm dilated. I can't check it myself."

"You want me to do it," he guessed.

"Could you?"

"I guess I'll have to." He smiled encouragingly and patted her on the knee. "I always wanted to be a doctor."

"I think the best place would be below," she said. "You'll have to help me out of here. It was a lot easier getting in."

Below decks, he went to the head to wash his hands while she rid herself of the life vest, then undid the drawstring and got out of her trousers and sneakers. Ross came back minus his shirt. They looked at each other and laughed.

"There's an air of depravity around the place," he laughed, helping her stretch out on the bed.

"Don't be afraid of hurting me," she told him, then explained what he was to expect. "You'll be able to tell," she assured him. "It's just a question of whether I'm dilated at all, or a little, or a lot. If it's a lot, we don't have time to do much of anything. If it's not at all, or a little, we'll probably be able to make it to the off-islands."

He had no qualms at all until the moment when she bent open her legs. Then it seemed to him impossible. "Are you sure?" he asked, hesitating.

"Go ahead."

He was about to proceed when she cried, "Wait!" and, startled, he straightened.

"I'm going off again," she whispered. "Just hold my hand for a minute."

He held her hand, awed by the lean strength of her grip, watching her face twist and flush deep red as the contraction gained, then peaked and passed. Her grip relaxed, she took a deep shuddering breath and said, "Okay. You can do it now."

It was painful, but she forced herself to relax, her eyes on the bulkhead, until his hand was withdrawn.

"I don't feel anything," he said.

"Then we'll have time to make it to the islands."

"You're sure?"

"As sure as I can be under the circumstances. Let's just hope I don't suddenly dilate when we're halfway there." She tried to keep her tone light but he suspected she was putting on a brave face. He washed his hands a second time then returned to sit beside her a moment. "I'm a little scared," he said. "I wouldn't want anything to happen to you."

"I'll have the baby, that's all." She looked into his eyes and felt caring for this man breaking through her system like countless small hemorrhages. He bent to kiss her.

"We'll get underway then," he said, on his feet but still holding her hand. "If you need me, shout." He covered her with the bedclothes then went topside back to the wheel. After checking his charts and the compass, he set his course for the tiny blue dots that would be a series of small sandy outcroppings.

She tried to relax, and dozed between contractions. The pain and discomfort were bearable, but something almost separate from herself. She'd grown accustomed to the monthly, then the twice-monthly visits to the obstetrician; accustomed to the probing of her interior. It was part, she knew, of the necessary process. But keeping herself gentle to accommodate Ross had been the most intimate experience of her life. They had joined, at that moment, into something far more than they'd previously been. A new bond had been welded, and in her half-sleep moments before contractions, she reexamined the dimensions of her emotional response to this man.

They were friends. Certainly he was the closest friend she'd had since her college years. They were friends who shared a bed, and a house, and time. They talked together, often late into the night. Sitting on the flagstone patio at the rear of the house, they watched the moths on their collision course with the citronella-scented candles designed to keep the mosquitoes at bay, and they talked. They laughed often and continued to discover more and more areas of mutual agreement and interest. Their hours spent together, whether in silent company, or in conversation, constituted a luxury she'd never dreamed of. There was no pressure—from any source. They were free simply to be. For the first time in her life no one else had a claim to her time or her thoughts; she was entirely at liberty. So was Ross. Their laughter and the frequent meetings of their eyes confirmed the extraordinary pleasure this freedom gave them both. Ross was teaching her to cook and, to her surprise, she liked it. He was also teaching her to sail, and she liked that too. They were, she thought, the best sort of friends: those with respect for privacy, but with forthrightness and honesty.

She and Alec had been married for seventeen years, but they'd never been friends. Love had come too quickly to allow room for friendship. They'd been many things to each other—surrogate parents, from time to time; and brother and sister; sometime antagonists, sometime supporters—but never friends; certainly they'd never been close confidants in the way she and Ross were.

The contractions came and went with increasing regularity. She thought of Alec and knew he'd be appalled at the situation in which she now found herself. That she could have been foolish enough to get herself impregnated—without knowing which of her two lovers was responsible—would have brought the full weight of his condescending scorn down upon her. She knew. She'd heard him speak often enough about the foolishness of some people, some women. She had become, it turned out, one of those foolish women. But she didn't mind. In fact, she was eager for the end result of her foolishness. She wanted the child more than she'd ever wanted anything. Beside her desire for the child, her former career diminished to paltry proportions, and her marriage to Alec seemed to have been something that had taken place between two other people, neither of whom she'd known particularly well.

Ross came down to say, "Not long now. We'll put in in another ten or fifteen minutes tops. How is it?"

"Getting worse," she answered, finding it hard to speak. Her brain seemed to be functioning as effectively as ever, but her senses had undergone a change. Everything in and of her was tuned to her body and its performance. Even her brain seemed to be becoming fogged by her body's enterprise. "Perhaps you should check me again."

He got up, went to wash his hands, then returned to position himself between her knees. It was easier this time, for both of them, and he could feel how the thinned-down ring of flesh had spread. "About this much," he said, making a circle with his thumb and forefinger.

"We'd better get there," she told him. "I don't think we've got much time left. I'll try to get a few things organized." She pushed herself upright and lumbered to her feet. Seeing him watching her warily, she made herself smile, and said, "You go back up and sail the boat. I'll see what I can find down here."

Reluctantly, he returned topside. She found a worn-thin white sheet that seemed fairly fresh and set it to one side. In the head, she unhooked the plastic bucket from the back of the door and carried it to the galley where she set it down while she put water on to boil in the biggest pot she could find. Pausing now and then to wait out contractions, she unearthed a small, sharp paring knife, and dropped it into the pot of water. She found a ball of string, some newspapers, and several clean towels. She stripped the bed, lay down a thick layer of the newspapers, then covered this over with the sheet she'd just taken off. The string, the remaining newspapers, the towels, and the bar of soap she placed on the fold-out table between the beds that served as their dining area.

"What else?" she said aloud, turning to look around the small cabin. Her attention turned instantly inward as another contraction spiraled through her belly. She held on to the edge of the table, feeling the weight of the baby bearing down as her body swayed with the boat's motion. When the contraction had passed, she pulled off the sweater. It was warm inside the cabin and she was perspiring. Her legs trembled and she moved slowly back to the bed. She spread another layer of newspaper over the sheet and covered it with one of the towels. She lay down, the newspaper crackling as she stretched out. She lay on her back for a time, then shifted over onto her side. The pain, when it came, seemed less forceful in this position.

The boat ceased moving and she heard, or felt, the abrupt final tug of the craft as Ross dropped anchor. He came below and stopped at the sight of her, curled naked on the bed. He took in the preparations she'd made and it was all at once inescapably real to him that they were alone, and were going to have to deliver this child.

"I was always outside in the waiting room," he said, dropping down on his haunches to take hold of her hand.

"I've never even come that close," she joked. "We'll manage. I've got a pot of water heating on the stove. We'll need it, for washing the baby, and me, I suppose. It's a good thing I did all my reading. Christ! This is *not* the way I had it planned."

"You're going to have to tell me what to do." He rested his cheek for a moment against her bare arm. Behind his closed eyes flashed visions of carnage, of her torn and bloodied body, of an infant needlessly dead. He lifted his head and gently squeezed her hand. She gripped his hand hard, her nails digging into his palm. Instinctively, he reached to massage her belly, cowed by the muscular pull he could feel in her abdomen.

"I'm getting tired," she said almost inaudibly. "It feels like this has been going on for days."

"Just hours," he said, in what he hoped was a consolingly positive tone. "I'll just go have another wash. Is there anything I can get you?"

"A wet washcloth."

"One wet washcloth coming up!" He went into the head, leaving the door open, and kept an eye on her while he scrubbed his hands and forearms. It was hot in the cabin, now that the breeze had died down. Lynne's entire body was shiny with perspiration, her hair clinging damply to her face and neck. He wondered if it would be wise to open one of the portholes, then decided against it. The baby would have to be kept warm, and so would Lynne. When it was done, he'd work on creating some cross-ventilation.

Emerging, he checked the pot of water in the galley, asking, "What's the knife doing in here?"

"You're going to need it. Is it boiling?"

"Yes."

"You can turn the heat off, and let it cool. When it's cool enough to put your hand in, pour some of the water into the bucket and bring the knife in here. You can put it on the table with the other things. There's a sheet . . ." She broke off in a low moan that brought him hurrying to her side. "I think it's getting ready to come," she gasped. "I'm starting to feel as if I want to push, but I think it's too soon for that."

"Should I check again?" he asked.

She nodded and eased over onto her back. Her legs, weighted by exhaustion, splayed open.

"I can feel its head," he said, astonished.

"I must be fully dilated," she said hoarsely.

"I'll . . . what should I do?"

"Nothing yet. Just wait."

He sat down at her side, taking hold of her hand, aware, in the silence, of the gentle rocking of the boat. He guessed, from the boat's motion, that a slight breeze must be rising. She gazed unblinkingly at the bulkhead, only the sudden increase of pressure in her hand indicating when another contraction was occurring. After a time, he said, "I'll get that water. It should be cool by now," and went to the galley to pour some of the water into the bucket. He returned to set the bucket and the knife on the table.

Red-faced, she cried, "I want to push!"

He dropped to his knees at the foot of the bed, in readiness.

"Ross?"

"What is it?"

"They're coming faster and faster. One hardly finishes before another one begins." She ran the wet cloth over her face, then sucked at a corner of it, grateful for the moisture in her dry mouth. She thought longingly, for a few seconds, of a cigarette. She hadn't had one in five months. "I plan to celebrate with a cigarette," she said with a bark of dry laughter. "God! It feels as if this is a dream. I really have to push!" she cried again.

"Then go ahead, push!"

She pushed, straining, until she was positive everything inside her would come spilling out.

"The head's starting to come down," he said excitedly, thoroughly caught up in what was happening. "Push some more!"

"I have to rest for a minute."

"Keep pushing and it'll all be over."

"I can't! I'm so tired."

He stroked her belly, encouraging her. "A few more good pushes and you'll have your baby. Come on, Lynne!"

"Oh, *God*!" she groaned. "I'm going to turn inside out."

He laughed. "Of course you're not. You're going to be just fine." He could literally feel her gathering her strength together for another massive effort. Every muscle in her body went tight and she emitted a strangled scream as she heaved downward, her heels digging deep into the mattress. The baby seemed to hover for a moment at the apex of her thighs and then, in a rush of blood and fluid, slid into Ross's hands. He gaped at the whitely waxy, slippery infant, for a moment rendered so awestruck he could neither move nor speak. The baby squirmed in his hands and his thought processes seemed to spring back into action and he wondered if he should hold the baby by its feet and slap its bottom.

"Take the washcloth," Lynne said weakly, "wet it in the

warm water and clean its nose and mouth, make sure it's breathing all right. Is it breathing?"

"She certainly is. It's a girl," he said, gingerly cleaning the infant's face.

"I knew it would be," she said mysteriously, holding out her arms. "Let me see her."

"Just one second. Aren't we supposed to cut her free?"

"Use the paring knife. Give her to me. I'll hold her." He laid the baby on her breast and she laughed softly. "She isn't even crying," she said wonderingly. "I thought babies always cried the second they hit the air."

"Maybe it's because some doctor always gives them a whack on the ass. Tell me what to do." He thought of all the evenings when he'd watched her sitting reading books on childbirth and wished now he'd taken the trouble to join her in her reading. He felt hopelessly ignorant, and marveled at not only how well-informed she was but also how calm.

"Get a piece of the string and tie off the cord, close to the navel. When you've got that done, just cut the cord above the tie with the knife. You'd better hurry. I'm starting another contraction."

He did as she'd instructed, then watched her body ripple as the contraction delivered the placenta. Automatically, he wrapped it in the newspaper, towel and all, and set it aside. "You're torn," he said, wincing at the visible tear in her flesh.

"I don't care," she laughed. "Isn't she beautiful?"

"I think I'd better get you both cleaned up. Who has priority?"

"She does," Lynne said promptly. "Use the washcloth and a little soap, then wrap her in one of the towels. We can clean her properly later. I can wait."

The baby began to cry finally, as Ross delicately cleaned the waxlike substance from her skin. Her tiny fists waving, she emitted gusty cries that mildly intimidated Ross and incited Lynne to further delighted laughter.

"She's real," she declared happily. "I made a baby!"

"I'll say," he concurred, wrapping the infant in the towel and returning her to Lynne.

Seeing the baby make fishlike motions with her mouth, Lynne decided to hold her to her breast. With some difficulty, she managed to connect nipple to baby and sighed, startled, as the infant at once began sucking, creating further mild contractions. "I can't believe it!" she whispered, vaguely aware of Ross applying warm soapy water to the lower half of her body.

"That makes two of us," he said giddily, pausing to study again her torn flesh. "How do you feel?"

"Tired and sore, but happy. Stop that for a minute and come here! I want to tell you something."

"What?"

"First, I'd like a kiss."

He bent to touch his mouth to hers, caught offguard by the ferocity of her kiss, and by her arm going tightly around his neck.

"I love you," she said, tears leaking from the sides of her eyes. "It frightens me because I think it's the first time. But I love you. You're the finest friend I've ever had. It's what I was thinking about all that time down here."

"You're worn out," he said solicitously, stroking her eyelids with his fingertips. "Sleep now." He removed her arm from around his neck and stooped to collect the bedclothes, tenderly covering her and the infant. "You sleep," he said softly, kissing her forehead. "I'll be here."

MARCH, 1982

✦✦✦✦✦✦✦

❖ *Twenty-two* ❖

HE CAUGHT THE midafternoon train, settled himself in the bar-car—relatively empty and almost pleasant at this time of the day—and opened the early edition of the *Post*. He wasn't sure exactly when it had happened, but at some point about five years earlier, he'd become a five-newspaper-a-day man. On the train into the city in the morning he read both the *Times* and the *Wall Street Journal*. On the ride home he read the *Post*. Upon arriving home, he'd find the Stamford *Advocate* and the Greenwich *Times* waiting. In the course of the evening he'd read these two local papers, fitting them in where possible. It seemed all his waking hours were spent reading—either manuscripts, or books he was sent to review, the many daily newspapers and sundry magazines to which he subscribed and, of course, his own work when time permitted.

His work had, in recent years, taken second place. That no longer bothered him. It certainly didn't trouble him to the extent it might have had someone told him sixteen years earlier that other people's writing would take precedence for a time over his own. Back then he'd have been devastated by the idea; he'd have denied that even the possibility might exist. He had been then, he now acknowledged with some fondness for his former self—as if that younger version of the present man were some sweetly naive friend he'd had at college—overwhelmingly idealistic and untried.

After the publication of *Opening Doors*, his first novel, he'd learned a great deal not only about himself but also about the publishing business. The book did not, as he'd privately hoped it might, leap to the top of the *Times* bestseller list. With a first printing of five thousand copies and a handful of fairly enthusiastic reviews, the book in hardcover had sold just over twenty-six hundred copies. The paperback rights were sold for a small sum and the ensuing reprint sold tolerably well. The surprise aspect of his publishing experience had come some ten years after the book's publication, in its success with college students. In the past six years the paperback had gone back to press eleven times, and continued to sell well on the backlist, thereby providing him with a twice-yearly royalty income that relieved some of the financial pressures. Granted, it wasn't a great deal of money, five or six thousand a year, but it had been enough to allow him the time and confidence to commence work on a long-delayed second novel. He'd been at work on *Love Song* for close to two years and was going home early today to begin corrections on the galley proofs.

Due to the delayed success of the first novel, and its continuing sales, his hardcover house had offered a good advance for the new book, and the paperback rights had already been sold for what was, to John's mind, the astronomical sum of fifty thousand dollars. The book had been picked up by the Book-of-the-Month Club, and negotiations were underway for an option on the film rights.

It all struck him as ironic that at the age of forty-three he was about to begin earning what might be construed as a decent living from his writing. He'd already informed his employers that he intended to swing over to part-time editing and his thoughts were pulling together a concept for yet another novel. He contemplated his future with a degree of satisfaction. With his share of the paperback money on *Love Song* he'd be able to pay off the mortgage on the house and have some long-needed major repairs made.

Altogether, he was feeling very good. He lit a cigarette, opened the *Post* and began to scan the contents. He was aware of people occupying some of the other seats in the open-plan bar-car, but continued his reading of the paper without looking up. He knew it was ridiculous, but he could never leave anything unfinished, not even a newspaper, to go on to something else. The something else in this case was the fresh set of galleys in his briefcase. The moment he set aside the *Post* he intended to get them out of his case and spend the thirty-minute train ride having a look at them.

He completed the sports section just as the last passenger rushed into the compartment and, with a jolt, the train began its route through the underground tunnels leading out of Grand Central. He looked out the window, able to see very little, thinking, as he did every day, of the plotting one might engage in with these tunnels and the myriad passageways and pedestrian ramps connected with the station. There were work lights he saw here and there that illuminated the low-ceilinged darkness and he studied the belowground emptiness as the train moved slowly toward the light.

He turned from the window and was about to reach for his briefcase when his eye was caught by a woman seated several chairs away on the opposite side. She was exceptionally well turned out, in a white mink coat with a matching hat that completely hid her hair but framed perfectly a very beautiful face, only slightly made up. She wore brown leather boots that came to the knee. A pair of brown leather gloves rested in her lap. She was smoking a cigarette and gazing into space, preoccupied. Her hands were long and wide, well cared for. On her right hand, she wore two rings, a square-cut diamond solitaire on the ring finger and a simple band of diamonds on her middle finger. Her left hand was bare of rings but a heavy gold chain bracelet was visible at her wrist. She had unbuttoned her coat but it was difficult to tell what she was wearing, since the sides of the coat overlapped.

The longer he looked at her the more familiar seemed the long line of her throat and the set of her jaw. When her eyes connected briefly with his he felt a jolt of recognition that rendered him suddenly overheated and excited. He wasn't quite sure what to do. The seats on either side of her were vacant. He could move, sit down beside her and reintroduce himself. Or he could wait until her eyes again made contact with his—it seemed inevitable that this would happen—and then he'd smile. No, that was no good. There was no guarantee she'd recognize him. It did bother him somewhat that recognition hadn't been immediate. But then he'd failed to place her. Why should she instantly remember him?

The train was pulling into the station at 125th Street. Now would be the moment to shift seats. He knew if he deliberated much longer, he'd do nothing more than spend the ride gazing at her, then he, or she, would get off the train and they might never see each other again.

He picked up his briefcase—his coat would do well enough where it was, on the overhead rack—and moved to the seat to her left where he was at once pleasantly enveloped in her perfume, the same perfume, with spicy overtones that well suited her. She paid him no attention but simply recrossed her legs in order to allow him more space.

"Excuse me," he said, his voice emerging with the tinny thinness of an adolescent. She turned to look at him. He smiled. "You're Lynne, aren't you?"

She nodded and then smiled suddenly, her eyes filling with recognition. "John!"

"That's right. You do remember."

"I thought you looked familiar," she said. "But people on trains always seem to look familiar. How nice to see you! How are you?"

"I'm just fine. How are you? Have you moved back here?"

"I'm visiting my daughter. She goes to school in Greenwich."

"Your daughter," he said. "So you're still in Florida?"

"Still. Where are you living now? I read your book, by the way. Actually, Fee read it, and raved about it so much that I picked it up out of curiosity. It really was very good."

"Greenwich, too. Fee is your daughter?" he asked, not so much ignoring the compliment, as missing it altogether in the urgent rush of his need to find out all he could about her.

"Fiona. Originally we'd planned that she'd come home

for her spring break but at the last minute she decided to stay on. So I came up.''

"What school does she go to?"

"Low-Heywood."

"Hmm. Good school. You look wonderful," he said, warming more and more to the reality of seeing her again, feeling the response whizzing through his bloodstream.

"Thank you. So do you."

He paused to light a fresh cigarette—he was nervous, he realized—and used these few moments to run through the long list of things he wanted to ask her all at once. She had to be in her late fifties, he thought, and looked at her again, deciding she didn't look it. Late forties, perhaps, at most. There were the same lines about her eyes and mouth, maybe more of them and deeper, and her flesh had the softness of middle age. How, he wondered, must he appear to her?

As if having read his thoughts, she said quietly, "We're both a lot older."

"You don't look it," he said truthfully. "*I* look it."

"No, you don't. Do you honestly think you do?" she asked interestedly.

"I know I do. Does your sister still live in Greenwich?"

She smiled. "Always. Amy intends to go out of her house feet first. It gets a little shabbier every year, but she's happy."

"And what about you?" he asked. "Are you still working in television?"

"God, no! I quit just before Dianna died, and never went back. And, no, I don't miss it."

"You married, I take it."

"Yes."

"And how is he, your husband?"

She paused just for a second, then answered, "Oh, he's fine." She looked at the man seated beside her and saw the younger man she'd known superimposed upon this older man's features. Despite what he believed, he hadn't changed all that much, nor had his effect upon her. He was a bit heavier, and there was some gray in his hair, but he still had that earnestness, that wide-open-eyed way of ask-

ing questions. His voice had deepened, and he'd lost that
freshly-scrubbed look; his hands were no longer work worn
and roughened, but he was essentially the same. And her
response to him was, too: instantly, urgently, she wanted to
touch him.

"Did you marry, John?" she asked.

He relaxed a bit and crossed his legs, resting the ankle of
his right foot on the knee of his left leg. "I did, years back.
It didn't work out. The whole thing only lasted about three
years." He'd married Lizzie on the rebound—a bad idea,
but it had seemed to make sense at the time. She'd been so
eager and, for a time, her eagerness had strongly appealed
to him. "Actually," he said, "I got married about a year
after you left. It was a mistake."

"That's too bad," she said politely.

"Not really. Lizzie's done very well for herself, got what
she always wanted: A *Times* posting in Europe as a foreign
correspondent. We're still in touch. She remarried, a Ger-
man photographer. They live in Paris and have three kids.
She sends Christmas cards."

"You didn't have children?" she asked.

He shook his head. "None that I know of." He grinned
at this little joke, and the younger man was more clearly
evident. "Are you staying with your sister? How long are
you here?"

"I go back on Sunday. Fee's term starts on Monday."

"And you're staying with your sister?" he asked again.

"That's right."

"Could we have dinner?" he asked abruptly.

She laughed. "I think so."

"Great! What's a good night?"

"Actually, tonight would be good. Fee's spending the
night with some friends in Darien, and Amy's playing
bridge in Stamford. I'm not going to be hungry for quite a
while, though. I just finished a long lunch in the city with an
old friend I used to work with. Did I ever mention Gloria to
you?"

"The production assistant."

"My God! What a memory! That's right. She produces a

soap now. We try to see each other whenever I'm up this way."

"The time's no problem. I could make a reservation somewhere and pick you up about eight. How would that be?"

"Fine. Tell me, are you still writing?"

"I've got the new one in here." He patted the side of his briefcase. "A long time between drinks, but it's finally finished."

"Well, congratulations!"

"I've been working as an editor for years now. After the first one floundered and finally kind of died, and after Lizzie moved into the city, I decided it was time to get a job. So I made the rounds, sent out the résumés, and was hired as an assistant, worked my way up to senior editor. Now, I'm about to cut back to a part-time basis so I can spend more time on my writing."

"What's the new book about?" she asked, turning slightly toward him so that the coat opened to reveal a smart-looking burgundy wool suit under which she wore a cream-colored silk shirt, opened to the upper curve of her breasts. He felt the response in his groin to the sight of her white flesh. Several gold chains circled her throat. She looked wealthy, he thought, indulged and elegant.

"It's a love story," he replied hesitantly, all at once aware that the subject of his book and the book itself were in close proximity. When he'd written the manuscript it had never occurred to him that he might actually see this woman again. It struck him now that his physical description of her was, at least, accurate. He was terribly curious to know if he'd properly represented the woman herself. "How old's your daughter?" he thought to ask.

"Fee's sixteen, going on forty-four." She laughed again, showing her teeth.

"Sixteen," he repeated trying to imagine a daughter of Lynne's. "How long's she been at Low-Heywood?"

"This is her third year. She wasn't doing well in the public school system at home, so we decided to send her up here to school."

"And is she doing well here?"

"Oh, very. She's made a lot of friends, and she's hoping to get into Yale when she graduates. She wants to go into medicine."

"You don't miss your career?" he asked, his eyes probing hers.

"I have moments. In the past couple of years, with Fee away at school, it's been a little quiet. I did it all backwards, you see. I had the career first, then the marriage and family. It worked out well, though."

"But you were married before."

"Yes," she said. "That's true, I was."

When she failed to elaborate, he asked, "Don't you count the first one?"

"I count it. It's just that in retrospect it wasn't the marriage I thought it was." She looked out the window, then said, "We're coming into the station. I'd better give you the address, and the phone number in case there's a problem."

He jotted down the information she gave him, then tucked his notebook back into his inside breast pocket. The train was slowing. Lynne had fastened her coat and was pulling on her gloves. He was freshly overcome by his feeling of urgency. "Eight o'clock?" he asked.

"Fine." With a smile, she got to her feet and moved toward the door with the other passengers who were leaving the train at Greenwich.

"I'll see you later," he called out over the heads of the people between them as he reached for his coat in the overhead rack. When he turned back she was gone. As he emerged onto the platform he caught sight of her climbing into a dark-colored car. The passenger door closed after her and the car drove off. He was unable to determine whether it had been a man or a woman at the wheel.

As he drove toward the address she'd given him he couldn't help feeling slightly mystified. While she'd talked readily enough with him on the train, when he reviewed the conversation it seemed she'd told him very little. Perhaps it was because they'd talked of facts, not feelings. What he needed now was to speak more deeply with her, to get some intimation of her feelings. He was, he'd discovered in the course of his lengthy preparations for this evening, still in love with her.

For months after she'd left, all those years before, he'd walked about with a pain in his chest, missing her, mourning her as if she'd died. To the extent that he felt deprived of any pleasure in life, she might just as well have died. He'd spent years trying to recover from those few weeks of knowing her. His marriage to Lizzie had been farcical: both of them overly anxious to prove that they could make the marriage work, when neither of them were seriously dedicated to the effort. Lizzie's attention had constantly wandered, her thoughts on foreign fields of a greener hue. His own attention, for large chunks of time, was fastened to an endless examination of the hours, the days he'd spent with Lynne. He'd thought often of the accident on the turnpike and how she'd sat afterward with him at the Japanese restaurant, her clothes bloodstained and dirtied, unbothered by the curious eyes of the other patrons. She'd commented only once on the fact of her outfit having been ruined, then never mentioned it again. She'd been more concerned with the injured boy she'd cradled in her lap, and had worried aloud about the child until, giving in to her need, she'd excused herself and gone to the telephone to call the hospital and ask after the child's condition.

Thinking of that incident now, he could readily picture her as a mother. Yet he couldn't conceive of it. His mind seemed to have split in two; half was actively reviving the past, the other half surged about in the present, trying to make sense of the things she'd told him, and why she'd disappeared from the train the way she had. He'd been so fuddled by the mysterious way in which she'd slipped away that he'd tried to check the address and phone number she'd given him in the directory, just in case it didn't exist. Naturally, that had been an entirely useless effort since she and her sister had different names, and he didn't know, had never known, her sister's last name.

Now, he was driving along Round Hill Road wondering

if there actually would be a house at this address, and if Lynne would actually be there.

He was relieved, and vexed with himself for his over-imaginativeness, to find that the house did indeed exist. He pulled into the driveway of the large, white-painted brick house and sat for a moment trying to pull his excitement back into control. He studied the place—the black shutters on the front windows, the black roof, the front door. After a minute or so, he got out and walked up the salted and sanded front walk to the door.

She had changed out of the burgundy suit into a black silk dress that showed her to be still slim, but slightly, appealingly, fuller in the hips and breasts. The gold chains were still in place at her throat and dipped temptingly into the low neckline of the dress. She'd put on a bit of makeup that served to heighten the blue of her eyes and the fairness of her skin. Her hair, which had been covered by the fur hat, had silvered. But rather than aging her, the loosely coiled hair at the nape of her neck made her look even younger.

"You're not tanned!" he said with a smile. "I forgot to ask you why not."

"Come in!" She laughed. "Do we have time for a drink or are we going right away?"

"We can have a drink at the restaurant."

"All right. I'll just get my coat." She opened the hall closet and he helped her on with the white mink. "I'm not tanned," she said, looking into the mirror as she wrapped a scarf around her neck, "because at my age a little sun gives a lot of wrinkles. I've grown vain in my old age. I'm all set," she announced. She picked up her gloves and bag and followed him down the walk to the car.

"Vanity becomes you," he said, once they were on their way.

"I lied," she said. "I had a melanoma and I'm no longer allowed to sit in the sun. It happens quite often," she explained, "with people who spend a lot of time on boats in the sun."

"Is that what you did?"

"We sailed constantly until Fee started school. After that, it was only during school holidays. A few years ago, Ross finally sold the boat."

"You don't have a scar," he said, glancing over at her.

"I do. I cover it with makeup."

"Oh!" He glanced at her again, then said, "It's not far."

"Good." She looked out the window, wondering why she found herself being flip with him. Not all the time, but in response to several of his questions, she'd either lied outright or evaded the truth. She looked at the snow banked on the sides of the road and shivered. "My blood's thinned after all the years in the south," she said. "I'm always freezing when I come up here."

"I'll put the heat up," he said, and set the blowers going full blast.

"Thank you." His profile, she thought, was as pure and beautiful as ever. He was still wonderfully good-looking, still eminently attractive. John Grace, she thought, and smiled. She'd wondered for years if she might someday run into him on some street in Manhattan, or on the train. Now it had happened and she was glad to see that time hadn't been unkind to him. There was a certain cautious light to his eyes that time and, undoubtedly, experience had placed there. But he was so overtly enthusiastic that she found it warming to be with him.

"I'll have to be sure to buy your new book," she said. "When does it come out?"

"In a couple of months. I'm not so sure you'll want to read it."

"Why?"

"In a way, it's about you."

"Really?"

"Well, it's about that time we . . . uh . . . spent together."

"When I made love to you in the bathroom." She laughed at the memory.

He turned toward her, trying to decide if she was laughing at him. "Was it funny?" he asked.

"No. It wasn't funny. I was terrified, and that was funny."

"Terrified?"

"Corrupting the morals of a youth, that sort of thing," she tried to elaborate.

"I was twenty-six, hardly a 'youth.'"

"You were to me."

"Do I still strike you that way?" he asked, directing the car into the parking lot adjacent to the restaurant.

"No," she answered. "But then, I'm no longer terrified."

Once seated in the restaurant, with drinks, he asked, "What did you mean by that business about no longer being terrified."

She ran her finger around the rim of her glass, then raised her eyes. "I was terrified by what I thought I wanted."

"Which was?"

"I don't know anymore."

"You're hedging," he accused.

Her eyes narrowed slightly for a moment, then she smiled. "You're far more direct than you used to be."

"I've had a lot of time to think. I never thought I'd see you again, but now that we're together, I don't want to waste time making social chit-chat. I've been wanting to talk to you, really talk, for seventeen years."

"Why?" she asked.

"It's too soon for that particular conversation," he said, retreating. "Would you like to order?"

"In a few minutes. I'm more interested in the conversation you think it's too soon for. Tell me," she urged.

"You know what I realized in the car, driving over to pick you up tonight? I realized that I'm still in love with you. How do you react to that?"

She shook her head. "It's a romance novel. You don't stay in love with someone you scarcely know for seventeen years."

"Here I am!" he insisted. "Living proof that it does happen."

Her eyes remained on him for quite some time before she said, "I can't argue with how you claim to feel."

"You look the same," he said, "just exactly the same."

"Of course I don't," she disagreed. "I'm fifty-seven years old. I've got the requisite gray hair and wrinkles."

"You, sitting there talking about gray hair and wrinkles, are the best ad I can think of for getting old in a hurry."

"What is it you find so appealing?" she asked, curious. "I mean have you any idea how much of an effect gravity *has*? Everything," she said, laughing, "falls to earth."

"You look the same," he said, "but you've changed. I don't remember you being quite so funny."

"I don't think I was. I'm not particularly funny now. I just find this a little—awkward."

"How?"

"Think about it! You're here claiming to be still in love with me, and I'm here inside me trying as hard as I can to imagine why. I believe that constitutes an awkward moment."

"All right. I'll drop it. Would you like to order now?"

"I think so." She picked up the menu, feeling a little tired. She'd forgotten John's need to complicate matters by overanalyzing them. She couldn't help but feel a need to defend herself, yet couldn't think why the need existed.

They ordered, and after the waiter had left the table, John watched her lift the glass of Scotch to her mouth, finding everything about her even more alluring than he'd remembered. Except that there were certain things that jarred, things that weren't quite as he'd recalled. They stared at each other, each trying to think of what to say next.

She broke the silence at last, saying, "This could go on for hours."

"I enjoy looking at you."

"That much," she said carefully, "is mutual. You were a very beautiful young man."

"I'm forty-three," he said, looking at his hands. "It's sometimes surprising to think of it."

"I know. I feel it in most of the things I think I can do that I discover I can't. I don't have the same kind of energy."

"I know what's different!" he exclaimed suddenly. "Your eyes. You've lost that look you had."

"What look?"

"You looked so sad. It was what I first noticed, the sadness in your eyes."

"Let's change the subject," she suggested. "I'm really not comfortable with all this."

He could see her discomfort, and could accept the words she spoke at face value. Yet he simply couldn't leave it alone. The issue of his love for her required settling, somehow. He wasn't sure how. After all, she was, he reminded himself, married to someone else. She had a life about which he knew very little; a life that involved boats and a warm climate, a surfeit of money and comfort, and a child. The child threw him almost as much as her presence across the table. He could not, no matter how hard he tried, connect Lynne with a child.

"Do you have any pictures of your daughter?" he asked.

"I'm not one of the ones who carries around a miniature family album in her handbag," she said with a smile.

Another silence fell and she allowed it to continue until the waiter brought their salads. Then they both began to speak at once. They stopped, and then laughed.

"Go ahead," she said. "What were you going to say?"

"I was about to apologize for coming on that way. It was absurd. What were *you* going to say?"

"I've forgotten. It doesn't matter." She picked up her fork, then said, "We don't know each other. Perhaps that's why it feels peculiar to you."

"Do you find it absurd?"

"No, because you take it so seriously. That much hasn't changed: I remember you as terribly serious."

"If you have memories," he said, "and some of them strike you now as appropriate, then it proves that we did know each other once upon a time, even if we don't know each other present tense."

"Possibly." She wished he'd stop pushing his way back to this one central theme. He seemed obsessed. "Do you live in town?" she asked.

"I have a house in Old Greenwich, near the beach. I bought it after Lizzie and I split up. I've done quite a lot of work on it, but it needs more, a new furnace, new septic tank. Now that this new book's done, I'll be able to pay off the mortgage and get some of that stuff done.''

"Wouldn't you be wiser to hang on to the mortgage for the sake of the interest deductions?''

"I might be wiser," he said, surprised by her business acuity, "but I'd like to feel I finally own the place. I'll probably live in it for the rest of my life.''

"Now you sound like Amy.''

"Maybe I should take up with her," he said with a wide smile. "We sound totally suited.''

They ate, and talked, and managed, throughout the rest of the meal, to stay safely away from the matter of their brief-lived affair and John's claims of love. They both declined dessert and coffee.

"I only drink coffee in the morning now," she said. "It tends to keep me up all night, makes me vibrate.'' She held her hand in the air and made it tremble, to illustrate.

"Would you like to see my house?'' he asked clumsily.

There it was, she thought, what she'd been expecting all evening. "Another time, perhaps.''

He was disappointed, but covered it by paying close attention to signing the American Express slip, and calculating the tip.

The trip back to Amy's house was made in relative silence. Lynne huddled inside her coat, shivering, and John apologized. "It takes a little while for this car to heat up.''

"It's quite all right. As I told you, I'm never warm here.''

He pulled into the driveway, put the shift into neutral then turned to lean with his arm on the steering wheel. "I'm . . . uhm . . . sorry it wasn't quite the . . .''

"Stop apologizing," she said kindly. As had happened years before, her hand reached out to touch his cheek, and she remembered going with him to his funny apartment. It had been an innocent invitation, just as the one he'd made in the restaurant had been. "It was a lovely evening," she said. She made contact with the cool, firm flesh of his face and was jolted by her internal reaction and the understanding that it would again, as it had years before, fall to her to initiate whatever was to happen. If anything was to happen. He caught hold of her hand and held it warmly. She began to shake her head but he was already moving closer to kiss her. She held on to him hard, kissing him deeply, then abruptly freed herself. "You want to make love to me." Her words emerged gluey, thick with response.

"Don't let's go through it all again," he said quickly. "All the words about age and differences and how we're strangers, people who don't really know each other. We do; we always have."

He was wrong, but she had no desire at this moment to correct him.

"You'd better come in," she said soberly.

"What about your sister?"

"Amy won't be home for hours. I'm not going to fight with you, John. Do you want to come in?"

He switched off the ignition and hurried around to her side of the car to offer his hand. She stood for a moment with her hand in his, then kissed him again. It was no good telling him, she thought. Let him see for himself. And what was she proving? she asked herself, drawing warmth from his enclosing hand. Was there something that needed to be proved? She found her key and opened the front door, then turned to confront him.

"Take this for what it is," she cautioned.

"Don't say that."

"I have to say that. It's the difference between us." Without waiting for his reaction, she walked into the living room, dropped her coat and bag on a chair, then started up the stairs.

Bemused, he followed, watching the seductive slide of her hips as she ascended the stairs. She walked into a bedroom and he went after her, coming to a halt to watch her draw the curtains.

"Close the door," she said, sitting on the edge of the bed to remove her boots. "If it makes you feel more comfortable, you can lock it, too."

He closed and locked the door, then went to sit beside

her. The entire encounter had a dreamlike quality. He kept having the feeling he'd wake up at any moment to discover he'd imagined all this. "Let me do it this time," he said, stopping her hands. "I've dreamed of undressing you."

She wanted to protest that he'd dreamed of undressing the woman she'd been seventeen years before, but she took a deep breath and said nothing. She would take this pleasure—it would be a pleasure, she had no doubt of that—and, unlike him, she wouldn't question it or analyze it, or attempt to make it anything more than it was, just as she made no attempt to hide from his eyes the slackened flesh at her belly or any part of her aging self.

If he found her sadly altered, neither his words nor his expression betrayed it. He held her and touched her with the same hands, the same loving interest and intensity as before. Grateful, she closed down the thinking part of her brain and found herself still greedy—for the heated potency of his flesh, the urgency of his mouth and hands, for the welcome thrust of his body. She bound him to her with her arms and legs, oblivious to everything but the exquisite motion and the grinding, familiar desperation to have him dance within her arms, within the lock of her flesh, until it was ended. For as long as it lasted, she savored the thickness of his hair, pushing her fingers into the curls and feeling them wind, tendrillike over her skin; she cherished his lean, jutting hips and long, pale legs. All of it, everything.

He whispered, "I love you, I love you," and subsided into her arms.

She held him, weaving her fingers through his hair, relishing the weight of his body. The minutes whirred past, altering constantly the face of the digital clock on the bedside table. Lazily she looked at the numbers and felt herself returning.

"Amy will be home soon," she said.

He pulled away slowly and at the instant the contact was broken, he said, "I want to see you again."

"It's not a good idea." She slid away and reached for her robe, belted it tightly, then looked around for a cigarette. She'd left her bag downstairs. She'd have to wait.

With resignation he bent to retrieve his clothes from the floor. He dressed quickly and followed her down the stairs to the living room where she picked up his coat and held it out to him.

"Wait a minute!" he protested. "We've got to talk."

"Call me in the morning. We'll talk then."

"No, now," he argued. "I can't do this!" He looked around the living room, as if hoping to find the words he needed painted on the walls. "This is so . . . casual . . . something. I don't know."

"I asked you to take it for what it is."

"No. You loved me," he said. "I know you did."

"John," she said sadly, "I liked you, I wanted you, I was fond of you."

"No," he insisted. "It was more."

"It was more, perhaps, for you. Making love to you . . . How can I make you understand? It's something extraordinary, something that exists outside of time. It's like being famished and suddenly seeing a table heaped with food. You want to eat and eat until you burst. I could make love with you for the next six months, and I'd adore every moment of it. But I don't love you. I don't even *know* you. And you certainly don't know me. There's also something you're forgetting: I'm married. I have a husband, and I *do* love *him*.

"Meeting you today was an accident. I'm not sorry it happened. I would happily go back upstairs with you right now and do it again, if this weren't my sister's house, and if I didn't have a conscience. Making love to you is *wonderful*, but I don't love you. I scarcely know how to talk to you. It's entirely your fantasy, John," she said gently.

"Then why . . . ?"

"You don't have to love someone to make love to him. Surely you know that. You're a beautiful man, a beautiful lover. I sensed the very first time I ever saw you how you'd be. Tonight was probably something I shouldn't have allowed to happen, but I thought it might help you to see things differently. I'm *not* sorry it happened. But what you don't seem willing to accept is that I have a life, and I'm happy. What exists between you and me is a splendid chemistry. The problem is that it seems to blind you to certain realities. I'm not in a position to ignore those realities. I have a husband, and a daughter, and a life that pleases me more than I could ever say. Please don't spoil what we just had by trying to force it into something it could never be. Amy's due home any minute and I'd be embarrassed to have her find us this way. It's obvious what's gone on."

As she spoke, something odd seemed to be happening to his vision. It was as if a blindingly bright light had been illuminated somewhere overhead and it cast her features into entirely different definition. The idea that she wasn't the woman about whom he'd written began to infiltrate the edges of his awareness.

"I love my husband," she was saying, "and you're in love with my capacity to respond to you. That's all it is. Go home and forget about me. I'm not who you think I am. It's time to go, John, and I think it's time to put the fantasy aside. I'm sorry if I contributed. I never meant to mislead you."

"Whatever you say," he said with less than his former conviction, "I do love you. And I won't forget you." Did this mean, he wondered, that the book was of less value than he'd previously thought? He felt suddenly desperate to get home and look at the galleys. "I won't forget you," he repeated.

"Oh, you will." She smiled. "Tomorrow, you'll begin to recall details of tonight and the dream will start to dissolve. You can only stand just so close to the fire, my dear. Thank you for a lovely evening." She placed her hand on his arm and kissed him on the lips. "Go home and write another fine book and forget about me. I'm just a middle-aged housewife from Florida. Put it into perspective and it'll be a lot easier to deal with."

"I'll remember you," he promised, no longer at all sure of that, then he opened the door and went out.

Cold in the brief blast of air from the door, she wrapped her arms around herself and gazed at the front door. She turned, finally, and started up the stairs. She'd call Ross, and after that, she'd take a hot bath and go to bed. In the morning, she'd drive up to Darien to pick up Fee, her and Ross's daughter.

Critically acclaimed works from a bestselling author!

Charlotte Vale Allen

Few authors today have explored the emotional landscape of women's lives with the depth and precision of Charlotte Vale Allen. Her bestselling books, Promises, Daddy's Girl, and Destinies have touched millions. All are sensitive accounts that probe the very soul of today's woman—as only Charlotte Vale Allen can do!

_____ 06591-X	INTIMATE FRIENDS	$3.95
___ ___ 06167-1	PROMISES	$3.50
_____ 06749-1	DESTINIES	$3.50
_____ 05964-2	MEET ME IN TIME	$3.50

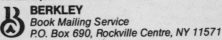